C

PRICE: $22.37 (3797/   )

Jamaica Street

SALLY WORBOYES

Jamaica Street

Hodder & Stoughton

Copyright © 2004 by Sally Worboyes

First published in Great Britain in 2004 by Hodder & Stoughton
A division of Hodder Headline

The right of Sally Worboyes to be identified as the Author
of the Work has been asserted by her in accordance with the
Copyright, Designs and Patents Act 1988.

1 3 5 7 9 10 8 6 4 2

A CIP catalogue record for this title is available from the British Library

ISBN 0340 73499 X

Typeset in Plantin Light by Palimpsest Book Production,
Polmont, Stirlingshire

Printed and bound by
Mackays of Chatham plc, Chatham, Kent

Hodder Headline's policy is to use papers that are natural,
renewable and recyclable products and made from wood grown in
sustainable forests. The logging and manufacturing processes are expected
to conform to the environmental regulations of the country of origin.

Hodder and Stoughton
A division of Hodder Headline
338 Euston Road
London NW1 3BH

This book is dedicated to Juanita and Urban Turner

Prologue

In 1953, Errol Turner, a brave seventeen-year-old, had left his homeland in the West Indies to begin a new life in Great Britain. With a suitcase in one hand and his grandfather's old cased sewing machine in the other he stepped, with other hopeful migrants, off the ship to disembark. His destination was not the core of the Caribbean settlement in South London but the East End. Errol's uncle Joe, a shoeshine man, together with cousin Malcolm, had arrived here two years before with five hundred or so Jamaicans and had been temporarily housed in a large air raid shelter on Clapham Common, before being moved into nearby Brixton. The condition of the cramped lodging rooms had not come up to his uncle's expectations, nor did they compare favourably to what he and the majority of his countrymen from back home had been used to. Lodgings that left much to be desired.

Taking a bold and brave step for the time, Errol's uncle had moved from his South London lodgings almost immediately to the East End, where he knew and understood that the majority of residents would be white. It was clear that he and his son would stand out more than if they had stayed comfortably with the flock in Brixton and he also realised that they would be a greater and easier target, for those who were colour prejudiced, without the solidarity and support of people from his own background. Led by a strong will and determination the risk he was taking seemed a fair exchange for the chance to make something of himself in this country.

By the time Errol had arrived in England his uncle's post office saving account was modest but both he and his son were prepared to work the long hours that success demanded. In case his relatives had not been able to meet him at the dock, Errol had held firmly onto the Hackney address scribbled on a piece of paper in his pocket. To come to Britain had been his dream ever since the day his uncle and cousin had made the journey and had written a letter encouraging him to pack his bags and join them. Errol's aspiration to make his mark as a tailor had been with him from the age of eight, when his father had begun to teach him the trade. Having always been a keen reader of any news to do with Britain, he had known only too well of the problems which lay ahead of him: the most pressing of all being limited housing and overcrowded tenement dwellings.

The mere fact that he and the other passengers had been allowed ashore had given him faith that things in Britain were changing for the better. He had been aware that hundreds of other Jamaicans who had arrived in the June of 1948 on the old troopship *Empire Windrush* had been told, once the ship had moored on the Thames, that they were not allowed to disembark. Unbeknown to them at the time of their departure from their homeland the disillusioned passengers were to find out too late that the British Nationality Act had not actually been passed through Parliament: an unfortunate and costly mistake had been made at high level.

Arriving in the mid-fifties, with the new law passed Errol realised that he would be greeted with prejudice and suspicion, but his determination had been stronger than his anxiety over racial intimidation and he had done his homework and kept up to date on current affairs in England. He had read a report in which the Colonial Secretary, Arthur Creech Jones, had claimed that objectors to mass immigration had nothing to worry about, because those from a hot climate would not last one cold winter in England. Needless to say this had not proved to be the case. The people from the Caribbean were hardly ignorant of the British climate and so had naturally protected themselves against the harsh winters with warm clothing and while the women brightened grey foggy days with their colourful clothes and bubbly attitude, the clean-cut men brought with them a style of their own: light, wide-lapel over-coats and suits, dove grey trilby hats, sparkling white shirts and jazzy ties.

Apart from having to deal with the sometimes freezing cold weather, most had to come to terms with a lack of interest in people from their part of the world. Practically nothing had been done to acknowledge the arrival of West Indians to help them settle in, even though they would balance the population figures. The vast flow of people moving out of London to other parts of Britain together with those emigrating to Australia, Canada and South Africa, meant a hefty decline in the city's population. Seeking a better way of life, thousands had continued to leave throughout the fifties while the redevelopment of war-damaged towns was in full swing. It might not have struck the government that the departure of the working classes and the huge loss of lives during the war was leaving a void and that our ambitious friends coming to this country were an asset to be welcomed rather than a problem to be solved.

At least eight thousand immigrants were employed in Britain inside the public transport system alone. The smile of a Caribbean ticket collector was like a beam of sunshine on a cold foggy morning and went some way at least to counter the discontented mood of London born and bred passengers who wanted to be far away from England, in a hot sunny place across the oceans.

With high hopes for a new life, Errol passed through Passport and Customs officials a happy, excited, young man. His only assets were his sewing machine, a few pounds in his pocket and a touching faith in Great Britain. The piece of paper with the Hackney address on – now slightly limp and crumpled, having been nervously opened and refolded several times – had luckily not been needed, as his uncle Joe, who had travelled to Southampton on the dawn milk train, had been at the quayside to greet him. Joe, a friendly, hard-working chap had become quite a character in London's Soho district, where he had secured a small square of pavement as his regular spot outside the old Cameo cinema. Here he pitched up at the crack of dawn as the Cherry Blossom shoeshine man, happy in his work and happy that his own son Malcolm had found employment within the British Railway. In their rented rooms close to Victoria Park in Hackney, father and son had eagerly placed a fairly comfortable second-hand put-u-up for their new guest in a corner of their sitting room.

From the moment Errol shook his uncle's firm hand at the dockside, some of his worries disappeared and he knew above all he had a welcoming, friendly relative to rely on. During his first few weeks so far away from home, Errol found that like most strangers to London he was in awe of the ancient city. The beautiful imposing buildings and monuments, the hustle and bustle of street life, the lively markets and the milk and coffee bars were all so new to him. The culture was different, as was the music, and he drank it all in like a cold beer on a summer's day. He also found he was rather partial to what his uncle had referred to as 'eye candy' – the white girls who caught his eye and held his attention. His cousin Malcolm, however, preferred the beautiful dark skin and luscious curves of their own women. The highlight of Errol's first week had been his walking and bus-hopping tour, within the heart of old London town. Once he had witnessed the majestic changing of the guards at Buckingham Palace any small doubts that he might have made a mistake in leaving his beloved homeland had dissolved. He had arrived and he was happy.

Soon after he had settled down Errol, together with his cousin and uncle, had been given a pleasant reminder of home by the colourful street parties held in celebration of the new Queen's coronation as they walked through East London. They had watched the coronation of Queen Elizabeth II on a tiny television set at a friend's home in Hackney which had been packed with their own people. As it turned out, that historic day was special for more reasons than one. Errol had met two lovely girls, arms linked, in the excited crowd – Maggie Baroncini and her best friend Rita – a girl with lovely blonde hair and blue eyes who had swept him off his feet.

Having finally agreed, after some flirtatious persuasion, to meet him outside the Hackney Empire, he had been disappointed and disillusioned when the girl had stood him up. But a few years later he had met up with Rita again. At first he hadn't recognised her but thought her familiar and very attractive. Giving her the eye and smiling at her across a crowded room it had dawned on him where he had seen her before. No different from other girls of her age, she had changed the colour of her hair to brunette, but she couldn't change the colour of her light blue eyes or her lovely smile. Mingling with a small group of well-heeled Italian young men with Tony Curtis haircuts in a dance hall in Bow, she looked radiant, even though that beautiful blonde hair which had attracted him in the first place was gone. He lost no time in asking her to join him on the floor and she was happy to slip into his strong arms and rest her head on his shoulder as they moved slowly around the floor to the wonderful soft voice of Nat King Cole and 'Unforgettable'.

Now aged twenty-three, in the final year of the nineteen fifties, having won Rita over since that evening Errol was still deeply in love. Wary at first because of his black skin, Rita soon realised that their hopes for approval from both their families were no different from thousands of others who had fallen for someone from a different race, and since Britain was becoming a multiracial society, with immigrants having come from India, the West Indies, Italy, Greece, Cyprus and Malta, neither Errol nor Rita could see why their courtship would not eventually be accepted.

In these so-called 'modern times' however, there continued to be a rumbling of racial prejudice, stimulated by the articles on the Union Movement. The message they were delivering was that Britain was an overcrowded island. The attitude of Oswald Mosley had not changed either; he was continuing to insist that people the world over, black or white, had to maintain and perpetuate their cultural and religious identity by keeping foreigners out and races pure. This was mostly seen as claptrap by the ordinary man on the street.

It came as no great surprise in the summer of 1958 though, when riots broke out in Nottingham and London. Fuelling the fire had been the *Black and White News* with headlines to incite: 'Blacks invade Britain', 'Blacks milk the Assistance Board', 'Bone idle and work shy'. More poignant, where Rita and her boyfriend Errol were concerned, was the most recent headline: 'Blacks Get the White Girls!'

Living alone in two rented rooms in a terraced house in Cornwall Avenue, Bethnal Green, Rita was neighbour to a Pakistani family who had helped her move in; carrying packing cases and bags up two flights of stairs to her rooms. Next door to the Pattel family lived Jock McGregor and his wife Mary. A stevedore in Canary Wharf, Jock was similar to hundreds of other dockers in that he had kept his distance until he realised that, colour and religion apart, the foreigners were not so different from his own kind.

Music in this new era played a great part in bringing people together from all creeds and classes. While most of the young were raving over Elvis Presley and the hit parade, Rita enjoyed her time with Errol in their favourite nightclub, listening to lively jazz created by an American Negro, entrepreneur Buddy Bolden. With its infectious rhythms, his music continued to brighten the times. This barber, born around the year 1900 in New Orleans, was a natural born musician. A talented man who had managed to get hold of an old battered cornet and had blown the first stammering notes of jazz. He blew so loud that on a still clear night, he could be heard ten miles across the Mississippi delta.

Errol loved his music and was never happier than when dancing to a slow tune, cheek to cheek with his beautiful girl, in the small cellar of the Moody Blue in Brick Lane. Even though he had gone against strong advice from a friend not to court Rita in this nightclub, where most were like himself, young and black, the couple thought they would be free of intimidation and pressure to conform. Standing out amidst the West Indians, she, with her pale skin and blue eyes behaved with a natural indifference to those who gave her disparaging glances. And when Errol's friend, Louis Robinson, a cool, handsome young man had swaggered over to their table for two and stood looking at Rita with half-closed eyelids, showing mild disapproval, she had simply sniffed and then said, 'Great tie . . . shame about the knot.'

'Really,' had been the slow drawn out response. 'And do you think the knot should be smaller . . . or larger?'

'Tighter,' had been her somewhat curt answer. After a short silence as the two of them stared each other out, Louis had flicked the brim of his light grey trilby and smiled, showing admiration for her refusal to be intimidated. His perfect white teeth flashing against his brown face, he had begun to softly laugh. Then strolling away he called back over his shoulder, advising Errol to get a curry into his white woman's bones. From that moment on Rita knew she would be accepted into the tight-knit West Indian group of people who lived for their music; jazz and swing in particular, and singers and musicians such as Count Basie, Duke Ellington, Jelly Roll Morton, Muggsy Spanier and his Ragtime Band, and Louis Armstrong.

Rita was in love with Errol and he was clearly besotted with her. He enjoyed the fact that his girl did not run with the crowd, and rebelled in her own small way, like enjoying a Marlboro cigarette which was no longer seen as a ladylike thing to do. Since Marlboro had acquired its cowboy with a tattoo on the back of his hand and the message, 'A man's cigarette that women like too' it had been clearly marked as unfeminine. But Rita was not alone in rebuffing the message. Sophisticated young ladies from the upper classes in their West End nightclubs that seemed a million miles away from Rita and Errol's caverns, were also drawing on them, all be it through their gold-rimmed amber cigarette holders.

The fight for the emancipation of women was not yet over. In the February of 1958, when the campaign for nuclear disarmament was launched, women enrolled in their droves. 4,000 of them, several carrying their babies, gathered in London's Trafalgar Square before marching from London to Berkshire to confront the atomic weapons research establishment.

The young were working hard in their attempts to realign their goals to fit new facts of life while the older generation were clinging on to their old hopes: that since Britain had triumphed over Hitler, the future would from then onwards be one of peace. For the young, this was a time when life was pleasant and it was good to be cynical and mildly rebellious. There was great optimism across all youth culture and class, that solutions to all things could be found through the voice of the new generation. This was a time when the hydrogen bomb and rock 'n' roll were the topics of conversation and action. A time when those who weren't dancing were marching.

I

1959

On this special day, with the early springtime sun on her face, Maggie Baroncini held the small hand of her little boy, Peppito, and smiled as the memory of his birth, this time five years ago, came flooding back. At the time she had only just turned sixteen and in becoming a mother she felt as if all the worries of the world had been placed on her shoulders. Even though she had shown a brave smile while carrying her boyfriend's child, from the very beginning and all through her pregnancy, Maggie had been on a high tide of emotions. Her mood was volatile one minute, impassive, euphoric or in the grip of panic the next. She had been terrified at the thought of giving birth and confused by the flood of conflicting advice, as to what she should or should not do, from the day she broke her shocking news – three months after conception. Edie, her mother, had been the first to be told and then her much loved great-aunt Naomi. By the time Maggie had made her confession however, Edie, who had brought Maggie up as a single parent had recognised all the signs which had pointed in only one direction, that her fifteen-year-old child had given herself to her very first boyfriend. An Italian. Tony.

Without her father around, Maggie had at least been saved from a plethora of rage which might have come from that quarter. The one thing that she had stood firmly against from the very beginning of her confession had been the hints and suggestions to have an abortion. Adoption, the most talked about option, had come second to keeping her baby. But along with this had come controversial opinions: should she give her baby to complete strangers never to be seen again, or keep it in the family. If the baby was to be kept, Maggie's uncle Jimmy and aunt Helen had been the obvious ones to become its parents. As fond as she was of her uncle, his ambitious wife Helen, desperate to be middle class and forget her roots in Plaistow, was the last person that she would have wanted to bring up her child. So, after much deliberation and tears all round it was judged to be right that Maggie follow her own maternal instincts and mother her offspring come what may.

On Maggie's worst days the fear that Tony would turn from her made her think about ending it all. This tendency to seek relief from reality had been one of her failings since a young girl, when she had gone into her classroom with a clumsy brace on her teeth. Torment and sneering had all but crushed her confidence. At the age of fourteen however, her world had turned around. The brace was off, her teeth were beautiful and her wonderful flamboyant great-aunt Naomi had cut and styled her red hair and showed her how to wear make-up. From then on Maggie was one of the most popular girls where the lads were concerned. Wolf whistles had become normal to her.

Now, enjoying married life with Tony, Maggie was content. Strolling under the nearby arches on her way to visit her best friend Rita, she brought to mind the night when she had delivered Peppito into the world. She recalled the voices below her bedroom window, just after midnight, when two policemen had been chatting under a street lamp. There had also been a distant echoing sound of a dog barking. Unlike this pleasant early March day it had been extremely cold with a fine layer of frozen snow on the ground.

All things considered it had been a smooth delivery with nothing going wrong. Even though Maggie had only just passed her sixteenth birthday the question of risk had been the furthest from her mind. The midwife who had attended her had been young, but in her uniform with its cuffs and ruffs and pinched-in waist and little pert cap, she had instilled confidence. Her gentle but efficient ways soon eased Maggie's worries.

She remembered her bedroom as it was on the night before she gave birth. The council flat where she lived with her mother had become a small maternity ward and the surface of a pine chest of drawers in her room had become a place for the midwife's utensils; forceps, scissors, stethoscope and cord clamps.

With all of this swimming through her mind, Maggie squeezed the chubby hand of her son and smiled into his innocent face as he looked up at her saying, 'Will Aunty Reet 'ave a present for me? And a toffee apple?'

'She'll have the toffee apple, Peppie, she always does. Don't know about a birthday present, though. She might have forgotten it's today,' she teased. She hadn't and Maggie knew it. 'She might not even be in for all I know.'

'Can we go to where she works?'

'No. Mustn't disturb 'er while she's at the library. We don't want to get 'er in trouble, do we?'

'I want to show my watch,' he said pushing the cuff of his duffel coat up with a finger and raising his arm to show her, as if she had never seen it before. 'It's real silver.'

'I don't know about that sweetheart, but Roy Rogers is your favourite cowboy, so there we go. Your grandfather did well to know what you want.'

'I said I wanted it.' He was still admiring it as he murmured. 'Roy Rogers on Trigger. It's my bestest present. And my scooter.'

'Two favourite presents, eh? Lucky boy,' said Maggie. 'And it's three, if you count the little train set from Aunt Naomi.'

'I know. *Will* Aunty Rita be in?'

'I think she *might* be in but we can't be certain, can we?'

'She's up the clinic,' he murmured, gazing at his watch.

Taken back by this Maggie stopped in her tracks and looked directly into Peppito's innocent face. 'What do you know about the clinic?'

'I heard it. Will they cut 'er open to look for a baby?'

Maggie shook her head in wonder at the way her child's mind worked. 'No, Peppie, they won't.'

'It might be a bun,' he grinned.

Maggie lifted her eyes to the sky, sighing. 'I think I know who *you*'ve been listening to.'

'She might not have chewed it proply. Aunt Naomi said—'

'I don't want to know Peppie! I think we might 'ave to cut down your visits to Nao.'

'She'll cry,' he murmured, anxiously shaking his head. 'I brighten her day,' he added proudly.

'Is that right? Well, no more talk about buns and babies then. Or I won't let her look after you any more. You can go to Grandma Baroncini instead.'

'Why did we give Grandma my cot? Is she going to have a baby?'

'No! It was your daddy's cot once. We've given it back now we don't need it any more.'

'Will she scrub the pictures of birds off? Grandfather said we could paint cars on it.'

Maggie let his chatter go above her head as she recalled the first time she had held him in her arms, wrapped in a soft white towel. Her new-born child. Her perfect baby who had inherited his dad's Italian looks with his black hair and long eyelashes. At least he had Maggie's green eyes and freckles. She recalled the expression on Tony's face when he had gazed at his baby and it made her smile. There had been tears in his eyes when he whispered . . . 'I love you, Maggie Birch. I love you both.' And now she was Maggie Baroncini. A young married woman and still very much in love with Tony who she had been too young to marry at the time. But marry they did as soon after her sixteenth birthday as possible – in Gretna Green. And now her baby was a bright intelligent five-year-old too sharp for his own good and Maggie and Tony were living with Edie in her council flat in Scott House. And while Peppito's fifth birthday party was being prepared by his gran and great-aunt, Maggie was taking a break from domesticity. She turned into Cornwall Avenue and politely smiled at a couple of shabby-suited men wearing flat caps who clearly did not want anyone to know what they were discussing. Speaking out of the side of his mouth, his eyes moving rapidly as he checked his surroundings, Jimmy the Fence, a familiar figure in this neck of the woods, was holding a cheap gold plated ladies' bangle watch, insisting it was pure gold and a bargain to be snapped up. His uncomfortable victim, eager to be away was shrugging and doing his level best to escape. Enjoying the banter Maggie stepped up her pace before she became a target.

Arriving at the terraced house in which her best friend had taken rented rooms, she pushed her fingers through Peppie's hair saying, 'Don't go reminding Rita that it's your birthday. She won't 'ave forgotten.'

'I wouldn't,' he said, splaying his hands and shaking his head. 'Can I knock on the door?'

'Course you can.' Maggie heaved him up into her arms. 'Only once though.'

'Twice. Aunt Reet said I could knock twice when I was five.'

'Go on then. Get on with it. You're a ton weight,' she groaned.

Once he had banged on the knocker, Peppito ordered Maggie to put him down. He didn't want Rita to see him in his mother's arms as if he were a baby. Waiting for the door to open, an expectant smile on his face, he could hardly contain his excitement. Being his godmother, Rita felt it her duty to spoil him rotten. The sound of footsteps from inside coming down the stairs caused him to chuckle before saying, 'I fink she *has* got me a present.'

'Peppie . . . what did I tell you?'

'I'm not 'specting it!' he whispered loudly to the sound of the door opening.

'Blooming heck!' Rita grinned. 'Who's swallowed one of Jack's magic beans then? You must 'ave grown an inch overnight Peppie. I swear it. I can't believe you're only four.'

'I'm *five!*'

'Course you're not. I should know,' she teased, standing aside. 'Go on, up you go. And don't stomp on the staircase or you'll wake up the black man.'

'You mustn't say that,' murmured Peppie as he passed her. 'I'm telling Errol of it. And I *am* five! It's my birfday!'

'Is it? I never knew. I would 'ave got you a card,' she said with mock sympathy.

'I've got cards. And a scooter. And this real watch.' He pulled the cuff of his duffel coat up and held his arm out proudly. 'It's Roy Rogers.'

'No it's not. It's Hop-along-Cassidy,' she jibed.

'It's not!' Peppie pushed his wrist under her nose. 'Look?'

'Stop teasing 'im, Reet. He's bin driving me mad since he woke up,' moaned Maggie as she arrived in the living room and flopped down on the old sofa. 'You've bin winding 'im up all week. Getting 'im excited. You're as bad as Aunt Naomi in your own way.'

'*And* she said *black man*,' Peppie chimed in, pleased to have his mother on his side.

'Well,' said Rita looking earnestly at her godchild, 'if we don't make a joke of it Pep, they're winning.' She then tapped a sheet of paper which she had pinned onto the wall. 'This came through the letterbox today. Some people 'ave got nothing better to do.'

'What is it?' asked Peppie, his familiar frown capping his eyes.

'Nigger Lover? Well . . . depends what you read into it I s'pose. But in plain English . . . whoever wrote that . . . has got suet pudding for a brain.'

'What?'

Rita tapped her temple saying, 'Nothing between the ears. No intelligence.'

'I don't know what you *mean*,' said Peppie, shaking his head and getting agitated.

'She doesn't know either, sweetheart,' said Maggie, attempting to end this. Her five-year-old was too young and too innocent to be drawn into racial intimidation.

'I wish I did know who wrote it, Mags. I would send Errol to their front door so he could smack 'em in the face,' she said with a mixture of sadness and anger.

'Don't talk like that in front of him, Reet.'

'Why not?' said Rita, now in the tiny kitchen, filling the kettle, and talking through the open doorway. 'Best that he knows and has it explained while he's young, eh Peppie?'

'I don't know what you mean!' he said again, splaying his hands.

'I don't agree, Rita, so change the subject and take that down. You should 'ave put it straight in the waste-paper bin. I would 'ave done.'

'I will when I feel like it. D'yer want a cup of tea or coffee?'

'Coffee,' Maggie replied, grudgingly.

'Wot about you, Mister Baroncini? Do you want a glass of Welfare orange juice?'

'Yes, please. And a toffee apple.'

'Haven't got none. Forgot you was coming.'

'Oh.' Peppie's bottom lip curled under. '*And* you forgot what this day is.'

'It's yesterday's tomorrer. That's all I know.'

'How comes you've got Welfare orange juice?' asked Maggie, accusingly.

'I found a box which 'ad fell off the back of a lorry.'

'It's my birfday,' murmured Peppie, pursing his lips.

Putting on a convincing show, Rita opened her mouth in surprise. 'It never is your birthday for real, is it! I thought it was a lark! You can't be four already?'

'Five. I'm five *today*! I've got . . .' Peppie splayed his fingers and thumb. 'This many birfday cards. Same as how old I am. You can come to my tea party.'

'*Five* cards! You lucky boy! Well . . . it won't matter that I never got you one then, will it?'

'No.' Peppie lowered his eyes. 'I'll 'ave another one anyway – when Emma comes 'ome from her work.'

'I hope there's jelly and ice cream at your party. So Emma Smith's got you a card eh? That's the sort of neighbour you want.'

'She gets four *pound* notes and a ten *shilling* one on Fridays!' exclaimed Peppie, wide-eyed.

'No flies on you, is there?' laughed Rita bending over him. 'Now, give us a kiss on the cheek and then go in the bedroom and see what's on my bedside table.'

Losing no time Peppie raced out of the room and within seconds the sound of ripping paper could be heard through the open doorway. Giving Maggie a sly smile Rita confided in a whisper that she had managed to find a beginners' Meccano set for her beloved godchild with nuts and bolts big enough for his chubby fingers to cope with. The glow in Rita's eyes said it all. She adored Peppito as if he were her own son. This was not so unusual as she and Maggie had been best friends since they had started junior school at the age of seven and were like sisters. Rita knew that the five-year-old would be totally absorbed with his present and leave them in peace. He had always been spellbound when watching his dad enjoying his hobby of carving end pieces of timber he picked up from a local wood yard.

Leaving Peppie to himself, the girls were soon curled up on the old comfortable sofa sipping their coffee and quietly chatting about the much debated subject of Rita's boyfriend, Errol. It was obvious to Maggie that Rita and Errol were beginning to feel the outside pressure of people who were against mixed courtship no matter the race or religion. The note which had been put through Rita's letterbox was clearly doing what it was meant to – unnerving her. Maggie shrugged off Rita's worries, telling her not to let ignorant people get under her skin.

'It's never bothered you before, Reet, so why now? It's just two words on a scrap of paper.'

'I know . . . but it's the fact that whoever wrote that can't live far from us, can they? No-one in their right mind would walk any distance just to put that through the letterbox. That's what really gets to me. The fact that someone down this street must 'ave done it. It gives me the creeps. You think you know your neighbours but you don't, not really. I feel like moving out.'

'What's to stop you?' said Maggie.

'And play into their hands? Sod off. It's obvious that's what they want. Well, stuff them. I'll flaunt Errol all the more. In fact, this coming Sunday I'll invite his cousin and uncle round for tea and we'll play some Blue Beat music . . . nice and loud. Or get his friend Louis Robinson to come and play his trumpet at midnight with the windows wide open.'

'That should make everything all right, then,' said Maggie. 'Just the ticket for mutual understanding.' She couldn't help her gentle sarcasm. Knowing Rita's temperamental side it was entirely possible she would follow through her joking threats.

'Well, what do you suggest then?' Rita lit a cigarette. 'That Errol puts bleach in his bath?'

'Put up and shut up or move.'

'No. Why *should* I move?'

'You want a reason, how about Notting Hill?'

'What about it?' Rita sighed. 'And don't preach. I'm not in the mood.'

'You know very well what I'm referring to, Reet. Five blacks were beaten up. A house was petrol-bombed. Is this what you want?'

Rita knew what Maggie was saying and she had hit home. The race riots in London had made her feel ashamed to be English. More than 150 arrests had been made during three days of rioting in North London in the August of the previous year. Gangs of up to 2,000 white youths and children had attacked black houses, breaking the windows. Even though it was known to the police that the instigators had been the extreme political groups, nothing had been proved.

'Errol wants us to stay in East London once we're married. He prefers it here to north or south of the river.'

Maggie smiled. 'So together for ever, then?'

'Course. And tell your aunt Nao that I'm *not* pregnant. I've put on a bit of weight with all the rice and curry, that's all.'

'Take no notice. She was going on to me about it yesterday and big ears in there was listening. Don't be surprised if he tries to look up your skirt to see what's growing under there.'

Smiling as she pictured it, Rita sipped her coffee. 'I've got some interesting news. Errol's uncle, the shoeshine man, 'as picked up some info about cheap terraced 'ouses for sale in Jamaica Street.'

'And?'

'Errol might buy one for us. Get a mortgage.'

'Before you're married?'

'If he has to get in quick, yeah. Why? You're hardly one to lecture.'

'I wasn't going to! And anyway, me and Tony never slept in a bed together before we got married.'

'He got you up against the wall though, didn't he?' Rita grinned.

Maggie chose to ignore that. 'What about your mum? Would she mind if you share a place with 'im before you're married?'

'Who said anything about that? I said *he* might buy one. It'll take months to make it liveable. Anyway, she'd be all right about it. She likes Errol. He used to make her laugh . . . and she cracked him up with the fings she said behind my stepdad's back. You wouldn't believe what she came out with. She got worse by the day, turned into a totally different woman, from the very day my dad buggered off.'

'She was a bird in a gilded cage.'

'Gilded? I don't fink so. Old and rusty and stinking of 'im more like. Miserable old bastard. Once she was free to say and do what she liked she went too far at times – but that was because of Errol. He encouraged 'er. You should have heard the jokes they used to tell each other. Filthy.'

'Do you still miss her, Reet?' said Maggie, cautiously. She was quite aware that when her best friend's mother emigrated with her new husband a year since, Rita had cried almost non-stop for a week and then avoided any discussion on her leaving England.

'Sometimes,' murmured Rita. 'But she writes all the time and I've got your mum to talk to, haven't I. She's been like a foster mum.'

Maggie leaned back on the old sofa and tucked her legs under her. 'She sees you like a second daughter, that's why. She thinks the world of you.'

'I know she does. And I couldn't ask for much more than that, could I? Anyway . . . one day me and Errol will go on a cheap voyage to see my mum.'

'Does she ever mention in her letters that she might come home?'

'No. She loves it out there, Mags. They might visit though . . . in a couple of years or so. They're saving up for it.'

'Good. We'll chuck a party in their honour. In St Peter's church hall. So . . . Jamaica Street. How can Errol afford to buy his own place?'

'His uncle Joe will go half with 'im.'

'His uncle Joe? He's a shoeshine man,' said Maggie. 'How can he afford it?'

'Don't knock it. His uncle does all right and sod the tax man. And his son Malcolm, Errol's cousin, has got a steady job on the buses as well as helping out Sunday mornings on a stall in Petticoat Lane. I always thought he was a bit on the tight side but he 'ad a good reason for putting any spare cash into a post office account. He's been saving for a deposit.'

'Why Jamaica Street of all places? Nostalgia?'

'No. A Jew boy where Errol works told him about the demolition and rebuilding plans and reckons that to buy one now would be smart thinking.'

'But if they're gonna be pulled down . . . they won't be up for sale.'

'Those owned by landlords will be – and most are. And with the paying tenants moving out and into new flats there'll be no rent coming in. And on the face of it there's no plans for houses on the southern end of the street to be demolished. And there's a little radio shop at the end of the street that might be up for grabs as well.'

'What would you and Errol want with a shop? And I think I know the one you mean. It's run down surely?'

'Ah, that's just the point. It looks old-fashioned and could do with a lick of paint, but inside, apart from a bit of damp and rot in the floorboards, it's sound – apparently. And it would make a decent tailor's shop. There's one big room upstairs for cutting and making up and a smaller one out the back. Downstairs you've got the shop at the front and a living room with a kitchen out the back.'

'And a bucket to pee in,' Maggie teased.

'No, actually. An outside lavatory that flushes and there's a little window that opens, thank you very much.'

'So you and Errol would live where?'

'The 'ouse next door. A two up two down. 'His cousin Malcolm would get a mortgage to buy the shop, number fifty-six. He'd use the upstairs back room of the shop as a bed-sit and use the kitchen below to do his cooking and that. Errol would rent the other upstairs room as a workspace . . . and then there's the shop front which could be used for measuring up and that.'

'And the uncle?'

'Shoeshine Joe?' Rita smiled and then clicked her teeth. 'He's already done a deal for a little one up two down just a few doors along. He'll live there.'

'So that's three places?'

'Yep. But . . . let's not get too excited. The bank might not lend 'em the money and . . . would we really like living in the middle of a row of boarded up 'ouses? In Jamaica Street?'

'You tell me,' said Maggie, pushing a hand through her hair. 'It's all above my head. I never thought in a million years that any of us would be talking about buying property.'

'Why not? Look at your mum's friend, Jessie. And her sister and brother-in-law. They did it in the thirties and they're gonna do it agen. All right, in bloody Norfolk but so what?' Rita sipped her coffee and looked at her friend over the rim of the cup. 'Things are changing, Maggie. It's no longer a case of class any more whether or not you buy your own property. It's all about grafting and cashing in on the changes that are goin' on. We've got something to thank that bloody war for.'

'So, if the London County Council decide to rebuild there, later on, they'll still 'ave to compulsory purchase it.'

'Yep. And for more than Errol's family'll be paying now. Then again, the Council might not want more blocks of flats or might not 'ave the funds for a while, to keep on building. Either way, we can't lose.'

Impressed by all of this and a touch envious, Maggie was beginning to feel as if she and Tony weren't going anywhere. They had been married for almost five years and were still living with her mother and waiting for a council house. Her best friend was on the brink of moving on to new and exciting horizons, while she would be over the moon to get a council house. Which in the bigger picture wasn't really all that much to write home about. Maggie had been friends with Rita for a very long time and had always known that she was more ambitious than herself. But now, she felt the gap widen and divide them and it made her feel uneasy.

Prior to a brief spell of helping Maggie run an Italian café in Islington, when Maggie was pregnant, the girls had been employed at the Bethnal Green library. Rita was quick to get back the position she once held as general assistant. It hadn't taken her long to realise, once she had started to help run the café, that she missed the ambience, the people and the books. Now, five years on, Rita had risen in rank to Assistant Librarian and had set up and established public readings involving fresh new London authors and poets, to promote their work.

As she listened to more of Rita's plans for the future, Maggie grew more and more despondent while trying to look positive and encouraging where her friend was concerned. Helping Tony in the fish-and-chip shop that he was managing in Roman Road seemed dull and drab in comparison to the future that Rita was enthusing over. Purchasing a house had been the furthest thing from Maggie's mind. Her name now down for a two-bedroom council place on the nearby Ocean Estate in

Mile End, she had come here with what she had considered to be her own good news. Now it hardly seemed worth mentioning. She had received a letter telling her that a house had become available.

Snapping herself out of this invasive mood of envy, she clung on to the world in which she belonged and which she loved: her marriage and her five-year-old son. Glancing up at Rita who was flicking through the *East London Advertiser*, she realised that she hadn't responded to her news about the purchase of a house as she should have.

'So . . . if Errol *is* to buy a house for the pair of you to live in . . . you'd better make a start with planning your wedding.' She grinned cheekily.

'I have already. It's gonna be a registry office. I'm taking a leaf out of your book. Me and Errol wouldn't want a proper white wedding without my mum and his parents being there and they can't afford to come over for it. And what we'd save we can put towards a deposit. Errol's already been to see a bank manager who'll arrange the financial side of it once a deal's been struck.'

'And will he keep on his job at the tailor's in Mile End once you've got the shop spruced up?'

'Course he will. But he'll do some private work as well. He's already got a couple of private customers. Two Jew boys who like a pukka finish. Hand stitched and all that.' Rita looked up from the newspaper, her face earnest. 'He deserves to get on, Mags. He slaved alongside his dad in Jamaica since he was a boy learning the trade. The first thing he was taught was to make sure that every pin was picked up from the workroom floor after a day's sewing and wiped clean. Every cotton reel was kept covered to avoid any dust from settling. And every scrap of material, off cuts, put into a box for shredding which was then sold on to mattress makers. Nothing was wasted and it was painful back-bending work, all of it.'

'Of course he deserves to get on but he'll need a bit of luck as well. If he wants to build up his own business in tailoring.

The East End's packed with Jewish tailors who're excellent
when it comes to the sewing machine and hand stitching. You
see them in Whitechapel of a Sunday morning hoping to be
taken on. Piecework is what it's all about.'

'Errol knows that. But he's going down a different route.
Work'll come his way. He's a grafter and tailoring's in 'is blood.'

'I know he's a grafter. So's my Tony. Except his love is food.
He'll own his own restaurant one day.'

'Exactly. We've done all right for ourselves, Mags. The Prime
Minister's been saying that we've never 'ad it so good and I
think he might be right. We *are* on the brink of better times
and good job as well. And do you know who, in her own way,
'as been telling us that for years? Your aunt Naomi.'

'Don't remind me.' Maggie smiled. 'The older I get the more
I realise that what Nao's been saying hasn't been a load of
hogwash after all. It's just that the things she's told us in the
past seemed a bit too much for one person in one lifetime to
'ave experienced. But now I don't think so.'

'Well, we're not talking about an ordinary person, are we?
She's special, your great-aunt. A one-off. And still glamorous
in 'er own way – even though she's old. She can wear something out of her box of tricks from the nineteen twenties and
make it look fashionable. She's got a style of 'er own, that
woman.'

And truer words could not have been spoken. As to Maggie's
aunt Naomi's penchant towards the roaring twenties . . . as far
as she was concerned, there had never been a time as magical
as then and she never held back from saying so. To Naomi,
glamour had been at its peak and the 'moderns' had looked
just as stunning off stage as they appeared on it. Her treasured recollections, often described to Maggie and Rita however,
were of a different period – the 1890s. As a ragged street urchin,
Naomi had sneaked into the stage entrance of a small West
End theatre and viewed from a secret place, the beautiful actress
and mistress to the Prince of Wales, Lily Langtry on stage.
Exuding charisma as she reclined on a plush red silk chaise-

longue, her long trailing gold satin gown decorated with pearls to match her hairpiece, Miss Langtry had been the epitome of all that any young girl could wish or hope to become. Maggie and Rita had loved listening to wonderful accounts of that era while curled up in Naomi's cosy home for one.

'The strange thing is,' said Rita, 'if we was to dress up in Naomi's lovely sequinned flowing clothes we'd look ridiculous.'

'I know. And it's just as well because she wouldn't let us get anywhere near 'em. Anyway, they're practically museum pieces now.'

Coming into the room, Peppie offered a metal triangle to Rita which he had bolted together. 'You can hold this. But you can't keep it.'

Taking it from him, Rita admired it. 'Well that is definitely a triangle. And it's right that you don't give it to me. You need to look after every nut and bolt so you can add to this and make a car one day. But thank you for letting me hold it.'

'It's my best present. Thank *you*!' said Peppie taking it back. Then, looking sheepishly from Rita to his mother, murmured, 'Except for my scooter from Mummy and Daddy.' He then turned smartly around and went back into the bedroom to make something else.

'We've got to move out of Mum's flat soon, Reet,' Maggie sighed. 'The six months has turned into five years in no time.'

'Why? What's the hurry? I thought it was all working out okay.'

'It is but we should have a place of our own.'

'You and Tony should have moved into the flat in Islington. I don't know why you didn't.'

'I wanted to be near Mum and Aunt Nao. And you. And in any case one of Tony's cousins was in there like a shot once you and me moved out. Anyway, it won't be long now and we'll be in our own place on the Ocean Estate. A little house with a front and back garden. Can't ask for more than that, can we?'

'No, you can't. Lucky to get one. It's only 'cos of little

Peppie. Without a kid you wouldn't stand a chance at the moment with the Borough when it comes to housing. Not that I mind my little nest for one. It's cheap and I think the world of Errol but am I ready to share a home with another person *all* the time? I just hope we don't get any more of them notes through the door. I'm not sure whether to let Errol see it or not.'

'Not,' said Maggie.

'Best ignore it altogether then?'

'Definitely.'

'People do get bored with tormenting after a while if they don't get a reaction. Your mum pulled the best trick of all and fooled 'er neighbours. They actually *believed* that it was her who was pregnant and not you and then accepted it when he started to call *you* Mummy instead of your mum.'

'Most knew the truth though, Reet. It was obvious really. Me disappearing for six months like that and then being there when he was born and staying on . . . before and after me and Tony were married. The two old gossips never twigged it, though. All that time when they used to whisper behind their hands that it was a disgrace the way we let Peppie call me mummy and Mum grandma. They had no clue as to who was having the last laugh. They honestly believed that he was Mum's illegitimate baby. They called her the merry war widow, you know. Jessie Smith told us. Never said it twice, though.'

'I still can't believe that your mum had the nerve to walk about with a cushion under her clothes and you hiding your big fat belly in Islington 'til it was due. Brilliant. Thank God you never listened to me, eh? Little Peppie wouldn't be here now if you had of done. I'm usually right about most things but I was wrong there. You was right not to 'ave an abortion. It don't bear thinking about now.'

'And now it's your turn to listen to me. Chuck that note in the bin and forget it.'

'I already said I would. I'm not worried for myself over it.

It's Errol. Too much of this kind of thing and he might stop coming round.'

'He won't stop. He might carry you off sooner than later, though. To your little house in Jamaica Street. And how bad's that?'

A sudden chilling sound of a bottle smashing against the outside of the house stopped them dead. Raising an eyebrow, Rita got up from the sofa and walked casually from the room to look out of the front window. She needn't have worried that the noise might frighten her godson. Peppie was too engrossed with his Meccano set to care. Back in the living room, she drew breath and slowly shook her head. 'I couldn't see anyone but that's not the first time it's happened. I s'pose it could 'ave been kids. Sometimes I'm terrified that Errol will get beaten up when he goes back from here to Hackney. The Bethnal Green and Roman Road boys are okay. They've got mates who're black. But you never know who's waiting to kick the shit out of someone 'cos they're different.'

'I used to think that about Tony. Him being Italian and looking it.'

'This is different. People are used to ordinary foreigners . . . Italians, Jews, Polish, Russians and Germans.'

'Well, excuse me . . . but I'm not married to an *ordinary*. This is Tony we're talking about.'

'You know what I mean. But you never get notes through your letterbox, do you? Or bottles thrown against the front of the house. What if they was to come and kick our door in? I've seen what a gang can do, Maggie. Once they become a mob. They turn into vicious animals, out for the kill.'

'Well . . . if we're to live in the East End and marry who we want, we just 'ave to put up and shut up 'til it all dies down.'

'And how are we supposed to do that? When I'm faced with this?' She ripped the note off the wall and threw it into Maggie's lap. 'Well?'

'I don't know,' Maggie shrugged. What else could she say?

The sound of another bottle smashing against the front wall of the house made her go cold.

Later on, once she was home and her son's party was over, with the excited and exhausted Peppie put to bed Maggie slipped into her and Tony's room and lay on top of the bed thinking about all that Rita had said. She herself had been on the receiving end of barbed comments from neighbours when she had first started to court Italian Tony, but once she had learned not to react, the dirty looks had gradually eased off. It seemed like it happened only yesterday one minute, and a decade the next. So much had happened during the past few years. Her mum had found and then lost the love of a man, Dennis, who turned out to be someone who liked to have a woman in every hamlet. Tony's family had moved out of their home on the third floor of the block of flats in which she lived, Jessie, her mother's closest friend had mourned the death of Max, her partner of several years and Rita's mum had divorced her husband, remarried and gone to live in Australia. And now Rita was talking about moving into Shadwell; a twenty-minute walk through the back streets would see Maggie there but it wasn't the distance so much as the area. It was alien to her. It was not somewhere to walk alone at night. It was dark with poorly lit narrow turnings and only a stone's throw from Commercial Road and the core of gloomy dockland in the far reaches of Stepney. She didn't want her best friend to move there. She wanted her to stay right where she was – a few minutes' walk away through the arches.

She was so deep in thought she hadn't heard Edie tap on the door. Coming into the room, a radiant smile on her face, Edie said, 'Sonny Jim's out like a light.'

'I'm not surprised, them party games 'ave worn me out as well. I just heard the front door close. Was that Naomi going home?'

'It was, Mags. She said to give you her love. She thoroughly enjoyed herself and so did I. What would we do without that grandson of mine? He's a real treasure.'

'I just wish that Tony had been here to see Peppie's face at the tea table. His first real birthday party with friends from the nursery school instead of just us lot.'

'Work must come before pleasure at the moment, sweet-heart. And not only is Tony a worker but ambitious. And we can't knock that. Do you fancy a cup of tea?'

'Yes, please.'

'Come and sit by the fire, then. I've got something to tell you.' With that, Edie left, closing the door quietly behind her. She and Maggie were particularly close and this was probably because Edie had brought her up without her father around to help. They had come a long way together.

Lifting herself up onto one elbow, Maggie looked at her great-uncle's army uniform from the 1914 war hanging from the picture rail on the wall and smiled. This had been there since the day she and Tony had married when he had worn it for the ceremony, courtesy of war-widow, Great-aunt Naomi. A faint smile on her face she recalled how proud and hand-some he had looked in it. Getting off the bed, she pushed her feet into her fluffy white slippers and went to the window and looked out, imagining the phantoms of those past watching from their place on high. The sky was a dusky blue; a mixture of light and dark as the early evening began to draw the day to a close.

In the sitting room Maggie sank into the small red sofa by the gas fire and curled her legs under her. It was an in-between time, when streets were still and people were indoors after a day's work before going out for the evening to the local pub or cinema; a time when small children were in their beds and older children watching television. She welcomed this quiet time now that everyone had gone home. It was just her and her mum and she loved it when they could sit by the fire and quietly talk, woman to woman, sharing private moments without anyone or anything disturbing their time together. This was something they had enjoyed before they had moved out of their old terraced house in Cotton Street and onto this more sociable council estate. Since moving into the flat her mother, Edie, had made more friends than she ever had in the old house and one or the other of them had often taken Maggie's place in this living room.

Edie arrived with the tea tray and set it down on a low table. Unusually quiet, she poured a little milk into each cup, wondering how she could even begin to tell her daughter something that was painfully close to her heart, often coming into her thoughts when she least expected it. But Maggie was no longer a child but a mother of a five-year-old son and it was time for her to learn the truth. About her father.

'Rita's not very happy, Mum.' Maggie spoke in a quiet voice. 'She covered it well at Peppie's party, though.'

'She did seem a bit troubled and distant,' said Edie. 'I thought it was the noise of the kids. So what is it, then? Is she pregnant?'

'Of course she's not. Why must you jump to that conclusion? There are a million other reasons to bring people down, apart from *that*. Or was it meant to be a dig at me?'

'Don't be silly. I've had nearly five years to get over you gettin' in the club at fifteen. So what is wrong, then? With Rita?'

'She had another nasty note through the door and another two bottles smashed against the wall today. She thinks the note might be from one of her neighbours.'

'About Errol?'

'More or less. There're only ten houses along 'er turning and she knows all the families and landlords. Now she's not sure who she can trust.'

'That's a shame. But you know . . . I doubt it will be one of her neighbours if, as you say, she knows them. Rita's a friendly girl and people react to that. Especially neighbours.'

'I can't believe anyone would do such a rotten thing.'

'Well . . . it takes all sorts, Mags but . . .' shrugged Edie.

'But what?'

'Well . . . Rita's got a good brain. She will 'ave known the kind of reaction she'd get. Going out with a black boy is one thing but getting serious is something else.'

'Don't call 'im that. His name's Errol. And he's not black. No more than we're white.'

'You know what I mean. I can't say a brown boy going out with a pink girl, can I?'

'No . . .' said Maggie, lowering her voice, 'but you could 'ave said Errol instead of black boy. Don't forget that I'm married to an Italian, Mum. That kind of thing hurts, you know.'

'Well, it shouldn't do. Italians 'ave been living in this country for decades. They're part and parcel of the community. And anyway . . . all I meant was that she should 'ave known and been prepared for nasty comments. That's all I'm saying. She's bound to be criticised for walking out with a Jamaican. And she's been with 'im long enough now to have got used to it. A note through the door *is* nasty, mind you. Does she have *any* idea who posted it?'

'No. She gets on all right with her neighbours. Not in and out of each others 'ouses like you, Jessie and Laura but friendly enough.'

'Maybe she should move to Stratford for a while . . . in with her aunt and uncle. They've had a box room with a small bed in it for her since her mum left for Australia. Too much independence is not always a good thing.'

Struck by the suggestion Maggie was thoughtful. 'You know . . . that just might be the answer . . . until she moves into the house that Errol is gonna buy with his uncle – in Jamaica Street.'

'*Jamaica Street*? They're all being pulled down surely? To make room for new blocks of flats? I thought that everyone'd been moved out and they were boarded up.'

'Not all of 'em. The northern end's been flattened but the southern end's not been, and them that are left standing are going cheap.'

'And that's why they've chose that street. Not because of the name.'

'It might 'ave bin the reason Errol's uncle went scouting around there in the first place or one of 'is mates told 'im about it. I don't know.'

'Well . . . we can only wish them well. Owning property can be expensive . . . they'll have to live on a tight budget but so long as Rita realises that, she can't go wrong. And anyway, her background will stand her in good stead. Meals can be cooked cheaply. But she won't need me to tell 'er that. Eileen did a good job of bringing her up on very little.'

'So you think that her and Errol buying a place is a good idea, then?'

'So long as they're both prepared to mend and make do once they're married. Bricks last for years and property goes up in value.' The room went quiet until Edie said, 'So she is definitely gonna marry him, then?'

'Of course she is! They've been courting for ages. Why? Nothing wrong with that, is there? You like Errol don't you?'

'That's not the point; in these times, with people still colour prejudiced, they might be courting more trouble than they can handle.'

'They know that but they love each other, same as me and Tony, and we're all right. You wouldn't 'ave preferred me to marry a nice English boy, would you?'

'Don't be daft. Tony's lovely and so are 'is family and I miss them now they've moved, to be honest . . . and look at the beautiful grandson you've made between you. Can't knock that.'

'And it'll be the same for Rita and Errol. I think they look good together when they walk along arm in arm, her pale skin against his brown . . . and his short, black curly locks next to her white straight hair. She's letting that awful colour grow out now, thank God. Going back to her natural blonde again. They could 'ave brown babies with blue eyes. Anyway, you said you wanted to 'ave a little talk and it sounded a bit serious. Me and Tony are not getting on your nerves, are we? Under your feet all the time?'

'Course not.' Pouring herself a second cup of tea, Edie was in two minds as to whether to mention Maggie's dad or not.

'Well then? If it's not us getting on your nerves, what is it?'

'Don't rush me, sweetheart. Give me time. What I've got to say isn't easy.'

'Surely nothing you've done can be this bad? Come on, smile,' Maggie coaxed, a worry now lodged in the pit of her stomach. 'Mum . . . you're frightening me.'

Leaning back into the cushions of the comfortable second-hand red settee she had purchased when moving into this flat Edie bore the expression of worry. She was reluctant to own up to what she had been keeping secret for so long but it was time to let the truth come out into the open before Maggie stumbled across it herself. Edie drew breath and then spoke in a quiet voice saying, 'It's about your dad.'

'Skeletons in cupboards, eh?' Maggie showed a faint but nervous smile. 'Come on then, out with it. I'm all ears.' The room went so quiet she was aware of the ticking clock. 'Mum . . . you're not gonna cry are you?'

'No. No, I'm not going to cry.' Edie moved her head slightly to glance at her treasured daughter's face, to gauge her expression. 'You'd best prepare yourself for a bit of a shock though and whatever you think of me after I've told you . . . remember I'm not made of stone and none of this was any of my fault. If I'm guilty of anything, it's being chicken-hearted for too long and putting off something which should have been said a few years back.'

'Why 'ave I got to prepare myself for a shock?' Maggie felt a chill down her spine as fear and suspicion crept in. 'It's nothing to do with us two, is it? We're all right . . . aren't we?'

'Yes, it is to do with us . . . or more to the point, your father.'

'Go on, then. I'm listening,' she urged.

Edie took a deep breath as she straightened her back and tipped her chin forward. 'He's alive, Maggie. He wasn't killed in the war.'

Maggie stared at Edie as a silence hung in the room. When

she finally spoke it was no more than a whisper. 'My dad is *alive?*'

'Yes.'

'He *wasn't* killed in Turkey . . . during the war?'

'No. Your father made a decision . . . a very long time ago . . . not to come back to us. His boat did crash, but he was nursed back to health by a young Turkish woman.'

'Who he fell in love with?' Maggie could hardly believe her mother was reeling off without emotion something so heavy and serious.

'Apparently so.'

'And you're one hundred per cent sure about this? You couldn't have possibly got it wrong.'

'Sweetheart, please don't talk to me as if I'm a child. Of course I'm sure. It's not the sort of thing to get wrong.'

Maggie leaned back in her chair and stared up at the ceiling, slowly shaking her head, unable to take this in. Pinching her lips together she looked into Edie's sorry face saying, 'So Dennis wasn't the only one to take advantage of you. The two men in your life have treated you like a dishcloth.'

'Don't say things like that. I'm not made of stone. I know this has come as a shock for you but the last thing I need is you to turn on me. And as for Dennis . . . I don't know why he left me just before we were married. Maybe he got cold feet. And your father . . . Well, who knows? He's behaved totally out of character. Unless I didn't really know him the way I thought I did. The worst thing we can do is feel bitter over it.'

'Well, what am I supposed to feel then? Am I supposed to be happy or sad? Happy that he's alive or sad because he never even wanted to see what I looked like. I couldn't 'ave been that ugly.'

'Of course you weren't ugly.' Edie gently smiled. 'And I don't know why he didn't want to come back to see you or me for that matter. We were in love, Maggie. When he went off to war we were both broken hearted at having to be apart.' Then, only just managing not to cry, she all but whispered, 'Last heard of, he was living in the Canaries.'

'The *Canaries*?'

'That's right.'

'Oh well, he's obviously not suffered at all, has he? And he certainly can't have a conscience. Sunny Turkey and then the Canary Islands. Feathered 'is nest very nicely by the sound of it. Not bad, eh? Not when you compare it to the kind of a life you've had.'

'I'm not grumbling about my life. Once I'd got over the grief of thinking he had been killed I found peace. I never carried a torch for him exactly but lived off the love we once had. The memories. Once I found out the truth mind you, that all went down the drain. I was angry and hurt – but not any more. That's all in the past. I don't care now. I don't care what he does or where he is. I don't crave for the companionship and love we once had any more. It's over.'

Maggie reached out and squeezed Edie's hand, saying, 'You didn't have to pretend to me that he was dead, Mum. I would 'ave understood.'

'I thought he was dead . . . until a few years ago when he came back to England. Five years ago. After ten years or so of living a pleasant life. According to what I've been told his main reason for running away from where he was . . . because the young woman who nursed him and he'd been living with, was pregnant . . . with his child.'

'Oh, right . . . great . . . He likes to make the babies but won't stay for the show. And when he came back, did he visit you? Did you go out and 'ave a nice meal together? Did he even ask about me? What I was doing? What I looked like?'

'I never saw him, Maggie. He came back from Turkey and turned up on your aunt Naomi's doorstep. He would have caused me a lot of grief if Nao and her friends hadn't seen him off to the Canaries with his back pocket lined. Ben and Joey organised it all. His passage, everything.

'Your father thought he could sail back into our lives but he was wrong. He was sent packing before he had had a chance to try and worm 'is way back. Ben and Joey helped us more than we can ever thank them for.'

'And where was I while all of this was going on?'

'Where were either of us? I never knew he was back either until a year or so after he'd left. He must 'ave changed a great deal after that boat crash is all I can say. He wasn't perfect but he was a good husband and he would have made a good father. He looked after my brother – your uncle Jimmy – once we were orphaned and not many men would have done that. Anyway, at least I get a war widow's pension out of it – that's something.'

'Except that now you know he's alive it's illegal.'

'That's true. I never thought about that to tell the truth.'

'Well, don't start worrying over it now. Anyway . . . why are you telling me all of this after so much time has passed? Has something happened to make you?'

'Aunt Naomi always thought I should 'ave told you everything and I'm still not sure that I would have now . . .'

'Why? Has something happened to bring it about?' A silence hung in the room as mother and daughter looked at each other. 'I can tell by your face, Mum. Something's happened, hasn't it?'

Edie finished her tea and put her empty tea cup back onto the saucer, determined that no matter what Maggie wanted she was going to stand by her own convictions and have nothing to do with Harry. 'Nao heard from Ben who heard from Joey that your dad has been back in this country again, and recently and before you say anything – I will *not* see him. Not to please you or anyone else. He's dead and buried as far as I'm concerned. I'm not interested in him any more.'

'Back in this country? Since when?'

'I don't know. He's been seen, that's all I can tell you.'

'Where?'

'In Petticoat Lane,' murmured Edie, gazing at the floor, 'on a Sunday morning. Not shopping but selling off the back of a lorry and the things he was selling were going like hot cakes.'

'So we know where to find 'im then . . . if we want to.'

'He was only there that once sweetheart and it was a month ago. He's not been heard of since but Joey reckons that he'll be back with more goods. Hand-made goods from the Canaries made by peasants for peanuts.'

'If it was worth his while, of course he'll be back,' said Maggie, masking the feelings which were going on inside . . . a natural yearning to see him. 'Would it bother you if I went down the Lane and found him?'

Taken aback by this, Edie felt frightened. Fearful that she was about to lose her daughter to her father. 'Why would you want to do that?'

'Because he's my *dad*. I think I would like to ask him why he left us. That's all. I wouldn't let him know where you're living if you didn't want me to. And I wouldn't see him a second time if it upset you. I just feel that . . . I need to see that he's real I . . . s'pose.'

'It's up to you, Maggie. But *I* don't want to get involved. I can't be bothered to go through listening to his excuses and I certainly don't have any questions to ask him. He should have stayed away. But you go and do what you have to. He is your dad after all.'

'And Peppie's grandfather.'

'Exactly. Just think very carefully about it before you go charging in. Don't forget he might not want to know you.'

'I think that's why I have to do it. To feel something. Angry or pleased. I'm in-between feelings right now and it feels wrong.'

'Natural reaction, Maggie. That's all it is. You might feel differently tomorrow or in a couple of days. However long it takes.'

'If I do that'll be good. I'd prefer that. To go back to how it was before you told me. One thing I do promise. If I do it, I will tell you afterwards. I won't keep it a secret. I promise you that, Mum. I won't go behind your back a second or third time.'

Edie sighed with a touch of relief. 'I am so glad you said that, darling. Don't ask me why. I just am. Maybe it's instinct. But I don't want to share you and Peppie with him.'

'Don't worry, Mum,' Maggie smiled, 'that could never happen. Not in a million years. One Sunday I'll maybe take a stroll through Petticoat Lane by myself to see if he's there and I won't even tell Tony about it . . . yet.'

'If you're sure you can handle it . . . then follow your heart.' The expression in Maggie's light green eyes reminded her of the time when her father was fired up by something or the other. Yes, she was her father's daughter all right. And she would be a match for him – her youthful fiery spirit had not gone away, she knew that – it had simply been lying dormant. Now it was back and showing on her face and Edie secretly welcomed it . . . as she would a lost child.

'I don't feel anything for your father now, Maggie, so nothing he does or says can hurt me. I kept myself for that man when he went to war and then I mourned 'im . . . while he was loving a woman in sunny Turkey. If you want to find your dad that's up to you. But I've washed my hands of him.'

Maggie's face broke into a smile. 'That's the spirit, Mum. Good for you. At the end of the day we've got each other and Peppie and Aunt Naomi. Not to mention our friends. I'm not exactly intending to fall into his open arms . . . if they are open. He never bothered about me, did he? And I couldn't wish for a better grandfather for Peppie than Tony's dad.'

'I'll make a fresh pot of tea,' said Edie, patting Maggie's hand. 'Let's not forget that this is a very special day. Your son's fifth birthday.'

Standing in the kitchen with the door between herself and her child, Edie allowed herself a quiet private moment of self-pity for all the years of sadness and all the hurt that she had felt and kept to herself. But at least she had told Maggie now which meant that they could talk about her long-lost husband freely, if and when either of them wanted to.

2

After several disturbed nights and now waking in a sweat after a bad dream, Maggie knew that she was not going to push the news of her father being alive to the back of her mind. She had had too many formidable dreams centred around him with herself being dragged away from either her mother, her aunt Naomi, her husband or her treasured son. Now, with the flat silent and Tony sleeping soundly next to her, she carefully eased herself out of bed, crept into the narrow passageway and went into the kitchen to quietly close the door behind her. It had just gone five thirty and the early morning sun was coming in through the window. Having lain silently in her bed for over twenty minutes hoping to get back to sleep again she was now quite awake and gasping for a fresh hot cup of tea.

Her shadowy father, at the root of her nightmares and always in the forefront of her mind when awake, was going to have to be approached in the flesh. Since Edie's confession that he was alive and well Maggie had not been quite free to get on with her life as normal. The worry of her mother who wasn't a war widow after all, even though she was drawing a pension, conjured up pictures of court rooms, a stern judge and Edie thin and white in a plain grey frock crouched in the corner of a cell having been sentenced to a term in prison for fraud and deception. Having struggled with changing thoughts as to whether to face her father or not she now knew that this was something she had to do soon or forget it altogether. The more she thought about the web of deceit he had created and dragged her family and her mother's friends into the more she felt justified in confronting him.

Pouring boiled water from the kettle into the brown teapot

with the Sunday sun coming in through the window and onto her face she began to feel lighter inside. She toyed with the idea of taking a stroll down Petticoat Lane the very next morning, Sunday, and perhaps continue to do so on and off over the next weeks or months. She would have a quiet word in Tony's ear and leave Edie to work it out for herself as to why she had to go. The fact that her father had forced himself upon her great-aunt Naomi, on his first trip back to England a few years ago while hiding from the authorities, had showed him to be entirely selfish. His own welfare at heart, he could not have thought about the jeopardy he had placed her aunt in when she had, after all said and done, hidden a criminal from the justice of law.

Curled up in an armchair in the living room and sipping her tea, Maggie could not believe that those older than herself and who she presumed to be wiser, had behaved as if they were a law unto themselves by not only sheltering her father, but arranging and assisting him to escape from the threat of arrest when they had secured him a passage out of England and sent him to the Canary Islands. Having questioned Edie further, since she had broken the news that he was alive and living close by, Maggie had been shocked to hear who had been involved in first her father's homecoming and then in his eviction from this country: her great-aunt Naomi and her close circle of friends including Ben, Joey and old Harriet Smith, with whom Nao had lived rough on the streets as a child, once the two of them had escaped from a horrid children's home in Bethnal Green.

Maggie had asked herself over and over how they could possibly think they could keep something so serious a secret from the authorities. Her father had not only faked his own death during the war and deserted in the face of the enemy, but had forged documents and a passport in order to return to England and not only this, but he was trading goods from one country to another. She realised that he had not been the only man to have gone AWOL during the battle to keep Hitler from ruling the world and was hardly the first to have changed his name to avoid arrest, but this business of him coming and going was laughing in the face of the law. He was either totally irresponsible or incredibly self-assured. She couldn't work out which.

Later that day, with Edie and her small circle of friends in the sitting room enjoying a tea-time gossip, Maggie was in the kitchen scrubbing at the neck of one of Peppie's white school shirts which had been soaking in the kitchen sink. She warmed to the sound of Edie softly laughing in the other room. Her mother deserved to be happy, no-one in their right mind would go against that, and considering all that she had been through, she also deserved a medal for endurance. But her law-breaking thought-less father, who had placed her mum in jeopardy, was back in the country and putting her at risk for a second time. She felt as if the life she and Edie were now enjoying was in danger of being blown to smithereens and that blinkers had been worn for too long. As far as Maggie could see if they didn't tread care-fully, her mother could end up in serious trouble for receiving an army pension, knowing that she was not a war widow and that her husband had faked his death. Edie's natural honesty would, she felt, see her humiliated in a courtroom if she were to find herself there being cross-examined. And what of her aunt Naomi? If it came to light that she and her gentle chums had each at one time or another given Harry a roof over his head to hide him, would she be in trouble, too?

The more Maggie thought about it the more she could see a dark horizon for *everyone* who had taken part in her father's selfish cover-up. He had, after all, been seen recently and there was no reason not to believe he would turn up once he knew he had a grandson, his paternal instincts to the fore. It was a *grandson* that Maggie had produced for her parents and not a granddaughter. A *boy*. A lad who would turn into a *man* just like his *granddad*. Maggie could not be sure that he would not come sneaking back if for nothing else other than vanity to see if the boy looked anything like himself.

More maddened at the way her mum had been dragged into her father's seedy life, Maggie's thoughts flew to the second bastard she would like to punch in the face. Dennis. A bachelor who, after having promised himself to Edie, had also vowed to Maggie that he would be like a father to her and had then slunk off without a word before the marriage banns had been read. He, just like her real father, had been a liar and a philanderer and her mother was clearly better off without both men, but Maggie was bitter at each of them having got off scot free.

Having found unconditional love with Tony, she knew that Edie had been deprived of the friendship and caring that comes hand in hand with marriage – never mind the love and passion. It wasn't fair and it wasn't right. Her mother was only forty and this should be a prime time for her, a time to enjoy life with her husband, being grandparents and going on summer holidays and not spending every evening alone or with her old aunt or daughter and son-in-law for company.

In the sitting room with her friends Edie could have no idea what was going through Maggie's mind as she listened to Gloria, the somewhat shy and simple neighbour who lived alone on the fourth floor and who she and the others had taken under their wings. The woman, in her late fifties, had been tormented by children who had teased her from the first day of moving into this block of flats, when they were brand new.

Naomi, who had felt an affinity towards Gloria had managed to bring her out of her shell because she herself knew what it was like to live alone with sometimes only silence for company. Worse than this it appeared that Gloria had no family. She certainly had no visitors. The mocking of children whenever they saw her passing time on her balcony watching the world go by and taking pleasure from all the comings and goings, had done little to install self-confidence. But to this lonely woman it had been some form of contact with the outside world and was a preferred option to having to sit in her living room with only the wireless for company. Being on the fourth and top floor of the block of flats where she lived, she at least had a lovely vista of the heavenly sky and when the sun shone into the room she could fancy herself to be wherever she wanted and she mostly wanted to be in a sunnier place. So, with her view of the sky and the sounds of birds singing above her on the rooftop she had little to lose when there was nothing much else to cherish.

It was through the kindness of Naomi that Gloria was gradually coming out of her isolated world. Since her first evening out in a very long time, when Naomi had coaxed her into going to the opening night of an Afternoon Tea Dance Club at the local church hall, she had begun to shine. Before this, the woman had given numerous excuses when asked as to why she was so alone with no family. She had fabricated incredible stories about her late husband: from him having been tortured in a prisoner of war camp in Japan, to being a Casanova. Whichever the story and no matter how each of them had begun, the ending had always been the same: her husband had committed suicide by way of an overdose and it was she who had found him lying next to her in bed, a cold corpse. Nobody had really known for sure whether the woman lived in a world of fiction or fact.

More recently however, Gloria had kept to a new and more likely version to any she had told previously. She had confided in Naomi that soon after she was married, her husband had shown himself to be a man who liked an easy life with easy money. Her adult son, who she hardly ever saw, had also, at an early age, slipped into a world where to do a day's honest work was not on the agenda. This she had confessed to Naomi in her own kitchen during one of their little tête-à-têtes. Living on her widow's pension, Gloria, up until now, had lived a frugal life, making a joint of meat last an entire week. The routine throughout being exactly the same. Roast on Sunday, cold on Monday, casserole on Tuesday, stew on Wednesday, soup on Thursday and cold again on Friday. As ever, caught up in her own world, she hadn't heard her hostess ask if she would like another cup of tea.

Looking from Gloria to Jessie, Edie quietly said, 'She's away with the fairies agen.'

'I know.' Jessie smiled, then reached out and tapped Gloria on the arm, offering her a chocolate biscuit.

Her face lighting up, Gloria smiled broadly and then said,

'Oh, yes please, dear. That would be nice. It's like a party, isn't it? And it's not even Christmas.'

'Thank goodness. It comes round quick enough as it is,' said Laura, Edie's other friend from along the balcony. 'I don't wanna be dragging them time worn Christmas decorations out of the cupboard for a good while yet.'

'No, but I bet you can't wait to drag them hop vines down though, eh Laura?' Jessie gave her friend an artful wink. 'All right for some. A nice long holiday in Kent.'

'It suits me,' was the bland answer, Laura not being one to rise to her baiting. 'I've got a few months yet before I trundle off. Anyway Jess . . . you'll be living life as if you're on a permanent holiday soon. Living in a lovely village in Norfolk with Tom and the kids. What more could you want?' Turning her face from both Jessie and Edie's knowing smiles, Laura looked out through the open back balcony door and watched as a sparrow pecked at the remaining crumbs of stale bread that Edie had put out that morning. Longing for late August to come along, when she would be on the back of her brother-in-law's lorry, with three or four other families heading for Kent, she could hardly wait to see her part-time lover, Richard the land owner. The memory of their love-making now invading her thoughts she only just heard Edie say, 'I might just climb up on that lorry and go with you, Laura.'

Snapping herself out of her private world, she shrugged. 'You say that every year but never do anything about it. You can come up for a weekend once I'm there and settled in. You know that.'

'I wouldn't dream of cramping your style or space but I might come down there with a tent.'

'You haven't got a tent, Edie.'

'My brother-in-law Stanley has though,' said Jessie. 'He'd let you borrow it. Now that his cottage in Norfolk is all but finished, he won't be needing it for a while. No more camping out now. Now that the thatch on the roof's been patched.'

'So it's not leaking like a tap any more, then?'

'Not according to my sister. Dolly reckons she'll be as snug as a bug this winter and tapping away on her typewriter in the attic room . . . writing that book she's still working on. One about us lot but set around the square where Laura and Jack lived before they moved here.'

'It should be an interesting read if she ever gets it finished,' laughed Edie. 'Sexy and full of gossip.'

'Or a television serial. That's her latest idea. To write it like a play and send it to the BBC. She reckons they'll want a series one day about ordinary people.'

'Let's hope they take it on,' said Laura. 'I can't see it though. A bunch of East Enders on the tele? The posh nobs at the BBC won't go for that. We're seen as the scum of the earth in some quarters, don't forget. It would be good, though. Me and Jack could star in it. The couple who are always at each other's throats. And our Kay could be the cantankerous only child. And Jessie the local sex kitten.'

'Cheeky cow. Mind you . . . if I could flirt the way you do I would.'

Bemused by all of this but more interested in the move to Norfolk, Edie asked Jessie if she thought that Dolly would really settle down in a quiet village in the back of beyond, saying, 'They reckon that Norfolk's flat and windy, never mind isolated and cold. Be a bit of a shock in the bitter winter, wouldn't it?'

'Log fires, Edie . . . don't forget that part of it. Old beams, log fires and a thatched roof,' Laura mused. 'It's got to beat bricks and mortar and smog. Good luck to Dolly is what I say. Good for her.'

'What do you mean good luck to Dolly? She can't wait but what about me? Tom reckons we could be in our cottage before Christmas. I'm not so sure I'm ready to give up my flat, that's the trouble.'

'Well, don't then, Jess. Keep it on for a couple of months until you're really sure.'

'We'll see. It's a different world I'll be moving into once I do make the leap. I can't imagine there's much office work to be had in the local town, Diss.'

'I think you should let Tom go and live there while you stop here in the flat with your Billy and Emma. Wait until next spring. You'll 'ave had plenty of visits up there by then to make up your mind if it's the life for you or not.'

'We're going up there soon for a weekend. I'll 'ave a better picture by then,' said Jessie quietly. 'Perhaps you're right. My sister wouldn't be none too pleased about it, though. She's looking forward to us living next door to each other. My Tom and his brother Stanley'll be fine. They've got plenty of work up there already. A contract with the Norfolk Council to upgrade houses built in the nineteen thirties as well as private work on a manor house.'

'Well, that should sort your son out then, shouldn't it? Your Billy could work alongside his dad and uncle.' Edie smiled. 'All the men up there together.'

'I don't know. He's twenty now, Ed. I think he's planning to stay put in our flat. He's dropped a couple of hints. So have 'is mates. Three young working bachelors in there? Parties every weekend I should reckon.'

'Well, at least it would be a way of keeping it just in case you want to come back home to live. If you turn out to hate living like a country bumpkin.'

'I know.'

'Oh, right . . . so you've already worked that out for yourself, then.'

'Course I have. Me and Tom are fine now but since we got back together, he's spent a great deal of the time with Stanley doing up the cottages. Us living under the same roof all of the time might prove a bit of a strain. My flat can be a bolt hole if I need one.'

Laura nodded in agreement. 'I love going down to Kent for a month of hop-picking but would I want to live there? No. I'd miss the East End.'

'I was tempted to accept a council house in Harlow when we were moved out of Cotton Street,' said Edie wistfully. 'But I didn't want to be far away from Aunt Naomi and my brother Jimmy. Apart from Maggie . . . they were my only family. I'd lost everyone else by then.'

A pitiful hush filled the room until Jessie cut gently through it, saying, 'So, Laura . . . we can come down to see you in Kent then, in late August?'

'You know you can. I don't mind if you come to take a peep at my boss who can't keep 'is hands off me.' Little did she know that she was in for a rough ride this year.

'Oh dear!' shrieked Gloria, suddenly laughing. 'The things you girls come out with! You make me blush even though I know you're only fibbing. I feel as if I'm in another world. In a film in the picture palace.' She continued to quietly laugh as she gazed into space and visualised herself dancing around with a handsome man under sparkling revolving lights to a romantic song.

'He swept me right off my feet!' Gloria startled them with her sudden joyful outburst. 'I didn't even know he was there. At the dance. I was always a wallflower. But I wasn't the only one who was shy! No. Me and my friend Tilly used to get so flushed if we was asked to dance.'

'Who are you talking about, Gloria?' Jessie was pleased that this normally shy woman was seeking a little of the limelight.

'The young man who asked me to dance. See! I remembered that, didn't I Jessie?'

'You certainly did. Your first love, was he?'

'Oh no, dear. No, he only danced with me that once but it made me feel that I wasn't such a wallflower. I danced quite a lot after that. Especially when it was the Ladies Excuse Me. I used to wait for that. So did my friend. We dragged all sorts of men up onto the floor.

'I never met my husband in a dance hall, though,' Gloria continued, as if she didn't want to let go of the attention now that all eyes were on her and her alone. 'He was my first love. I only ever loved one man and that's all you need really, isn't it. One's as good as another so why swap? I don't know why my husband turned bad. The bit in the newspaper said he was born bad. But I don't think he was. I think he was cleverer than a lot of people. He earned such a lot of money. It's a shame I mustn't spend it yet.'

'Why ever not?' Maggie had come into the room and caught Gloria's tail end of her oratory. 'It's what money's for. Use it to make a better life for yourself is my way of thinking.'

'Oh Lord bless me dear, I wouldn't do that! No. My husband was very adamant that I wasn't to touch those gold sovereigns. Nor the money. Not even to give them to our only child. Our son. Even if he went away on a long holiday I was to leave it be.' Her face breaking into a smile again she pushed her face forward and spoke as if she was telling a secret. 'And he is away on a long holiday. A very long one!' She laughed out loud and then within seconds became serious. 'It's all still locked away under my bed in a very old trunk.'

'A small fortune is it then, Gloria,' Laura smiled.

'Thousands of pounds my husband said. And then there's the sovereigns as well. Not that I would open it 'til I really need to. No. He might come back to haunt me so no, mustn't do that. And in any case. I was a very disciplined child and learned very early to do as I was told. There are quite a few bundles of fifty-pound notes my husband said but I don't know what colour they would be.'

'Well, why don't we force the lock open and have a butcher's?'

'Maggie?' Edie gave her daughter a black look and then relaxed into a smile for the sake of Gloria. An expression of worry had fixed on the poor woman's face.

'I don't think I was meant to tell you about the trunk. We'll forget about it, shall we? Silly me. Going on about the past. Nothing we can do about that now, is there? It's got nothing to do with today has it, so best not go down that road. Enjoy the day you're in . . . that's what Naomi tells me and she knows best.'

'Oh . . . so you told my great-aunt about the money, then?'

'No! I never! I never told a soul! Not even my son, James.' Quiet and thoughtful for a few seconds Gloria smiled again, saying, 'Naomi's my friend. When I get sad because I've got no family coming to visit she gives me kind advice to cheer me up. You can choose your friends but you can't choose your family can you? Which is a shame really. Except in the children's home. People used to come to choose a child they took a liking to. They never chose me, though.' She began to laugh again while the others remained solemn. 'Well they wouldn't! I was too pale and scrawny!' Her smile dissolved as she stared down at the floor, remembering. 'That's what Matron said. Too pale and scrawny,' she muttered before suddenly breaking into a smile. 'My son might come again, though. Soon. I've seen him once this year already!'

So far as Edie knew, no-one had yet been told that Gloria had spent her childhood in a home and it wasn't another fabrication that she wanted to hear. It was a bit too much to take. She glanced across the room and saw that Jessie had her eyes raised to the ceiling and her hands were tightly clutched together. The talk of a children's home and when she had had to place her daughter Emma in one during the war had been dragged back by Gloria's oration.

'My husband never minded me being a bit on the slow side,' the woman continued. 'I was twenty-two when we met. He put a half-crown in my collecting bag when I was in the Army.'

Trying to steer the conversation to a more normal level, Edie sported a look of surprise and interest. 'I didn't know you had joined up, Gloria. During the war was it?'

'Oh, not that army, silly!' More laughter. 'The Salvation Army!' She slowly shook her head, remembering it. 'I had to give all that up, though . . . once I was courting my husband. He wanted me to himself. That's what he said. I was his and his alone. I couldn't even have any friends. He loved my cooking and the perfect way I ironed his shirts and pressed his trousers. I was very house proud. Still am.'

'Do you see much of your son, Gloria?' said Laura.

'No, dear. He's a very busy important man in business. I expect he will come and see me again, though. Once or twice a year.'

'And where might your husband be now?' said Maggie, feeling as if she would like to give the man and his son a kick in the shin for neglecting this sad mad soul.

'Dead and buried, dear. They hanged him. For murder.'

A silence that could be cut with a knife filled the room. With all eyes on her, Gloria was clearly relishing her moments in the sun. 'I think that's kinder than the electric chair that the Americans use.' She looked from one to the other, a faint smile on her lips.

'They allowed him to wear his own clothes, which was nice, wasn't it? And it only took fifteen seconds from the time the hangman put the noose around his neck until he was in the cell below. They told me that. So he wouldn't have had time to worry over it. And on the death certificate it said, "Injuries to the central nervous system . . . consequent upon . . . judicial hanging." I thought that was a nice way of putting it. Much better for the grandchildren to know. If there are any. But I don't think that my son will marry. I don't think he's the type.

'The prison officers were kind and so was the priest who came to see me once it was over. He said that my husband, even though he wasn't a church-going man, had turned to God in his final hours. That made it better. Made me feel nice and warm, inside. Better to go quick like that instead of a long terrible illness in pain and agony. Like a lot of people have to put up with.'

With an expression of holiness on her face, Gloria smiled at Jessie. 'That's why I said to you that that lovely man of yours, Max, had a nice quick ending and you should thank God for it. You didn't appreciate that at the time dear, but now that the years have gone by you probably realise I was right.'

Jessie felt her heart lurch at this sudden reminder of how she had lost a partner whom she had known and thought so much of since she was fifteen. This remark would have been cruel had it come from anyone else but this barmy woman. She lowered her eyes to avoid Gloria's, hoping she would drop the subject but it was futile. The woman looked around the room at each of them and bore the resemblance of a gentle nun. 'A quick heart attack is the best way to go. And so is execution if it's under the watchful kind eye of the priest. So there we are. We've got something in common, Jessie. Haven't we?'

The women could only gaze at Gloria, speechless. She was making Max's heart attack and car crash sound like some kind of wonderful act from God. Max, who had such plans for the

future. Max who lived for tomorrow. Max who had been cruelly
cheated of having any of his much deserved dreams come true.

Picking up on Jessie's sinking mood, Edie wasn't quite sure
whether to contrive a quick end to this gathering and lead the
completely mad Gloria out or say nothing and wait for someone
else to end this macabre scenario. She could hardly believe that
anyone was capable of making up such stories off the cuff,
and especially not this simple-minded woman. And Maggie
was feeling something deep inside. Her inner voice was telling
her to get out from under her mother's roof. Having heard
more than enough for one day, she stepped in with her forthright manner and firm expression which was bang on target.

'Right, you lot. I'm expecting my Peppie to come in any
minute now so with the best will in the world . . . you know
where the door is.' She then winked at Jessie, softening her
voice and saying, 'Your Emma's the best child-minder in the
world. Peppie adores her.'

'Thanks for that, Maggie,' said Jessie, rising to the occasion.
'That's a lovely thing to say. Emma thinks the world of him,
too.' She then stood up, took a deep breath and said, 'Come
on Gloria, I'll walk upstairs with you. To our balcony.'

'Oh, that's all right, dear. I'm quite comfortable here. This
is a lovely room. Homely.'

'Maybe so, but Maggie's expecting her little boy and—'

'Oh, don't mind me. I'll fetch him a few sweets next time I
come.' Smiling innocently and somewhat childlike, Gloria made
no attempt to get up. In fact she looked as if she was there for
the rest of the week. Jessie looked from her to Edie, lost as to
how she was to get the message across. She needn't have worried.
Maggie bore a different expression, one of defiance.

Jabbing her thumb towards the open doorway, she said, 'Come
on, Gloria. This is a family home not the Women's Institute.'

'Goodness me, Edie,' was Gloria's smiling response as she picked
up her handbag from the floor. 'What a strict daughter.' Pulling
herself to her feet she gave a little shrug of her shoulders. 'Thank
you very much for the hospitality. I've had such a lovely time.'

'You're welcome,' said Edie. 'We'll do it again.'

'Will we? Oh, that would be nice. Next week?'

'No,' said Maggie. 'At Christmas time, when we'll invite the neighbours in for a quiet, quick drink.'

'All of them, dear? I shouldn't think we'll all fit, will we?' she asked innocently.

'She means those who we're friendly with,' whispered Jessie, taking Gloria's arm and walking with her to the street door and out of the flat. Edie followed in their footsteps.

Flabbergasted by all that had been said, Maggie flopped into an armchair. 'Can you believe that woman, Laura?'

'It takes all sorts.' Laura gently smiled. Then, lowering her eyes to the floor, she drew breath. 'All sorts.'

'So she got to you as well, then?'

'No. I wasn't really listening to tell the truth. I was preoccupied with my own problems.'

'New ones or time worn?' said Maggie, as always comfortable in her neighbour's presence.

'New . . . I think.' She looked into Maggie's face and said, 'I think that my Jack's got serious with one of his women on the side.'

'Oh, come on,' said Maggie, quietly. 'He doesn't have women on the side, Laura. He just flirts a lot, that's all. And . . . well, if he does get his leg over occasionally, you can't really point the finger, can you?'

'I've always got hop-picking, you mean?'

'That's one way of putting it.' Maggie tilted her head and waited. 'Come on. It can't be that bad.'

'I think that it's been just the one woman all this time. The flirting's been a clever cover-up. I've spotted little clues here and there. Her name's Patsy. I'm not going to let him know that I know, though. That way I'll find out more.'

'Well, if this *is* the case then, yeah, you should do something about it. Blow that for a lark. Who does she think she is? Jack's your man. Your husband. Kay's dad. Get rid of her and soon. Go and find her and tell 'er to sod off. I would. Blooming cheek.'

'We'll see. Don't say anything to your mother or to Jessie though, will you? You know what they're like. They'll want us to form a spy ring.'

'Course I won't say anything. I'm not like you lot.'

Edie came back into the room and their conversation stopped as Maggie tactfully changed the subject, saying, 'Mum, you do know that you can't pick your family . . . but you can pick your friends, don't you?'

'I should think I do, Maggie. It's what I've told you more than once.'

'I'm not blaming you for Gloria,' Maggie continued, 'or for having a lunatic masking as a nice if not daft woman in our front room, but, Christ, where is she from?'

'It was a bit of a turn up for the books, wasn't it? Who would have thought that someone so frail—'

'I don't think she is as frail as we first thought,' said Maggie. 'She might be small boned and skinny, but she's not frail. Manipulative, maybe. She did manage in her own way to get all the attention. Look at all that stuff she came out with. It was enough to shock Jack the Ripper himself. Or herself as the case may be. Rumour had it at one time that it was a woman that had carried out them murders and after hearing Gloria going on, I think I can believe it.'

'Yeah, all right Mags. You're making my blood run cold. Never mind what Laura's making of all of this.'

'Exactly my point. Why are we discussing dark and horrible things because of one fragile old woman?'

'She's not that old, Maggie. And don't forget she's had a hard life and it shows in her eyes.'

'So have you, Mum, when it's all taken into account.'

'I was never in a children's home thank goodness. It could have happened though Mags, once my dad had left home and my mum passed away. Had I been younger.'

'And you're not round the bend, Mum, are you? And you went through enough. We all treat Gloria as if she's made of porcelain and then she comes out with stuff like that.'

'Well, we won't have to so much now. She's come out of her shell. I must say that stuff about murder, hanging and a quick death made me go cold.' Hugging herself she added, 'And poor Jess. Did you see the look on her face?'

'Of course I saw it. Max has been gone for four years or so now. Fancy her bringing that up and bloody well equating it to someone who's been hanged for murder.'

'Well, let's not be too hard on her, Mags. And stop cursing. Rita swears too much lately as well. I hope it's not her boyfriend's mates you're hearing it from. I know that Tony would never—'

'Oh, what her black mates, you mean? Errol's cousin and family who're darkies?'

'Oh, be quiet. You know I never meant that.'

'That woman's got to me I s'pose. Even after she's gone she's got our attention. I'm telling you Mum,' said Maggie, showing the flat of her hand. 'Keep a long yard between you and that neighbour. I'm sure she is innocent and a bit simple, but there's something going on in that world of hers. Maybe it's not her own fault that there's a dark aura round her, I don't know. But she's made my flesh creep.'

'Don't be silly. She's upset you with all that talk of her husband hanging for murder,' said Edie as she lay her head back into a cushion and closed her eyes. 'I don't believe a word of it and apart from all of that she's harmless enough. Tell 'er, Laura,' she said.

'No way. I'm not getting dragged into it.' Smiling, Laura got up from her chair. 'I'm going home. I've got some pockets to go down.'

'Pockets?'

'Never mind, Edie. I'll see you tomorrow and don't worry, Mags. Naomi's not backwards in coming forward. She'll soon pull Gloria up if she gets carried away with her bizarre fantasies again. See yer.' With that Laura was out of the room.

'See you, Laura! And leave no stone unturned!' Maggie called after her.

'Leave no stone unturned? Am I missing something here?'

'Oh it was just a joke we'd been having, Mum. Forget it. We were just trying to lighten the atmosphere.'

'Come on, sweetheart,' Edie smiled. 'Gloria might be too simple to know what not to say, but she's all right. She rarely socialises, that's the trouble. Who else has she got to talk to? No-one.'

'I'm not surprised.'

'She's got to learn how to make conversation, that's all. Can you imagine what it must be like? Living on your own with no-one popping in and being too frightened to go out by yourself. She hasn't got a television like we have; that would make a little difference. Just to hear other people's voices in the room, albeit from a square box with a screen.'

'Well, according to her she's got a little fortune under her bed. Why don't she spend some of that and get herself a telly? Or buy tickets for a show and take you and the girls out for a night? She could do, couldn't she?'

'Girls are we now?' Edie smiled.

'Women then. Whatever. But she could.'

'So you believed that bit then?'

'I think so. Why would she want to make that up? It wasn't as if she was using it to buy your friendship or anything. All right, there might not be much more than fifty pounds in there but—'

'No,' said Edie, stopping her flow. 'If it's for real she was talking about a lot more than that. A great deal more. Fifty-pound notes in bundles? Never mind the rest.'

'Well, it must 'ave been another silly fancy, then. Not as dark as the hanging by a noose bit. God.' Maggie shivered.

It made Edie shudder too. She cleared away the empty teacups, saying, 'Well then, best we don't think about it any more.' She left the room and went into the kitchen, the word 'manipulative' now on her mind. Placing the dirty crockery in the sink she shook her head and, talking to herself said, 'No . . . she's just a sad and lonely soul, that's all. And that's more than enough for anyone.'

Aware that Maggie was standing in the open doorway she said nothing and kept her back to her. There was an atmosphere in the flat now and it was understandable. Gloria's gentle face came into her mind again, her expression when she had told them about her husband having been hanged for murder. She didn't seem the type to lie so outrageously but there was no disputing the fact that she had seemed to have enjoyed being at the centre of it for those few minutes.

'I'm not gonna harp on about it, Mum,' said Maggie, cutting into her thoughts, 'but I really don't think you should have Gloria in here when you're by yourself.'

'Oh, stop being silly. I asked her in simply because I met her on the stairs and felt sorry for her. She was so pleased with herself because she'd walked all the way down four flights and taken a five-minute walk to the green and back. It had been a huge thing for her. She'd walked beyond her realm and climbed a mountain.'

'I realise all of that and all I'm saying is—'

'I know sweetheart! I know what you're saying. We'll leave her to Jessie and Laura and Aunt Naomi. Now put the wireless on and see if you can tune in to something decent we can listen to. Something cheerful.'

'You'll be lucky. Peppie's on his way.'

Turning around, Edie smiled. 'How did you know? I never heard him and I'm closer to the window than you are.'

'Because I'm like that lovely little puppy who belonged to the Smith family in Cotton Street. Remember him?'

'Course I do. He used to wag his tail and wait by their front door before Mrs Smith could see her husband coming home from work. I always thought you had more of your aunt Nao's blood in you than I have. Two white witches in one family. God help me.'

'So you'll listen to me then and stop treating me like a school-girl?'

'Yes, Maggie. Now drop the subject of Gloria, please.'

'Consider it done.' She placed her hands on her hips and grinned. 'See. I told you.' They could both hear Peppie talking ten to the dozen now. 'I don't know how Emma puts up with him. You couldn't lend me half a crown could you?'

'Take it out of the jar.'

'Or do you think that's too little? She's only had 'im for a few hours.'

'She might not want anything, love.'

'Maybe not.' Maggie tipped five sixpenny bits out the jar while Edie went to open the door, before her grandson banged on the knocker three times loudly. She couldn't wait to hear what he had on the tip of his tongue this time. Peppie adored Sid the Singing Tramp. The friendly old gentleman could always be found in Barmy Park performing to his free audience as they sat on the low, brick wall that circled the large outdoor paddling pool. The old boy would play his lovely old accordion while singing a kind of song which nobody could quite make sense of. But it didn't matter. It was enough to watch his performance, his own kind of slow, stamping dance. A vacant smile on his sun-weathered face. His battered trilby always on his head and hardly ever placed on the floor to receive coppers. Sid the tramp, with the inside of his old belted gabardine mackintosh packed with newspapers to keep him warm in the winter and cool in the summer, had the appearance of a happy down-and-out. It had always been rumoured that he was in fact a wealthy eccentric from an old, aristocratic family. No-one knew for sure what Sid was or where he came from and it mattered not one iota. He was their local singing tramp who was like an old Uncle Christmas. Always content, sometimes smiling and never cross. And Peppie, like so many other children, was in awe of him.

Pouring lemonade into two glasses for Peppie and Jessie's lovely daughter, Emma, Maggie grimaced when she overheard her little boy telling Edie, somewhat excitedly, that Gloria had seen him coming along from her view on the balcony in the sky and had waited for him on the stairs where she had given him a pound note to buy some sweets. Bounding into the kitchen the five-year-old looked up at Maggie with a huge smile on his face, saying, 'I've got a real pound note!'

'I heard you the first time, sweetheart, telling nanny at the door. The lady upstairs gave it to you.' She looked from him to Emma who was now standing in the doorway and suddenly realised that to give this young working girl a palmful of sixpenny bits would be insulting. 'Thanks for taking him Emma,' she said. 'Can I pop in later with the baby-sitting money? I don't want to give you loose change and I've only—'

'It's all right, said Edie, butting in. 'I've got a half-crown in my purse.'

'No, I don't want anything,' said Emma. 'And I mean that. We went for a walk over the park. It's not the same as when I babysit. Anyway, if anyone is to treat anyone, it's money bags here. What a turn up for the books, eh? A pound note.'

'Indeed.' Maggie sported a sorry look as she smiled down at her son. 'And now, we can expect a flood of tears because you, my darling, will have every reason to have a tantrum. You've got to give it back, sweetheart.'

'I haven't got to,' said Peppie, stamping his foot. 'She said I could keep it. She put it in my hand and pressed my fingers round it.' He looked to Emma for support. 'Tell Mummy, Em. Tell her I'm not fibbing!'

'She knows you're not, silly. But it is a lot of money, Peppie.'

Going down on one knee, Maggie pushed her fingers through her boy's hair and smiled into his sulky face. 'I'm sorry babe but . . . you know what the other children say about the lady. That she's a bit like simple Simon. If she wasn't, she wouldn't have given you the pound note in the first place. People don't do that sort of a thing. It's a lot of money. So . . . you're gonna be a good boy, an honest boy, and go with Emma to the lady's door and give it back to her.'

'But it's mine! It's a present . . .' he pleaded.

'Presents come wrapped in parcels, darling.' Maggie was beginning to wish she had never heard of the woman on the fourth floor. 'So . . . either you take it back or I'm going to have to. And if I do, she might be sad over it. But if you hand it over she'll think you're a very good boy. And one day, when she goes out to the shops she might buy you a present with the money. A proper present.'

Peppie narrowed his eyes and creased his brow, puzzled. 'What kind of a present?'

'I don't know, darling. A toy of some sort. Just do as I say, there's a good boy.' Maggie pulled herself to full height and glanced at Edie, mouthing the words, 'Bloody woman.'

'I wasn't naughty for taking it, was I?'

'No, of course not. But if you don't give it back it might look as if you are. All right? It's not your money, Peppie – it's hers. Okay? But if you don't want to go up there, I'll take it for you.'

'Come on, Peppie,' said Emma, winking at him. 'We'll go back up and if the lady refuses to take it, maybe your mum will let you buy some post office stamps with it. Save it for a rainy day.'

'Sounds reasonable,' said Edie, grateful as ever for Emma and the way she handled her grandson. 'Can't argue with that, Mags.'

'All right. If you both think so. Go on then – before bath time.'

'It's not bath time yet,' moaned Peppie. 'It's time for Sooty and Sweep. Emma said so.' With that he took his babysitter's hand and sauntered out of the flat with her.

Taking a moment to wonder if she had done the right thing by sending him up to the woman who was obviously a penny short of a shilling, Maggie felt her heart lurch. 'Maybe I should have gone with him?'

'Don't be silly. You're over-reacting. He's fine with Emma. She's sensible. She's not a kid any more, is she? Turned seventeen, now. She might look young for her age but she's got a good head on her shoulders.' The echoing sound of Tony and Rita's boyfriend Errol laughing on the staircase stopped Edie in her tracks. 'Right. His dad is back now so no more on the subject or this will grow out of all proportion.'

'He's not going to like it, Mum. I can tell you that for sure.'

'Well then, don't tell him.'

'Oh . . . and you think that Peppie won't?'

As soon as Tony stepped into the kitchen and before he had said a word, Maggie smiled sweetly at him. 'You'll never guess what? The Sink Lady only gave our Peppie a pound note. He's gone up there with Emma to give it back. I told him to.'

'Whoa!' whooped Errol. 'Girl . . . the woman can give me a pound note any time. Why you looking so worried?' he said.

'I didn't think it was right,' said Maggie, her eyes on her husband's face. 'What do you think, Tony?'

'That the woman should have given it to me!' joked Errol, giving Edie the teasing eye.

'Why did she give it to him?' asked Tony, his voice flat. 'Did he ask her for it?'

'No, of course not. He was coming back from the park with Emma and she met them on the stairs and gave it to him. For sweets.'

'A pound note for sweets?' Errol's expression showed concern. 'Well . . . we kids at home were warned not to take a t'ing from those whom we didn't know. Does a neighbour count as that?'

'How long have they been up there?' said Tony.

'Not long. They went just before you came up. I'm surprised you never heard them.'

Preoccupied with his own thoughts Tony slowly shook his head. 'Maggie . . . if he asked her for money he's going to feel the back of my hand on his rump.'

'He never asked for it! Emma was with him and she said the woman pushed it into his hand as happy as Larry. And anyway . . . Peppie wouldn't do that.'

'He's a kid, Maggie. Five years old. I would 'ave done if there was a rich old woman as a neighbour when I was his age. I can't see him handing it over too keenly. I'll wander up there and see what it's all about. And no, I never heard them. Errol was bending my ear as usual – about Jamaica Street.'

'Eh? I don't t'ink so. Eh eh. I never said anyt'ing about it.' Errol was exaggerating his accent as usual.

'That woman makes me feel creepy as it happens,' said Tony. 'Always has done. My mum used to say that she had an aura of death around her.'

'She never said that Tony. Surely not?' said Edie.

Quietly laughing at his mother-in-law, Tony squeezed her cheek. 'We're talking about my Italian mama, don't forget. Had she ever had any *real* reason to worry she would have been there with her rolling pin. She wasn't *that* bothered. She thought she was a bit of a mystery that's all.'

'She is Tony, trust me,' said Maggie, her face breaking into a smile. 'You should have heard the things she came out with today.'

'No, thanks. It's bad enough the way she smiles at me if we ever pass on the stairs. As if she's known me all her life. As if I'm her long-lost son or something. Keep me company Errol and your fingers crossed and a smile on your face in case she's a witch. She might make and then burn an effigy of you. Come on, move yerself!' he said as he made his way along the passage.

'You see what I mean?' crooned Errol to Edie. 'He the boss and it gettin' me down.'

'Go on, the pair o'you,' Edie laughed. 'Before I slap one of you on the back of the legs.'

'Oh woman, don't talk dirty, eh? It could be our future in the making. And what I gonna tell my Rita?' Following Tony along the passage, Errol, humming a tune of an old-fashioned honky-tonk began to sing: *'What a beau . . . tiful thought, I am thinking . . .'*

'He's as bonkers as Rita,' said Edie, laughing. 'It's lovely that him and Tony get on so well though Mags, eh?'

'Yes, Mum,' said Maggie, noting the colour rising in her mother's cheeks and the sparkle in her eye. Errol was a handsome young man and clever with it. He had lifted Edie's spirits as usual by flirting with her. But to her mind there was nothing wrong with that. It showed that there was passion in Edie waiting for the right man to come along and rekindle the flame.

'Do you know what I think would be good?'

'What's that?'

'If you, Laura and Jessie were to go to the jazz club in Brick Lane one night. You'd love it there.'

'I'm sure we would but we'd look a bit out of place, wouldn't we? A bit too old for that sort of place?'

'Don't be daft. There's no age limit. Everyone goes. All ages and all creeds. It's the music and atmosphere that draws people in. You could dance 'til the cows come home. Sound the girls out and let me know. I'll make sure I'm not there. Errol and his friends will take care of you.'

'You make us sound like old women. Take care of us?'

'You know what I mean.'

'And why wouldn't you, Rita and Emma be there to see us enjoy ourselves?'

'You must be joking. I would die of embarrassment. My mum jiving or dancing all smoochy with a bloke? My cheeks are beginning to burn at the thought of it.' Maggie quietly laughed. 'Imagine yourself in my shoes. If it was your mum letting her hair down in a West Indian nightclub. With gorgeous young men all over her.'

Visibly shaken, Edie tried to picture it. Tried to remember a time when her mother was smiling and in any kind of mood for dancing. She couldn't. All she could see was her wasting away with no illness other than grief being the cause. Whether Edie would ever be able to talk about her mother's suicide was something she chose not to think about. But she had a grandson now and soon he too would want to know more about his gran who was dead. She went icy cold at the thought of telling any of them the tragic truth. Especially her daughter.

'See?' Maggie chuckled. 'You can't answer me, can you? You know you would have hated it.'

'In those days,' said Edie, her voice flat. 'People like us didn't go to nightclubs. They went to the local pub. But even so, my mum and dad never used to go out together, socialising. They drank a glass of stout with Sunday dinner but that was about it. Dad was always in the pub, though. Not a drunk. Nothing like that. Just having a drink with his mates,' she said, matter of fact. 'I don't think it would have occurred to him to ask my mum to go with. But then . . . he had been seeing his other woman. Seeing your stepbrother's mother. My mum never had much of a life outside the home. It never seemed to bother her though, but then, who knows? To be in every evening while he was out for an hour or so must have affected her.

'I sometimes wonder if she knew what was going on and chose to ignore it. Hoping it might go away. I wish that I had been more aware. I can't tell you how many times I've wished that. It's a terrible thing to be too late to change the course of things that lead to tragedy. I just didn't see it coming.'

The expression on Edie's face was upsetting Maggie. 'Seen what coming? What tragedy? Your dad leaving you all?'

Deep in the past and her thoughts, Edie hardly heard Maggie. 'I just didn't see it coming. The neighbours did. They said so afterwards.' Suddenly shaking herself out of that mood, she looked at Maggie and shrugged. 'Take no notice of me.'

'Your dad seeing someone else you mean? You never saw that coming?'

'Something to that effect.' Edie kissed Maggie on the hand. 'One Saturday afternoon in the winter we'll sit by the fire and I'll tell you more and we can talk about my mum. What she was like before it started to go wrong.' She wiped her eyes with the back of her hand. 'I loved my dad but my mum was every-thing to me. I lived in her shadow. She was my mum. Mine. Soft and kind. I couldn't 'ave been more content when I was curled up on her lap with my head snuggled into her breast. Even that far back I can remember her. Her soft voice and her smell of talcum powder when she was holding me and gently singing. The warmth and the soft heart beats.'

Choked by this unusual baring of her soul, Maggie only just managed to speak. 'Is that why you used to love getting Peppie off to sleep for me? It brought back memories?'

'Probably.' Pulling herself out of that mood Edie lifted her head and listened to the outside sound of footsteps echoing on the stone stairs. 'And if I'm not mistaken that's them coming back. Go and open the door for them love, while I powder my nose.'

Directly her daughter was out of the kitchen Edie lifted her handbag off a hook behind the door and found her compact. In the tiny mirror she could see that her face was flushed and knowing her grandson as she did she could expect him to see she had been tearful. Once she had patted the powder puff against her hot cheeks she snapped her compact shut. But she needn't have worried. Peppie was sulking and keeping his eyes fixed on the floor when he came into the kitchen. It hadn't been easy for him to part with the money. Tony followed him in with Emma and Errol in his footsteps trying to lighten the mood as he joked with Edie that both she and Maggie were going to have to stop spoiling his sulky son.

'Fair enough, Tony,' said Edie, supporting her grandson's grumpy mood with a bemused smile. 'But Grandfather Baroncini's worse than me when it comes to what Peppie wants or doesn't want. He runs rings round him.'

'That's because Italians are like that. It's in the blood to spoil children.'

'It wasn't my fault,' murmured Peppie, tears trickling down his face and neck. 'She give it to me. It was mine. My real pound note.'

Errol's light-hearted voice drifted in from the passage. In the same mood as earlier he was still talking like his uncle. 'Gloria is one very *strange* woman. But she make me laugh and that no bad t'ing.'

'She wanted to give me the money for being a nice boy,' wailed Peppie. 'She said it.'

'Never you mind, sweetheart. We all think you're a good boy for giving back the money. Daddy agrees with that, don't you, darling?'

Tony, a touch guilty now said, 'Course I do. Never mind, son. One day Daddy's going to own his own café and you can work in it and earn lots of pound notes.'

'When?' sniffed Peppie before wiping his nose on his cuff, cheering up at the prospect.

'One day. Come on. We'll go round Riley's and buy you some sweets. That'll make up for it.'

'I don't want jelly babies.'

'Fair enough.' Tony lifted his son off the kitchen chair and onto his back. 'Come on, Errol. Let's get away from the women.'

Once the door had closed behind them, Edie sank into a

chair and sighed. 'Well, that seemed easy enough. I hope Gloria wasn't offended.' She looked across to Emma. 'Was she?'

'No. She took it as if it was a present from us. As if she'd forgotten she'd given it in the first place. She's not bright enough to be offended. It was right to take it back.'

Maggie filled the kettle at the sink and then said, 'Fancy a cup of tea, Em?'

'Yeah, go on then. I'm ready for a cigarette as well.'

'Emma?'

'Whoops. Sorry Edie – slip of the tongue. Don't tell Mum though, will you . . . and speak of the devil, here she comes. Hot on my tail.' She had seen Jessie pass the kitchen window. 'I promised I would tidy my bedroom and do my pile of ironing.' At the sound of the doorbell she raised an eyebrow, saying, 'Here we go.'

'Go and let her in love, would you?'

'On my way out. See you!' With that Emma was gone and Edie reached out and took hold of Maggie's hand. 'You were right, Mags. The table was turned there without me fully realising.'

'What d'yer mean?'

'Well, if it had been a fifty-four-year-old man who had given you a pound note when you was Peppie's age, I would have screamed blue murder.'

'Honest to God,' said Jessie, coming into the room, 'if you saw that girl's bedroom you'd have a fit. Untidy little mare.' She looked from Edie to Maggie. 'Who's dropped dead, then?'

'Glory Glory Alleluia gave Peppie a pound note,' rushed Maggie. 'Emma took him back upstairs to give it back and when Tony came in and heard about it he went straight up there as well. Him and Errol. So that was four people that woman got the attention of, once again.'

'I've never seen your eyes blazing so, Maggie.' Jessie chuckled as she sat down. 'Gloria's all right. Just a bit oblivious to real life going on around her. Where is Peppie, by the way? I've got a comic for 'im indoors. I forgot to pick it up on my way out. He can go and knock for it.'

'Tony's taken 'im round Riley's the sweet shop to make up for giving the money back. Poor little sod couldn't believe it. I've never seen 'im grip anything so tightly.'

'Have you got time for a cup of tea, Jess?' asked Edie.

'No, I mustn't stop. I only came to nudge madam into action. I'll be blowed if I'll do her ironing.' Jessie turned to Maggie, a different expression on her face as she said, 'Does Peppie have bad dreams?'

'Sometimes. He soon goes back off though, once me or Tony gets up and pats his back. Why?'

'I just wondered. Only I can't be sure if Emma's dreams are so vivid that she lives them or she's not even dreaming. She always seems to be in a kind of a half-awake trance. Her sleep-walking's started up again. It wasn't so bad when she was little. I used to find her in all sorts of places. Asleep at the foot of Billy's bed. On the settee. Curled up in a corner of the room. You name it, I found her there. Even in the empty bath once with a pillow and my coat over her.

'She let 'erself out of the flat the other night – about three in the morning. I thought I heard the street door but wasn't properly awake and carried on dozing. Then, for no particular reason I sat bolt upright and knew she'd gone outside. The front door was open. I looked over the balcony and there she was; I could just see her under the glow of the lamppost. Sitting on that low wall down there where the kids play hopscotch. Sitting there as if she was awake and watching everyone coming and going.'

'You're joking?' Maggie's eyes showed her horror at the thought of such a thing happening.

'I'm not. I wish I was. I put a little bell on the front door catch when I go to bed now. So I should hear if and when she goes out agen. But what if I'm in a sound sleep?'

'I don't know, Jess. Does she remember it the next day?'

'Bits of it. Tiny little snippets. She'd go spare if she knew I

was telling you, by the way, so don't say a word. It embar-
rasses her. The next morning she said she remembered walking
down some stairs but not ours. And could remember looking
for someone. Matron.'

'Matron?'

'From the children's home in Ongar. She's had nightmares
about it before. She must have thought she was back there.
She said she could remember sitting somewhere waiting for
me and Billy to come along. She thought the wall was a bench.
So there we are. That's the ghost that's come to haunt me. I
should never have agreed to place her there, Maggie.'

'Oh stop it, Jessie,' said Edie, 'or do you want a stick to beat
yourself with?'

'I never knew she was in a children's home, Jess,' said
Maggie, taken aback.

'No-one on this estate knows except your mum and Laura,
Mags.' A haunted look on her face, Jessie pinched her lips
together. 'I only hope she never sleepwalked while she was
there. She wet the bed . . . that much I do know. She was three
years old by then and had never wet the bed before then. Poor
little cow. Things we do, eh?'

'For the good of our children, Jessie,' said Edie. 'It was war
time. Your house had been hit. You did the best thing for Emma
. . . and you know it. Deep down you know it. So, she wet the
bed. Had she have moved in with her gran and granddad she
might 'ave been blown to bits instead. How would you feel
now if you'd taken that option?'

'Oh, don't . . .' said Maggie, 'I've gone icy cold. I think I'll
go round Rita's for half an hour. This is too much for me. Tell
the boys that's where I am when they get back, Mum. I won't
be long.'

'Oh, and who's gonna give Peppie his tea?'

Calling back over her shoulder from the passage, Maggie
said, 'Tell Tony to go out and get him a bag of chips. See you
Jess!' With that Maggie was gone – the street door slamming
shut behind her.

'Well, how do you like that?' said Edie, each of her hands pressed against her hips. 'Is she taking me for a mug, or what?'

'Oh shut up, Edie. You know you love to be in charge of that grandson of yours when you can. You worship the ground he walks on.'

'But why leave all of a sudden?'

'Because she's not made of stone, Edie. What was you talking about before I came in? Gloria, wasn't it? And then me going on about Emma and sleepwalking and the children's home. It's all a bit on the dark side.

'I sometimes wonder about the ancient building that stood on this site before it was pulled down and these flats were built. Maybe there are ghosts of the past around who are not too happy about us being 'ere. I've been aware of a peculiar feeling on that staircase once or twice.'

Edie sighed loudly. 'Stop it, Jess. And if you really believed that you *would* take Emma to see a specialist. Never mind evil spirits – anything could happen to her out there. There are enough weirdos around in the flesh to be wary of.'

'Well . . . we'll be moving out soon.'

'Well, that's a comfort, I'm sure. Give me the creeps and then sod off and leave me to the devil.'

'Then agen I might have second thoughts and not go.'

'Well that's up to you but . . . I will miss you, Jess. That's for sure.'

'You can come up for weekends. By train. Liverpool Street to Diss. Tom or his brother'd meet you at the station.'

'I know.' Edie smiled at her friend. 'You'll be okay. Once Emma gets settled into an office job in the local town. Not so sure about your Billy, though. He was telling Tony about it the other day. He's not keen. Lads of his age don't care about sweet-smelling fresh air.

'I wish it was me in your shoes. My husband Harry always said we'd move out one day. The war got in the way, though.' A part of Edie wanted to tell Jessie that Harry was back from the dead.

'Well then, why not come up with Laura for a few days

and try it out? You never know . . . you might both decide to opt for the village life. The council houses are lovely. Got an old-fashioned feel to 'em. And back gardens that back on to farmland. Can't ask for more than that.'

'We'll see. You're going up there this weekend, aren't you?'

'If Tom doesn't change his plans by then we are. He wants us to see how well they've done. Ours are practically ready, apparently. I'll believe that when I see it. Dolly and Stan's cottage and extension is finished. She can't wait to get up there. Nor can her kids. All four of them.'

'Who would 'ave believed it? You and Tom back together agen . . . and beginning a completely new life in a cottage in the heart of the country.'

'I know,' said Jessie, not wishing to be reminded of the past when talking about the future. 'Anyway, I'd best get back. I've got to sort out the right things to take with us. Jeans and wellingtons in case it rains and summer cotton and sandals in case it's boiling hot. I'm worn out already.'

'Get out of here,' Edie smiled. 'You're loving it.'

'Maybe. And I will think seriously about taking Emma to see someone about the sleepwalking. She should have grown out of it by now.'

'Never mind that. Just remind yourself of the danger of her roaming around in the middle of the night in her nightdress. You never know what's lurking out there.'

'Point taken,' said Jessie. 'Oh and tell Maggie that the twin set she ordered from the catalogue should be here by Monday.'

Once by herself Edie pictured Emma walking around in the grounds below in the dead of night. She shuddered at the thought of it. And well she might. A dark, if not black, cloud was on its way and destined to put the fear of God into all of them. And in the centre of the horror would be none other than Jessie's daughter, Emma.

3

During the long journey of Tom driving his family to Norfolk, Jessie had things on her mind other than the village of Elmshill. Her friend Laura had invited Emma to stay with her and Kay for a week in Kent during the coming hop-picking season and by her reaction, it looked as if her daughter might take her up on the offer. The girls had forged a friendship but weren't exactly close buddies so Jessie had thought that Emma would turn down the invitation straight away. But Kay had made it sound like a lot of fun, telling Emma about the handsome young gypsy travellers there for the picking season and one lad in particular – Zacchi. She painted a tempting picture of the lovely old colourful horse-drawn caravan wagons; the evenings under the setting sun around camp fires; the lovely voices of the gypsies as they quietly sang in the background. Emma had certainly warmed to the romance of it all but she had not yet fully made up her mind. Up until now Jessie had not disclosed to any of them the fact that she herself had once been hop-picking at a different farm to Laura in Paddock Wood, Whitby's Farm, over a decade ago, during the war.

This was something she had chosen to forget. Her short time spent there had been wonderful but the reason for her going had been quite the opposite. Up until now Jessie had managed to put the short episode in her life where it belonged – in the deepest archives of her mind. But with all this talk of Emma going hop-picking, memories which both she and Tom wanted to forget, were surfacing.

Her unpremeditated trip to the hop fields in Kent during the early part of the war had come about because of an accident which had happened to her landlady in Stepney and which had resulted in her death. The house-proud woman had slipped on a rug on her overly polished floor in the passage and although it had been nobody's fault other than her own, Jessie had in a sense been part of the cause of it. A row had broken out between herself and the cold-hearted woman, to whom, in a moment of sheer frustration, Jessie had raised a threatening flat hand. This had caused the woman to step back and slide on the mat covering the lino which was more akin to an ice-rink than an ordinary floor.

The only other tenant in the house, a character called Edna, had heard the rumpus and knew it could only have been an accident, but in her wisdom, she had told Jessie, who was in a state of panic, to disappear that same day. She had suggested that since it was the hop-picking season, she should get herself down to Kent where her own brother and sister-in-law would take care of her and her boy, Billy. In shock, Jessie had agreed and Edna, a true East Ender closing ranks, had spoken to the police once she had left, as if she were the only witness. In her usual forthright manner she had told them that it had been an accident waiting to happen and that she was only too relieved that it had not been herself lying in the mortuary, instead of her landlady, who was addicted to the high smell of lavender polish. Death by accident had been recorded.

With Billy in his pushchair, Jessie had sat on a bench at the station, next to a woman surrounded by three scruffy children and a home-made cart which contained their belongings. Cardboard boxes filled with pots and pans, bedding, clothes, wellington boots, a couple of chairs and a small table. She too had been on her way to the hop fields. The spirit and strength of the woman had given Jessie heart and when the shrill sound of a station master's whistle had pierced through the platform announcing the forthcoming arrival of her train, she had been ready to face the unknown, feeling as if she were a fugitive on the run.

After what seemed a very long, slow ride the train had finally pulled in at Paddock Wood and her then small child, Billy, having slept for most of the way was in a good mood. Happy, even. Whitby's farm, to which she was bound had, luckily, only been a walking distance from the station, just over a mile down a long winding lane. Even so, further good fortune had been on her side. A farm tractor and trailer had pulled up and offered Jessie a lift. The driver, a South London man, was also there for the picking season. And this is how Jessie had arrived onto the common where the hop and apple pickers lived as a community. By then it was early evening with the sun going down and she had been tired and hungry and out of her depth. The families living in the row upon row of huts, black tin, brick and pastel painted huts, had settled into their neighbourly scene and she felt like an intruder.

Her hero, who had come to her rescue in the lane, was the son of a woman whom on first meeting, Jessie had felt as if she'd known for years. Nelly. The lively woman from Stepney had carried two kitchen chairs from her hut and placed them by her outside fireplace. A tin mug of tea was placed in Jessie's hand together with two doorstep slices of bread with a filling of extra strong Cheddar cheese cut thinly. Soon after this she had been shepherded to a row of black tin huts, to Edna's brother and sister-in-law, who from then onwards had taken care of her. There was a spare brick hut for visitors which had a straw bed, a chair, oil lamp and a little table, and had seemed like heaven to Jessie at the time. For a week or so she was happy, picking hops by day and sitting by the camp fire in the evenings, talking and sometimes singing with the other hop pickers. Her days, sitting on the timber frame of a hessian bin, the mid-morning autumn sun on her face as she picked hops from a bine, wearing her cotton fingerless gloves given to her by Nelly, she had loved. But this lifestyle and new-found peace of country living while a world war was on had been cut short.

The baker, who arrived daily in his van, on a sunny morning, had had a passenger on board. One who had also arrived by train from London. Tom. His brother had been killed at Dunkirk and he had been wounded by a bullet to the knee. Once restored back to health in Britain, Tom had had no desire whatsoever to go back and fight with his regiment bound for Italy. So he had gone AWOL instead.

He had found out where Jessie and his son Billy were from her previous neighbour, Edna, and had decided to join her. Of course, she had been happy to see him and had enjoyed the few days of them being together again; quietly making love in a cosy hut on a mattress which smelled of sweet fresh hay.

But Jessie's short burst of happiness had soon ended, just a few days after Tom had arrived and after a Sunday drink at lunch time, in the village pub. With others from the common, they had strolled over a bridge and into trouble, stirred up by someone who had drunk one pint of stout too many. Leaning on the rail of the bridge a woman had sung to the Italian prisoners of war below, who were clearing the river edge with only one British guard watching over them. And this little part of the ditty, Jessie had never forgotten.

> *Oh Mr Fuh-rer whatever shall they do?*
> *They wanted to stay and fight your war but we*
> *   dragged 'em to Waterloo.*
> *Mr Mussol-ini, whatever will you say?*
> *Your hero's fucking Hitler . . . but we know he's had*
> *   his day.*
> *So . . . Mr Mussolini, whatever will you do,*
> *your lovely Mr Hitler doesn't give a toss for you.*

While the second rendition was given by all of the happy boozy London women, the bemused soldier on guard duty happened to glance away from his charges and up at the lovely array of ladies, but it had been Tom who had caught his eye. He had wondered why he was hanging back and then wondered why he was there at all. He was a young, healthy man and looked fit for fighting for his country.

Slipping further into the background, Tom had lit a roll-up and planned his next step. The enquiring looks from the guard, who was craning his neck to get a better view, confirmed his fears. He had to get away and quickly and without arousing any suspicion from the Londoners. They believed that he was there on sick leave due to the injury to the leg.

The following day, he and Jessie and Baby Billy had arrived at the station to catch the train to London as had plain-clothed military officers. A description of Tom had been sent to London police as a suspected deserter. The information which came back was that this man was canny and had already slipped the net twice. Settled in a carriage, and just before the station master had blown his whistle, the smart and official-looking gentlemen boarded – two carriages behind theirs.

'I'm going to the lavatory, Jess, before the train pulls out and there's a queue as long as you like,' Tom had said. Then, giving her a wink he had ruffled Billy's hair before he casually strolled out of the carriage and into the next and lit a cigarette by the open window. He had been waiting for the train to start up before he made his escape and all that Jessie could do was watch him get off as it began to move and slam the door shut behind him, to disappear over the station wall.

A few minutes later the military police were strolling along the aisle checking both sides and Jessie's cheeks had burned bright red as they closed in on her. Once they had passed her by she had breathed easy again. She had realised then, why her husband had been cagey, hanging back from her when she purchased the train tickets, and why he kept his distance until they were on that train and seated. He had done it again. Appeared out of the blue, taken her away from somewhere where she had felt safe and was in good company – and then left her to get on with it.

And now, the idea of Emma going hop-picking made Jessie feel strange. It was all too close to home and she didn't want those things which she had buried to float back up to the surface. But worse than this, playing on her mind, was the fact that there had been another sleepwalking episode with Emma. Tom had stirred in the night to the sound of the front door

opening and the tinkling of the bell, purposely fixed there.
Going silently from the bedroom, so as not to disturb Jessie,
he had grabbed his dressing gown from a hook on the back
of the door and crept into the passage. Once outside he had
followed Emma along the balcony and down the stairs to the
grounds below. This was the first case of him actually *seeing*
her sleepwalk. Previously, Emma had woken up somewhere
other than where she had fallen asleep, and been guided back
to her room and her bed.

When Tom had explained to Jessie what had happened it
had sent a wave of dread and fear through her. He had said
how Emma had walked down the stairs quite naturally as if
she were awake and knew exactly where she was going and
with no sign of arms raised in front of her. Neither had she
crossed the grounds to sit on the wall where she had once been
found by Jessie, but strolled casually along in the dim light of
one or two lampposts, taking the usual route out of the estate,
as if she were on her way to catch a bus to work.

Taking her hand Tom had gently coaxed her back home and
back into bed without any problem but the thought of Emma-
Rose, wearing only her nightdress and walking through the
dismal backstreets alone, past slum dwellings, on her way to
catch a bus in Whitechapel was too serious to ignore.

And now, the idea of her daughter sleepwalking in the pitch
black of the Kent countryside where, according to Laura, there
was a river close by and also a swamp, was in itself a living
nightmare. Jessie had dropped broad hints to her daughter
about her having to sleep on a bed of straw infested with beetles
and spiders and staying in a hut which was used for cattle
during the winter months. But Emma had simply laughed and
said that she already knew that the huts were in a dire state
from January to June but that they were hosed down and
scrubbed clean before the hop pickers arrived. And that the
Londoners, Laura and Jack included, always distempered the
insides of their huts or pasted wallpaper onto the brick walls.
Jessie knew all of this to be true for she had experienced it

herself. She was also aware that not only did the hop pickers decorate but they also laid cheap lino on the small concrete floors. As for the bedding, the straw and hay was supplied by the farmer, in square blocks, and had been stored in an oast house to be delivered to the huts on the day of arrival. This filling made quite a comfortable bed once drawn and pushed into a sturdy twill mattress case with fresh plump hops thrown in to ensure a good night's sleep.

When Emma had told all of this to Jessie she had listened as if it was all news to her and now, not only was she agonising over what might or might not happen to her daughter should she sleepwalk while away from home, but was having to face a bit of past which had lodged itself back in her mind. That dreadful period during the blitz on London when she had felt like a refugee going from pillar to post.

'You all right, Mum?' said Emma, quietly breaking into Jessie's thoughts.

Bringing herself sharply into the present, she said, 'Course I am, sweetheart. I'm just thinking about lovely, lazy summer days with no sound of traffic and waking up to Norfolk birds singing.'

'And bats in the church belfry,' murmured Billy, not so struck on the idea of living in Norfolk as the others.

'Bats are okay if you leave 'em be,' said Tom, as he drove slowly through the small sleepy neighbouring village to Elmshill. 'Your granddad was gettin' all excited yesterday when I mentioned us keeping chickens and ducks. I wouldn't be surprised if we end up finding a little place for the pair of them, as well.'

'Your mum wouldn't leave the East End, Tom. Be realistic.'

'Don't you bet on it. She don't stop moaning about how much traffic there is now in Stepney and how crowded the place is. I wouldn't be surprised if they've been talking seriously about moving out.'

'I wish they would. They could sell their two up two down and buy a place up here.'

'You what?' Tom chuckled. 'No. That's their grandchildren's inheritance. Billy, Emma and Dolly's four kids. She'd rather get tenants in there and live in a council place up 'ere.'

'They wouldn't give 'er a council house, Dad,' said Billy. Not if she's a property owner in London. You should know that.'

'I do know that. And I've said so. Told 'er to sell it and buy a cottage and let *that* be your inheritance.'

'Can we stop talking about things like this? It's morbid. Nan and Granddad 'ave got years yet.' Emma was too sensitive for all of this.

Tom glanced at her through his rear-view mirror. 'Not that many years, Em. You should tell them to make the most of what's left. They'd listen to you. They could enjoy a bit of life living in the countryside. What d'yer reckon, Billy? Think they'd settle for it?'

'Whatever you think, Dad. Whatever you say. Just don't include me in all your plans.'

'Fair enough,' said Tom as he turned the steering wheel of his old Wolseley at a tiny crossroad which showed the sign he always loved to see. Elmshill. Jessie was hardly surprised at her son's confession. She knew that Billy was having second thoughts.

Enjoying a pint with Tony and Errol earlier while in the Carpenter's Arms, Billy had listened with interest and piqued curiosity when Errol had enthused over the terraced houses in Jamaica Street. Excited at the prospect of having his own place, Errol had got carried away with his glorious vision and plans of what he would do to the house once a deal was struck. Billy had probed further, wanting to know more.

Once explained to him it all seemed quite simple. And with the wages he was earning as an engineer for the railway he could just afford the repayments that Errol had talked of. The conversation had then turned to the idea of Billy lodging for a while in the house that Errol's uncle was going to buy, and in return, he could help with the renovations and act as night watchman, making sure that the local kids didn't break in and vandalise the place and the down and outs did not use it as somewhere to doss.

The thought of being independent appealed to Billy. He quite fancied having a pad of his own where he could take his girl-friends. The more he had thought about it since the chance conversation with Errol the more he had come to like the idea. And now that he was in Elmshill he knew that living in a dead quiet village was not for him. With the cottage nearing completion, there was the possibility of Jessie and Tom moving in during the next few months or so. Billy was going to have to break the news soon that he definitely didn't want to live amidst people who thought that a Saturday night in the local pub – a small run-down house with a licence to serve beer – was a great night out.

'Anyway . . .' said Billy, his voice quiet and thoughtful. 'You won't be short of company, Dad. You'll 'ave your brother to share a pint with and Mum'll 'ave 'er sister. Dolly and Stanley will be in their little house before you're in yours by the sound of things.'

'We won't be lonely, son,' said Tom, only too aware of what Billy was driving at.

'And if I was to decide to stay put in London . . . I could always nip up on my motor bike for a weekend.'

'What motor bike?' said Jessie.

'The one that Uncle Stanley's mate is selling. At a good price. I might buy it.' The silence could be cut with a knife.

Knowing about the bike on offer and her mother's dread of them, Emma stretched and yawned loudly for attention. 'I can't wait to get in that river for a paddle. I hope there're no water rats in there.'

'Wait until you can afford a safe little car, Billy,' said Jessie. 'Motor bikes are death traps.' Too many accidents had made the headlines showing pictures of mangled motor bikes.

'Did you fetch your swimming costume, Em?' said Tom, who like Emma, wanted to change the subject.

'I did shove it in my overnight bag, just in case. But that don't mean I'm going in.'

'You will. It's deep enough and as clear as the Lido in Victoria Park. Me and your uncle Stanley are in there every day after we've finished work.'

'That's because you probably need a river the state you get in.'

'Well, what d'yer expect? After we've knocked down walls and ripped off mouldy hardboard from filthy beams and taken up brick floors to clean and relay?'

'Stop boasting, Dad. We all know how hard you work. I came up when you was in the thick of it, remember? When you was knee deep in old plaster and rubbish and it stank of mould and damp.'

'It's not much different from that now, Em.' Tom smiled inwardly. It was a lot different and he couldn't wait to show it off. 'But what does it matter? It's gotta be better than being in dirty old London.'

'So we won't be stopping overnight after all then, if it's in a state,' said Billy, ever hopeful.

'It's up to you, son. You can camp out overnight like me and your mum and Emma or get the train back to London.'

'Camp out? You can't expect Mum and me to do that?' Emma was aghast at the thought of it.

'Why not? Plenty of families go camping for their 'olidays. It's called *fun*.'

'It's one of Dad's jokes, Em,' droned Billy. 'Take no notice.'

'It had better be. Because if it's not – I'm gettin' the train back. I'm not sleeping in a make-shift tent.'

'Shut up, Emma,' said Jessie. 'Your dad's pulling your leg. I know from Aunt Dolly that he's bought camp beds on the cheap. And there's inside running cold water.'

'So we'll be camping inside,' said Billy. 'With cold water to wash in. Great.'

'What about electricity? Or is it all oil lamps and candles?'

'Candles, Em. Nice and romantic.' Tom grinned. 'Billy'll soon eat his words and sneak up here with one of his girl-friends, you wait and see if I'm wrong.'

'I don't think so,' said Billy. Keeping his thoughts to himself, that he would rather take them to Jamaica Street and light candles. 'Thanks all the same.' He tried to imagine his latest girlfriend in this village with her bouffant hairstyle and shocking pink coat. 'Let's hope you don't go sleepwalking, eh Em? You might slip on a pile of steaming cow shit.'

'I *don't* sleepwalk, thank you. I just go out for a stroll when I feel like it. That's all,' she said defensively.

Billy glanced at his sister, sorry that he had made the remark. 'You think I don't know that?' He gave a brotherly wink. 'Just winding Mum and Dad up.'

Once they had reached the small village church, Jessie's mind was filled with the vision and memory of when she had once before arrived into this lovely setting where time had stood still. She had loved her short stay here when she and Billy were evacuated from London with a coach load of other cockneys during the blitz on London. But would she feel the same now? Eighteen years or so later?

She hadn't been married many years at the time but was a responsible young soldier's wife and mother, with just Billy, in a pushchair. On the day of arrival most of the villagers had come out to welcome the coach and several had spent days preparing to receive families from the war-damaged capital. They had even hung a string of Union Jacks across the front of the village hall. And now, as Tom steered the car away from the church turning right into the winding lane, that day warmed Jessie's heart. She could see it clearly in her mind's eye and remembered how happy everyone on the coach had been when they found themselves in this sleepy unspoiled village where peace and quiet reigned. The healthy glow and smiling faces of the locals as they stood in their small groups to welcome them was the best greeting anyone could have wished for.

'It all seems so quiet now,' Jessie murmured. 'You won't remember Billy, but when we came during the war, when you was in a pushchair, the home-dwellers put on a lovely afternoon tea for all of us, in the village hall. I don't think the kids 'ad ever seen so many different kinds of cakes. All home-made.'

'Yeah, I know, Mum,' said Billy, peering out of the window and up at the sky. He had seen a hawk hovering above. 'You told me . . . more than once.'

'Not lately though I 'aven't.'

'Tell Dad about the retired colonel,' he grinned. 'I don't mind 'ow many times I hear that. I hope *he*'s still alive.'

'Your mum's boyfriend, was he?' said Tom, giving Jessie a foxy look. Little could he know that the colonel's attractive son, Rupert Maitland, might have become her lover had Tom, on sick leave with his supposedly unhealed wounded leg, not found out where Jessie had been evacuated to that time and arrived unannounced to take her back to Stepney. Shortly afterwards she and Billy had almost been buried alive. A bomb had dropped on a house in Westminster in which they and other homeless families were lodging.

'Actually the colonel was too old for me,' said Jessie, remembering the little bit of romance she had relished with his son, Rupert.

'Ah, but was he though? Methinks you do protest too much, Muvver,' said Billy, grinning. 'I should keep an eye out for 'im Dad, if I was you.'

'I've already done that, son. He's not exactly confined to a wheelchair but should be. Old, grey and round-shouldered. Posh and loaded, though. I'll give you that.'

'Oh,' said Jessie, a touch concerned. 'So you've met the colonel and his son, then?'

'Not 'is son, no. But I've had a drink or two with the colonel in the pub. He's all right. Bit of a bore but you can take the piss out of 'im and he don't know you're doing it.'

'I'm sure he had a son. Rupert. I can't quite remember,' Jessie fibbed.

'Oh, he's always narking on about 'is bloody son. Lives in some bloody mansion somewhere. As if I cared one way or the other.'

'So where is this pub, then?'

'A five-minute walk away, Billy. That's all.'

'Oh, right. Well, I know where I'm going soon as we stop.'

'You should go, Billy. It's good for a laugh if nothing else. Old timers chewing on straw and drinking pints of cider.'

'The colonel was all right,' said Jessie quietly. 'He wanted to be lord of the village that's all. When we arrived into *his* domain he wanted to make sure it all went without a hitch. He'd be striding from one group to another apparently – telling evacuees all that he'd read in *The Times* to do with the capital and people like us who were arriving. As if they didn't know already.'

'They probably didn't. Half of 'em can't read now Jess, never mind then.'

'Most *could* read and them that couldn't either listened to the wireless or had it all told to them by someone else in the local. They knew exactly what was going on in Britain, Tom. Don't you worry.'

Arriving at the muddy track which led up to the two cottages, theirs and the one next door which was going to be the home of Stanley, Dolly and their four children, Tom nodded towards the old sign which was swinging on a bit of old fencing. 'What d'yer reckon then, Billy? Still fink we should keep the original name or change it?'

'Whatever you say, Dad. Who gives a toss, anyway? It's hardly a grand hall, is it?'

'"Tom's Nest",' said Tom. 'Sounds all right, don't it?' Mocking laughter filled the car. 'Jack Davey thought it was a good idea,' he said, his voice trailing off. 'So that's what I'll call it. Tom's Nest.'

'I think he might 'ave been pulling your leg, Tom. You're gonna have to get to know the Norfolk humour if you're to keep up.'

'There's not much to know about this lot, Jess. One Friday in Diss, on a market day, and you'll get the picture in half an hour. You can buy anyfing from a scrawny live chicken to a bloody big wardrobe. Brick Lane all over agen.'

'It's not gonna be that easy to be accepted, Dad. If you can't take a bit of micky taking,' said Billy. 'You'd best keep your 'ead down and your mouth shut 'til you know what's what.'

'That's what Willy Belcher said last week as it 'appens. The local builder.'

'So did Alice Davey's brother, Jack,' said Jessie. 'During the war. "Step by step, my girl, step by step."'

Alice Davey. The very sound of the name brought a glow into Jessie's heart. The gentle but wily woman who was now in her seventies. She, along with Cyril the lay preacher and Mrs Hilldrop who ran the post office, were the chief officers of the social club during the war and the chief organiser in the village hall. Before she and the coach of evacuees had arrived, between them they had set up trestle tables covered with sparkling white starched table cloths and bowls of fresh cut flowers before the spread of food was brought in or prepared in the village hall kitchen.

Almost everyone in Elmshill had contributed in some way to put on the welcoming spread for the London folk. Cakes, quiches and sausage rolls had been baking in ovens the day before and piles of sandwiches made up on the day of arrival. All of this, carried out in a community spirit by people whose own loved ones were across the seas fighting the enemy.

Apart from those taking part in the war, the rest of the villagers had experienced nothing by way of attack. They had prepared themselves against it of course and the Home Guard and Wardens had taken their role *very* seriously and had been nicknamed locally as 'The Dad's Army'. The paraphernalia had often been comical but at least the presence of the ARP had been a constant reminder of what was going on outside of their domain, across Britain.

Pulling up in front of the two cottages, Tom looked around for any sign of the couple of local lads who had promised to be there to dismantle rusty old corrugated iron from a decent timber frame outbuilding, which Tom planned to turn into a workshop. 'Typical,' he said as he pulled on the hand brake.

'Lazy sods ain't turned up agen. I tell you, love nor money will make this lot go faster than a snail's pace.'

'Well, someone's inside from the look of it,' said Billy, leaning forward and peering out and across the front garden into the window. 'There's a light on in the back. Stanley's coming later on, ain't he Dad? Following us up?'

'Yeah – won't be that far behind – an hour or so.' Tom lowered his head and looked across Jessie's shoulder. 'You're right. There is a light on in the kitchen.'

'I thought you said there was no electricity,' said Emma.

'Did I say that?' Tom kept a straight face. 'Well . . . if some poor old tramp's moved in and lit the oil lamp we'll 'ave a job chucking 'im out. He'll 'ave to kip down in a room with you, Billy.'

'He bloody well won't,' grumbled Billy, pushing down the handle of the car door and getting out. 'After that jaunt in your old banger I'm not in the mood to argue with a dosser.'

'Mister Big Man.' Jessie chuckled as she got out of the car.

'Take no notice,' said Tom scratching his ear. 'He'll have the wind taken out of 'is sails.' Then as he stretched to full height he took a deep breath and then said, 'Well, Jess? What do you think of the outside? We was gonna paint it pink but I couldn't bring myself to do it. Sod tradition.'

'I'm glad you never. I like it. I would 'ave chosen this as well. It's not green exactly and yet it's not cream.'

'Bang on. I mixed the two colours and got this. It goes with the new thatch.'

'Yeah, all right, Tom. I noticed. And it's lovely. That must 'ave cost a few bob.'

'No. Me and Stanley helped the thatcher. A young kid of eighteen who'd bin working alongside 'is old man since he was ten. He was 'appy enough taking half what 'is dad would 'ave charged. And his dad was 'appy for 'im to have a go by 'imself. Local family. I let 'im do Stanley's first so I could test him out.'

'I'm sure. Stanley probably nabbed 'im first in case he got sloppy by the time he got to our one.'

'Our one?' Tom smiled as he looked into Jessie's face. 'Well, that's a first. Up until now you've always referred to it as *Tom*'s cottage.'

'Oh, right . . .' said Jessie, containing her laughter. 'That's what the changing the name of it was about. You just can't resist a bit of sarcasm, can you?'

'And you really believed I would call a cottage by my own name, did yer?'

'Yeah. I thought it was all going to your head, Tom. Come on then. Take me inside and show off a bit more.'

'What? Carry you over the threshold you mean?'

'No, that's not what I mean. I'm too old and it's too late for all that. You should have done it years ago.'

'I did, Jess. Our little house in Grant Street, Stepney?'

'True enough.'

'Go on in, then,' said Tom as he pulled his tobacco tin out of his pocket. 'Let someone surprise yer. Don't spoil it for 'er.'

Unsure as to what he meant Jessie cautiously followed Emma up the old brick pathway towards the old oak door thinking how romantic it would be if Tom were to carry her over the threshold to make up for his past wrongs. Once inside the beamed front room she could hardly believe her eyes. The walls and ceiling in-between the elm studs had been given two white coats of distemper and the old red tiled floor scrubbed clean and polished to a lovely sheen. And in the inglenook fireplace, next to a log fire, set and ready to light, was a large pair of old black wrought-iron tongs, a chunky copper scuttle and a polished brass poker on a stand. And coming from the big old-fashioned kitchen was the delicious smell of smoky roast chicken and the sound of familiar high-pitched laughter and then the strong accent of a Norfolk woman. She was calling Billy by name and saying how he'd grown. It was Alice Davey.

As she turned around to look at Tom standing in the doorway watching her, Jessie heard the familiar voice of Alice calling out, 'Where is she, then? Where's my Jessie?'

'She's looking forward to seeing you, Jess. She helped me clean up and that.'

'Tom . . . I can't . . .' Jessie only just managed to speak. Tears were welling in the back of her eyes and her throat felt as if it would close under the strain of her trying not to cry.

'Go on in, Jess.'

'In a minute,' she said, pinching her lips tightly together. Being with Alice during the war had been the best days of her life and hearing her voice again was almost too much. That lovely singsong voice that had drifted into her dreams over the years. Taking a deep breath, she willed herself through the living room of what was to be her new home and then into the farmhouse kitchen to face the most wonderful woman in the world.

'Oh my, Jessie. Well, just look at you. If you ent a sight for my sore eyes, I don't know what.'

'Hello, Alice,' was all Jessie could manage to say as they held out their arms to each other and hugged. Words were not important. Being close again was. It was Emma's excited voice which pierced through emotions.

'Mum, look at all this! I thought I was in the wrong 'ouse! The beams are not black any more. Dad's stripped 'em back to the timber. And look at the old copper boiler – all clean and polished. And the iron door on the old oven's not horrible and rusty. And look at the floor. I can't believe these are the same bricks. Uncle Stanley took them all up, cleaned 'em and then—'

'Oi oi oi!' said Tom waving a finger. 'Me and your uncle Stanley if you don't mind.'

'I've got eyes, Emma,' said Jessie, watery eyed and laughing. 'Calm down.'

Turning to Alice, this lovely rosy-cheeked rotund woman wearing a pink and green flowery frock with a big white apron over it, Emma said, 'Thank you for doing all of this cleaning and everything. Can I 'ave a cuddle, too?'

'Course you can, my dear!'

'If the upstairs is as good as the down, Dad,' said Billy, avoiding the emotional stuff and taking the stairs two at a go, 'I owe you an apology.'

'Oh, right. I've impressed the unimpressable then, 'ave I?' said Tom, his face showing his joy. He then turned to Alice. 'So you decided to cook the chicken in the Dutch oven, after all?'

'Course I did! All cleaned up again I thought I should christen it! And that ent no ordinary fowl in there. It's one of my specials. Corn fed and fancy free. And I've fetched a lovely wrapped sliced loaf of bread! Baker delivered that not one hour since.

'I shall have to be getting along now Jessie, love, but you know where I live. You'll be all right here. You've got electricity put on . . . *and* running hot water. But then I expect you'll be used to all of that in London.'

'It looks lovely . . .' Jessie murmured, tears still flooding her eyes. 'I love it. And I love all you've done for me. *Again*. And that roasting chicken smells lovely.'

'And pie, Jessie. I put an apple pie in, too. Shouldn't want to waste the heat.'

Turning around and looking about herself, Emma repeated her mother's sentiments, saying, 'I just *love* it here, Mum.'

'Well Emma-Rose . . . our ways may be a little different from town folk,' said Alice untying her apron, 'but don't you go worrying your pretty head over it. You'll soon get the hang of things. And look you out of that window, my dear. That back garden, well that hev been a *blaze* of colour this year! It's been waiting for you, I shouldn't wonder. There're some pretty little shrubs out there. And a pear tree. I shouldn't think you'll ever have to pull a drink from that well now you hev water piped into the house . . . so you can fill it in and hev some flowers growing there. I seen one jes like it up at the colonel's house.'

'Is there *really* a proper bathroom?' said Emma, biting on her bottom lip.

'I should say there is, Emma! Ooooh . . . them boys hev done well up there. Turned the old hay store into a proper little bathroom. Now that I *should* like! A proper bathroom like that one. And I *shall* have one – so I shall.'

'I should reckon so, Alice. Tom and Stanley can put one in for you, later on.'

'Well then, we shall make sure they do, Jessie. And now . . . I must love and let you be.'

'You're an angel, sweetheart,' said Tom, coming back into the room and pulling Alice into his arms. 'An angel sent down from heaven to look after me and my family.'

Blushing, Alice turned back to Jessie. 'Now you know where I am Jessie. If there's anything you need . . .'

'I'll be straight round. But am I allowed to just pop in later on? Just to see you and Jack? And catch up?'

'Course you are! I don't know where that lazy brother of mine's got to. I did ask him to check on Tom and Stanley's fire in the field. But there, I expect he forgot. They did hev some rubbish to burn Jessie . . . stripped all the old rotten wood out from everywhere I should say.' She bent over a little and peered out of the window. 'Oh ah . . . here he comes now. Slow as you like. They don't call him lazy Jack for no reason.'

'Still limping?' Jessie smiled.

'Course he is. Daft old bugger. He limp all the more when your sister Dolly's about the place. She took the mickey out of him and he loved it. Oh, ah. Jack think the world of your Dolly. They make each other laugh, so! She say he look comical from behind in them old baggy trousers.'

'They're not the same ones. Surely not?'

'No, but he must hev had this pair for over ten years. And I wouldn't say he ent wearing the same braces as when you were here, Jessie. Moth-eaten old things.' With that, Alice left them to it, happy to have seen Jessie again after all this time.

That evening, while Tom, his brother Stanley, Billy and Emma were enjoying a drink in the local, Jessie and Dolly, in Alice and her brother's parlour were sipping home-made sloe gin,

made by none other than Alice. The room reminded Jessie
of the London two up two down that she and Tom owned
before the war. The house which, once Tom had left her way
back for a life of luxury somewhere else, she had sold. This
living room of course was heavily beamed and even though
it was a warm evening a small fire was smouldering in the
open brick fireplace. Above the fire hanging on an iron chain
was the same black kettle that Jessie remembered and on an
iron stand next to the fire grate, a light blue smoky enamel
teapot.

Set around the inglenook fireplace was the worn but clean,
faded pink and red rose patterned loose covers of the suite
that she had fallen in love with and which had caused her to
have her heart set on living in a cottage herself. Several pieces
of furniture were still crammed in the room, taking up any
available wall space. Ornaments handed down or won at fair-
grounds still bedecked every surface and shelf.

'I don't know why the men hev gone to that blooming pub,'
Jack grumbled. 'You can't get a decent pint in there, that you
can't. Ale? Why it tastes more like cat's—'

'That'll be enough of that, Jack! Ta very much,' said Alice,
interrupting her brother. 'We've got company, so mind your
tongue.' She turned to Dolly and rolled her eyes. 'You hev a
word with him. He'll take more notice of you than me. He
sometimes forget his manners, Jessie. But then you'll most
likely know that from having lived under the same roof. It was
quite a few years ago but he ent changed.'

'Oh, yeah. I soon 'ad your number eh, Jack?' Jessie grinned
and winked at him. 'How's that bad leg these days? Still playing
up when it feels like it?'

'Mustn't grumble,' he said, stretching a leg and wincing.
'Can't complain.'

'This drink's lovely, Alice,' said Dolly, covering a smile.
'What's it called agen?'

'Sloe gin, my dear. I picked the sloes myself from the
hedgerow.'

'Pity she can't brew whisky, Doris,' said Jack. 'Blooming expensive, that is.'

'It's Dolly and you know it. And I think that might be against the law, anyway. But then I s'pose there's one law for London and one for up 'ere.'

'You could say that, Dolly. Then agen, you couldn't. We hev to be careful. Don't want to go upsetting our local policeman. He live in the next village, you know. In Garblesham.'

'Blooming daft bugger,' said Jack, massaging his knee. 'All uniform and no sense.'

'He's all right,' said Alice. 'Keeps his eye on you and that's no bad thing.'

'Keeps his eye on the ladies more like.'

'So . . . Dolly . . . how's it coming along then? That cottage of yours?'

'Lovely. And thank you for letting Jess know about them being up for sale all them years ago. It took us a long while getting around to it but I'm glad we did.'

'It weren't her that let Jessie know. It were me! I said she was to write a letter. Don't s'pose she said so though. But then I'm used to that. Treats me like I'm invisible. Never mind my leg.' Jack gave his knee another little rub and then stretched it. 'Just as well they did take your husband's arm off, Dolly. I wish they'd take this blooming thing away and give me a plastic one.'

'There ent much wrong with your leg,' said Alice. 'Take no heed, Dolly. He talks daft when he's been at the cider.' She looked across at her brother and gave him the evil eye. 'And don't you go telling me that you ent hed a drop cos I know full well that you hev!'

'Course . . . You ent seen the upstairs of our place, Dorothy, hev you? Alice can show you round if you like. You need to watch your head, mind. There's a beam up there which sit an inch too low for my liking. I crack my head on it every blooming day. I shouldn't wonder at the aches and pains I get when I lay my head on the pillow. But she won't let me take it out.

Bloody beam. Hev your Sidney got that chimney stack swept yet?'

'Stanley. You *know* it's Stanley. And yes, he's had the sweep in.'

'Oh, Mick the Irish was it?'

'I think so.'

'He's no more a sweep than I'm a bank manager.' Jack laughed. 'Rub a bit of soot on his face and then says he's a chimney sweep. Money for old rope I should say.'

'Don't talk so daft!' said Alice, her cheeks now flushed. 'Course he's a sweep!'

'Your Sidney should hev got Lenny from Three Wells cottage. Now he is a proper chimney sweep. Got all the brooms he hev.'

'And no sense!'

'He got more'n Mick the Irish, woman, that he hev.'

'Take no notice of 'im, Dolly love,' said Alice. 'He's in a snit 'cos he's been up all day agen.'

'Oh? I didn't know you was a night-shift worker, Jack,' said Dolly, clearly enjoying herself in this somewhat bizarre atmosphere created by two lovely old Norfolk characters.

'Course I don't work at night. I ent no bloomin' owl. No. It's this leg. I must rest it more'n a couple of hours on my back. Day and night. As my sister do *know*.'

'Night worker,' joshed Alice, 'He ent done a *day's* work in years.' Turning to Jessie, she said, 'But I don't need to tell you that, Jessie, love. You've lived with the old bugger as well.'

Jack sniffed and leaned back in his rocking chair, his cheeks bright red and his cap pulled down over his sleepy brown eyes. 'Now you know *why* I hev a rest during the day. She wear me out with her tongue wagging in my ear all the time.' He winced in pain to get sympathy, saying. 'Blooming *war* wound. Them that fought in the second world war hed no idea what we hed to go through in the first.'

'You should give a talk on it, Jack,' said Dolly in earnest. 'In the village hall. I'd come and listen. I'd want to know the inside and out of the nineteen-fourteen war.'

'You would,' Jessie laughed. 'She's a born writer, my sister. Always looking for a story.'

'Take no notice of my brother, Dolly. He was a farm hand and needed back here. He never went to no war.'

'No,' said Jack, 'but it were because of the blooming war that I damaged my leg. Hed to do the work of three or four men! You could write a story about that.' Jack went quiet and there was a certain look in his eye that his sister recognised only too well. 'Do they pay much for writing a book, then?'

Slapping her knee, Alice laughed out loud. 'Never you mind writing one! I can read *you* like a book, Jack! That I can!' She glanced at Dolly, still chuckling. 'There ain't no flies on him, my dear.'

'Well, I'm up for working with you on a book, Jack. You talk and I'll type. We'll go fifty fifty, how's that?'

'Sixty forty,' sniffed Jack. 'Because without what's in here,' he tapped the side of his head with a crooked finger, 'there would be no book.'

'And wivout me you'd never get it out of there. Fifty fifty.'

'Well, I shall hev to think about it.'

'You do that.' Dolly glanced at Jessie who was gazing out of the window, at the setting sun, which was creating streaks of pink against a blue and orange sky. 'You coming Jess or staying for a bit longer?'

'I'm in heaven,' said Jessie, gazing up at her sister. 'But yeah . . . we'd best get back.'

'When will the fish-and-chip van come round, Alice? I'm starving,' said Dolly.

Alice peered at her mother's old mantel clock on the shelf. 'In about twenty minutes' time I should think. But you've got a lovely chicken to eat, Dolly.'

'You reckon? That was polished off as soon as we got 'ere. My four kids and a skinny 'usband? Mind you, I don't know what we'd 'ave done if you 'adn't of shoved that bird in Jessie's oven like that. Bloody 'ansome it was. Lovely.'

'It was like a free for all, Alice. I only just managed to grab one of the sandwiches I made,' said Jessie. 'Did you want us to pick you and Jack up some fish and chips?'

'Yes, please,' said Jack, quick off the mark. 'I shan't be able to pay 'til pension day, mind.'

'Take no notice, Dolly. I know what he's got in his pocket. Cod and chips twice, would be lovely.' She held out a hand to her brother and wiggled it. 'A two bob bit if you please, Jack.'

'That's all right, Alice.' Jessie smiled. 'Our treat.'

'Oh, well, in that case I should like a bit of skate. It's not every day I get treated. Thank you very much, Jessie.' A contented smile on his face, Jack sighed and sank his head back into his old feather cushion. 'And if them men of yours are calling in at the pub . . . a jug of ale would wash my supper down very nicely.' He then looked slyly at Jessie and said, 'I expect your old friend Rupert'll be in there tonight – eyeing up the goods. He's a decent fellar mind. Always puts half a pint on the table for me. But there . . . they say the rich are tight by birthright, and I just so 'appened to meet one that isn't . . . I s'pose. The ruddy colonel is though. He ent bought a drink for anyone that I know of. I don't think I've ever sin him put his hand in his pocket. Unless he's looking at a pretty face, of course. He hed his fair share of rolling in that hay. Dirty old sod.'

'I thought Rupert had moved away? Into Suffolk?' said Jessie, not quite casual enough to mask the joy in her voice.

'He has. But then it's only that little ole river Ouse that split the county. They do say that the divide sorted the men from the boys. Them that couldn't swim hed to stay over the other side. Too daft to know how to blooming swim!' Jack slapped his bad knee hard and roared with laughter. 'That's how they got the name Silly Suffolks. Couldn't even blooming-well swim. Mind you. He's a good-looking chap that Rupert, I'll say that for 'im. But there . . . I shouldn't be saying any such thing. You being a married woman, Jessie.'

'You can say what you like, Jack. I don't even know the man – only to look at.'

'Course you don't,' said Jack, giving her a sly smile. 'Course you don't know the man.' He rubbed his chin thoughtfully and then said, 'Mind you . . . he did seem interested . . . when I just happened to say that you was coming back to the village . . . to live.'

Once she was back in her and Tom's cottage enjoying a few minutes by herself in the house that was soon to be her new home, Jessie let her mind wander back to when she had first met and come to know this village and the people. She had discovered from Alice and Jack during her time of staying with them way back in the late 1930s that while she and the other Londoners were on the coach bringing them to Elmshill, the locals had been debating while in the village hall, as to what they should expect from the migrants. Mrs Hilldrop who ran the post office had apparently voiced her concerns loud and clear, that the London kiddies would be smelly and running alive with fleas which could be carrying the plague and the humorous report had not been far wrong. Speculation had been running high since the day the parish council had announced the news and asked those interested in earning a few pounds extra a week to put their name on a list pinned to the wall. It hadn't taken long for the empty white piece of blank paper to be filled with candidates.

On the day of arrival as the locals waited for the coach to arrive, Alice, striking a match under the Calor gas stove on which she had placed a huge brown enamel kettle of water, had quietly laughed at the debates going on between the women. Raising her singsong voice she had spoken loudly so that most of the other helpers in the hall could hear her say that they mustn't go putting down their paying guests before they arrive. Of course she knew that it was the government paying them to take in the Londoners but Alice liked to give respect where respect was deserved, and as far as she had been concerned, those having to leave their homes to come to a strange place of safety merited a bit of consideration when it came to pride. 'I dare say they'll be hot and bothered when they do arrive,' she had told the others in her usual no-nonsense way. 'And not altogether happy that they've hed to leave their homes and their neighbours.'

That said, a free-for-all had followed with opinions and points of view from the various helpers. A tiny percentage of them had shared the feelings that urchins and ragamuffins from London shouldn't be allowed and that they would contaminate the rest of the young ones, if not the entire village. When the coach-load of tired travellers finally arrived, all fears were put to rest. The people aboard, Jessie included, were no poorer than themselves and in the main were clean, and once afternoon tea had been taken and the billeting papers handed out, all that the weary trekkers had wanted was a comfortable, clean bed. But Norfolk people could not be hurried and it wasn't until seven-thirty in the evening that the Londoners had finally been marshalled into small groups and taken off in cars, carts, trailer and tractor, to their temporary homes.

Jessie, who had pushed Billy in his pushchair, had followed in Alice and her brother Jack's footsteps, with him graciously carrying her hold-all bag and small suitcase.

'My cottage is no palace,' Alice had said, a touch defensive. 'But there's a welcome mat at my door and I shouldn't like it if you didn't make yourself at *home*.' Too tired for much else, all that Jessie had wanted at that time was peace and quiet and a room of her own for Billy and herself. Alice had borrowed a cot bed for the boy and there was an old brass bed for Jessie with white cotton sheets as clean and fresh as daisies in springtime. Little did Jessie know then that once back in London, she and Alice would become pen friends. Or that the two old cottages, then up for sale in this village, would one day become a home for her and Tom and she would be sitting in this beamed room by a smouldering log fire.

Later on, once night had fallen, Jessie, Tom, Dolly and Stanley sat on wooden crates sipping cocoa around that inglenook fireplace, which was by then burning two large logs. They were joking over the fact that while they were in Tom and Jessie's cottage making do, their offspring were next door and very comfortable as they played cards next to their fire on two second-hand feather-cushioned sofas, purchased at the auction yard in Diss. Furniture from a large Victorian rectory had gone under the hammer and Stanley had been lucky with his bids for a couple of decent beds, an oak dining table and chairs, lamps and decent linen as well as an old-fashioned larder fridge, crockery and cutlery. And all at a fraction of the price they would have to pay had they bought new.

But here, in this lovely historic room, Jessie felt as if she had stepped into a fairy story that was real and she knew that Tom was experiencing similar emotions. His tired face said it all. He was relaxed and content even though his seat was no more than an apple crate.

'Well,' said Dolly finally, her voice soft, 'I don't think I'm gonna 'ave any trouble sleeping over. I'm all in.'

'Me neither,' said Tom. 'Don't forget to put a candle and a box of matches by your bed in case you do wake in the night. It's pitch black and you won't even be able to see to get to the light switch. I learned that the hard way. Fell arse over 'ead and kicked my big toe.'

'I don't think I'll wake before the sun comes up,' said Stanley, yawning.

'Nor me. This'll be a first for you, Jess. Waking up to the dawn chorus.'

'I'm looking forward to it,' said Jessie, not wishing to remind them that she had woken up in this countryside to the dawn chorus several times, when lodging with Alice and Jack.

'Right,' said Dolly, stretching and yawning, 'I'm ready for my bed.'

'Me, as well.' Stanley eased himself up from the crate and groaned. 'My poor old back's killing me. Still . . . it's bin worth it eh, Tom. Knocking ourselves out all week and then going back to fetch this lot up.' He was searching for well-deserved appreciation and praise. But both Jessie and Dolly stayed quiet, tormenting him.

'Let's 'ope so,' said Tom. 'But there you go. What do women know about back-breaking work and long hours?'

'And what do men know about delivering babies?' said Dolly as she stood up. 'Come on, you. My little hero. Carry me over the threshold and into that lovely old-fashioned feather bed.'

'Dream on, sweetheart. Dream on.' That said, Stanley reached out and took his wife's hand, saying, 'I'll give you a piggy-back if you're that tired.'

'No, ta.' Dolly laughed and then bade her sister and brother-in-law goodnight as she left hand in hand with her adorable husband to go next door into their dream cottage.

'She seems happy enough,' said Tom, staring into the flames of the fire.

'Course she's happy. And so am I. You've done wonders, Tom.'

He slowly turned his head to look into her face. 'But 'ave I made up for the past?'

'Nearly,' she teased, 'nearly. Ready for the camp bed?'

'I'll say I am. I could sleep on the floor the way I feel.'

'Come on, then. Let's go up before the kids come back.'

'That sounds like an offer, Jess and I'm not sure that I've got the energy.'

'I've heard that before,' she said, reaching out and taking his hand in hers. 'And . . . before we leave this lovely fire I want to hear something else I've heard before. Make it a perfect ending to a perfect day.'

'What's that.'

'Can't you guess?'

'You know I do, Jess. There's no need for me to say it.'

'Yes, there is.'

Pausing, Tom looked back into the flames and then, in a quiet voice said, 'I never stopped loving you, Jessie.'

4

Alone in her kitchen, ironing with the late afternoon sun coming through the window, Edie was trying to imagine her daughter coping as a full-time housewife. She wasn't a lazy girl but so far, apart from Tony creating Italian meals now and then, Edie had done most of the cooking and most of the washing and pressing, too. There had been times when all she had wanted was her flat all to herself, but those times were few and far between and she was in no hurry to see the back of Maggie, Tony and her treasured grandson. But the time *had* come for a parting of the ways. Today, on this glorious May Saturday, having listened to Jessie and Tom's daughter's excited account of her trip to Elmshill and now enjoying her own company, Edie imagined Maggie living in her own home, the house on the Ocean Estate. She and Tony had taken Peppie and Emma to their second viewing which was to be Peppie and Emma's first look.

Edie knew from Maggie's first reaction to the house that she could not wait to move into it. The new two-bedroom terraced property with all modern conveniences, a small front and back garden, sounded ideal. A dream come true for a young couple with a child, especially since a purpose-built community hall for those living on the estate would be on their doorstep, just beyond a small hedged green. Peppie had been thrilled when it had been explained to him that once they were settled into the new home, he could attend the Young Children's Club for an hour after school and on Saturday morning. It was mainly for this reason that Emma had gone with them today. She was hoping to see someone at the community hall to offer her services as a voluntary helper.

Since spending more and more time childminding Peppie, she had come to realise that she loved taking care of children. For Emma, there was small joy in sitting at a desk in the offices of the London Hospital, where she worked as Girl Friday: filing, typing and filling in endless forms. She was ready for a change, so being able to practise at the community hall, where, of course, her cherished Peppie would be going, seemed like a good idea, *if* she could persuade the person in charge to let her have a go. Both Edie and Jessie were a little tongue in cheek about it; looking after one small boy now and then was a very different thing from being semi-responsible for a hall full of energetic children.

Smiling to herself, Edie hung Tony's freshly ironed white cotton work coat onto the back of the kitchen door, her feet aching and her throat dry; she was ready for her armchair and a cup of sweet tea. She pulled the plug of the iron out of the wall socket and placed it on the draining board to cool and glanced up at the light blue clock on the wall to see that she had ten minutes or so before her aunt Naomi came to pay a visit with her old cronies: Joey, Ben and Larry. The three musketeers who she used to love to watch as they strolled into the turning in which she lived before moving onto this council estate. Their arms waving as they debated this, that or the other, the men had been, and still were, part and parcel of the old East End.

As she put the kettle on the gas stove, her old life in her thoughts, the face of her father, as he had stood in the doorway of their old house, came to her mind. The difference now was that it no longer upset her. Not since he had recently returned to England after being away for a very long time. Resting back in her chair, sipping tea she warmed to the sound of her aunt Naomi and her motley group of friends filing past her kitchen window. She knew they were here to discuss one of Naomi's crazy ideas that so far Edie had avoided getting involved in herself. When she opened the street door to them, Edie quietly laughed. They were all in their mid to late seventies and enjoying life. Ben was wearing a thick padded raincoat on this hot dry summer's day, Joey looked smart in his suit and tie and Larry, tall and lanky wearing his summer slacks with a blue and white open-neck check shirt and navy chunky-knit cardigan and check peaked cap. Larry liked to think there was an aura of mystery about him. Was he a London villain or a gentleman from the country? He was neither and no-one actually gave a toss in any case.

Wearing her old comfortable flat shoes, her daughter's old three-quarter-length green coat and a baggy pink cardigan over a floppy blue crepe blouse and a short-brimmed straw hat perched on top of her wiry grey hair, Harriet also looked a picture. Naomi of course was lovely in one of her sunny delicate flowery frocks with a straw hat bound by a chiffon scarf to match.

They had been debating the ways of the world on their way here and were still in disagreement as to the rights and wrongs of life in general as they filed in, each of them trying to score a point. Edie, so used to them, was not going to ask questions. Harriet was the first into the living room and onto what she considered the best chair by the gas fire and next to the veranda doors. She took off her straw hat and then eased off her shoes and wiggled her stiff toes.

'Make yourself at home, why don't you?' said Larry in his usual deadpan voice, his eyelids at half mast. 'You know why she only takes off her hat and shoes?' he said, looking sleepily at Edie.

'To air my brains and my feet,' said Harriet unbuttoning her coat and waving it to let the heat out, filling the air with the scent of Lifebuoy toilet soap. 'I'm still 'aving hot sweats but Nao won't 'ave it that I'm in my change.'

'Silly cow,' said Larry, sitting down on a high-backed chair. 'Nearly bloody eighty and she thinks she's going through the change.'

'Tea all round, then?' said Edie, bemused as ever by this bunch of cronies.

'In a china tea cup, thank you,' said Harriet.

'As if I didn't already know that,' said Edie as she turned to Joey. 'Camp coffee?'

'Yes, please, Edie. Thank you.'

'Coffee.' Ben grinned. 'He thinks he's a blooming teenager.

And it's murder on the gnashers. Look at mine.' He curled his lips to show his sparkling white and pink false teeth.

'You look like a gorilla doing that. One day you'll stop like it. Anyway . . . you are what you are,' Joey sniffed. 'And compared to you I *am* a teenager . . . as a matter of fact.'

Leaving them to it Edie went back into the kitchen and closed the door. To her this was like a rerun of an ancient cinema film. They seemed determined not to change. The hatch door suddenly opened and Larry peered in at her saying, 'I wouldn't mind a drop of Milk of Magnesia if you've got it, Edie. Harriet's give me indigestion. She's not stopped talking since we left the house. What do you think? You think it's a good idea?'

'Milk of Magnesia?'

'No! A pantomime this coming Christmas. At the Grand Star. I wanna get rid of the bloody place but she says I should keep it. That it's money in the bank.'

'It wasn't my soddin' idea!' boomed Harriet's voice from behind him. 'It was Rosie's! She reckons we could make some money putting shows on!'

'It's up to you, Larry,' said Edie.

'But what would *you* do? Keep it or sell it?'

'At your age – sell it. Sell it and enjoy the money. Take Harriet abroad. To Spain.'

'I would rather send her to Coventry for a week. That in itself would be a holiday. There're enough foreigners in England without having to go abroad to look at them . . . and having to pay for the pleasure. I don't think so. Milk of Magnesia?'

'It's in the bathroom cupboard. Go and help yourself.'

Larry rolled his eyes and closed the hatch door leaving Edie to enjoy a minute's peace while she made the tea. She could hear their sometimes muted and sometimes raised voices, arguing the toss about the Grand Star. Of course Naomi was all for keeping it and turning it back into what it had originally been built for, a music hall. And in this instance, Edie was in agreement because too many of the lovely old theatres and music halls had already been turned into bingo halls and those that hadn't were either boarded up and running alive with rodents or had been razed to the ground.

The previous year, Harriet's granddaughter Rosie had put on a show, *Love in Lavender*, which she had written and produced herself, using appropriate published songs of the period. It had been a super night out and a lovely show and the rave review in the *Evening Star* written by one of Larry's old contacts had been good for morale. Edie remembered how much she enjoyed the musical and had loved hearing old songs as well as those from the hit parade which had been performed by a local band. To lose a lovely old music hall for a place where people could play bingo seemed a shame. Shaking her head, Edie murmured to herself, saying, 'It would be a pity.'

'What d'yer mean?' said Larry as he came into the kitchen with the bottle of white medicine. 'What would be a pity?'

'The Old Star turned into a bingo hall.'

'Grand Star, if you don't mind. And yes, it would, but why should I bloody care? I don't live there any more. It smells of damp and shit. It's like a bug hole now.'

'No, it's not. It was only last year that the show was on and it looked lovely. New stage curtains and everything. But then . . . you don't have to make excuses.' She turned her head to look into his solemn eyes. 'Larry, if you want to pass it on, then do so.'

'I would, don't you worry. But not for bingo. I would give it away if I thought it would be brought back to its former glory. We tarted it up for the show for Rosie's sake but the place needs a lot of attention and a lot of money spending on it. The rising damp's come up and gone back down again but you could live off the bloody mushrooms growing there.'

'What about the Arts Council? They might be interested.'

'Do me a favour. They never put anything into the Theatre Royal so they're not likely to pass any lucre over to a bug hole. I wouldn't mind if it was their own money. Grants come from the government and if it comes from the government it comes from us – the tax payers.' He took a dessert spoon off the draining board and filled it with the creamy white medicine. 'Banks and blooming investors. They know what they're doing. What they're about. It's in their interest to let the East End run down. Give it another fifty years and you won't recognise your birth place. It's already begun . . . you've seen the skyscrapers.'

Edie laughed at him. 'A few tower blocks don't make New York.'

'We'll see,' he said, 'we'll see. Not from down here, though . . . from up there on high. From the clouds. We'll all be dead by then, thank God. It's a changing world, Edie. A changing world. Money – that's all anyone thinks about now.'

'Not in this block of flats – we're all working just to make ends meet.'

'Not everyone,' said Larry, licking his medicine spoon clean. 'A chap came down from upstairs as we came up, wearing a very nice navy serge suit and gold cufflinks and smelling like a woman. I felt sure I had seen him before.'

'Well, I don't know who that would 'ave been.'

'Course you wouldn't, they're like ships in the night that sort. Someone up there has got a spiv for a relative or a friend with a bit of ill-gotten gains in the back pocket if you ask me. Maybe it's your Italian relatives?'

'They moved out, Larry, I already told you that before. Did the man look continental then?'

'He wasn't dark skinned if that's what you're saying but in that light on the stairs who could say? Does it matter?'

'Exactly my point. It doesn't. Don't forget that some of Maggie's friends are West Indian and she's married to an Italian. You shouldn't go on about foreigners.'

'Why not? I'm a Jew. I was always called the Jew boy. What's the difference? People are too bloody sensitive these days, if you ask me. You expect it from women but grown men getting offended? It's all a bloody act.' He hunched his shoulders and left the kitchen muttering. 'I'm glad they've all come over. Took the bloody torch light off us.' With that Larry left Edie to herself and went to join the others – to stir *them* up a bit. He couldn't help having a bit of fun and it was in his nature to torment and tease. Shrugging at what he had said as being the ramblings of an old man Edie opened a packet of biscuits to the sound of the older generation in the other room discussing whether they should put on a pantomime at Christmas or a musical.

Placing her full tray on the table in the sitting room, Edie passed a cup to each of them, listening to Larry as he went on about the dilapidated music hall he had inherited from his father. He glanced from Harriet's bored face to Edie saying, 'My father left it to me and it's been a bloody burden ever since. I could never bring myself to let it go but I couldn't afford to open it. The rates had gone up and the bank wouldn't lend me another penny on it. Developers had been after that plot for years. I've held on for as long as I could, though.'

'My heart bleeds for yer,' said Harriet. 'What a rotten thing it is to own property.'

Larry studied her face and rolled his eyes. They had been mates for years and he knew her better than anyone. Had they not been such good friends, they might have married years ago. Now, too old for romance or sex he liked their present arrangement, he the lodger, she the dodger. Hers was an old rented house with a bit of character and he loved living there. A moment of silence passed and Larry waited for another quip from Harriet but she was gazing up at the ceiling, avoiding his eyes, sitting him out.

He turned to the others and said, 'They want to turn it into a bingo hall. With roulette tables.' He slowly shook his head and then cautiously eyed Naomi who was unusually quiet for a change. Sensing his eyes on her, she smiled graciously back at him, 'Do go on, Larry. It's quite fascinating.'

'You would bleedin' well say that,' sniffed Harriet.

'Of course, I hadn't had the purchase offer until Rosie was well under way with her rehearsals for the show and so on . . . last year. And she did do a marvellous job of cleaning the place.'

'Her and whose army? I scrubbed my fingers to the bone,' sniffed Harriet.

'Everyone did. I never had the heart to tell her about the offer at first but then what choice had I? I searched for weeks looking for a new venue for her.' He flapped a hand. 'What does it matter now?' He paused for a thought and then added sadly, 'But that look on her face . . . it broke my heart. She soon cheered up, mind you, when I turned down the offer to sell the place.'

'And you're breaking mine. Anyone would fink it's *your* granddaughter you're talking about. Still, don't mind me,' Harriet sniffed.

Larry continued as if he hadn't heard her. 'I told her. I said, Rosie, if I could be one hundred per cent sure that the show would be a success and that other companies would follow in your footsteps . . . I would persuade the bank to give me a loan. I had a bit to tide me over. Enough to pay rent to Harriet for my room and so on.' He looked around at his captive audience. 'I had only just moved in as her lodger, of course. If I knew then what I know now I might have thought twice. I've never heard snoring through a wall before.'

'I don't snore.'

'Let him tell his story, Harriet,' said Ben, waving a hand. 'I haven't heard this before. It makes a change.'

Larry shrugged and then said, 'I'll try not to go too fast for you.' He glanced slyly at Harriet. 'Not everyone's as quick as me. Anyhow . . . I told the developers that I needed more time to think about their offer. I said I had had another bid and needed time to think.' He leaned back in his chair and relaxed as if he had all the time in the world. 'I'd fought the greedy bastards off for years. So what difference would a few more months make?'

'And that's it?' said Harriet, looking from him to the others. 'I've heard more interesting tales from a tramp sitting on a park bench.'

'And are you not sorry now?' said Naomi, her head tipped to one side, her expression one of admiration. 'Others in your shoes would have *surely* taken the money and run, Larry?'

'If there 'ad of bin a wad of notes on the table he'd 'ave had it never you fear. It's all a load of fanny.'

'Darling, you can't *possibly* mean that. If I thought for one moment that you did I would think you *horribly* cruel. Do *try* and be nice to Larry.'

'You're like an old record that's got stuck yourself, Nao. Create a stage and you're right back up there. Performing.'

'Take no notice of her tormenting, Larry,' said Naomi. 'I know it's difficult but one can get used to a heckler.'

Larry was no longer paying any attention; he was in a world of his own, back in the Grand Star on the opening night of the show. In the lovely old theatre that had been left to him by his father who had inherited it from an uncle. Theatre had been in the family blood for generations. 'Rosie looked stunning,' he murmured, as proud as if she *were* his own granddaughter. 'She was the first to come on stage, looking out at the audience like a rabbit that thinks the fox is about. Then the band began to play and she danced as if she was Isadora Duncan reincarnated. Different music of course.' He gazed across at Harriet and said, 'I can't remember what the song was now.'

'"Fever,"' she said, having not forgotten one moment of that wonderful evening.

'"Fever." That was it.' Larry quietly chuckled. '"Fever." She swirled and spun and danced around that stage as if she was born for it. She stretched herself to the limits. I don't think she wanted that song to end. She would have danced 'til midnight. And the applause! What can I say? Words fail me.' Again he looked at Harriet. 'You remember the applause she got when she took that bow?'

'No. I can't say I remember any of it, Larry, except for when the clock in the bar struck midnight and someone popped the cork of a bottle of champagne.'

'I remember that opening scene actually,' said Naomi. 'Larry has a point, Harriet. Your granddaughter *is* gifted. And I speak from history and a long time in show business.'

'Well, there we are then. So speaks the voice of wisdom and experience,' said Harriet, rolling her eyes. 'Naomi knows best.'

'It was a good party, though. I'll give you that,' said Larry, unyielding. This was *his* story. His drama recalled. And he wasn't going to let Harriet or Naomi take the limelight off him.

'It was a good *show* is what it was,' murmured Harriet. 'My Rosie filled that music hall. And she'd weathered a storm doing it as well.'

'We all did. Only God knows how many bloody leaflets we gave out the week leading up to it. And on the day,' said Larry. 'Weathered the storm? She was flying as high as a kite.'

'Takes after me,' said Harriet. 'I used to fly high in my youth. From one market stall to another, pinching a bit of fruit or bread to keep the wolf away from the door.'

'On the stairs,' murmured Larry, 'that's where I once saw him.' He rubbed his chin thoughtfully. 'I remember now. Where I'd seen the man before. It was on the night of your Maggie's last birthday party, Edie. He looked out of place in his mohair suit and diamond tie pin.'

'Who're you talking about now?' said Ben, yawning.

'The spiv I saw not half an hour ago. When we were coming up. We passed him on the stairs. He looked like an Italian. One of the mob. But not Italian. Just trying to be.'

'I know who you mean,' said Ben. 'The bloke who wouldn't look us in the eye. So? What about him?'

'Nothing.' Larry glanced from one to the other as they sat there gazing at him. 'What did I say?'

'He was just a bloke coming down the stairs,' said Joey. 'Why mention him if there's no point to your story?'

Larry narrowed his eyes thoughtfully and shrugged. 'There was something about him. Too shifty for an East London man . . . as if he didn't belong. You know what I mean?'

'Does the description ring any bells with you, Edie?'

'No. I can't say it does.'

'Does it matter?' asked Ben. 'In the big picture who cares about a stranger in the background, unless it's Alfred Hitchcock in one of his own films.'

'He struck me . . . that's all. Not someone you'd expect to see in this building. Don't ask me why.'

Larry's instincts were bang on. The man he had seen had just come from his mother's flat with every intention of extracting from Gloria the information he knew she had lodged some- where in the back of her feeble mind. But he had failed to get anything sensible out of her and now needed a drink and twenty minutes by himself before he went back to squeeze the facts out of her brain. This man was James Drake junior. A young man who had the blood of his murderous father running through his veins. His father who had left a small fortune hidden away and the only one who knew where it was, he had left just a quivering wreck. Poor Gloria.

'So . . . what about this panto then?' said Edie, glancing at her watch.

'At last,' said Joey. 'Someone has answered my question. Do we put a show on or don't we? And if we do, should it be a pantomime or a musical?'

'With us lot on stage?'

'Why not?' Larry smiled. 'We'll be working alongside profes- sionals. Naomi. Then there's Harriet's connections. Her Rosie's bloke, George, has got mates in a band. But the place'll 'ave to be spruced up. There's the back staircase that could do with a coat of paint . . . etcetera, etcetera, etcetera.'

'Crafty bastard.' Harriet smiled. 'It's why he's set this up.'

Larry looked at Harriet through half-closed eyes. 'What are you talking about now?'

'You know bloody well. If we put the show on . . . and you knew we'd be up for it . . . we'd 'ave to smarten it up first . . . all nice and ready for when your buyer comes in to 'ave a look.'

'It never crossed my mind,' he sniffed. 'But now that you've mentioned it. Maybe it would be killing two birds with one stone. I suppose I would have to make it worthwhile for the lot of you. A slap-up meal in Joe Lyons.'

'In the Savoy more like.'

Larry splayed a hand and shrugged. 'Somewhere in-between the two.'

'So is it set in stone then?' asked Joey.

'Course it bloody well is,' said Ben. 'We needn't 'ave come to this meeting. Larry and Harriet 'ave decided it for us.' He looked across at Naomi. 'What's up with you?'

'Why, nothing at all, Ben. Should there be?'

'No – but there is. You can't see your face. I can.'

'Well . . . as a matter of fact I am a *little* offended. I have never, up until now, mentioned the word *professional*. The reason being that I have not had cause to. But . . .'

'Oh, here we go,' said Harriet, butting in. 'She wants us to pay 'er for 'er performance.'

'Indeed I do not. But . . . since Ben happened to notice that my feelings had been hurt . . . I shall tell you what the matter is. It is common courtesy, when one is in the company of a professional . . . who has played against many a famous actor, in the very best of our theatres and in film, to ask if she *would* be prepared to work alongside amateurs in an amateur production.'

All of them, with the exception of Harriet found this a touch amusing and couldn't quite manage to keep a straight face. Harriet had known Naomi since they were both ragged urchins, so knew she had been and still was talented and someone who had worked her way up, from singing and dancing next to a chestnut seller's glazier, to performing in West End theatres. She *had* been something of a star and, as with all actors, had been depressed when good parts no longer came her way. And for this little elderly group to assume that she would jump at a chance to be on stage again with inexperienced amateur actors was a bit of a let down. Someone like Naomi had to be approached properly.

'Did you really expect us to believe for one second that you'd get up on a stage with a bunch of amateurs, Nao?' Harriet sighed. 'It was a joke but you missed it, as usual. You should know Larry by now.'

Quick off the mark, Larry chuckled. 'No flies on you is there, Harriet? Course I was sowing a seed – but only a quarter hoping that it might lodge in your mind, Naomi.' He looked at Ben and winked. 'Can you imagine the poster? With Naomi's face and name spread across it? And a list of the famous actors she's worked with. The tickets'd sell like hot cakes.'

'You can't go using her name like that. I wouldn't do it in her shoes. And I put a pound note on her not wanting to.'

'A pound note? Well I must say that is very generous.' Naomi looked across to Ben. 'Will you match the bid or double it?'

'Match it. You think I'm a millionaire?'

'Go on, then,' said Larry. 'I'll double it. Providing you all agree to help clean it and that.'

'Never mind the Ritz, though. Larry should treat us all to a week at Butlins once we've done the show and he's done a deal on the Star. Once he's sold it.'

'*All* of you?'

'Not me,' said Edie, laughing. 'I'm not quite ready for a holiday with pensioners.'

'I like the sound of that,' said Joey, standing up ready to leave.

'Count me in.' Ben eased himself up from his chair. 'But I won't share. I want a room of my own.'

Ten minutes later with the men gone and heading for the pub, Naomi and Harriet were by themselves in the living room while Edie was making a second pot of tea. There was no more mention as to whether or not Naomi would star in their show this coming Christmas; it could now be taken for granted that she would. There was no doubt in Harriet's mind that, given two or three weeks, her friend would be presenting them all with a selection of publicity photographs of herself in stunning costume taken while on stage or in a film-set from the early days.

A peaceful calm now reigned and Naomi thought this a good opportunity to broach Harriet on the diary she had been keeping safe for her. Easing her shoes off of her tired feet she knew she was going to have to be tactful because Harriet was still edgy about any mention of a particular period of her life, towards the end of the nineteenth century. A time when as a child, she had been left to fend for herself, bedding down at night in a coal man's stable, on a bed of hay with old blankets given to her by the caring old man.

'You've got a good heart, Naomi,' said Harriet quietly. 'I shouldn't think I've ever come across anyone as generous as you are. I'm glad you've agreed to be in the show. There, I've said it.'

'Oh, Harriet . . . and what a lovely compliment to pay. I'm sorry if I was a touch sulky earlier on.'

'I'm not. If we can't be ourselves, what else is there to get up for in the mornings?'

'Fresh air and sunshine, poppet. Fresh air and sunshine,' replied Naomi.

'Or rain and thunder.'

'Oh?' Naomi tipped her head and looked into her friend's face. 'What's the matter, Harriet?'

'The conversation made me think of my husband Arthur to tell you the truth. He would have loved to have seen what our Rosie had achieved. Seen her up on that stage. She's got star quality, you know.'

'Of course she has darling – I've always said so.'

'Perhaps he did see 'er, eh? Him and my grandson Tommy who was cut down in the prime of his life. It's practically a year now, you know. Since that Maltese bastard pushed the knife into his heart.'

'I know it is, Harriet . . . but I didn't want to bring it up. It must be terribly painful for you. I wish I could say something to make you feel better but I can't. No-one can.'

'You already have. Now we'll drop it.' Harriet pulled a sparkling white handkerchief from her pocket and blew her nose. 'I wouldn't mind a bit of Butlins holiday camp.' A faint smile crossed her face. 'Be a lark, wouldn't it? Us lot there together. Long lanky Larry in a one-piece swim suit.'

'Don't be silly. He'd wear trunks. Wouldn't he?'

'Don't bet on it. He never throws a thing away and never buys anyfing new.'

Naomi nodded and smiled with relief. Her friend had managed to pull herself out of the dumps so bravely. 'Yes,' she murmured, 'it would be a lot of fun. We must keep Larry to it.'

'So? What's on your mind then, Nao?'

'Mine? Why nothing, darling. Whatever made you think there was?'

'Oh, don't give me all that bollocks. I know you better than you know yourself. Out with it.'

Naomi leaned back in her armchair and relaxed. 'So you do, Harriet. So you do.' Her expression altered as she looked into her friend's face. 'The diary.'

'Oh. That. The reporter covering my Tommy's funeral wanted my life story, you know. He didn't look as if he could afford it. Worth a fortune to the right paper. No-one's come up with anything near the truth so far. Jack the Ripper. Dozy buggers.' She shook her head despairingly and continued.

'It was the midwife and her nephew who wasn't right in the head. He was all that woman had in the world. Her beloved nephew . . . who started the whole ball rolling. He murdered that first whore out of passion, you know, and the second out of anger. Then his aunt Jacqueline had no choice but to take care of the others. They were gonna blackmail her. And the pair of them gave little away, aunt and nephew, two ordinary, everyday people you would pass in the street without batting an eyelid.

'Pass the diary of the midwife onto your Edie. Once I'm dead and buried she can get it published and share out the money between herself and my Rosie. Or give the diary to that woman's sister.'

'Which woman, darling?' said Naomi, tipping her head to one side.

'Jessie . . . the one up on the fourth floor. Her sister writes books, don't she? Let 'er make something of it. But make sure she shares the money three ways if she does wanna have a go at it.'

'And you really do mean it this time? You've said so before but then changed your mind. Is it what you want? Your story to come out in all of the national newspapers?'

'No. In a book.'

'But darling . . . reporters would be in like a bee to the honey pot. It will make headlines should it come out.'

'What does it matter? Once I'm out of the way? Let the world know what 'appened to them poor Whitechapel women. Poor cows. You'd 'ave to be desperate to let some of them filthy smelly drunks touch you.'

'I'll talk to Edie and if she's willing I'll pass on your instructions.'

'Good. But you make sure you tell 'er that she's to go to a publisher herself. And not to let it out of her hands until she's bin made a good offer. What's in that diary is worth a fortune. It's the plain truth.'

'And there really was no Jack the Ripper?'

'No . . . but there was a Jacqueline the Ripper – who my Arthur's sister Mary only just escaped from . . . by the skin of 'er teeth. Once it's published in a book . . . you just make sure that you tell Edie not to let go of it without a solicitor witnessing an agreement for a payment for my Rosie as well as whoever writes it up. I've got no money to leave my granddaughter. Only that diary. Promise me you'll do that?'

'Of course I promise. Rosie will have children one day and she will need—'

'But whatever you do,' said Harriet, interrupting her flow, 'don't ever let my Rosie know that that woman, that midwife, tried to murder me. Promise you won't ever mention that to a soul in case it gets back to her. She'll agonise over it and I won't rest in my grave. She's 'ad enough misery in 'er life. Her mother never wanted nor loved the poor cow when she was a child and her father had run off. All she had in the world was me and her Tommy. He worshipped that girl as no brother could. And now *he*'s dead.'

'All right, Harriet. I promise. You have my word.'

'Good. That's got that out of the way. Now then . . . what's all this about your Maggie's friend Rita and a black man?'

'Harriet! His name is Errol. And he's a lovely, sweet and charming young man. I'm afraid I don't find that amusing. We must either change the subject or have a terrible row.'

'Who lives next door to me, Naomi?'

Naomi sniffed and looked away. 'Point taken.'

'Not good enough.'

'Juanita and Urban and their three children.'

'And are we at each other's throats that you know of?'

'No, of course not.'

'Thank you. Now then. I asked for a reason. Tell Rita to be careful and to warn her black friends that trouble's brewing in the East End now. I don't think it's spread to Bethnal Green yet but it might 'ave done. If not, it won't be long unless it all dies down – which is possible.'

'And what am I to tell him? To go into hiding?'

'Don't be daft. Where can he hide?' said Harriet, her feet now up on the sofa, a cushion under her head. 'Where can any of 'em hide? But he might want to think about leaving this business of buying property for a little while. Wait 'til it's all died down.' She yawned and closed her eyes. 'It's probably just a flash in the pan but since the fascists lost interest in the Jews they look elsewhere for someone else to pick on. Oh and your Edie's Harry is back for good by the way.' She yawned again and then spoke in a sleepy, slow voice. 'Got 'imself a flat in Holborn. Running a proper little import business now. Selling onto shops and stallholders.'

Stunned by this, Naomi stared at her friend who was within seconds of sleep. She knew that Harry had been seen selling off the back of a lorry in Petticoat Lane but presumed that he was to-ing and fro-ing from the Canary Islands. She wanted to know more but as history had proved over and over again, Harriet had gone out like a light and there was no point in trying to wake her. She was out for the count.

Her niece Edie filled her mind instead. She had only just moved out of her house in Cotton Street when Harry had first turned up out of the blue five years back. Harry was spotted by Ben and Joey, who were still living in Cotton Street, each in their separate small terraced houses, which they had refused to move out of – neither of them fancying the idea of living on a council estate. Edie's husband, Harry, had been stunned to say the least to see the house boarded up and his wife and child gone. They had taken him to Joey's house for shelter.

It hadn't taken the two close friends long, however, to find out that Harry had done Edie an injustice and his confession of why he had come home to England at that time did nothing to re-ignite the fondness they once had for him. Turkey at that time was getting involved in the Korean War and Harry had had enough of any talk to do with battles. He had also let it slip that the Turkish woman he had shacked up with was pregnant with his child.

Remembering all the effort that Ben and Joey had made to send Edie's husband packing five years ago she gazed at the fast-asleep Harriet and wondered if she could possibly have got it wrong about Harry being back for good. She would have to wait and see. Get Ben to find out what was going on. She leaned her head back and, to the sound of her friend Harriet softly snoring, fell into a lovely, if not troubled, light sleep. And while Naomi dreamed of footlights and theatre and Harriet struggled with a nightmare of a maniac midwife stalking her in the dark streets of Whitechapel, on the fourth floor, Gloria, listening innocently to a play on the wireless, was about to be subjected to the worst of any mother's fears. Her son, James Drake, had just parked his Jaguar under the arches and was here again to bully her, but this time, at the end of his tether, he was prepared to do whatever it took to get information from her that would change his lifestyle – and was prepared to cause her a heart failure if necessary.

The most striking feature about Gloria's son was his dark blue eyes that were only a few shades lighter than his black pupils and the slight cast in one eye gave the impression that his mind was always somewhere else. His black hair and dark eyebrows, his straight nose and thick shaped lips set him apart from other men where looks were concerned. But this handsome-looking man could do little to hide the dark streak which permeated his soul, something that he himself was not even aware of. His hands were almost always clenched into a fist, his jaw bone tense and there was hardly ever an expression in his eyes other than a cold unemotional look. If he had a soul and conscience it was so deeply rooted as to be almost lost. In short, he had inherited the worst of his father's traits – and his father, after all was said and done, had been hanged for murder – unpremeditated though it was.

Tall and broad, on the face of it this twenty-seven-year-old could be viewed as any woman's dream lover and with his good looks had managed to lure, bed and extract money from those wealthy women who liked to spoil themselves wickedly. Even his dispassionate expression had been a turn on. But there had been a swerve in trend to be promiscuous and it was now being seen as fashionable for the rich to have lovers openly. There was no longer a need to pay men such as himself to be discreet.

Clever enough to have lived the way he had wanted and charm most people into believing he was an upstanding citizen, he had so far never been under threat of arrest, never mind suspicion, for any of the crimes he had committed. His sin of extracting money from wealthy women, after he had satisfied them in bed, had given him a sense of security for too long. Now the daunting realisation that it was over filled him with rage and filtered into his sleep at night causing him to wake in a black mood. He believed that society owed him something since it had been no fault of his that he had been spawned by the devil and cursed for the sins of his father. Having followed in those paternal foot-steps he had been pleasantly surprised to see how game society ladies were to pay for his pillow talk and love-making.

Unlike his father, James Drake hadn't had to resort to black-mail to extract hefty payments for his favours and this he had put down to himself being something of a romantic Casanova with aristocratic blood running through his veins. His father had come from old stock and a family who, although by no means lacking in funds, had lost a substantial chunk of their fortune in the notorious stock market crash some years back. And as history often showed where the gentry were concerned, the family were tight with their money and had used the excuse of teaching Drake's father a lesson, by stopping his allowance because of his reckless youth: gambling, whisky and women.

Once he married Gloria they cut him off completely because he had dared to marry beneath himself.

Having been brought up in rooms in Shoreditch in a dingy street, James, from boy to man, had learned how to be street wise and clever in order to survive in his vermin infested world, which was a huge contrast to the upbringing his father had had. One of four privileged children, born and bred in a grand house in Knightsbridge and educated in the best private schools he had enjoyed exeats and summer holidays in the family country mansion. In short, James' father had been fed from a silver spoon, until he had been cut off completely to fend for himself.

All things considered it was no wonder that Gloria's son had followed in his father's dark footsteps.

Drake was aware of everything his father had got up to during his lifetime, from the court case reports in newspapers, as well as hidden journals and diaries that he had found amidst his late father's belongings. Before he had been arrested and executed, his father, after a few shots of whisky, had hinted to Drake, when he was no more than a boy, that he had a few thousand pounds stashed away for emergencies, money which had come from blackmailing wealthy married women. Where the small fortune had been hidden he hadn't said, but Drake had always felt that his harebrained mother, Gloria, knew exactly where it was even though she insisted otherwise. The only bit of information Drake had gleaned from his father was that his mother held the key to a safe deposit box at a railway station and in that box was the key to his fortune. No matter how hard or persuasive Gloria's son had been when visiting his mother of late he had not been able to find out where that key was – and so as this afternoon drew into early evening he had every intention of getting the information out of her – whatever the outcome.

Half listening to soft classical music coming through the wireless and half dozing, Gloria hadn't heard the doorbell ring at first but then, with her son's finger resting on the button she came to with a start and rushed to open the door to at least stop the shrill sound of the bell piercing through her brain.

Her face breaking into a smile of relief when she saw who it was standing there, she believed, in her own innocent way that her son had come to make amends for shouting at her earlier on. Realising by her expression that Gloria was still not taking him seriously, Drake inhaled slowly and decided to change tack. Using all he had learned throughout his life, he smiled innocently as if butter would not melt in his mouth. He then gently cupped her face with one hand saying, 'I'm sorry I lost my temper, Mother.'

'Did you? I don't remember,' she beamed, holding onto this rare moment of physical contact. She could not remember the last time he had reached out and touched her. 'I was just going to make a pot of tea. She floated a hand through the air while singing, *'Tea, for Two . . . Cha Cha . . .'*

'That would be lovely,' said Drake, rubbing his chin as he walked into the sitting room, wishing he didn't have to be in this flat. At least his mother seemed to have forgotten that he'd been hostile towards her earlier on. His charm and acting ability to the fore he slid open the hatch into the kitchen and spoke to her as if he was a caring son. 'The veranda windows are sparkling, Mother. I hope you haven't been overdoing it?'

'Are they? That's nice. Would you like a digestive biscuit with your tea?'

'No, thank you.' He closed the hatch and drew breath. It wasn't easy for him to have an ordinary conversation with someone he had not the least bit of respect for. But if he was going to be successful in dragging information from the deepest crevice of her dull mind he knew he had to keep a grip. So long as she didn't touch him or worse still try to give him a kiss on the cheek he felt he could cope. He looked around the room at the armchair and sofa and wondered if Gloria might have hidden the key to the safe deposit box down the back of one or the other and had forgotten. Lowering himself into the armchair and not the sofa in case she sat next to him he pushed a hand down the side and slowly drew his fingers along until he touched a dried up apple core which made him

go icy cold. Pulling his hand out believing it to be the remains
of a dead mouse he felt himself shudder.

'I've brought the biscuits just in case,' said Gloria, coming
into the room, carefully holding a tray. 'You always loved them
when you was little.'

Watching as his mother placed the tray on a small round
table in the middle of the room he felt his stomach churn and
wondered why she always looked as if she smelled of moth-
balls and lavender. He half listened to her babble on about
nothing of importance while she poured their tea. Then, when
she paused for a few seconds he said, 'I was just sitting here
wondering where I might hide something away from burglars
if I lived in this flat. Something small that is. A piece of jewellery
. . . a key . . . a five-pound note . . .'

'I wouldn't trust tucking a five-pound note in the hem of
the curtains, dear. No. I always keep my bit of pension in my
purse, in my handbag, down there, where I can see it. And I
take it to bed with me at night. You never know, do you . . .
who might get in through a window while you're asleep.'

'Hem of the curtain?' he said, an impressed tone in his voice.
'That's very clever, Mother. You don't think that that's where
you might have put the key to the safety box, do you?'

'It might be, dear. What a clever boy you are. Why don't you
have a look and see?' She knew the key wouldn't be there but
was so enjoying the little game she thought they were playing.

'I suppose it's worth a try.' He smiled as he pulled himself
up from the chair. 'After all, there might be money around
somewhere. We could buy you a television with it.'

'That would be nice.' Gloria sipped her tea and watched as
Drake ran his finger along the hem of the curtains until he felt
something and stopped.

'I don't think this can be a key,' he said, hoping it was, 'but
who knows.' He eased the hidden treasure out of the hem to
find that it was a gold half sovereign. Stunned by this, he turned
to his mother. 'Did you know that this was in there?'

'What is it, dear? I can't see.'

'A half sovereign.'

'Oh, goodness me! I must have slipped that in there years ago. Before I moved into this flat. I fetched all my curtains with me.'

'Why do you think you placed it there before and not after you'd moved in?'

'I don't remember putting it there so it must have been a long time ago, mustn't it? Before your father was hanged. I must have taken it out of the little bag it was in with the others – for the funeral – and then forgot I'd done it. Silly old me. It won't buy a television set though, will it?'

'Out of *what* little bag?' said Drake, constraining his short temper. Then, checking himself and sporting an amused face, added, 'There couldn't possibly be more of them, Mother. You would have told me about them. Surely? We were very poor once Father had passed on.'

'That's because he said I wasn't to spend it. But I suppose that was because he didn't really believe they would hang him. I never went to see him on the day. I stayed at home, with you, with the lights off. But I think he would have told me to spend it on myself if I had gone. So when I remember where I put that key I'll use the money and go on a long cruise with lots of lovely frocks to wear. My friend Naomi said I should make the most of myself. She said I had lively blue eyes and a healthy complexion. There. I remembered that without even thinking!'

'Ah,' smiled her self-centred son, 'so all we have to do – is find that little key to your fortune. And this is a small flat so it shouldn't be difficult. Should it?'

'No. I'll have a really good look one of these days. Don't let your tea get cold, dear.'

Drake, grinding his back teeth held up the half sovereign and then said, 'How many of these do you think might have been in the little bag?'

'Oh, quite a few I should say. All shining like real gold.'

'This is real gold, Mother.'

'Is it? I didn't know they made coins out of gold. You'd think that a penny would be worth a lot more than it is then, wouldn't you?'

'Pennies are made out of copper.' He sat down next to her and leaned close, his eyes fixed on hers. 'Did you put any more of these in the hems of any of your curtains that you brought with you? The bedroom, for instance?'

'Now then,' Gloria said, smiling and wagging a finger at him. 'Stop trying to trick me into telling you things. Because even if I do find the key to the safety box I won't let you have it. It's not your money, it's mine. Your daddy said so.'

'Of course it's your money and you should spend it on yourself. Do you think you might have put the key in a hem, too?'

'Not telling,' said Gloria, treating this like a game. She had her son back and was behaving as if he were her little boy. But Drake had already had enough. His temper was rising to such a pitch that he could hardly contain it.

'If I don't find the key tonight, Mother . . . I fear I shall be very angry.'

'Naughty *boy*!' Gloria shrieked, her face alive with laughter. 'No more tantrums! What did I tell you a long time ago? That tantrums cause tears? And that if you were a good boy Mummy would treat you? Well, I shall. One day. Scout's honour!'

Drake had spent enough time in this woman's company. He could no longer be patient with her. 'You're not a scout and I think you do know where the key is.' He tapped her head hard with one finger. 'In there . . . inside that thick skull . . . is the key to the key . . . and you are *going* to tell me where it is.'

'Oh . . . you've gone and got all cross with me again. Silly boy. Don't get your pants in a twist over nothing.'

Gloria's only child . . . now a man, placed a hand on her arm and could feel her bones through her cardigan sleeve. 'You *stupid* woman! This is *my* future we're talking about! I *need* that money and you wouldn't know what to do with it! Where – have – you – hidden – that – key?'

'Tut tut tut,' said Gloria, wagging that finger again. 'No getting cross with Mummy.'

Infuriated by her naiveté Drake brought his other hand to her neck and gently squeezed it. 'You are going to tell me where the key is,' he said. 'You are going to if I have to squeeze the life out of you. You will tell me. I promise you.'

'I won't,' she said. 'I won't tell. You're a naughty boy. Yes, you are. A naughty boy!' Still, she believed this to be a game. She began to make up a ditty, singing as if it was a nursery rhyme: 'It's under the sink, behind the bed, don't look now or you'll be dead!'

'Shut up,' he snarled. 'Shut up!' He tightened his grip and glared into her puzzled eyes. 'Where – is – that – fucking – key?'

'King's Cross station! Safety box!'

'I know that! But where is the key to the safety box? Where is it?' He tightened his grip.

'Wallpaper,' she only just managed to whisper as her red face began to swell. 'Up there.' Drake let go of her as if she were a bundle of rags in a sack and followed her line of vision to see that she was staring above the door of the room – at the green flowery paper border. Then, as his repulsion towards his mother got the better of him he pushed her aside as if she were a rag doll and left her crumpled on the floor gasping for breath. Sweeping his hand along the paper border he felt the telltale bump. He had found the key. Once she heard the street door slam shut behind her son, Gloria curled up into a ball and quietly cried.

5

Oblivious to the outside world and all its problems, Naomi lay on her sofa, a feather cushion propped under her head, looking through one of her many early fashion magazines with her sad friend on her mind. She had promised herself that she would take Gloria to see the lovely talented seamstress, Shereen, for a fitting. To have a special evening frock made to measure had been Naomi's suggestion and Gloria had waved it off as if she wasn't pretty enough to wear a long gown. It had in fact been her dream since a child and especially when she discovered that she had a natural flair for dancing. She had surprised everyone at the afternoon tea dances, started up by Naomi and her friends. Since then, on cold winter afternoons, Naomi had sometimes sat with Gloria, entrancing her with stories of when she had been in the theatre and telling tales of the stars she had been on stage with, from the twenties until she had retired from acting and singing.

Gloria's favourite tale was not of a famous star but when Naomi told her of a particular designer and a particular mode of fashion. Christian Dior being her topic of criticism and in particular his New Look spring collection in Paris in 1948. Little slim tops that Gloria could remember and full skirts from waist to ankle. A fashion which had, in high places, been thought to promote immorality because of its hourglass shape. Naomi could still not believe that ancient members of the House of Lords would not recall the voluptuous seductive vamps of the nineteenth century who were far more daring.

Dropping her fashion journal from the early thirties to the floor, Naomi sipped her glass of brandy and snuggled down into her sofa, musing on all the changes which had come about since then. This had become a weekly ritual after a long soak in a lovely warm bubble bath followed by golden melted cheese on toast. Opening the first page of her newly published journal, she was aware once again of the change within the Arts sector and those working in shops and factories. With wages and salaries continuing to rise there was now an opportunity to earn more for those prepared to work extra hours. A taxi ride to a favourite nightclub, pub or dance hall was becoming part of the way of life.

There was a buzz in the air that even the down and outs were picking up on and benefiting from when it came to clothing themselves for the changing climates. Charity shops where interesting clothes could be purchased cheaply were opening in all boroughs in most towns. The small article in large print publicising an Oxfam shop in Portobello Road lodged in Naomi's mind. She allowed this second journal to slip to the floor too and then closed her eyes for a five-minute cat nap with the frock she would most like to see Gloria in on her mind – one which she would help her design for the next tea dance in a month's time. Once in her favourite state of a light sleep she dreamed of herself in one of Lily Langtry's gowns, spinning around the dance floor with Ben.

Still living in his old house in Cotton Street, Naomi knew that deep down Ben was ready to move onto this estate should a flat or maisonette become available, even though he, just like Joey the old die-hard, protested with might and main against it. The row of terraced houses all boarded up apart from theirs were damp, dark and mice infested. Naomi was certain that once they were in a new modern dwelling they would be sorry they hadn't let go of their old bit of London before now, while they were still lively enough to enjoy a bit of luxury. A lovely new fitted gas fire and light at the touch of a switch. Electricity not gas. Other terraced streets everywhere in England were being smashed to the ground to make way for exciting tower blocks as the trend towards high rise became more and more popular.

The motor car, especially the Morris Minor, advertised in

Naomi's magazine for women, in itself was innovative, since driving a car up until recent years had been seen as the man's prerogative. In the home comfort pages, central heating, washing machines and refrigerators were filling the space with pictures of up to the minute sparkling white, cream and light blue machines.

This was the time of Britain at another peak of industrial wealth but it was no longer a case of the rich becoming richer and the poor, poorer. Noble country landlords were being hit by high taxation and death duties wearing down the landowners, ex-officers and gentlefolk. Those living in stately homes were feeling the pinch and to make ends meet were opening to the public – causing the aristocracy to become an offshoot of the entertainment sector.

The barrier was slowly lifting on all fronts and it was thanks to writers such as Shelagh Delaney who set her play *Taste of Honey* in a Salford slum to great success and to Alan Sillitoe for *Saturday Night and Sunday Morning* in which he featured the terraces of Nottingham. The working man's culture had become fashionable again.

Television commercials with their alluring advertisements were showing that image was all-important and women who had been encouraged to go back to wife-and-motherhood after the war were now waving the feminist flag and in their own subtle way eroding male dominance, with hardly a male being aware of it.

In working-class pubs, corner shops, swanky Knightsbridge pads, coffee bars, jazz clubs and in the King's Road where bohemian students gathered, the topic of conversation continued to be the emancipation of women. The pressure to marry young was at an end and it seemed that changes were taking place everywhere. Locally, Rita was beginning to think that it would be easier to live by herself for a while, rather than rush into marrying Errol just yet and Billy Smith, Jessie and Tom's son, caught up in the talk of purchasing cheap property had now given up all ideas of moving with his parents and sister, Emma, to Norfolk. He too wanted to hang on to his independence.

★

Arriving into Jamaica Street on the back of Errol's cousin's motor bike, Jessie's son Billy was determined to get himself two wheels and soon. But his choice of a bike had changed; he was now saving up to buy a moped instead. It suited the image he preferred to sport; the Italian style rather than the teddy boy. Easing off his helmet he gave Malcolm a pat on the shoulder and thanked him for the ride.

'No problem, man . . .' said Malcolm, showing his lovely unaffected smile. 'Is ten to one you gonna buy one of these machines, eh?'

'We'll see,' said Billy, not wishing to offend his new mate. 'I might start off with a moped. I dunno.' He glanced along the turning and at the few old folk dotted around either gossiping or coming and going from the local market. He felt as if he had gone back in time. There was no buzz here and no young people, nothing. 'D'yer reckon Errol's 'ere yet, Malcolm?' Billy asked. 'I can't see your dad's old banger.'

'They bound to come soon. But what we care? I have a key. We can look around the property. You would t'ink this place a palace the way Errol go on about it.'

'And you don't?' said Billy, having listened earlier on, in a café, how Malcolm was going to do this, that and the other to the house, now that it was his.

His helmet tucked under his arm, Malcolm unzipped his mock leather biker's jacket. 'I can't say that I excited over it.' He glanced at the front of the terraced house and sniffed. 'It all right.'

'It's a slum, Malcolm. Needs bulldozing.'

'You t'ink so?'

Billy broke into a smile and quietly laughed. 'I was kidding you. Stop begging for compliments. You did well to get it. No flies on you, is there?'

'No . . . I can't say there is.' Malcolm slapped Billy on the shoulder. 'Things do level out you know. I older than you. Give it a year and you be looking to buy a little bit of England.'

'We'll see,' said Billy. 'Move yourself, then. Or do you want me to carry you over the threshold?'

'You? Carry me?' Malcolm pulled back and peered at Billy. 'You need some good West Indian food before you can even t'ink on it. You is so *skinny*.' Malcolm held up the Yale key to his house. 'You t'ink you can manage to open the door? It one heavy key, you know.'

Swiping it from Malcolm's hand, Billy pushed it into the keyhole and opened the door to a dark narrow passageway. 'Gawd . . . it stinks of cat piss!' He turned around to breathe in fresh air. 'Here . . . take the key. I'll be in, in a minute.' His head tilted up, Billy sucked in fresh air.

'A good West Indian clean and it will be just fine,' said Malcolm, preoccupied as he peered along the turning at a man in a smart navy suit who had just got out of an old dark blue Jaguar. Letting himself into a house six doors along, the man glanced sideways at Malcolm, showing no sign of neighbourly hospitality. He went inside and slammed the door shut behind him.

'My aunty Irma and her friend coming tomorrow with the scrubbing brush and bucket,' said Malcolm, slowly shaking his head, his forehead creased, 'You know . . . I sure as I stand here know that I see that man somewhere.'

'What man?'

'He gone inside the house but I tell you I *know* his face and I can't say I too impressed wit' de neighbour. He 'ent all dat friendly. No sir.'

'You're like an old woman at times. And stop talking like that. And does it really matter anyway if your neighbours don't kiss you 'ello?'

'No . . . I can't say it matter too much . . . and yet . . . I can't say it don't.' He turned to face Billy. 'Where I see him, eh?'

'I don't sodding well know! And I don't particularly care. Now get inside and open them windows! 'Cos I'm not coming in there 'til you do.'

'You have a very loose tongue you know . . . and a weak stomach, too. You curse in front of Aunty Irma and you sure in trouble, boy.'

'Go and get me a glass of water. I feel sick.'

Malcolm burst out laughing. 'You a baby – that for certain.'
He went inside the house, laughing. And while he was waiting
for a drink Billy strolled along to the car, the old Jaguar. He
had recognised the man too, but didn't know from where so
presumed that it had been in passing in this street. It wasn't
the first time that he and Malcolm had been here, after all. He
didn't give a toss one way or the other but he did like the car.
Admired it. This was what he wanted one day. A brand spanking
navy blue Jaguar saloon with chrome you could see your face
in. As he turned around to walk back to Malcolm he caught a
glimpse of the man staring at him through the filthy window
of the house. He nodded at him but all he got in return was a
defiant stare and a clear silent message: *Get away from my car.*

'Fair enough,' said Billy. 'Suit yerself.' He then swaggered
off and looked forward to tormenting the bastard another time.

'So . . . you t'ink you could live here?' Malcolm handed his
young mate a freshly opened bottle of beer and a glass. 'You
t'ink you could look after my home till I move in?'

'Yeah,' said, Billy. 'No problem.'

A joyous smile breaking out on his face, Malcolm gave Billy
a friendly punch on the shoulder. 'Man . . . you one *hell* of
friend.'

'I know I am. But listen. Keep away from the Jag. That bloke's
trouble. You don't need it.'

'How come you know it?'

Billy tapped the side of his nose. 'I just do. Call it the white
man's instinct. He'll be all right. Stay out of 'is shadow and
he'll leave you be. Don't even think about trying to be neighbourly. He won't wanna know.'

'Whatever you t'ink, my friend, eh? Whatever you t'ink. I go
along wit' it.'

'Good. I'll see you later on.'

'How you mean? You see me later on? You ain't gonna come
in *now*?'

'Nar. I'll wait till it smells of carbolic. Tell your aunty to
scrub the floors good and proper.' He looked at the outside of

the house again. 'And get them bloody windows cleaned.' With that, Billy turned away and sauntered off leaving Malcolm to gaze after him, bemused. Then, as he turned around to go back into his house, he almost bumped into an older woman pulling a shopping basket on wheels.

'Eh? What?' she yelped. 'I never said anyfing. I never said a word!'

'Sorry, love,' said Malcolm dropping his accent and smiling affectionately. 'Never saw you coming. You okay?'

'Yeah. Just. You wanna watch what you're doing. Who are you, anyway? And what you doin' going into Mrs McCarthy's?'

'This house?' he said.

'Yes. *This* house.'

'But she don't live here no more.'

'I know that.'

'I gonna be moving in,' he said gently teasing her with a wink. 'Once I got it all *spotless* I give it a little coat of paint . . . and I doubt you even recognise it. Eh?'

'Oh. It's yours now, is it? I might 'ave guessed. Another darkie moving in. How many of you are there?'

'Oh . . .' he said, rubbing his chin, thoughtfully, wishing to tease her. 'Just me and my aunty Urma and some cousins . . . and de pink boy, Billy, who jus' leave. We share the house. You know what I'm saying? When he here – I somewhere else. When I here – he at his mother's house. He a good white boy. There be a lot of us coming and going . . . but we give you *no* trouble.'

'You'd better not. I live at the end of the street. Tell your aunt, what ever 'er name is, to come and knock, so I can put 'er straight about a few fings. I don't want no loud jungle drum music. And no women if – you – know – what – I – mean? We're respectable in this street. And I know exactly 'ow many cats there are as well.'

'Cats?' said Malcolm, now acting the English gentleman, cupping his chin. 'I don't quite follow.'

'No . . . I'm sure. I know what *you* lot get up to. And I know the difference between the smell of *chicken* cooking and *cats*. You're as bad as the Chinese. Gawd knows 'ow many dogs 'ave gone missing since *they* moved round this way.'

Leaving Malcolm totally dumbstruck, the woman said no more but walked away muttering, her trolley bouncing on the uneven paving stones as she went. 'Well . . . I can't say this move is gonna be a dull one.' He went inside his house shaking his head and laughing.

And while Billy Smith made his way home wondering how best to break the news to his mother that he had definitely decided to stay in London, Jessie, worried about Emma's sleepwalking, was on her way to see her family doctor, whose surgery was practically next door to her local cinema, the Foresters. Stopping to look at the publicity poster showing the forthcoming film, *Some Like it Hot*, she made a mental note to suggest to Edie and Laura that they have a ladies' night out, with a couple of drinks in the Carpenter's Arms before going in to see this film. Glancing at the highly polished brass handles on the sparkling glass entrance doors into this bug hole with its old timber floor, which had been covered in lino and seen better days, Jessie couldn't help but smile. In its time this had been a beautiful old two-tiered music hall and then a smart small picture palace. Somewhere along the way, whoever had inherited it, or purchased it cheap, had lost interest. It was a flea pit now with creaking worn and torn seats and nicotine stained walls. But as with all antiques, it had gained character with age and continued to draw the locals who wandered in to see old black and white films from a past era as well as a dated Technicolor.

Ticket prices were reduced on two afternoons during the quiet week days to a few coppers for pensioners and complimentary tickets given to the regular down and outs providing they had had a wash and shave in the Seamen's hostel beforehand. An empty house was something that the manager, Mr Clark, could not cope with. He took great pride in this cinema and liked to keep up certain standards by wearing his slightly worn and faded black uniform with gold epaulets and matching hat. During miserable wintry days when the Foresters was only a third full he had felt as if he had let the side down. He also felt personally responsible for his staff and the appearance of the ladies who worked under him – the usherettes, especially the young women personally trained by himself to walk gracefully alongside the aisles of battered seats in their little off-white pert hats and matching wrap-over uniforms with navy trim.

These attractive ladies, chosen for their pretty faces, bore the image of film stars themselves when they stood either side of the big screen, in the spotlight. During the interval, when music chosen by the manager came softly through the loudspeakers, his ladies would seductively entice the men to buy the women choc ices from their trays. Spotlessly clean trays strapped across their breasts and around their lovely necks left their hands free. Tipping was not compulsory but the threepenny bits slipped into their pockets by gentleman admirers soon mounted up as did the love notes. Men of all ages and religions could be so easily mesmerised by the seductive smiles of Mr Clark's beautiful ice cream ladies.

'Would that you were seeking work here as an usherette,' said Mr Clark, breaking into Jessie's thoughts as he flicked nothing off the shoulder of his meticulously brushed jacket. 'I presume that I could not be so fortunate?'

'I'm not looking for work, no,' said Jessie. 'But my mother-in-law might be interested.' She was thinking of Emmie and the time she was going to have on her hands once her family had moved to Norfolk.

The man splayed his hands theatrically. The last thing he wanted in what he saw as *his* picture palace was someone's ageing mother-in-law. 'What a pity,' he said, willing to lie through his teeth for the sake of his palace. 'Only last week did I employ a new cleaning lady who is terribly good.'

'She wouldn't be up for a cleaning job,' Jessie chuckled. 'Be a pity if you lose whoever you've got, though. She's got the brass shining like gold.'

'And the oak doors waxed to a deep shine,' smiled he. 'Which is no less than any of our patrons would expect of their grand old Victorian *picture palace.*'

'I'm pleased you've got *West Side Story* coming,' said Jessie, backing away. 'I'll be in to see that with my chums.'

'And I shall keep an eye out for you,' he said, lifting his hat gracefully to her. And show you to the very best seats . . . in the *gallery.*'

'Sounds good,' said Jessie, moving on. 'I'll take you up on that.'

Softly laughing at the old die-hard ladies' man, Jessie pressed a shoulder against the heavy door which led into the waiting room of the doctor's surgery. Characters like the manager of the picture palace were a dream and just like dreams, they were disappearing overnight. Even in this part of the East End. She glanced around the surgery to see that apart from the few young children rummaging in a cardboard box filled with old toys and comics, there were only three women and an old man to go in before her. She sat on a wooden bench, folded her arms and fixed her eyes on the floor. She didn't want to get involved in the hushed conversation that was going on between the women. Women who spoke to each other from across the room, talking about the headline in the local newspapers, giving graphic details of a boy who, while playing with his mates, had fallen into the Cut in Old Ford and drowned. Of course, there were other things in the newspapers to talk about, but for some reason which Jessie had never been able to fathom, the waiting room in a doctor's surgery seemed as if it were a place where disease, fatal injuries or painful deaths were the main if not the only topics up for discussion.

Content to sit quietly and think about things in general, Jessie was surprised when someone was nudging her arm, telling her to go in. She shook her head as if she'd been asleep. It was a different set of patients around her. She had been aware of the quiet comings and goings but it seemed as if only a few minutes had passed. She was quickly off her chair and smiling at the doctor who was in the doorway, waiting.

Once inside his small surgery and on the cushioned tub chair she felt comfortable in her surroundings; the panelled walls and the wooden cupboards and small drawers with tiny brass knobs were by now very familiar to her. This room looked and felt every bit an old Victorian surgery without trying. She had been coming here since a small girl and it was almost homely. The doctor found her file in his tall slim polished mahogany cabinet and then sat down.

'What seems to be the trouble, Mrs Smith?' he said, pulling the buff coloured medical card from its envelope. He glanced at her to see a faint smile on her face. 'I know, I know. You still think I should call you Jessie. Protocol nowadays determines what we doctors may or may not do.' He looked at her over his bifocals and waited.

'I know you don't like this kind of thing, Doctor and normally I would never 'ave come, but I'm really worried. I'm not here for myself. I need to talk to you about my Emma.'

'Ah. You should have said so. Before I drew your card. Never mind. Never mind.' He shuffled in his seat and peered at her over the top of his bifocals.

'I won't take up much of your time. I know there're sick people out there waiting to come in. It's just that Emma's sleep-walking has got worse.'

The old gentleman leaned back in his chair and looked thoughtfully at her. 'How old is she now? Sixteen, seventeen?'

'Seventeen. And I know what you're thinking. She's no longer a minor. I just want your advice as to what I should do. That's all.'

'Why didn't you bring her with you?' he said, his eyes and tone showing the strain of his tiresome long hours.

'I didn't want to pass my worry onto Emma. I'm probably making more of it than I should.'

The doctor leaned back in his chair and rubbed his eyes. 'Give me an example. A recent one.'

'Tom woke up in the night to find the street door open. He knew it would be Emma so went out and followed 'er. And there she was, in her nightdress, in the middle of the night, walking through the council estate as casual as you like. As if she was on 'er way to work.'

'And when Mr Smith caught up with her?'

'He guided 'er back home. It's not the first time it's happened. But it's the first time either of us have actually *seen* Emma sleepwalking. I've found 'er here, there and everywhere. Last time, she was sitting on the low wall in the grounds. As if it was a perfectly natural thing to do.'

'And you think it's got worse lately . . . or you just hadn't noticed it?'

'Got worse.'

'And does she seem worried about anything? Is there a boyfriend on the scene for instance?'

'No. She's a bit of a loner, really.' Jessie looked up at the ceiling and tried to think of a best friend. But none came to mind. 'She's very family orientated. Her gran and granddad mean a lot to 'er. So do her cousins and her aunt and uncle. Tom's brother and sister-in-law. I s'pose her cousins 'ave always been her best friends.'

'I'll need to see her.' The friendly family doctor of years spoke caringly. 'Tell her you came to see me about yourself and happened to mention her sleepwalking. Then you must leave it to her.' He shrugged and raised an eyebrow. 'That's all we can do.'

'She won't come, Doctor. I can tell you that now.'

'Well then, what do you want me to say?'

'Does she need to see a specialist?'

'Possibly she does but first she must see her family doctor. I can't recommend anything unless I've seen and spoken with her. You should know that.'

'But you *know* her history. The stammering that started in the children's home. I think that the sleepwalking began when that stopped. More or less.'

'Since puberty?'

'I think so.'

'Well . . . there's nothing I *can* do . . . unless she comes in. I can't recommend her to see a specialist without seeing her myself first. I don't think you should pressure her. A suggestion perhaps, but no more than that.'

'Well, if you think so . . . I'll do my best. I'll tell 'er I'm a silly worried mother. She's sensitive. She might come just to stop me from worrying.' Jessie lifted herself from the chair. 'She is a touch on the worried side, mind. Now that we've told her that she was walking around out there in 'er nightdress.'

'I'm sure she is. Worried and frightened. Which is why you *should* try not to worry. She'll pick up on it. Be more relaxed. Make a joke of it. Give her a way out. Let her be the one to say she should come and see me.'

'I will. I promise. And I'm sorry to 'ave taken up your time. And thank you agen.'

Just as she was about to leave, the doctor told her to wait. He then reached out and pulled a slim hardback from his book shelf. 'You might find this helpful, Jessie. Return it to me once you've read it. I would be obliged if you didn't let anyone else see it . . . or know that I've loaned it to you.'

'Thanks. I'll look after it.' Jessie said goodbye to the old gentleman and left by the side door. She knew what the book was about and couldn't wait to get home to read it in private. She wanted to know everything about the disorder, understand it.

So, in the sitting room, curled in an armchair with only the soft ticking of the clock on the mantelshelf, Jessie began to read and before she realised an hour had passed and she was halfway through the book. She had already learned that when asleep and the mind relaxed, fears and emotions are free to roam out of their dark corners and that sleepwalking was far more common than people realised. This, in some way, had eased her worries. The innocent sleepwalker, according to the author, was often wrestling with inner turmoil which in the light of day amounted to very little. Teasing from school friends or cross words from a strict teacher might worry the child deep down and so haunt them at night. It described the way Tom had said that Emma carried herself, a blank expression in the eyes while seeming to be awake.

According to the professor who had written the book, when children hear parents quarrelling, fear permeates their dream-state and the worry over losing one or both parents engulfs them. It was becoming obvious to Jessie that Emma, when she was little, had shown signs of being a disturbed child. Often quiet and having difficulty in pronouncing her words. The stuttering had gone but had the sleepwalking simply taken over from her earlier failings?

After making herself a cup of tea, Jessie began to read again, and again the book all but described her daughter. That, while some children simply wandered harmlessly around the house, others may go outside to walk in the street and return to their beds without realising they have ever left them. Had Jessie read on she would have been relieved to learn that most sleepwalking stops in the late teens.

The sound of the doorbell was a welcoming side-track. Jessie slipped the book under a cushion and went to open the front door to find Laura standing there, smiling radiantly. In her hands were samples of pale blue and lavender flowery curtain material and wallpaper with tiny lavender flowers. Jessie managed to show interest once settled back in the living room with Laura and listened to how she had found washable wallpaper for the kitchen. Lemons, limes and bananas on a white background.

'Jack reckons it'll be like sitting in a fruit shop,' she said. 'But I'll get my way with it. I've let him have his way with the sitting room. I hope to God it'll look all right. Black and red wheeltracks on a light grey background. With one wall, where the fireplace is, red with tiny dashes of gold here and there.'

'Contemporay?' said Jessie, impressed. 'You'll start a trend in the flats if you're not careful.'

'So you think it'll look all right, then?'

'I think it will look lovely, Laura. Make a nice change. I'd love it but it won't exactly go in an old beamed cottage, will it?'

'The bedroom paper would. Little lavender flowers?'

'We'll see. So far it's white paint in between the beams everywhere. Once we've moved in . . . I'll work on Tom to put up some cottagy paper.'

'That's gotta be a must, Jess, surely?' Laura rested her head back and tried to visualise the thatched house in the country. 'I do envy you at times you know.'

'Do you?' said Jessie. 'I wouldn't. Everything seems to be up in the air.'

'Does it? Why do you say that? Not 'aving second thoughts, are you?'

'No. I can't cope with a first thought never mind a second one.'

'Oh?'

'That's right, Laura, *oh*?'

'What? What have I said?'

'Nothing,' Jessie sighed. 'Take no notice. I'm in a funny mood.'

'I can see that,' said Laura, looking her friend in the face. 'What's happened?'

'Nothing. And maybe that's it. Nothing happened and yet I know that something is going to happen.'

'Like what?'

'I don't know.'

'Tom's not been playing up, has he?' said Laura, treading carefully.

'No. Good as gold.'

'Billy not wanting to live in Norfolk getting to you?'

'No. I expected it.'

'Emma?'

'Yes. Emma. Emma and her sleepwalking.'

'Oh, Jess . . . you worry too much over your kids. She's a young lady now, don't forget.'

'I know, but it doesn't make the slightest bit of difference. She's still my baby and so is Billy.'

'Oh, right . . . you have got a problem. Or maybe I 'ave? I never let Kay get to me. She's a right little madam, now. Not yet fifteen but telling me what I should and shouldn't do. You should listen to her at times.' She smiled. 'I can't believe Jack. She gives him what for and he takes it all.'

'Think yourself lucky. Emma's still like a child . . . in a way. I can't imagine her with a boyfriend and yet she's seventeen.'

'Mmm . . . I know what you mean.'

'Do you?'

'Well . . . you know . . . just an observation, Jess. She's lovely, don't get me wrong, but . . . a late developer perhaps? She does seem to walk about at times as if she's living in a world of 'er own, day-dreaming probably. That's all. I'm not saying there's anything wrong with it.'

Jessie pinched her lips together and then closed her eyes tight, saying, 'Take no notice. It's that time of the month, that's all.'

'No, it's not. I know you better than this. What's the matter?'

'The sleepwalking's getting to me.'

'I would be worried about that kind of thing if I'm truthful. It is a bit spooky. Tom was telling me how he followed 'er downstairs and that.'

Staring down at the floor, Jessie quietly sighed and then said, 'Let's leave it be for now, eh?'

'Whatever, Jess. Whatever.'

After a few moments of silence, Jessie said, 'It frightens me. I can't help it.'

'Oh, come on. It's not that bad. We all 'ave nightmares. Mine's usually a lion stalking these flats trying to find a way in.' Laura shivered at the thought of it. 'I don't sleepwalk but I do wake up sweating from head to toe.'

'The lion prowling. You know what that means?' said Jessie, having read a short piece on this in the book. 'That the shadows of our ancestors are still living in our souls. Living in dark caves and rough huts people knew that death could be stalking and that at night they might have to kill or be killed.

'That could explain something that Max used to do,' continued Jessie, smiling. 'It scared the life out of me at first but then once I got used to it, it made me laugh. It was a comical sight. Him with his belly hanging over 'is pyjamas and jumping out of bed to fight a monster. He could never remember it the next day. Well, tiny bits of it. When it was over, the big fight, he'd climb back into bed . . . as if nothing had happened.'

'And he couldn't remember it the next day?'

'No. Well, tiny fragments.'

'Poor old Max, eh? Who would have thought we'd be sitting here talking about him like this, Jess? In the past tense.'

'I know. But there we are. None of us know what's around the corner, do we? Which is just as well. At least it was quick and he wouldn't 'ave known anything about it. A second, that's all it took, and bang. I s'pose that's one blessing about a car crash. For those that don't survive it.'

'Anyway . . . on a lighter subject . . . what d'yer reckon? Shall I go for the limes and lemons and sod what Jack thinks?'

Jessie smiled saying, 'Oh, no. No way am I gonna take any blame for *your* decisions. It's bad enough I know about Mister Romeo.'

The smile faded from Laura's face. 'You don't really mean that, Jess.'

'What, the fruit on the wall or the fruit in the hay?'

'You know very well what I'm talking about.'

'Oh, shut up. Silly cow. You know me and Edie love to hear about it. It's better than a romance serial in *Woman's Own*. Anyway, who am I to talk? I was only a few steps away from a love affair with Rupert in Norfolk, don't forget.'

'Forget it, Jess? I don't think so. It's tucked right up my sleeve. Upset me and I'll tell Tom all about it. Listen . . . I'd best be going,' said Laura, glancing at her watch. 'I promised Kay I'd pick up a first size bra for her. She's at that fourteen going on seventeen stage.'

'As we once were. Now we're middle aged and sensible. I'm not sure which is worse.'

'Old age and a pension book.'

'Many a true word . . .' said Laura. 'Where have all those years gone to, eh? When I think how me and Jack used to be at each other all the time when we was first married. And now . . . we don't even share the same bed.'

After a quiet moment, Jessie looked into her friend's hazel speckled green eyes and said, 'Honestly, Laura?'

'Yeah. Honestly. But don't say anything will you? It was Jack who started it. I moaned a bit once 'cos of his snoring but it was a joke more than anything else. I think he used it as an excuse. In fact, I know he did.'

'God . . . I had no idea.' She leaned forward and took Laura's hand and squeezed it. 'How long 'as this been going on then?'

'Ages. After our baby died, he couldn't, you know . . .'

'Well, that is understandable but . . . it was a long time ago.'

'Exactly. It *was* the cause at first. Neither of us could cope with the grief and the only way to get a night's sleep was to take a pill and go out like a light. We used to wake each other up with all the tossing and turning and crying. Then it just became a habit. We'd get together now and then but even that phased out. No-one knows, by the way. Not even 'is sister, Liz . . . and I'm just as close to 'er as Jack is. Well, I say she don't know, I think she must do, she's told me more than once that me and Jack 'ave gotta break the daft rift between us. It's not that easy though, is it?'

'I don't know and who am I to advise? The way me and Tom 'ave gone on over the years.'

'You're all right now, though?'

'Oh, yeah. Better than we were. We 'ave our ups and downs, though. Everyone must do.'

'So maybe there's hope for me and Jack? Is that what you're saying?'

'It has to come from both sides, Laura. You'd 'ave to be prepared to . . . you know?'

'Give up my only bit of romance in the hop fields? I know. Anyway, I think that's on the cards. I can't imagine there'll be many more years of hop picking. Most farms 'ave flattened the huts because we're no longer needed. Machines. Hop-grabbing machines are taking over. As a kid I remember there being talk of robots taking over the work of man, well . . . in a way it wasn't as daft as it sounded was it? What are machines if they're not robots?'

'Don't talk like that. You've slipped into a low, that's all. There's been no hint of it at the farm where you pick, has there?'

'No. Only gossip as to how other farms have gone down that road. Anyway . . . we can't change the future can we and to be honest with you – mine's not really looking all that rosy.'

'Oh?'

'Jack might not sleep in my bed any more but I can still smell him when we're in the front room watching telly. And it's been the same perfume for a very long time. The way I felt earlier on I didn't that much care. I just brought Richard to mind and the love we had for each other. But now . . . it hurts . . . and I don't really know why. Not really. I found a letter when I was going down 'is pockets. I should 'ave known Jack wouldn't 'ave been living all this time without sex on a regular basis. And he hasn't touched me in years. Liz must know and that's why she's turned a blind eye to what I've got up to when we've gone hop picking. That really hurts. I could end up with no family and let's face it, Richard's never troubled himself to come and see me on the quiet in London, has he?'

'I don't know, Laura.'

'Well, he hasn't. I'm not blaming him. He's got a family himself.'

'And you really think that Jack's serious with this other woman?'

'The writing couldn't be clearer. I wouldn't be surprised if he's not been waiting for Kay to grow up. The worst of it is that Liz and Bert must 'ave been going along with it all this time. I feel like an outsider in their family now. From the letter I gleaned that she's been for a drink with Tom *and* Bert. That guts me.'

'Oh, don't . . .' murmured Jessie. She leant back into the cushioned armchair and went quiet. Then, with tears welling behind her eyes she said, 'Laura . . . I can't believe that this could be happening to you and Jack. You're *so* right for each other. Okay . . . so you've enjoyed a little bit of romance on the side once in your life as well but only because you must 'ave been feeling left out in the cold.'

'A bit of both, I s'pose. I can't lay all the blame on his shoulders.'

'It doesn't matter who started it or why it happened. I just . . . I just can't imagine how you must be feeling. I've got to know you, Laura, we've all got to know each other. You, me and Edie. This must be ripping you apart.'

'It is, Jess. It is. But what I can I do? If I start being loving agen, Jack will know straight away that I've seen that letter in his pocket. It wasn't the first from what I read, so he's managed to keep them under wraps all this time. One little mistake and I was in there.'

'What made you go down his pockets?'

'I don't know. This and that. I just started to get suspicious. Little things, you know? Adding up.'

'And you don't think that Jack wanted you to find that letter? That he'd been deliberately dropping clues?'

'So I'd be ready for 'im leaving, you mean?'

'Well, that's possible but it's not what I meant. No. That's not what I meant. So you'd *stop* him. Some men are like that. What they can't do themselves they'll get someone else to do. Maybe he needs a *reason* to tell the woman it's over, that you've found out . . .'

'And he's decided to stay with me?'

'Possibly?'

'Well I can't be bothered with all of that. Sod 'im. Let 'im go. I won't be second best to anyone, Jessie.'

'Men are funny creatures and none of us will ever get to the bottom of 'em but at least once you know your man's kind of game-playing, you can run rings round them. I really don't think that men are all that bright. Honest to God, I don't. But don't quote me on that.'

'Jessie . . . you're assuming that Jack don't wanna leave me? What if it's the reverse? Your theory – in reverse?'

'I don't think it is. I honestly do not think that that man would want to leave you, when push comes to shove. Never mind his Kay who he adores. Whether you can see it or not, he loves you.'

'Well, I'm not so sure. Let's see where we are this time next year, eh? Or at Christmas even. I've got a feeling that me and Kay might be spending it with my dad in 'is little cottage in Delemar Place.'

'No, you won't. It'll be the same as last year; your dad will be round your dinner table. Mind you . . . I wouldn't say no to Christmas in your dad's house. Who would believe that behind that ancient brick wall and that paint peeling green door there would be a small corner of old Stepney village tucked away. I often peep in there to look at the cottages and front gardens.'

'I was never happier, Jess, then when I was a kid living there in Delemar Place. It was so private and – charity housing or not – it was, still is, a special place and it's not changed one bit. The lovely old paved pathway under creeper covered walls is full of cracks but it doesn't matter. And the row of little front gardens are lovely and old-fashioned. Lilacs, roses, hydrangeas, wallflowers, lupins . . . and delphiniums and all only a stone's throw from Whitechapel Road and all the hustle and bustle.'

'Charrington's did well by their workers all them years ago when they were built.'

'I know. And what I love about them is that they never seem to change hands. Practically all the same families are still there since I was little.' Breaking into a warm smile, Laura had a faraway look in her eyes. 'Jack used to hang around outside that gate waiting for me. But I played hard to get in them days. He was too popular for my liking. He was full of fun but 'ad a reputation for breaking a girl's heart. So I played hard to get and it worked.'

'It's a bit late in the day for him to break your heart, Laura. You're both a bit past all that now.'

'Are we though? Anyway . . . I'm not gonna worry over it any more but let things take their natural course. I've got hop picking and Richard to look forward to. There're worse things happening at sea.'

And so there was, but where Laura was concerned, serious trouble was much closer to home than she realised. Patsy, Jack's lover, had had it confirmed that she was pregnant with his child and she wanted him to leave Laura and file for a divorce. The note found in Jack's pocket had actually been planted there by the woman, hoping that her rival would find it. In a state of turmoil, no matter how hard Jack had tried to persuade Patsy to give up the idea of having his baby, she had flatly refused, because this is what she had been waiting for, what she had planned. It had happened on a Saturday evening after a few drinks together when she had been teasing him all evening with only one idea in mind – to trap him into marriage.

After a drink together in a small, quiet pub in Stepney Green, Jack had gone back to Patsy's rented rooms and after she had peeled his jacket off him, giggling as if she was too tipsy to think of anything but making love, she had taken his packet of three from his inside pocket and hidden it. She then slowly peeled off his clothes in her own special seductive way that not many men would find easy to resist. To Jack's way of thinking it had to be a million-to-one chance that she would get pregnant on the one occasion when he hadn't protected himself, but Patsy had been planning the occasion for a while and had done all she could think of to conceive, even taking her temperature in the mornings before getting out of her bed, so that she could gauge when she was ripe and ready. And her careful manipulations had worked. She had already thought of a name should it be a boy. Jac. To shorten it by losing the letter k was deliberate. A reminder that should he not leave his wife for her, he had left things unfinished.

This attractive young redhead had made other plans too. Once the baby was born she was going to give it enough time for Jack to bond with his child and then move back to her roots in Leicester, certain that he would miss both of them so badly that he would follow in their tracks and leave his wife. She saw Laura as a rival, someone whom her man had made the mistake of marrying. As for Kay, the sister of the child she was carrying, *she* would be a target should Jack turn his back on her. She would be told that she had a baby brother or sister that could take the place of Kay's sibling who had died when only a few months old. She had told Jack in no uncertain terms that she would not be bamboozled into anything she didn't want to do and would do as she felt fit – whatever that meant.

This young woman was no soft touch and it had been her fiery nature and her hard-as-nails attitude which had attracted Jack in the first place. He sensed immediately that she had no time for weak men who had obviously annoyed her in the past and he had been right. Men that she had given herself to that slunk off in the night as soon as marriage was mentioned; men who had wanted her for their pleasure but not as their wife but now Laura's rival was determined to have her man. *The best lessons are learned through failures* was a bit of advice from her mother some years before and had lodged in the deepest crevice of the woman's mind. Now it had resurfaced and she was determined not to let Jack slip through her fingers. Whatever the cost. Laura was going to have to be very strong to be any kind of a match for this woman.

6

The ghastly ordeal of Gloria having her son bully her over the key to the safety box had left its mark. She had shrunk back into her safe corner of the world and had not been outside onto her back or front balcony since that day but had simply sat quietly in her living room with the wireless turned down low. She was afraid that if the key her son had taken away did not fit the box he would be back even more cross with her for sending him on a fool's errand. There had only been one knock on the door since that day, when the man from the London Electricity Board had come to empty the shillings from her slot meter. At first she had waited silently in the passage hoping he would go away but then when he banged on the knocker determined to get an answer she had crept forward and seen his shape through the two panes of frosted window in the front door and let him in.

Now with it being a sunny June Saturday she felt that Naomi would call for a cup of tea and a chat the way she did every fortnight which was marked on her calendar. Gloria was looking forward to seeing her. Naomi always called through the kitchen window as she passed by and before ringing the doorbell. So, perched on the edge of a kitchen chair next to her small yellow Formica topped table Gloria sipped a glass of sherbet water and thought about her late husband and what he would have done if he had seen the way their son had treated her. Even though he had been bad himself she didn't think he would have agreed with the rough treatment.

Just like their son James, her husband had been a handsome man but she hadn't truly got to know him properly when she had accepted a marriage proposal from him. In those early days she had been a very good cook and housewife. Washing and ironing had been like a hobby to her and she always kept the home ship-shape and because of this she hadn't missed his company when he was out all hours. Often he never came home at night at all, telling her that he had been on business.

James Drake senior had appeared every bit the refined gentleman and had given her a regular amount each week for housekeeping, and on the surface he looked as if butter would not melt in his mouth but he was a liar and a blackmailer. With his good looks, his charm and fine set of clothes, he had made it his business to have affairs with wealthy women who he had charmed into the bedrooms of exclusive hotels. Once he had built up a good relationship with them and had enough evidence of the affair tucked under his belt, photographs from his up to the minute box Brownie camera included, he had threatened to expose them publicly if they did not lend him large sums of money. Money which of course they realised they would never get back.

Each of his victims, all of them married women, had been terrified that their husbands would find out about their sordid affairs in the gossip column of a national newspaper if they did not pay up.

During the several years of things working out very nicely for him, Gloria's husband's hoard had risen to a few thousand pounds. Once one of his victims had paid up in order to save her reputation and marriage, another was soon found to take her place. There had been, it seemed, a rich seam of wealthy, bored, disregarded married women, waiting and longing for their dream of a Romeo to come along. But Gloria's husband had let his success with women build his confidence and arrogance too high and believed that he could do whatever he wanted where all women were concerned – young or old. This self-assurance, which had taken him to great heights, had been the trait which had brought him crashing down and seen him in a high court sentenced to death.

Remembering the newspaper report of how, while in a telephone box by Hampstead station threatening a lady of means, he had been arrested, Gloria shuddered. The woman had in fact been one of his victims. She had alerted the police beforehand, knowing which call-box he used, and consequently he had been caught red-handed. However, before the detective sergeant had had a chance to put on the handcuffs, Gloria's husband had shot him through the heart, slipped the pistol down a drain and escaped into the nearby Underground station to mingle, with calm and decorum, amongst other passengers. When his journey home on the Underground was at an end and he was strolling out of Aldgate station, smoking his pipe as if he had not a care in the world, two plain clothes detectives had stepped out in front of him and made their arrest.

Imprisoned for murder he had been tried at the Criminal Courts where he had put on a good show of the innocent gentleman, quiet, shy and reserved. But the automatic pistol had been found, with his finger prints all over it. Six months after the trial and appeal he had been hanged at Wandsworth Prison at 9 a.m. on a foggy November day. At the time, when he was taken from his cell, his hands strapped behind his back and led to the gallows, Gloria had been at home with her son James, then a small boy, breaking her heart over the man she believed she had known. Someone who had been leading a double life.

The image of her husband after execution, hanging from a noose, still haunted her dreams and sometimes woke her in the small hours of the night, shaking from head to toe. What she didn't know or could not even bear to imagine was the macabre scene which led up to his death. The white cotton hood with eyelets over his head, a noose around his neck and his hands and feet strapped as he waited for the clanking sound of the trapdoor to open beneath him and then the thud as he fell, hanging from a rope, into the cell below. Gloria had been told that everything had been done to make her husband's execution as speedy and humane as possible.

Knowing that there was likely to be a crowd outside the prison on the morning of his hanging she had stayed at home in Shoreditch, with her door locked and the lights off, trembling.

And here she was again, in the shaded kitchen of her new flat, shaking like a leaf as she waited for Naomi and at the same time dreading that her son would arrive to ring on the door-bell in one of his black moods. Since a very young child of three years, when she had been found huddled in a corner in Spitalfield Market with scrawled words on a piece of brown paper pinned to the rags she wore, Gloria had, without real-ising, closed off her emotions. Her only memory of childhood was going from one children's home to another until she had been left to fend for herself at the age of fourteen, in and around the East End of London. The scrap of paper which had been pinned to her at the age of three, had a message which was short and to the point. *Lost Child.*

And now, as she sat alone, hoping that her friend would call, Gloria looked and felt as lost now as she did then.

Standing in the front room of the corner shop in Jamaica Street, Billy Smith felt a tinge of envy as the sun streamed in through the filthy stained-glass windows and cast the room in warm light. The room, which was dirty and showed evidence of mice infestation in the old patterned tiled hearth, was covered not only with black droppings but a thick layer of grime. Above the ornate fireplace hung an old cracked mirror with thick cobwebs stretching from the top of it to the ceiling – a beautiful network of fine silvery thread. Looking into the mirror at his reflection Billy smiled as he imagined himself lodging here once the place was spick and span, with two coats of paint on the woodwork and walls. White paint. Brilliant white paint everywhere is what he could see . . . and red carpet . . . to blend in with the Victorian tiles either side of the black iron fireplace. He winked at his reflection, saying, 'One day in the not so distant future you'll get a mortgage for a place *just* like this one.'

This was what he had secretly aspired to once he had left school and earned a wage, thanks to his gran, Tom's mum, who had always advised him to save up for a deposit and buy a place of his own. She had sown the seed of his ambition of having somewhere to invite friends for a game of cards, or spend enjoyable evenings in the winter by a cosy fire with a girlfriend, or sun himself in the back yard on a hot July day such as this. His gran, unlike most women of her age and background had always been, and still was, forward thinking and ahead of her time.

But, even though Billy was earning a respectable wage now, he had no savings. His money so far had been spent on clothes that were 'the business' and socialising with 'the boys' who were part of the in-crowd. Now he was eager to take a leaf out of Errol's book and learn from all that his wise grandparents, dad and uncles had done in the mid thirties – own a square of land on which would stand his own bricks and mortar. It had not crossed his mind to put five or ten shillings away each week and now he was beginning to regret it. Errol and his cousin and uncle had the right approach to life. Live for today but save for tomorrow. A sudden high-pitched racket coming from a gang of lads in the street playing cricket, as they swore at each other and argued the rules of the game, brought Billy back into the land of the living. He was reminded of when he was young and played football in the grounds of Barcroft Estate, or tin-can-copper; Jimmy-Knacker and his most favourite of all, go-cart racing, with orange boxes on old pram wheels as a vehicle. Most of the games, just like the one taking place outside, would end in a fight. It was part and parcel of life on the streets.

Amidst the swearing and yelling he heard a twelve-year-old effing and blinding at Errol and his cousin, Malcolm, who he had left outside examining the exterior of their property with all its warts and bumps. He didn't want to begrudge his friends this day but he couldn't help the jealousy that was seeping in. Today, the cousins had the keys, not only to this property, but the one next door. The one which had been purchased solely in Errol's name, with the help of a loan from his uncle Joe. Both lads were older than himself by a few years and at least this consoled his envy. He was twenty and by the time he had reached his twenty-third birthday, he resolved that he too would have a foot on the property ladder.

For now though, he would have to be content to be a free lodger and act as night watchman while the place was being fixed up. It would be a while before Malcolm could call this rat-infested abode home and before Errol could use the room above as his workshop, where he would cut and machine made-to-measure suits for the smart fashionable East End lads – young men whose sole purpose in life was to have an image and impress the girls and their mates and just as important, their own close family. With the cousins outside Billy was ready to start clearing the place of all the old rubbish, because now he could hardly wait to move in and to have his independence. He walked through the house to the back and into the kitchen which, although covered in dirt and smelling of damp and mould, was something he could see brought back to life. Hot water and sugar soap, which his gran had been going on about for years was the best and cheapest way to clean away grease and dirt. No-one had lived in the property for months and yet the electricity and gas had not been cut off and from a quick inspection of the old cooker he could tell that once he had pulled in his gran and his mother along with Malcolm's relatives, it would be fit for use.

He turned on the hot water tap over the butler sink and after a few rumbling sounds the gas lit and soon the water pouring onto his hand was warming. The gas-fired hot water cylinder was antiquated but in working order and the boys couldn't ask for more than that. He turned off the tap and wiped the kitchen window with the back of his hand and peered out, surprised to see an old brick-walled garden rather than a back yard which he had expected. Overgrown rose bushes of varying species and colour were growing all over the place in between crazy paving and climbing up the fence either side of the property. Here, even in this corner of Stepney, June was bursting out all over.

Forcing back the iron bolt on the back door he put his shoulder against it and pushed it open. The scent from the roses and fresh air was mixed with the smell of old kitchen rubbish left in a tin dustbin and cooking in the heat. The time-worn brick shed at the back reminded him of his granddad and Emma, his sister. He remembered the time when she had been brought back from the children's home in Essex and how she loved to go in to the shed and pretend that it was her play-house. As he glanced up at the blue sky and to the south towards Commercial Road, Billy could just see the first of the planned 17-storey tower blocks of maisonettes and flats, brand new and thrusting upwards into the sky. Doubts that he had been harbouring as to whether or not he should stay put or move to Norfolk with his family diminished altogether. This was where he wanted to be. In Stepney, where it was all happening. He knew that he would miss his parents, Jessie and Tom and his sister, Emma, but felt sure that they would all benefit from living in the peaceful Norfolk village that would be safer where his sister was concerned. He was aware of Emma's recent sleepwalking and the thought of her roaming around in the dead of the night in the East End worried him.

Errol arrived in the garden with a look of worry on his face but soon relaxed when he caught the scent of roses growing in this garden. Breaking into a smile he said, 'Man . . . I got no pressure from afar it right out there in front of the house.'

'Take no notice,' said Malcolm joining them. 'He a bit on the low because he realise he no longer a street boy. He a grown man now. Eh.' Chuckling he landed a hand on his cousin's shoulder and squeezed it. 'Self-belief . . . you can lose it if you let it get to you.'

Before Errol could answer, the shrill voice of a thirteen-year-old echoed in the street. 'Fucking niggers! Get back to where you come from!' This was followed by a slow chant by one boy with the rest joining in: 'Eenie – Meenie – Minie – Mo . . . Catch – a – nigger – by – 'is toe. If – he – hollers – let – 'im – go. Eenie – Meenie – Minie – Mo.' This rendition was repeated as the word nigger was vocalised. The sound of a brick crashing through the window jolted all three of them.

'Little *bastards*!' said Billy, as he spun round to make his way back inside the house and out to the front. Errol barred his way by placing an arm across the open back doorway. 'For one split second I thought you were going to go out there and ask for a brick in the face.'

'Out of the way, Errol.'

'Eh eh,' said Errol, shaking his head slowly. 'Confidence is a dangerous thing my friend. You can lose your handsome looks if you not careful.'

'Do me a favour. I'm not interested in your fucking philosophy. Move out of the way. I'm a good runner. I'll catch one of the little bastards and drag 'im by the ear all the way 'ome to his father. Who will pay for that window. Now get out of my way.'

'You can't see what I'm saying?'

'I don't give a fig what you're saying. They're not getting away with this.'

Clicking his teeth Malcolm placed an arm around Billy's shoulder. 'You know I saw that nagging woman again. The one wit' wheels fixed to her shopping bag. She make me laugh so . . . and that no bad t'ing.'

'Shut up Malcolm – and talk properly.'

'She one *very* funny neighbour. You know what she call me? The Monkey's *Grandfather*.' He started to chuckle. 'I can't believe I look so old, eh?'

'Old women being colour prejudiced is a lot different from racist lads. We're gonna have to board up the window – you realise that, don't you?'

'And you know somet'ing?' said Errol, staying on track. 'That neighbour cut me more than a broken pane of glass ever could. What I supposed to do? Eh? Hit the woman for insulting me?' He paused for a moment as he looked his friend in the eye. 'There are certain limits I will go to. But old ladies and children? I don't t'ink so. You see what I'm saying?'

Billy relaxed his shoulders, sighed heavily and then went into the front room with his friends following in his tracks. He stood looking at the broken pane of glass and felt ashamed that something like this had happened before Errol and Malcolm had even moved in. 'I could kill the little bastards for this,' he murmured.

'Then it time you learned to turn the other cheek, my friend.'

Billy turned around to glance at the cousins standing behind him, brave and proud. 'Fair enough. I'll wander around and calm down while I'm doing it. But I can't just leave it be or they *will* be back. Trust me. The little bastards get a whiff of a weak link and they're in like sharks. I'll find one of their fathers once I'm calm and cool. Unless I'm mistaken they'll get a right-hander for it. This might be seen as a rough area but the kids do respect their parents, trust me. Some might look and sound tough but they wouldn't want this. Not this. You shouldn't have to put up with this kind of thing from kids round this way. You're hardly the first coloured men to be buying your own place. Immigrants 'ave been doing it, or saving to do it, for decades.'

'And you know why? Because we don't have any other choice. From what I see around me there are not enough new or old council homes to go round. We *have* to secure a roof above our heads. Landlords take it for granted that they can keep on putting up our rent. But . . . hey . . . it was our choice to come to this country. To come to England. And we will be just fine in our own quiet way, and turn our back when trouble come. If it come.'

'Well,' said Billy, 'each to their own.' He looked from one to the other. 'I feel ashamed. Can't help it. Kids shouldn't intimidate their elders. I was taught that and *that* lot who've scarpered, will 'ave been told the same by *their* parents. They know they're in the wrong. Why else did they bolt?'

'That makes sense,' said Errol. 'So what do you suggest we do, my friend?'

'Take the rest of the broken glass out of the pane and board it up 'til I can get hold of a glazier to come and put another pane in. And . . . from now on those shutters will be closed.'

'Ah . . .' Errol smiled broadly. 'I never notice those.' He turned to Malcolm. 'You want character and charm? It right here under your nose.'

'Yeah,' said Malcolm, smiling with his eyes as he eased the old paint-bound concertina doors apart. 'Oh God . . . this mean more to me than you can imagine. I dream of this you

know. I had a dream. I'm telling you. I saw *these* very shutters
... in a dream. It remind me of home.'

'Right, so you're happy. Good. Now then ... we need one
of them cardboard boxes from upstairs and one of you had
better put on them protective gloves. Be careful.' With that
Billy hitched his shoulders back and strolled out of the room,
calling out as he went. 'Don't cut yerselves!'

Walking along the turning which was now quiet with the only
evidence of the lads being three thick old coal bags folded to
form a goal post. The boys had planned to play football after
cricket but as often happens one or two of them had spoiled it
for the rest. Billy knew that if he were to spot one of the boys
and grab him by the scruff of his neck he would give the name
of the culprit who threw the brick to save his own skin. In fear
of Billy going to his father who would no doubt give the boy
a clip round the ear. No-one in this area wanted to have to
cough up for a new window and very few men wanted trouble
on their doorstep. All that Billy wanted was to put an end to
the kids taunting and trouble making. There was nothing unusual
about his bravado; this was common practice. His own dad,
Tom, had dragged him to a neighbour's door once or twice to
apologise for something or the other. Never a brick through a
window, though. But if he were asked, with his hand on his
heart, Billy would not be able to deny that he himself had called
a Jew a Yid, using exactly the same swear word before it as the
boy had done when calling after Errol and Malcolm.

Passing a couple of lads of about six years old who were playing
marbles, Billy gave them a friendly wink and carried on walking.
It was possible that the boys had seen and heard what had
happened but they were too young to be drawn into trouble.
Arriving at the house where he had seen the spiv who owned
the Jaguar, Billy slowed his pace and then stopped by the car
and pulled his comb from the inside pocket of his jacket. He
used the window as a mirror, hoping the man would be in the
front room again and see him. It didn't take much to put Billy
in this mild tormenting mood but neither would the owner of

the Jaguar rise that easily to his baiting. He was nobody's fool. With no light on inside his room the man had a better view of Billy than Billy could have of him and he watched as Billy ran the flat of his hand along the sleek bonnet of the car. Hoping that the owner would come out, for curiosity if nothing else, Billy was patient. Since the last sighting when he had looked at him as if he was worse than the filth in a gutter he had wanted a confrontation, to see what the man was about. Not a fight and no loud swearing or threats but to simply come face to face with him more out of curiosity than anything else. This individual, as far as he could judge from his behaviour, was not from this neck of the woods. He wanted to know what he was doing here, hiding away in Jamaica Street. But he was not going to be satisfied today for the street door remained closed and the house silent.

'Fair enough.' Billy smiled as he swaggered off satisfied that the spiv was too cowardly to be any trouble if he was that frightened to come outside and make his feelings known. He had seen the man briefly on three occasions now and each time he had acted as if he was hiding not only from the lawful but the lawless too. He was intrigued to say the least. Not concerned or too curious, just a touch interested as to why someone, who was soon to become his neighbour, was keeping a low profile while having the sort of car that was bound to attract attention. In this corner of the world man nor boy would be able to help themselves from touching the shiny dark blue bonnet of a Jaguar saloon.

In the normal run of things Billy wouldn't give this man a second thought but the Jag was the attraction, with that chrome you could see your face in. He recalled the expression on the spiv's face when he had first seen him, peering out of his window when Billy was harmlessly admiring his car. The look had said it all. '*Get away from my car*,' said Billy in a deep, formidable voice before laughing out loud. Then arriving at the end of the turning he glanced left and right along Charles Street. With no sign of the lads he realised that to be so frightened as to clear off the streets altogether, the boys knew that they had overstepped the mark. And with Arbour Square police

station and police flats so close by he imagined them running
for their lives into the turning opposite, Patterson Street, to
make the getaway and not be seen legging it by officers coming
in or out of the station. He quietly laughed as he visualised
the scruffy lot with their arses out of their trousers running as
if the devil was after them.

Turning on his heels to go back and report to Errol and
Malcolm, he stopped in his tracks, as the dark blue Jaguar
drove slowly along the road towards him. Stepping onto the
pavement, Billy pushed his hands deep into his trouser pockets
and watched as the car glided past, stopped at the cross-road
and then continued straight on into Stracey Street, with not a
flicker of expression on the man's face. He had behaved as if
Billy was invisible. 'Well, they say it takes all sorts,' he mumbled
to himself as he made his way back to his friends. Back to the
place where he would soon be lodging. 'White walls everywhere,' he said visualising his pad again. 'Brilliant white walls
and paintwork with plain red carpet and a couple of black
sofas. A bit of chrome 'ere and there.'

'I saw who done it, mister,' the small voice of one of the
little boys playing marbles broke into his thoughts.

'Done what?' said Billy, amused by the skinny couple of kids
with crew cuts and a couple of front milk teeth missing.

'Frew the brick fru the winda.'

Billy tapped the side of his nose, saying 'Right, well, keep it
to yerselves for now but keep an eye out as well.' Encouraging
the boy to become a grass was not the East End way of doing
things. He pushed a hand into his trouser pocket and pulled out
a handful of change. 'Here. A tanner each. For being good boys
and not throwing bricks at windows.' He had almost said the
word *sweets*. A tanner each for *sweets*. His life would be in more
danger than a spiv threatening quietly to run him down if the
lads had gone home to report that a stranger had given them
money for sweets. Continuing on his way his mind filled with
a dark time when a ten-year-old boy who had been seen getting
into a 'posh car' had gone missing, never to be found alive again

but floating in the local Victoria Park lake. Pulling himself out of that mood he went into the house, took off his jacket and got stuck in with the boys to make a start on clearing this house.

A few hours later, tired and grubby, he was ready to go home for a soak in the bath and a ten-minute sleep before sprucing himself for his Saturday night out. He had helped Errol and Malcolm to clear their property of bug-ridden beds, a settee and an armchair, as well as boxes full of old newspapers and rags which were now burning in the back garden. Leaving the boys to lock up Billy made his way through the back streets where it was quiet and where he could think about the lovely seventeen-year-old girl, Anna, whom he had met a few weeks ago at a party. He had seen her before, across a crowded bar at the popular pub Kate Odders, but hadn't been able to pluck up the courage to go over and talk to her even though she had returned his attention with a demure smile. Having flirted with love many times, Billy was keeping this latest romance close to his chest because he felt sure that this time he really had met the girl of his dreams. She was intelligent with a lovely personality and yet shy with him. Her eyes were blue and her hair natural soft wavy blonde. An English Rose by any standards. Now all he could think of was the date he had with her this evening when they were to meet outside the Troxy cinema which was known to be *the* cinema if a lad wanted to impress a girl. Others in the area such as the Ben Hur in White Horse Road, the Mayfair in Brick Lane and the Ranch House which had a corrugated iron roof, were known locally as bug holes or flea pits. The Troxy however with its thick, deep pile carpets, imposing entrance foyer and central staircase of marble could make any young man feel like a prince when he had a girl on his arm. The upper lounge was fitted out with deep plush armchairs and settees with plush red seats in the stalls and upper circle and apart from the luxurious feel of the place it was also known for its majestic Wurlitzer organ and stage shows.

He had taken Anna the previous week to the Lotus Dance Club in Forest Gate where, amongst hundreds of young people, she had stood out and he had had to shield her from his mates who continually asked her to dance, hoping to steal her from under his feet. Even though he had given in and let one or two jive to a Bill Haley or Chuck Berry record, Billy was the one who had danced cheek to cheek with her at the end of the evening when the slow and romantic records were played. It was during one particular song when the darkened hall was illuminated only by a round revolving mirrored light that he had felt his heart beat as it had never beat before. And when he had looked into his angel's face as they danced up close to Tony Bennett's 'Stranger in Paradise' he saw the look of love in her eyes, too. Since then he had not been able to get this girl out of his mind.

Strolling back home, oblivious to anything going on around him he had arrived at the busy Whitechapel Road before he knew it. His mind was filled with his new girlfriend; the things she said, the way she smiled; the way she blushed. He couldn't wait to see her and let her know that he had fallen in love. When he arrived at the top of Cotton Street, the turning in which Edie and Maggie had once lived he had to weave his way through a crowd of people and so stopped to see what the fuss was about. There was a distinct smell of burning in the air. Picking up on the various conversations from the groups mingling on the pavement he realised that one of the houses had a chimney fire. A woman wearing a patterned scarf over her hair rollers, her arms folded, was only too ready to tell him all about it. She was one of those people who loved a drama, revelled in it. 'We don't know yet if anyone *is* in there,' she said gravely. 'I doubt they'd know much about it by now in any case. Once that kind of smoke gets into your lungs you've had it. Thank God the smoke kills you before the flames. I wouldn't like to be burned alive.'

Moving closer to the end of the turning, where the air was filled with the sharp smell of sulphur as well as burning wood and crumbling bricks, Billy could see the dark cloak of smoke whisking around the rooftops. Beneath the sound of ringing bells of a fire engine close by he heard someone say, 'I think the old man is still in there. Silly old fools. Should 'ave moved out when the rest of 'em did.'

'Whose house is it, love?' said Billy, his heart sinking. He had come to see both Ben and Joey as part of Maggie's family. Two caring great uncles. Old East Enders.

'Ben the Jew,' said a man standing next to the woman. 'And old Nao. So I heard, anyway. They're both in there. Can't see why they don't just come out. Unless the smoke's got to 'em and they've already copped it.'

Wasting no time Billy forged his way through the growing crowd making his way to Ben's house to realise that the chimney stack was well and truly alight and by the look of things could come crashing down any minute. From somewhere behind him he heard someone say, 'If they don't come out soon there'll be a white cross of roses on that spot next week.'

With urgency and panic Billy lifted his right leg and gave the door one almighty kick, causing it to fly open. Sitting in his armchair in the small front room was Ben, his hands trembling as he clasped one of his many framed photos to his chest. A picture of himself when five years old holding his beloved Yiddisher mama's hand. Standing over him was Naomi, her face and neck red, her eyes glaring with mixed expression of fear, anger and determination as the sound of cracking bricks and crumbling mortar could be heard.

'What the fuck do you two think you're up to? Out! Now! The pair of you! Move!'

'It's only the chimney on fire,' said Ben, lifting his pale drawn face and frightened eyes to Billy. 'I've told her to go but she won't. I'm not budging. It's either what I said it was and it will die down – as it has done before – or the house will go with all my possessions in it. And with my possessions go I.'

'Over my dead body,' said Billy to the loud sound of bricks above him splitting under the heat of the fire.

'What else is there for me?' said Ben, tired. 'This house is all I've got. And my family are still here. I'm not leaving them. Naomi can do what she wants. Leave or stay. I don't care.'

Pointing a shaky finger at him as more dust and soot filled the room, Naomi's voice was strained. 'If you do not leave this house with me *now* it will be *suicide*. And I will not shed one single tear at your funeral or your grave once it's over!'

'I'm going nowhere,' said the old man, wiping a tear from his cheek. 'I'm staying where my memories are, thank you. I've been through two world wars. Did I tell you that, son? Two world wars.'

Billy stepped forward and picked Ben up as if he were a bag of laundry and threw him over his shoulder, telling Naomi to move herself. She too was in a state of shock and simply stood looking around and blocking his way. 'Get outside Naomi. *Now!*' screamed Billy.

Naomi answered in a trembling voice as she backed towards the street door. 'Please do be understanding, Benjamin. I don't want to leave you but I must think of Edith.'

'Go away, Naomi,' murmured Ben, struggling free and almost bringing Billy to the ground. 'I'll see you up there.' He raised his eyes to heaven. 'Knock three times.'

Pushing Naomi outside the front door to avoid a chunk of ceiling striking her, Billy turned back to Ben, to an awesome rumbling sound from above followed by the sound of crashing as the chimney stack finally gave way. Swooping Ben up for the second time Billy charged forward holding his breath until he was outside in the fresh air.

Ben was quietly crying, begging him to get his family. 'Don't leave them in there, Billy. Don't let them burn to death.'

Pushing the old boy into the arms of the stoutest looking man there to do whatever he could to help, he said, 'Get him to the end of the turning and lay him on the pavement!' He then took a deep break and went back into the smoke-filled house, spread his arms wide and with one clean swoop gathered the framed photographs from the sideboard, clutching them to his chest as he made for the outside again.

By now the fire engine had arrived and there was the sound of alarm bells ringing to indicate that a police car and ambulance was also close by. Within minutes the street was cleared of people when another rumbling, terrifying, crashing noise signalled the roof collapsing and the old bricks and mortar of the house tumbled noisily under the weight, causing a thick black cloud to umbrella Ben's old house and those on either side of it. The one thing that Ben could reap from this tragedy was that he had stood firm against authority when they had wanted to bulldoze this old row of houses. At least his pride was intact and he would be able to brag about it to his dying day. He had stayed put until God had deemed fit to move him out. God and fate.

In a wheelchair, a red blanket wrapped around him, Ben could only watch as his home, which he had lived in, man and boy, came crashing to the ground taking all of his parents and his own belongings with it. Holding his bony shaking hand was his closest friend and the woman he had come to love. Naomi. 'Think of it as a new beginning, my darling,' she whispered, herself in deep shock. 'You couldn't give it up . . . so *it* had to give you up. We must all move on, my precious. And we move on together.' Ben could do no more than gaze up at her, his face grey, his eyes showing his emotional pain. But when Billy pushed his way through and stood there grasping the old boy's precious collection to his chest, his lips trembled and then he smiled.

'My family?' he just managed to say.

'Your family. Every blooming last one of 'em. Every picture on that sideboard is here – in my arms – safe and sound.'

'Thank God for that. Thank God.' He then glanced up at the ambulance men who were waiting to lift him into the back of their vehicle. 'You'd best put my girlfriend in there as well. She's in a worse state than I am.'

Naomi knew exactly what Ben was doing. Or trying to do. Distract the attention from himself, which to her way of thinking was a step forward. The stubborn old codger knew that he had been wrong in not getting out of the house of his own accord before it came smashing to the ground. Of course he was pleased that Naomi was there to comfort him but he was also embarrassed and irritated by all the nosy bastards who had come out to see if death had taken another old timer. 'Load of bloody fuss over nothing,' he said as they lifted him in the wheelchair into the ambulance. 'I wouldn't mind a cup of tea. You would think that one of this lot would have got me a cup of tea.'

Naomi climbed the few steps into the ambulance and then turned to those watching. She had eyes only for Billy. 'Darling . . . would you let Edie know that I'm all right. Someone is *bound* to be scooting round to her now – to break the news. And I dare say it will be told in such a way as to make the best impact—'

'Shut up Nao and keep Ben company. I'm on my way 'ome now. And I'll keep this lot safe 'til he's out of hospital. Every last picture.'

'Excuse me, sir! said the driver. 'It's time to go!' He pushed the back doors shut on Naomi's strained face which bore a feeble smile. Billy turned away and kept his eyes in front of him and turned a deaf ear to those who wanted to know all the ins and outs. He simply ignored them and strode through the clusters of groups with one purpose in mind, to get word to Edie that her aunt Naomi and Ben were fine. With a hand cupped to his mouth as he coughed up dust, Billy felt tears welling in his eyes and forced them back. He didn't want to think of what might have been if he hadn't come along when he did. There was a tight pain in his chest, not from the smoke and grime but from a strong determination not to cry. Not to let go.

As he walked through the arches where sparrows and pigeons liked to nest, a dropping from one of the fine feathered friends splashed onto the shoulder of his Italian suit. It made him smile for this, he had always been told, was a sign of good luck. His suit was covered in dirt in any case and he knew that once dried the present from above would brush off and not leave a stain.

The fact that his smart, modern Italian suit was in a state mattered not one iota. While it was important in his part of the world to be seen by his peers all spruced up to the nines and immaculate, in the bigger picture bird shit on his shoulder faded into pale significance. He had just been part of something which had had more of an effect on him than he would ever let on.

Had he not been in the right place at the right time, two people, who meant a great deal to his close circle of family friends, would be dead and theirs would have been a horrible demise. He pushed it from his mind because he could think of nothing worse than being buried alive or burnt to death.

Walking trance-like into the grounds of Scott House to the sound of girls chanting a rhyme and skipping, watched by mothers and neighbours from their balconies as they soaked up the sun and gossiped, Billy knew that he was going to have to put on a brave face. Especially when he broke the news to Edie that her much-loved aunt Naomi had just escaped death and was now in the London Hospital with her closest friend and old sweetheart, Ben. Taking the stairs two at a time he passed two women reporting any comings and goings in the block of flats. Today though, Sarah James was not even aware of the drama she had missed and would love to spread.

As he pushed his finger on Edie's doorbell Billy heard the distant sound of laughter coming from inside and recognised it. It was his mother, Jessie. He was pleased she was there; she would be good for Edie once he had reported what had happened. With all that had happened to her in the past he knew that anything, anything at all, that put her aunt Naomi's life in danger, would strike through the heart of her. The door opened and Edie, as ever, gave her best friend's son a lovely smile. 'Talk of the devil,' she said. 'We've been going through old times and comparing things with the new.' She stood back, her expression changing as she studied him. 'Whatever's happened, Billy? Your suit's in a right state.'

He nodded and offered a compassionate smile. Then, taking her arm, he took a deep breath before quietly saying, 'I've got some bad news, Edie. Well, better than what it could 'ave been but . . .'

'To do with?'

'Ben . . . and Nao. They're okay. Your aunt's fine.'

'There's been an accident,' said Edie, going icy cold. 'Is that what you're saying?'

'Something like that,' he said.

'Why 'ave you got all of Ben's photos, Billy?' Edie's face was taut and the blood was draining from her face. 'What's happened to Ben?'

'Edie . . . I feel like a tally man standing in the passage.'

'I'm sorry, Billy. I wasn't thinking. Your mum's in the front room.'

'I know. I recognise her laugh anywhere. Where can I put this lot down, Edie? They must be solid silver the weight of 'em. Can I dump 'em down somewhere?'

'Of course. In there.' She nodded towards her bedroom. 'Put 'em on the bed and then come through into the living room. Do you want a drink? Something stronger than water or tea.'

'No, thanks,' said Billy from the bedroom. 'But hang on a sec.'

Waiting for him to come back into the passage, Edie spoke quietly, saying, 'Come on then, Billy. Out with it. What's happened?'

'Ben's house caught fire but we got him and Nao out in time. They've been taken to hospital Edie, but only as a precaution. They're old and Ben was in a bit of shock.'

'Hospital?' Edie peered into his face. She wanted facts. Nothing more. 'Why?'

'She's *fine*, Edie. She went in the ambulance to keep Ben company. I just wanted to get that bit out of the way first before I tell you all about it. I know what you women are like. Questions will come at me from all sides. And to be honest – I think I could do with a cup of tea and a sit-down after all.'

'Fair enough,' said Edie. 'Come on.'

'I thought that was your voice, Billy. Come to check up on me 'ave yer?' said Jessie, smiling at her son.

'No, Mum. I just wanted to—'

'There's been a fire, Jess,' Edie cut in. 'Ben's place. He's all right, though.' She glanced at Billy. 'You did say that Ben was all right?'

'I did. Yeah.' Billy flopped down onto the sofa and rubbed his eyes. 'I wouldn't mind a glass of water, Edie.'

'Course, I'll just get it. You've gone as white as a sheet, Billy.'
'Have I?'

'She's right Billy, love.' Jessie placed an arm around her son. 'All grown up but still with that little boy expression.' She kissed him on the cheek and then winked at him. 'Thanks for coming to let Edie know before the gossips got wind of it and came straight up here.'

The hatch door into the kitchen opened and as Edie passed through the glass of water she said, 'So do you want a drop of brandy, Billy, or a cup of sweet tea?'

'Yeah . . . go on then . . . I'll have a shot of Nao's poison,' said Billy, feeling the effect of it all, now that he had arrived into a safe familiar place. 'I do need a stiff drink as it happens.' He held out his hands to see that they were shaking.

'So what's happened, then?' said Laura, who up until now had been watching and waiting to hear the worst.

'Ben's house has gone, Laura. I was on my way back from Jamaica Street. Talk about being in the right place at the right time.'

'What do you mean? Ben's house has gone? Gone where?' Jessie could hardly believe it.

'Flattened. A chimney fire started it. A fire in June. Typical of that daft sod.'

'He is all right, though?' said Edie, coming back into the room.

'Shaken but was still talking non-stop. Why would anyone light a bloody fire in this weather?'

'Ben and Joey light a fire every morning, come rain or shine,' said Edie, handing Billy a small brandy.

'Crazy,' he said, drinking it down in one go. 'People everywhere outside and all they could say was Ben wouldn't come out. And that was it. They was just gonna leave 'im there. Any fool could see from the way the chimney was going that it was serious.

'I went in to find Naomi trying to persuade him to leave but he wouldn't. He was in an armchair clutching a family picture. I ordered Naomi out and then carried Ben over my shoulder whether he liked it or not. Then I went back for them bloody photos. That's why he wouldn't come out, can you believe that?

'He didn't have the wherewithal to grab them and run. They were on the sideboard. It couldn't 'ave been many minutes after I'd come out when the whole place went down. Caved in. There was thick black dust and smoke everywhere. Then it caught alight and did it roar. Jesus. Anyway . . . the firemen arrived and made short work of it. You should 'ave heard Ben when they lifted him into the ambulance . . . he was rambling on, trying to pretend he wasn't in a state. Naomi went with 'im for company.'

'Ben doesn't ramble, Billy. He's straightforward. If he didn't think he needed to go in an ambulance – he wouldn't have gone.'

'He was in deep shock, Edie. And the smoke must 'ave got into 'is lungs. The place was filling with smoke when I dragged them out. Mad or what?'

'Oh, Billy . . . you went in *seconds* before it collapsed and saved Ben and Nao. You deserve a medal.'

'I think Lady Luck was there for me today . . .' said Billy, his eyes glazed, his face taut. 'I'm bloody lucky, that's all I can say . . . and so are Nao and Ben. Very lucky.' He put his empty glass on the coffee table and covered his face with both hands. 'You should 'ave seen it. The air was full of the smell of sulphur and burning. The crowd seemed to be loving it. Someone must 'ave phoned 999 for the fire brigade . . . but that was it. The sum total of help. And Ben and Naomi were *inside*. They were *in* there! Ben in his old armchair saying he wasn't gonna leave 'is family and Nao acting as cool as you like trying to talk sense into 'im. Talk *sense*? At a time like *that*? If I hadn't of left Jamaica Street when I did they would 'ave been buried alive. I swear it. What is *wrong* with people! Why didn't one of the men go in and get 'em out? I don't get it! I – just – don't – get – it!'

'But you never stood by, babe,' said Jessie, stroking his sweaty hair. 'You got them out. And I'm proud of you. Really proud.'

'But what if I hadn't of come that way home, Mum? What then? Ben looked terrible and all he could do was sit there and clutch an old photo. I'm telling you . . . he could easily be laying in the mortuary now. They would 'ave been buried alive.'

'But you did come along. . . . and thank God for it. You can be proud of yourself as well as thank fate.'

'There's nothing to be proud about. I went in and fetched them out. That was all.' He pulled a sparkling white handkerchief from his pocket and wiped his perspiring forehead. 'I'm a bit upset of what *might* of 'appened though.' He looked at his wrist watch. 'I'll go up the London now. See how they are.'

'If you're sure you're up to it, Billy . . . I'd like to come to the hospital with you,' said Edie.

'Course.' Billy turned to his mother saying, 'If Errol comes round tell 'im I'll meet 'im in Jamaica Street tomorrer. To help him and Malcolm. Come on then, Edie. Let's go and see 'ow that daft old pair are getting on.'

'We'll let ourselves out of your flat, Ed,' said Laura. 'You go and me and Jessie'll lock up.'

'Thanks,' said Edie as she picked up her handbag and left them to it.

As he followed her, Billy stopped at the doorway and turned back to Jessie, saying, 'It's what happened to us, wasn't it? Over in Westminster. During the war. We didn't think that roof would come down on us either, did we?'

'Similar,' said Jessie. She was taken aback by this. He had never mentioned it before and he had been very young at the time.

'It was the cracking and crashing sound that did it. Brought it all back. That and the horrible rumbling above us when we was in that cellar.'

'I didn't think that you remembered any of that,' said Jessie, her heart sinking at the memory.

'Only the sound and that horrible acrid smell of smoke, soot and burning. I didn't know what it was I was remembering at first. Then I did. The sound of that mansion falling about us after the blast.' With that, Billy turned away and left the flat.

'God. There's always something that comes up to remind

me of that bloody war,' murmured Jessie and then, 'Do you think Naomi's all right?'

'Yeah. Billy would have said so if not.'

'That's true. I don't know, Laura. This feels like history repeating itself. We were all but buried alive, me, Billy, and other women and their children. Trapped in a basement when the bomb hit. I told you about all of that. Didn't I?'

'I think you have mentioned it.' She had and Laura knew it but she also knew that Jessie needed to go over it again. Her only son Billy had just escaped death for the second time and in similar circumstances.

'It's not the sort of thing you want to remember.'

'Well, leave it be then.'

'I just can't believe that Billy would remember it. He must have only been three or four at the time. I should think it's something he's heard me talking about to Tom or his gran and granddad.'

'The memory's a strange thing, Jess. They say that with the help of an expert we can go right back to when we were being born.'

'It's seems like an age ago now,' said Jessie, staring at the floor. 'You should 'ave seen that place me and Billy had to stop in the night before we left for Westminster. A hostel for the homeless in Aldgate. We had to share one room with three other women and two children with me and Billy on a single camp bed. The sheet I'd been given for the bed was clean but the blankets smelt damp and of cigarette smoke. The place was crawling with bugs and lice.'

'It's not worth dwelling on, Jess. You weren't the only ones in a hostel for the homeless.'

'I know. There were hundreds in my situation. Anyway . . . I soon made my way with Billy to Westminster to an address where we could stay on a bed and breakfast basis, for free. It was a lovely big old tired house in an avenue lined with trees. The woman who answered the door asked me if I was used to sharing a room with strangers. I was ready to turn around and walk away but she smiled at me and then said we could have the attic room. Just me and Billy. She must have seen the look on my face.

'It was really nice there. We both enjoyed a few months of normal life with others in the house while a war was going on. And then . . . one minute we were taking shelter in the cellar, which we were all used to . . . and then the lights went out and we could still hear the wailing of the siren until that horrible nightmare crash. The sound from above was terrifying. I thought we were gonna be crushed and buried alive. Me, Billy, and the other families.'

'Thank goodness there was a cellar, Jess. You might not be here to tell the story.'

'I know. And neither might Nao and Ben if Billy hadn't survived to be in the right place at the right time. My God . . . when I think back to it now it don't seem possible. The bomb that had hit us had mis-routed – a one thousand pound or something . . . which had been meant for an important building . . . had found the wrong target.

'The fire service finally managed to get through to us after hours of shifting a mountain from the door leading down into the cellar. I'll never ever forget that wonderful sweet taste of fresh air.'

'God, Jess . . . when you look back now . . . how on earth did we survive those heavy raids on London – and especially the blitz on the East End?' said Laura. 'And what was it all about, really?'

'Power,' said Jessie, pulling herself back into the present.

'Haven't really moved that far forward in the bigger picture 'ave we? We're still like cave men protecting or trying to claim territory.' She looked out of the window and up at the sky. 'I wonder if the self-same thing goes on with the birds? To us they're lovely to look at and sing pretty tunes. But are they pecking each other to death at night over a certain tree?'

'I don't think so. Anyway, we've got peace now and let's be thankful for it.'

'Until another leader of a nasty gang surfaces.'

'Oh, shut up, Laura. It's all over now. There won't be any more wars. Anyway—' The sound of the doorbell stopped her short. 'That can't be your Billy back already, can it?'

'No,' said Jessie, checking her wrist watch. 'He's not been gone long. I'll go.'

Opening the door to Nathan and Becky who, from their expressions, had heard about their friend Naomi and Ben having gone to hospital, Jessie smiled warmly. Standing there, arm in arm the old Jewish pair looked like the odd couple of the year. Becky in her old-fashioned green and orange paisley frock was wearing bright red lipstick and blue eye shadow and her new spectacles which had wings edged with marcasite stones.

'Is it true?' said Becky, a hand on her heart. 'Tell me it's not true.'

'Depends what you've heard,' said Jessie standing aside. 'In you come. Laura's in the front room. Do you want a cup of tea?'

'I would *love* one. It's been a terrible shock.'

'We won't come in,' said Nathan. 'Take no notice of her. At a time like this Edie needs bloody visitors? I don't think so.'

'Edie's not in, Nathan. She's gone with my Billy to see how Nao and Ben are.'

'As a matter of fact,' said Becky as she walked feebly into the passage. 'I could do with something hot to drink with a little something in it. It was *such* a shock when I heard. Cocoa with whisky would be nice.'

'See what I mean, Jessie? You shouldn't have invited her in. You'll never get rid of her now. I should know.' Nathan shrugged and rolled his eyes. 'Never mind. You'll learn.'

Jessie closed the door and followed them through to the living room, saying, 'They're both all right as far as I know.'

'I thought they had been burned to a cinder and that's the God's truth.' Becky lowered herself into an armchair. 'That's what they're saying. Burnt to a cinder. A girl friend of my mother lived opposite a man who was burnt to a cinder in his chair by the fire. I've never got over it.'

'He wasn't burnt to death you silly cow—'

'Did I *say* he was? I said to a *cinder*, Nathan.' She glanced across at Laura who had a wry smile on her face. 'It's all the wax in his ears. He's saving it up for Christmas so he doesn't have to buy candles. So what happened?'

'Ben's chimney caught fire and Jessie's Billy went in and got them out.' Laura was hoping that with this one-liner Becky would be content.

'So they didn't go in an ambulance? I can't believe it. Why must people tell lies?'

'They did go in an ambulance. To be on the safe side. They're at the London now having a check up.'

'A check up? Ha. That's what they told you? A cousin of mine went in for a check up and she never came out. And that wasn't even the London Hospital. If it was I could understand it. They're well known for taking people's kidneys and liver and God knows what. To do their experiments.'

'They don't pinch them to experiment,' said Nathan as he draped his clean white handkerchief over his little finger. 'They just like a nice mixed grill now and then.' He chuckled as he pushed his covered finger into his ear and gave it a quick whisk.

'Was there much blood?'

'No, Becky. None. From all accounts they're both fine. Trust me.'

'We were going to go to the Paragon to see a film. I've got two complimentary tickets.'

'Paragon. It's a bloody flea pit,' said Nathan, examining his clean handkerchief. 'They can't even give free tickets away. It's a bloody Charlie Chaplin silent film. Still . . . she don't understand what they're saying half the time, anyway. Loses the plot if you know what I mean. I wish to God I was single again.' He had another go at his ear.

'You know, I don't think we should stop,' said Becky, melodramatic. 'No. I think we should go now. If we leave it much longer they might be home before we've had a chance to go in and visit. If they need blood I shall give. You don't know whose you're getting otherwise. I shouldn't like foreign blood in me to be blunt and truthful. It's not right. You get a nice cup of tea afterwards and a couple of biscuits.'

'Come on, woman. Let's get it over with.' Nathan turned to Jessie saying, 'Is it worth my buying them a bar of chocolate?'

'What do you mean? Worth it?'

'Well, if we're sure they're gonna be kept in I would buy a sixpenny bar of Cadbury's between them but if they're coming out the same day there's no point.' He took the tea and drank it down in one go, emptying the cup.

'What about the house?' said Becky, the dramatic expression back on her face. 'And the furniture. Did any of that get saved?'

'The house and all the furniture's gone. Burnt to—'

'A *cinder*?' said Becky. 'Oh my God – I can't believe it! *All* of Ben's furniture! Did you hear that, Nathan? There's nothing *left*. The *entire* contents is charcoal.'

'I don't think he'll give a shit about the furniture but what about what's under the floorboards? No Jew would be seen buried dead without a wad of notes in a tin under the floorboards. It's tradition.'

'Your floor's stone,' Jessie teased. 'They won't be letting you into heaven then.'

'I do all right, thank you. My tin's where only God and myself know where it is. He's not fussy where I put it so long as it's there. I've not done so bad. They always gave a guinea Christmas box at Mann and Crossman. And I was there for twenty-odd years so that should tell you something. I do all right.'

'I wish I could say the same for myself,' said Becky, standing up and checking her new glasses in the mirror over the mantelshelf. 'I'm lucky if he puts his hand in his pocket for one sausage a week.'

'You see what a liar she is? But what should I care? She can lose her temper today. I'm in a good mood now I know that Nao and Ben are okay. And in any case . . .' Nathan looked slyly at his wife who could see him behind her in the reflection of the mirror. 'She sneaks out and has pies and mash. And fish and chips which she takes to the park and eats by the pond. I dare say she meets her man friend there.'

'You're like a bloody record, Nathan. But there . . . you were interesting . . . once upon a time.'

'At least she can put herself to bed, Jessie. There's a silver lining behind every cloud, Laura. So you want I should give a message to the invalids?' Nathan was by the living room door, his eyelids half closed. 'Or take anything?'

'Give them my love,' said Laura.

'And mine.' Jessie walked with them to the front door. 'And tell Ben that if he wants a room until they find him a flat—'

'They already did find him a place,' said Nathan. 'You think it might have been an insurance job?'

Laughing at him, Jessie gently pushed the old boy out into the passage. 'Tormenting sod. Tell him that he can have Billy's room until he's re-housed. Billy's gonna be stopping at Jamaica Street for a while.'

'I'm telling you. Ben had a letter. And Joey. They've been offered a two-bedroom place, close by to Nao.'

'Good. It's time they gave up living in that blooming street. It's due to be demolished in any case.'

'Who told you that? Bloody fools. I heard that they were going to leave them standing. Fix them up a bit. The landlord's got wind of property within a certain radius going up in price.'

'Oh, go away, Nathan. The places are not fit to live in. They're slum dwellings.' Almost pushing him through the street doorway Jessie gave his wife a supporting wink. 'You need a gold medal to put up with him.'

'Tell me something I don't already know,' said Becky, leaving. 'Tell me something I would like to hear.'

Back in the kitchen, Jessie could hear the couple and their gentle banter as they made their way down the stairs outside and felt a rush of sadness. The old ones were getting older and it was showing. In ten years' time she doubted that any of them would be alive. Ben, Joey, Harriet, Larry and Naomi. Five people who had been friends for donkey's years. They were all now in their late seventies or eighties and the saddest thing of all would be when the first one passed away. This would be the beginning of the end of an era.

7

A month had passed since the demise of Ben's house and as far as the landlord of the terrace in Cotton Street was concerned the chimney fire had been a blessing in disguise. The two old folk, Joey and Ben, had been the last remaining in the street and until they had gone the land owner who had all but sold the houses, had not been able to finalise his contract. What they hadn't known was that the property dealer, after exhausting all avenues to find a way of turning them out, would have paid them to leave. As luck would have it a ground floor two-bedroom flat had become available on Barcroft Estate close to where Naomi lived. Although at first they had turned up their noses at the offer of one place between two of them once they had seen the ground-floor apartment they were both pleased with it and happy to be living in a place which was easy to keep clean, draught free with plenty of natural light coming in through the generous windows.

Settled in and quite content with their new way of living they had marked out their territories and the two old soldiers were soon in a daily routine much like the one they had in Cotton Street. Each could come and go as they pleased and surprising everyone, Ben and Joey had taken advantage of the Meals on Wheels service for the elderly, with reservations, naturally. They found that the dinners which arrived hot and fresh were quite tasty and almost like mother made and they loved the afters: fruit pies, crumbles and steamed puddings *with* custard.

Unlike their friend Nathan, who had been looking forward to being a grumpy old man, and his wife Becky who loved to grumble, Ben and Joey went about their business and their life as normal and with a smile in reserve. By mutual agreement each of them had placed their personal things, photographs and ornaments into their own bedroom and from the modest grant given to them by the local Welfare & Social Services plus Ben's small house insurance claim for contents after the fire, they had managed to furnish the place modestly to suit both their tastes. A small pale gold three-piece suite had come from a factory in Columbia Road, Bethnal Green, two single beds from a local store, Blundells, and their new bed linen from a market stall in Petticoat Lane. The lovely Turkish lady, Shereen, who lived next door to Becky and Nathan on the Barcroft Estate, an excellent seamstress and a friend, had run up new curtains for them on her treadle sewing machine.

All things considered the two men who had seen two world wars and had lived in Cotton Street for all their lives were now quite content with their lot and, especially since Ben had escaped from the claw of death, appreciated each day of life. After his short stay in hospital Ben was eager to be out and to make the most of the final years of his life. Both he and Joey had taken a very big step in moving out of the old street where they had both lived as boys and men. Ben had come out of the nightmare scene unscathed, except for being a little slower on his feet and a touch less confident than he had been, but now, with Naomi's enforced advice of brandy in warm milk, he slept soundly through the nights to the low snoring of his friend in the adjoining bedroom.

On three evenings a week, Naomi, Larry and Harriet, the gentle team of elderly friends, came together for a couple of beers and a game of cards at Joey and Ben's and continued to be involved in the St Peter's church hall tea dances.

This evening Harriet had, as promised, brought to Ben and Joey's apartment a brace of pheasants poached from a big estate in Loughton, Essex and delivered to her by a friend who could buy almost anything on the cheap with a nod and a wink.

'You make bloody well sure you braise them birds with beer,' said Harriet, dropping the birds into the kitchen sink. 'And get every single one of them feathers off. We'll be 'ere for Sunday dinner.'

'And I suppose *I've* got to cook the mangy things,' said Joey.

'That's right. With roast tatters, Brussels sprouts and peas. Processed peas. I can't stand fresh ones. I'll fetch an apple pie with me. You can make the custard.'

'It's Thursday.' Joey gazed into her face and waited.

'I know. So?'

'You think in this heat they'll keep until Sunday? Flaming July?'

'You've got a gas fire 'aven't yer?'

'What's that got to do with anything?'

'You don't keep coal in the coal cupboard. I 'ad a look on my way in. Clean as the day it was built. Hang 'em in there. It's the coolest place. And don't pluck 'em 'til first fing Sunday at dawn.' Harriet sniffed and then went into the sitting room to join the others round the card table, very happy to be spending what she considered to be her last years with old friends whom she liked and could trust.

'So what's it to be, then?' she sniffed. 'Pontoon or rummy?'

'Actually Harriet . . .' said Naomi, 'I was rather hoping we might play poker for a change?'

'Suit yerself, Nao. I couldn't give a toss. So long as we get on with it and you don't give us a running commentary . . . of when you played with famous *actors* backstage after a brilliant performance by one and all.'

Leaning back in her chair, the early evening sun on her face, Naomi looked up at the ceiling, thoughtfully. 'How odd that you should mention that. I was just thinking about the last time I played poker with Victor McLaglen, Julius Hagen and Jack Buchanan in the Hoe Street film studio in Walthamstow. Betty Balfour too. The cockney with huge blue eyes and golden curls and sense of humour who was rather dim. I was quite a star that evening. On a winning streak one might say.'

Larry, sporting his bored expression, placed a pack of cards in the middle of the table. 'We'll have a couple of games and then read from our scripts. I ironed them after the last reading so try not to turn corners or curl them in your hands this time.'

'Too much hard work learning lines if you were to ask me,' said Ben, sighing. 'The show will only be on for one night. A bunch of actors on stage for one evening only, but it takes months to learn what to do. Bloody daft. Cut the cards. Lowest deals.'

'But should it be a success – and I'm sure it will be – we can put it on again another time, Ben. So please don't start moaning about it all through this evening as you did last time. It would be such a shame to take all of the fun out of our rehearsals.'

'Fun?' said Larry, rolling his eyes and chuckling. 'It's more like being at school. Having to remember from one week to the next what I mustn't forget. Reminds me of when we used to have them evenings doing similar at the Grand Star.'

'But you enjoyed that time, Larry. We all did,' said Naomi. 'Talking about shows which had been produced there in the old days and so on. Each of us reading from old scripts. It was fun, surely?'

'For you it might have been, Nao. Theatre's in your bloody veins. Always has been.'

'And yours too, Larry. Let's not forget. You always got right into a part when we were reading those old scripts . . . so much so that if I remember correctly you encouraged us to *buy* published plays for one or two of those readings instead of us keeping on using those found in an old box in the theatre. In your father's oak cupboard.'

'Did I? I can't remember,' said Larry, leaning back and folding his arms, enjoying the attention. 'I thought you all came just to keep me company. I won't say I wasn't lonely living in the rooms, tucked away.'

'Stop fibbing, Larry. The Grand Star was like a second home to you. It had been in your family for years and you were thrilled and very proud when Lita Roza sang there before she was quite as famous as she is now.'

Gazing up at the ceiling as if he wasn't listening, Larry spoke quietly but loud enough for her to hear. 'All I had was a two-bar electric fire, a small hob for boiling a tin of soup, a stock cupboard . . . and a put-U-up settee. Still . . . there we are. I managed . . . until I realised that Harriet needed me to move into her place. She was lonelier than I was.'

'I bleedin' well wasn't!' said Harriet, coming into the room, 'I took you in 'cos I felt for yer. And the bit of rent comes in handy. Now then . . . I've fetched a bag of coppers with me. Who wants change? I'll take a shilling for eleven pennies.'

'See what I mean? She can't do anything without having to make a profit. For every shilling she makes a penny. I wish I had her brain.' Larry shuffled the cards again, saying, 'Lowest card deals.'

'Darling . . . surely it's the highest card?' said Naomi, her head tipped slightly to one side. 'Not that I'm a more seasoned player than you.'

'Cut the bloody cards. Lowest deals. I'm in charge when there's a full moon and tonight there is one. I checked.'

'In charge for how long,' said Harriet, obeying his command. 'When Naomi's around we must all be subservient. Full moon or not.'

'Oh, I wouldn't say that, my darling,' said Naomi, flushed with pleasure at receiving a compliment from Harriet. To receive any praise from her closest friend from childhood was an accomplishment. Once the game had got under way the hours went swiftly by. Stopping now and then for light refreshments and a natter about nothing of importance the elderly gang, relaxed and happy, could have no idea of the wickedness and evil which was hatching outside of this house and within their realm.

Later that night, once the card games were over and the friends had taken their leave and the two old men had cleared things away, both Joey and Ben were ready for their beds. A little tipsy from the beers, each of them had sank their heads into their feather pillows in the silence of their rooms, quite satisfied with the sociable evening and the company. It had just gone eleven-thirty and was quiet on the estate with just the sound of echoing footsteps of those returning home late. On the face of it, this balmy warm night with its full moon showed no sign of disturbance and inside their flats in Scott House most people were either in their beds or getting ready to retire. The lights in most of the homes were off and by the time the church clock in the distance struck midnight, Edie was asleep in her bed as was Jessie and Laura's family. All sleeping soundly while the moon shone brightly in the navy sky. It was peaceful and it was calm.

Having parked his Jaguar in its usual spot under the darkened arches, Gloria's son pulled on a pair of fine black leather gloves and walked towards Scott House, forever glancing cautiously around himself for any sign of life. With only a dim lamp light and the moon to see by he could only guess that most people in Scott House were inside their homes and most in their beds. Constantly looking about himself, in all dark areas, he was aware of his own footsteps echoing, even though he trod as quietly as he possibly could. Once inside the block of flats, his heart beat rapid, he silently climbed the stairs until he reached the fourth floor, then listened again for any sound of footsteps or any sign of life. Other than a dog barking in the distance and two stray cats fighting, it was a very quiet night.

Outside his mother's front doorway and hidden in the shadows he switched on his small silver torch and as quiet as a mouse pushed the key into the lock of Gloria's street door hoping it would not creak. Then, closing it silently, he pointed his torch-light to the floor and crept through the narrow dark passage and into his mother's bedroom where she was sleeping soundly. With as little light as possible to see by, he crept close to her bedside and looked down at the vulnerable innocent woman who was sound asleep on her back with her mouth slightly open as she breathed peacefully. Then, placing the torch on the floor beside her bed to leave himself hands free he studiously looked at the pillow beneath her head and birdlike neck to see how easy it was going to be to pull it away without disturbing her. Accordingly, with care and caution he then began to slowly ease the pillow from under his mother's head, stopping dead still only once, when she moved and muttered something inaudible. His heartbeat now rapid, the adrenaline pumping through his veins, Gloria's only child, her treasured son, waited with held breath while she turned and twisted and then settled down again – onto her back. Once he had released the pillow he very carefully, and as slowly, lowered it onto her face to the echoing sound of her bedside clock ticking in this otherwise silent room. Just as he was about to put pressure onto the pillow however, she moved again and mumbled in her sleep. Taking no chances of her waking up before he had carried out this act of murder he pressed against her face and held down the pillow, his face taut and his eyeballs staring as her arms and legs began to fight under the bedclothes as she fought for air. With nothing on his mind other than to kill this woman, detached from emotion, he pressed the pillow hard until her struggle for sweet fresh air eased and her frail body trembled and then stopped moving. His heart beating in time with the second hand of the clock he eased the pillow from his mother's face and jerked backwards as she stared up at him, her eyes glaring as if she could see him clearly. Turning away, he controlled his breathing and collected himself.

Placing the pillow to one side he drew the key to the trunk from his inside pocket and then eased the old wood and iron trunk from beneath the bed and unlocked it. And there, at last, was his inheritance and his ticket to freedom and a richer way of living. His father's ill-gotten. A fortune which was destined to disappear into the void had his mother passed away naturally in her sleep and the place was emptied of her furniture with him possibly being miles away and knowing nothing about it. Carefully he withdrew the thick wads of notes and a velvet pouch which contained the gold sovereigns, and squeezed them into his pockets.

His heart beating rapidly, he detached himself in heart and mind from Gloria's corpse on the bed and reached out a hand to brush her eyes shut and hide the horror and petrified state during her last seconds of fighting for breath. He then continued with his plan, placed the small portable two-bar electric fire close to the old-fashioned silky bed cover to be just touching and switched it on. As soon as the electric bars began to turn orange and glow in the dim light he stepped away and left the rest to fate.

At the bedroom door he turned to look at her for the last time and felt nothing. No compassion, no regret. He then left the flat in the same manner he had arrived, as quiet as a mouse with nothing going on inside his mind and totally devoid of any feelings whatsoever. Outside, as he stood on the balcony, he listened for any sound coming from above and below the stairs and then glanced over the balcony to be certain that no-one was about in the grounds below. It was silent and it was eerie. Walking stealthily towards the stairs he was stopped in his tracks and momentarily shocked by what looked like a bundle of old clothes in the corner which was moving. Drawing breath he walked past the ragged heap repressing the urge to kick it in case any cry of pain from beneath it woke a neighbour. Drake despised tramps and thought that they should all be gassed at once. To his mind they belonged in the nineteenth century, down by the then stinking river Thames.

Lifting a corner of his grey blanket the old man peered out to see who had passed him by and saw the back of Drake as he continued on his way down the stairs, a shifty aura about him. 'No good,' the old man mumbled, 'up to no good.' He then pulled his cover back over him and went back to sleep in his new temporary place in this block of flats.

As he arrived on the second floor, now on edge, Drake was pulled up sharply for a second time by the deathly vision of Emma in her long flowing white nightdress as she all but drifted down the stairs to make her way out of the block of flats. Drawing breath, he waited until his heart beat slowed and the hairs on the back of his neck flattened. But the ghostlike vision of Emma as she raised her eyes to stare at him froze him to the spot.

Deeply unnerved, Drake collected himself and then followed cautiously in her footsteps, his mind racing. The ghostly girl had clearly seen him and even though not properly dressed was behaving as if she had somewhere to go. His worry, once the initial shock of her appearing before him like that had subsided, was that should anything go wrong with his plans tonight and for some reason his mother's death by fire would not be seen as a reckless accident caused by a simple-minded woman, the girl was witness to the fact that he was here at this crucial time of night.

Once below in the grounds he stood in the shadows and watched as Emma made her way to the low brick wall and sat down as if it was the most natural thing in the world to do in the dead of night. Pushing thoughts of strangling her thin white neck out of his mind, he walked slowly back to the arches, as if he had all the time in the world. The girl was clearly not right in the head and if he could be frightened by her then others in this block of flats had been too, at one time or another. So if anyone was going to be under suspicion for going into his mother's home and starting a fire, it could easily be her. The gods, he felt, had just offered up a suspect and a victim. He smiled at the thought of it and wiped the beads of sweat from his forehead.

Arriving at his dark blue Jaguar Drake checked his surroundings and apart from a couple of alcoholic down and outs coming along swaying and talking gibberish there was no sign of human life. Taking his spectacles from his top pocket he put them on and glanced at himself in the mirror inside his precious car. He hated wearing them, but without these glasses he was short-sighted, and he would do nothing to put his Jaguar at risk even though he preferred to view the world and all of its people, out of focus. He started the engine and slowly pulled away to pay a visit to one of his favourite whores in Shoreditch.

He would have preferred to have had his bags packed and in the car to leave this disgusting part of London for good, but that might have thrown suspicion on him, should this murder not be seen as an accident. He had to wait. Bide his time. Behave exactly as he would had he not just killed the woman who had given birth to him and brought him into a world not of his choosing. The pits of London, a place not for someone of his standing.

Pulling up outside an all-night café in Brushfield Street to the sound of the Spitalfields church clock striking the hour Drake suddenly felt hungry and wanted an early morning, full fried breakfast while things were quiet and before the market porters began to arrive. He knew there would be a few taxi drivers around but he had always managed to keep them at a distance by ignoring them or offering a brief smile and a nod if any of them were in a chatty mood. This small café was run by an Italian family who had been handing it down from father to son to grandson as if it was all any of them had been born for. The best thing about the area to Drake's mind apart from the convenient opening times of cafés, were the local women touting for work. Paid for, but cheap, sex.

After he had finished his hearty breakfast Drake paid his bill and left the café and as luck would have it recognised one of the Whitechapel girls swaying and singing from the effect of cheap gin. Walking in her footsteps he followed her into Commercial Street and along Wilkes Row to proposition her. Tonight he wanted more than one whore. He flashed a ten-pound note at the twenty-year-old and she was happy to oblige, knowing that one or two of the girls would by now be back in their rooms in the lodging house where she lived. Profit by commission was on her mind. Smiling inwardly as he strode along, the attractive prostitute linked arms to make him believe he was her knight in shining armour and it worked. He felt like a king and wondered if the prostitutes would believe him if he were to say that he had just murdered his mother.

★

Edie's friend Laura was the first in the block of flats to wake to the smell of smoke. Even though Gloria's flat was two storeys up it was directly above hers and had merged into her dreams of a small bonfire swirling across huts in Kent and filling the air. In her dream she could hear the dawn chorus and see the pink glow of the rising sun and smell the scent of hops tainted by the smell of acrid burning as the sound of a steam train on nearby railway tracks woke her with a start. She sat bolt upright and rubbed her eyes to the real smell of smoke and fire. She got out of bed and called out to her husband and then rushed from the bedroom calling out to both Kay and Jack as she went. Crashing open the door of the small spare room where her husband slept she shouted at him: 'Jack wake up! Get up! The fire bell's going!'

With half-open eyes Jack turned over and peered up at her. 'What are you talking about Laura? What fire bell? We haven't got a fire bell.'

'Well then, there must be a fire engine on its way! There's a fire somewhere in these flats! Move yourself!'

'Don't be stupid. How can these flats catch fire? It's all bloody bricks and cement.' With that he yawned and turned over. 'Go back to bed . . . or fetch me a cup of tea if you're gonna keep on making a racket.' He snuggled his head back into his feather pillow. 'Don't forget that I've gotta be up at half past six.'

Furious with him, she stepped forward and pulled the bedclothes back. 'Get up now! There's a fire! Get out of bed!' She then ran from the room to find Kay coming out of her bedroom and rubbing her eyes. 'Can't *you* smell it, Kay?'

'Burning?' Kay stretched and yawned. 'I can Mum, yeah. But it's not in our flat. It's outside. Probably a garden rubbish fire smouldering.'

'No. It's much worse than that. It might not be our flat but it's close by and that's no garden fire.' She pulled on her dressing gown. 'I'm going out there.'

'Don't be daft, Mum. Go back to bed.'

'No. I'm going up there. That's where it's coming from. Above us.'

'You can't go out like that, Laura. Get back to bed or get dressed.' Jack appeared in his pyjamas. 'I'll go and 'ave a look after a cup of tea. Put the kettle on, Kay. Now we're all up we might as well 'ave a hot drink.' He went to the street door and opened it, yawning. Stopping in his tracks he listened and then murmured to himself, 'She's right . . . I can hear a fire engine.' He called out for Kay to get his dressing gown off the hook on his bedroom door.

'I told you!' said Laura, rushing past him. 'Someone must have phoned for it.' Once outside on the balcony she stretched forward and looked above herself. 'It *is* coming from the top floor and from Gloria's flat. You don't think she's trapped in there, Jack?'

'We'll soon see,' he said, brushing past her. Others were coming out of their flats and lights were coming on all over the place as the echoing sound of the shrill fire engine bell grew close. Arriving at Gloria's door it was plain that a fire was well under way inside. Jack turned to Sarah James who for once in her life was standing back, her coat wrapped round her shoulders and silent. He asked her if her next-door neighbour was still in there.

'I don't know,' was all the gossip managed to say.

He peered through the kitchen window only to find it filled with smoke and went to the front door and placed a hand either side of the porch and then brought up his right leg to give the door an almighty kick causing it to fly open. The hallway was so thick with smoke he could hardly see a thing and had to back off to fill his lungs with clean air. Surprising him yet again, Sarah James was offering a small wet towel. Still she said nothing. Taking the towel from her Jack covered his mouth and went back inside, diving into the smoke-filled passage to see thick black smoke curling from beneath the bedroom door. He kicked it open to see the bed and curtains were burning and so too was Gloria's small bedside chair in flames. Struggling with the fumes and beaten back by dense smoke and heat Jack had to go outside for fresh air to find the firemen had arrived and one was charging along the balcony towards him. Coughing now, Jack pointed to the inside and just managed to say, 'I think she might be in the bedroom, mate,' choking on his own words.

Light-headed, he went back downstairs to his flat feeling giddy from the smoke and nauseated by what he could only presume to be the smell of burning flesh. Once he came to his senses it sunk in that the lonely soul had burned to death in her own bed. Guilty now, that he had not jumped up on first waking when he thought he could smell smoke but had turned over and tried to go back to sleep, he went inside to his kitchen where he could be alone and could freely shed a few frustrated guilty tears.

The following day there was a hushed silence and a sense of deep shame between Gloria's neighbours who had either ignored or made fun of her. Practically all of them had by now heard that she was dead. It was believed by one and all that the cause of this tragedy had been death by misadventure, that Gloria had left her heater too close to her bed and fallen asleep before turning it off. The gossips were making the very most of this surreal dark drama as they whispered between themselves the word *suicide* while others who lived in these flats were saying a quiet goodbye to a harmless woman who wanted nothing more in life than a few friends, a little company and a few home comforts. They, like everyone else, believed this could only be a tragic accident. To even imagine that a murderer had crossed their threshold would send them scurrying into their flats to bolt their doors.

As with all bad news it hadn't taken too long before the fire made headlines in the local newspaper which reported that the pathologist had found no trace of carbon monoxide in the blood and no sooty deposits in the air passages and so concluded that Gloria had died before the fire had started. Fear and wild speculation was about to permeate this council estate as was speculation as to why someone might have wanted to murder a pathetic woman in her fifties, who was as poor as a church mouse. Once the pathologist's conclusion that Gloria had been suffocated was written into his report, it had been passed to the police. Scotland Yard officers were called in and an investigation into the possibility of murder was opened.

It was a young and fairly new recruit who had noticed that even though the woman had been found lying in her bed, her pillow was on a small chest of drawers and it had been this that suggested that someone had gone into the flat that night who had a key and a reason for killing a woman, who to all appearances, had no possessions of value worth taking. The fact that a torch had been found in the mess after the fire was another indication that an intruder had been there and had placed the fire next to the bedclothes once the woman had been suffocated with her own pillow.

With this evidence and the results of the post-mortem the police were mounting a house to house enquiry to discover that the only neighbours who had been into Gloria's flat had been Naomi, Emma, Billy, Peppito, Errol and Tony. All from the same group of family and friends. Once this snippet of information had surfaced during a routine call on Edie by two police officers, the chief of police instructed that his men narrowed their search and focused on Scott House instead of the entire Barcroft estate. Their first visit had been fairly brief but their changing attitude from casual at first to dour the next had frightened Edie, especially when she had answered a question she had not been expecting to be asked: when was her husband likely to be at home? Edie had lied to them and as she did so she had felt herself blush. She had told them that her husband had been killed while in action during the war. She had now incriminated herself because she knew that he was alive and back in the East End. Fortunately her lies had been accepted and condolences given. Even so, this did not mollify the sickening sense of worry in the pit of her stomach. She felt as if a time bomb was ticking.

The second visit from the police – the very next day – came soon after Edie was home from work and it not only surprised but disturbed her. This time, along with the officer who she had already met came Detective Inspector Braithwaite who, like his assistant, was polite when refusing a cup of tea which she had offered. Inviting them into the sitting room Edie prayed they had not returned to ask more questions about Harry. Once they were seated she was questioned and asked how often she had paid visits to her neighbour on the fourth floor, how close she had been to her, had they been close friends or just neighbourly. Edie answered with a gentle smile.

'To be honest, none of us in the block were that involved with the poor woman. Gloria, God rest her soul, was a loner and a bit of a mystery. She came out with some strange things. Quite alarming at times.'

'Alarming?' said the detective inspector. 'In what way?'

'Well we, myself, Jessie Smith, Laura Jackson and Gloria, were having a little get-together. Tea and cake in the afternoon, that sort of thing, and she started to open up more once she was relaxed, telling us that she never mixed with people much. She told us about her husband and how he'd met his maker.'

'Met his maker?'

'The woman wasn't all there,' Edie sighed. 'She said that her husband had been hanged for shooting a police officer. Of course . . . we never took it seriously, we just thought she wanted a bit of the limelight. She did enjoy that little get-together.' Edie shrugged and bore a sad expression. 'We should have done it more often. Poor woman.'

The detective inspector remained impassive as he said, 'Did she mention any other relatives?'

'I don't think so.' Edie was thoughtful as she recalled that day. 'Or did she? Yes, I think she did. Yes, of course she did. Her son. She said she had a son.' Again Edie shook her head sadly. 'It was all fantasy. It had to be. She said her son was very busy and that even he didn't know about the money that was in a trunk under her bed. She went on about her husband telling her never to touch it. Bundles of fifty-pound notes, she said. I suppose she was trying to impress us. Just so she could be our friend.' Edie looked into the officer's face as tears welled behind her eyes. 'Sad isn't it? Living on 'er own like that in a fantasy world. I wish we'd invited her in more.'

'It was just the once then, was it?'

'Unfortunately. We're all working you know and we don't get that much time for afternoon tea sessions. We just pop in and out of each other's flats whenever we fancy a chat. But, to be honest, none of us would 'ave been like that with Gloria. I know that sounds mean but she wasn't really one of us. She was harmless and likeable but a bit bonkers and a neighbour more than a friend.'

'Bonkers?'

'Just a bit. When we all first moved in she used to sit in her kitchen sink, naked, and sing. She had nets up the window but well . . . you can imagine the kids, can't you? Still, let's not get too depressed . . . she enjoyed the attention I s'pose. It was better than the silence of 'er flat.'

'So how many of you would you say knew about this money she kept under her bed?'

'Oh, I don't think that was real.' Edie smiled.

'What makes you say that, Mrs Birch? Why so certain?'

'Well – that kind of thing only happens in books and films, surely?'

'So it was you and your lady friends she told – and no-one else. No-one else knew about the money?'

'I don't know. She might have said it to shopkeepers. Let's not forget that she wasn't all there. She smiled a lot though. Always pink in the cheeks and smiling.'

'So apart from yourself and your circle of family and friends you don't think that any of the other neighbours went into the dead woman's home? For a cup of tea, for instance?'

Edie shuddered at the words; dead woman's home. She still hadn't really taken this in. It all seemed to be going too fast. 'I couldn't say. Emma, our babysitter, took my grandson up there once. Gloria had caught the pair of them on the stairs after she'd seen them coming back from the park and gave my grandson a pound note. His mother, my daughter Maggie, told Peppie he couldn't keep it and that he should take it back to her. You can imagine how the five-year-old liked that. So Emma took Peppie up there for Maggie and had him give it back. Apparently Gloria accepted it as if they were treating *her*. She'd forgotten she'd given it.'

'Go on, Mrs Birch . . . this gets more interesting all the time.' The inspector smiled.

'Well . . . then Tony, my son-in-law, came in with his friend, Errol Turner, a young West Indian, and my daughter told him what had happened. He was concerned over it.'

'Was he? I would have thought he might have been pleased. A pound for pocket money?'

'No. It didn't bother me that much, not really. But Maggie and Tony were none too pleased. They likened it to a man of Gloria's age giving a little girl money for sweets – if you see what I mean.'

'That's a good point.'

'So Tony went up to see he gave it back and to let Gloria know this was Peppie's parents' wishes. So that it wouldn't happen agen, I s'pose. Errol thought it was amusing at first but then even he could see the sense in returning the money – once he'd met that poor woman.'

'So Errol Turner went up with your son-in-law? To see that the boy gave back the money?'

'You know Errol then?' said Edie, surprised.

'Good question, Mrs Birch. There are no flies on you, are there. In a case such as this we work fast and overlook nothing. The Smith family live in this block and their son is thick with the Turners too – the West Indian lads. You were telling me that Errol went with your son-in-law to make sure the money was given back.'

'Well, no . . . not to make sure it was given back. You make them sound like the Mafia,' said Edie. 'Tony and Errol just went up there together rather than sit here gossiping with me in this kitchen. You know what lads are like. They nearly always

seem to move about in twos or in small groups.' Edie looked
from the DI to his assistant. 'Just like you two. Except that
you've a job to do and they were just passing time. It was a
Saturday. And they go everywhere together.

'They're good mates. There's a small crowd of them: my
son-in-law Tony, Jessie's Billy, Errol and his cousin Malcolm.
Errol and his cousin are buying a place together and Billy's
acting caretaker 'til the house has been done up properly. In
Jamaica Street. They're all excited about it. God knows why.
We couldn't wait to get out of the slums and they can't wait
to get in.' Edie was rambling and going pink in the face. She
was in her own way trying to protect Maggie's friends, without
realising what she was doing.

'And Billy being Jessie Smith's son? Who also lives on the
top floor? Close to where the deceased woman lived?'

'That's right.'

'Tom Smith with a grown-up son.' The inspector smiled.
'How time flies. And Tom and his brother Stanley are giving
a bit of guidance are they? With the house in Jamaica Street.
They're in the building trade now, from what I gather.'

'Apparently so.' Edie could hardly believe they knew so much
about everyone. 'The lads will need a bit of advice, I should
think,' said Edie, the worry in her voice showing. 'Jessie's son
Billy wants one for himself but he can't afford a deposit, so
he's gonna be live-in night watchman. His own little pad where
he can take the girls back.'

'Errol, Malcolm and Uncle Joe. Of course, they don't live
on the estate, do they?'

'No. They live in rented rooms in a house in Hackney. Errol
is my daughter's best friend's young man. Are you sure you
won't have a cup of tea?' Edie didn't like this one bit. She knew
she was being interrogated and wasn't sure how to handle it.

'Billy Smith,' said the detective constable quietly, rubbing
his chin. 'Wasn't he the one who was at the scene of the fire
in Cotton Street?'

'Yes, he was. The hero who ordered my aunt Naomi out of

the house and then carried Ben out. Stubborn old thing refused to leave. But how do you know all of this?' Edie quickly checked herself and smiled. 'Don't you people ever get time off?'

'It's a small neighbourhood, Mrs Birch. A tight knit community? That's what people say, isn't it?' He offered a polite smile.

'I suppose so. I owe a lot to Billy Smith. My aunt Naomi's been like a mother to me. I wasn't there but from what I gather Billy saved my aunt's life. And Ben's.'

'So we heard. Strange how that young man was in the right place at the right time. Pity he wasn't around when the fire in this block started. He might have rushed in to save your neighbour, too.'

'I'm sure he would have done. Had he been here. But like I said . . . he's been staying in Jamaica Street.'

'Not all the time surely? Or has he fallen out with his parents?'

'Billy? Fallen out with Jessie and Tom? Course not. He's backwards and forwards. Turns up at meal times.' She smiled. 'Just like my daughter Maggie. And she's married with a family and a little place of 'er own now.'

'Kids, eh?' said the detective inspector as he rose from his chair. 'Well you've been very helpful, Mrs Birch. Filled us in very nicely.' He looked at the accompanying younger officer and raised an eyebrow. The DI then thanked Edie and bade her goodbye. Once outside he led the way out of the block of flats, speaking confidentially to his colleague. 'We'll come back this evening and visit the Smith family. The water's a bit muddy but I think we need look no further than this block of flats. We'll save the West Indian lads 'til later.'

'You think that Billy might be following in his father's footsteps, sir?'

'No. But something's not right. It doesn't add up – yet. Tom's son doesn't have one blemish on his character and he's been in the same profession since he left school. I think he's straight but that's not to say he might not have a screw loose. Maybe he's a bit of a pyromaniac. Who knows? Likes to light fires and then rush in and save the victims? But this time he didn't.'

'Maybe he's fickle?'

'It takes all types, son. The world's full of oddballs.'

By herself in the kitchen Edie felt as if she had, without realising it, dragged Billy into this murder enquiry. She ran some of the detective inspector's questions through her mind and knew that he had been digging deep. It seemed to her that he had been making casual conversation while questioning her and made it all seem like a general chit-chat about the people in this block of flats. But he had concentrated on one small group . . . the one in which she and her daughter's friends and family were involved. Pouring herself a glass of water she stared out of the kitchen window at the sky wondering if the police knew more about Gloria's death than they had let on and that this was why they were conducting a house to house enquiry. The more she thought about it the more she realised that they had not been treating the fire as an accident but one which had been lit deliberately and that this was possibly a case of robbery . . . and murder. Someone who knew about the trunk under her bed filled with money had gone in there with one intention in mind, to steal it.

'Jesus,' Edie murmured as it all sank in. 'Perhaps there was a fortune under her bed after all?' She pulled herself out of her chair and lit the gas under the kettle and then went into the sitting room and took her packet of ten Weights out of the drawer. Occasionally she did like a cigarette but right now she *needed* one. Smoking the cigarette she paced the room, thinking aloud and trying to make sense of it all and no matter how many times she ran the officer's conversation through her mind she couldn't come up with an answer as to what had been his motives for the questions other than to get factual information. The man had done his homework before he had arrived at her door; this was now clear to her. He knew of Jessie's husband Tom and he knew that their son Billy had been in Cotton Street and saved Nao and Ben. He had spoken about the West Indian lads, the Turners. She hadn't mentioned *their* surname to him so even *they* had been checked into and Tony, her son-in-law, being Errol's friend, she felt that he too might be under suspicion of foul play.

Finding this all too much, Edie sank into the armchair by the fire and squashed the cigarette into her one and only ashtray, kept there for when the girls came in. Leaning forward she rested her elbows on her knees and pushed her hands into her face and talked to herself in the silent room.

'Am I naive? Are there things going on under my nose that I can't see? Is it possible that the poor frail woman upstairs who lived alone and harmed no-one might have been murdered? With none of us here in the flats having a clue that she was in danger?'

Edie pulled the hem of her cotton summer dress to her face and dabbed the beads of sweat on her forehead. 'Cold-blooded, calculated, murder? No. I can't believe that. And why is all this revolving around *my* family? Why did the police come into my flat and get me to talk as if they *weren't* interrogating me when all the time they *were*? Worming information out of me. I should have known! I should have kept my mouth *shut!*'

The sound of the doorbell pierced through Edie, startling her. She went to open the door to find Naomi standing there, a red bulging shopping bag in each hand. 'Darling, I've been to the fruit and vegetable stall in the market and can't tell you how wonderfully fresh everything is and how cheap.'

'Stop making excuses for buying me some groceries, Nao,' said Edie, standing aside and waving her in. 'I stopped feeling guilty about it ages ago. You can spend as much on me as makes you feel happy.'

'How terribly thoughtful, my darling,' she said, smiling benignly as she swept by in her usual majestic fashion.

'Tea or brandy or both?' said Edie once they were in the kitchen.

'Oh. I imagined that my bottle of brandy had by now been emptied by you and your friends.' Then with a familiar soft sigh, Nao lowered her shopping bags to the floor and dropped into a kitchen chair. 'Tea would be lovely.' She studied her niece's face. 'Would you like me to make it for you? You look rather peaky, Edith.'

'No. I'm strong enough to brew a pot of tea.'

'Of course you are.' Naomi knew that something was wrong and waited until whatever was on Edie's mind came out in a stream of words. If she was wrong and there was nothing the matter she would be relieved. She was tired from her shopping expedition and grieving for her friend.

'I don't think I want to live on this estate now,' Edie said as she spooned tea into the pot. 'I don't like it here any more.'

'And where might you prefer to live, pray?' said Nao as she eased off her shoes.

'Out of the East End. I've had enough of it.'

'Really? Well, that might be something to look forward to. Shall I be visiting you in the countryside?'

'No. I'll stop in London. I don't suppose you feel like moving?'

'Well, actually . . . no. Especially not now that Ben and Joey have taken a place close by.' Naomi leaned back in the chair and let out a contented sigh and then said, 'But do go on and tell me what this is about. It's so refreshing to see that at last you're showing your feelings of anger over something which has happened to have disturbed you. A little late in the day but—'

'What do you mean? What are you talking about now?'

'Well . . . when lightning has struck – and it has struck more than once – you have simply smiled and said: "Never mind. That is life." '

'I've never said that. Not once in my life have I used those words.'

'No . . . but your expression and demeanour had spoken for you. False though the vibes you deliberately tried to put out were. You are made of flesh and blood Edie, like the rest of us, and there can be nothing wrong with that. Gloria's death has had an effect and it would be comforting for *me* if you were to admit that and let down your guard.'

Edie placed two bone china cups on saucers and said, 'The police were here. You missed them by minutes.'

'Well, of course they would have been in. If only to dispel the theory that Gloria had taken her own life which seems to be some people's opinion. Not mine I hasten to say.'

'That's mad. She wouldn't have done that. She wouldn't have set light to herself. She had no reason to. She'd made friends in us lot and the kids who once tormented 'er are now young adults. It was a careless accident. As simple and sad as that.'

'Had you let me finish, those would have been my exact words. Not suicide, possibly an accident, but probably murder.'

Edie turned and stared at her aunt, dumbstruck. 'If this is coming from people who like to dramatise things for the sake of it Nao I'm amazed that you're even repeating what you've heard.'

'Personally speaking and in the normal run of things, I would be of the same mind, my darling. But I fear that there is evidence to support foul play. I *have* tried not to think about it but it is on my mind constantly. In and out of bed. I woke in the night sweating rather heavily after a bad dream to do with it.'

Lowering herself into the other kitchen chair, Edie gazed at her aunt and this rare sight of a tear trickling down her cheek. 'I don't understand, Nao. You bounce in here as if nothing has happened . . . and then talk about poor Gloria having been murdered.'

'I was trying to put a brave face on it, Edie.' Naomi dabbed her eyes with her lace-edged handkerchief. 'I went to see the police before they took the trouble to come and see me. I imagined they would have been door to door in this block by now.'

'You've been to see the police? Why?' Edie was beginning to feel angry now. 'Why on earth did you do that?'

'Because from what I hear the police have deemed fit to man a flat to flat enquiry.'

'I know that. They came here. Two officers. Both quite charming and good listeners and clever at worming out information. They now know from me that Tony and Errol went into Gloria's over the treat she gave Peppie and by the way they looked at me they've marked them down as people to question.

'Here's me thinking how best to keep the police out of my life and you go and walk into their domain of your own accord. I think we might have to find you something to do, Naomi. You've got too much time on your hands.'

'Time which I fully appreciate and enjoy. Furthermore, by going to the station, I have found out something that will blow away the litter and dried up leaves which do tend to gather in the corners of this estate. My friend Gloria did not burn to death but was actually killed beforehand. Thankfully she would have known little about it. It is thought that her pillow was pressed into her face in order to suffocate her. We can only hope that she knew nothing of what was happening to her.

'Whoever killed the kind and innocent Gloria made a rather careless mistake. The pillow was found on a chest of drawers in her room once the fire had been put out. Scorched . . . but not destroyed. When the post-mortem was carried out the pathologist found no trace of carbon monoxide in the blood and no sooty deposits in the air passages which confirms that she was suffocated before the fire started.'

'But Aunt Nao . . . how can you possibly know all of this?' Edie was trying hard not to be cross with her aunt who it seemed was pushing the boat out with her theatricals.

'Because as you know, my darling, I do have a few old friends left who appreciate the remaining few of us who were stars in the old days.'

'Oh, right. An old fan down at the police station. I might have known. I suppose whoever it was knew what they were talking about?'

'Indeed. The pathology report as far as the police are concerned cannot be disputed.'

'God almighty,' said Edie, leaning back in her chair. 'I can't believe that such a thing would happen in our flats. And if it wasn't an accident . . . there's a murderer on the loose. A maniac.'

'A *maniac* does not kill for gain but warped desire. Our friend was murdered for her money. It is as simple as that. And whoever did it was not insane but rather cunning and clever.'

'What money? Gloria couldn't even afford to buy more than one piece of meat a week. One joint to last 'er seven days. Had you forgotten that?'

'Indeed not. But there was a lot of money in the trunk under the bed which she was too frightened to use.'

'Oh, that. Well, if you believed that load of tosh about thousands of pounds hidden away, you're mad.'

'That's as may be but Gloria showed me a folded piece of paper and asked me if the listed amounts came to very much. She wanted to buy herself a new summer coat and wondered if she might just treat herself without her son knowing.'

'She never had a key to the trunk. That's what she told us once when the subject was brought up agen.'

'She did have a key, Edie.'

'But she told us that she'd *lost* it.'

'She said many things that were not exactly the truth, my darling. We are talking of the simple minded and very lonely, Gloria.'

'So you really believe that there was something in that trunk?'

'I *know* there was. Which is the reason I went to the police. My dear departed friend once drew me into her bedroom to show it to me. She asked me to pull it out from beneath the bed which I did. Inside . . . was a small fortune.'

'You're joking?'

'No, Edie, would that I was. Our Gloria would still be alive now if that trunk had been empty, I feel certain. Her hands did more than tremble when she saw the money. They were shaking and she was deathly white. She had wanted a little of it for the new coat and hat but not any more. She asked me to lock it and put it back under the bed. Which I did. She was petrified at the sight of it – as if it was some kind of a monster which had surfaced. Her husband most likely. She had lived in fear of him and this to her was the devil's money submerged in evil. She said that it had come from bad things that her husband had done to women . . . and it broke her heart.

'She threw the trunk key out of the window but there had been a duplicate in a safe deposit box at King's Cross station but she had forgotten where she had hidden the key to the deposit box. At least that's what she said.'

'Why haven't you told me any of this before?' Edie was finding this all to hard to believe.

'Because I made a promise to Gloria that I wouldn't.'

Slowly shaking her head, staring down at the floor, Edie spoke almost in a whisper. 'So if the money under the bed was real and she hadn't lied when she blurted it out that day – then the rest of it must have been real as well.' She glanced up at Naomi and waited for her to answer.'

'I'm sorry to say that it was all perfectly true. Her husband was hanged for killing a policeman.'

'God almighty,' said Edie, dumbstruck.

'Perhaps now you will understand why I went to the police station. My fingerprints will be all over her bedroom and on the trunk, too. I told them everything I knew.'

'They wouldn't have accused an old lady like you, silly. And you should have told me that you've been worrying over it.'

'I saw no reason to mention it before but now is different. Now that I am no longer worried over it. I feel much better for going to the police before they came to me. I expect many people will be questioned over this.'

'Of course they will. Tony and Errol too. She invited them in on the day that Peppie took back the pound note she'd given him.'

'Yes, I remember you telling me that. But I shouldn't worry over it, my darling.'

'No? An Italian and a West Indian visiting an old lady? Don't bank on them not being suspects. Especially since they're both foreigners.'

'Tony was born in this country, Edith, and as for Errol . . . he has honesty written all over him. Racial prejudice will not come into this if that's what's on your mind. Not when such a serious crime as murder has been committed.'

'Don't bank on it.'

'As far as I am concerned there is only one person that the police should be looking for . . . Gloria's son.'

'To inform him of her death? Why bother? He neglected her for years.'

'No . . . not to inform him of her death. To arrest him for murder.'

'Oh, now you go too far.' Edie nervously laughed at her aunt.

Naomi tipped her head to one side and looked a little hurt. 'Do you really think so, my darling?'

'Yes!'

'But he is the only one with a motive. The money has gone from the trunk, let's not forget.'

'And how do you know he even knew about it? He never had a key. Gloria threw it out of the window. You said so your-self.'

'He knew about the key to the safety deposit box.'

'It's out of the question,' murmured Edie. 'What sort of a man would suffocate his mother in cold blood? No. It doesn't hold water where I'm concerned.'

'The kind of a man who is the son of a man who was hanged for murder.'

'That's hardly fair, is it?'

'His father's crime may not have been premeditated but nevertheless he carried a gun.'

Edie shuddered at the thought of it saying, 'I've gone icy cold.' She then lifted her eyes and peered at Naomi. 'Did Gloria tell her son about you being her friend, by any chance?'

'She didn't have to. I was there when he came on one of his flying visits. Just the once. He was quite evasive, going into the sitting room instead of joining us in the kitchen, but he saw me and I saw him – face to face.'

'And you told the police this?'

'No. I left that bit out quite deliberately. I don't want to be the one responsible for the demise of Gloria's one and only treasured child.'

'Child? He's a grown man! And why ever not? Are you mad?'

'Don't think I haven't thought this through, my darling. I have . . . trust me. I should think that he will be miles away by now, in any case. I certainly hope so.'

'What do you mean? You hope so?'

Naomi avoided her niece's searching eyes. 'Best to leave things be. He won't be back so good riddance to bad rubbish is my way of thinking. Whether he hangs or lives it will not bring Gloria back.'

'And what if the police arrest someone else for it? An innocent man. Such as my son-in-law, Tony or his friend Errol?'

'They will have no proof and no evidence. You are letting your imagination run away with you. The boys went up to Gloria's flat for a good honest reason. To see that Peppie gave back the pound note. I hardly think that that is a case for suspicion of foul murder.

'These young men are not exactly tender-hearted nor fragile, Edie. They will shake such a thing off and laugh in the face of justice. Once they have been released – if ever they are taken in. I think you're worrying for nothing.'

'Am I? Well perhaps it's me that's going potty and not you. It's just that I think that you should tell the police about Gloria's son having been to visit her. That's all. Simple as that, Nao. Is it too much to ask?'

Naomi, no longer listening, was off on her own track. 'Of course . . . I wouldn't wish Tony to be taken off in a police car but I have faith in justice. He and his friend Errol have done nothing to be ashamed of.'

'Faith in justice? What about my ex-husband, Harry? He's living a complete lie. And so am I. I'm not a war widow. I shouldn't be drawing a pension – but I am – and getting away with it. Is that the justice you have complete faith in?'

'Darling . . . you're letting your feelings run away with you.' The tremble in Naomi's voice was giving her away. She was not quite as sure of her convictions as she was making out.

'And I'll tell you something else while we're on the subject. One day, when I'm ready, I'm going in search of Harry myself. And if he is making money, I'm gonna have some of it. And if he doesn't have a woman and wants me – I'll take him on.'

'Edith, please . . .'

'And do you know why I'll do it? Because I'm sick to death of having to go to that dress factory day after day and sitting at that sewing machine with my shoulders bent over and aching. Just so I can make ends meet and be able to buy a few little luxuries. Talcum powder, a joint of meat, some lacquer for my hair, a night out at the pictures. What a life of luxury, eh? What an exciting life I live!'

'Darling, please . . . I can't bear seeing you like this.'

'Well, you're gonna have to get used to it, Nao. I love you and I love your friends. I enjoy their company, they make me laugh. But they're old and I'm not.' Edie swallowed the lump in her throat but there was little she could do to stop her pent-up tears from flowing. 'I want a life before it's too late for me to be bothered to find one. Jessie's gonna move to Norfolk. Laura and Jack might well split up and move away. Tony's family have bought a house in Islington. At last I have a circle of friends and then what? Off they all trundle to a better life.'

'I thought you liked your flat,' whispered Naomi. 'I didn't know you were unhappy.'

'I do like it. I love it. But I get lonely, Nao. Especially now that Maggie and Tony have moved out. I don't want to live by myself any more. I hope that Harry hasn't got anyone. I'll take him back if he wants me and we'll move away and I will spend the money that you lot seem to think he's making.'

'And if he is broke?'

'I'll find someone else who isn't. I'm not ugly, am I?'

'Not quite,' said Naomi, hoping that this outburst was coming from shock of knowing that someone dear to both of them had been murdered in her bed. 'And I do wish you wouldn't say such things. Why are you being like this, Edie? It isn't you.'

'It's been building up for a while, as a matter of fact. And if you want to know why I'm letting it all out now it's because a woman who really isn't that much older than me was murdered in her bed. Murdered when she had only just started to come out of herself and live a bit.'

'Ah . . . I imagined something like this might be at the bottom of it.'

'Good – we've come full circle. So . . . are you going to sit back and wait for Maggie's husband to be taken in for questioning or go back and tell the police about Gloria's son?'

'The police will not arrest Tony. How many more times must I tell you? There is no evidence and so no cause to arrest anyone other than the man who is guilty. And I suspect the police will catch up with the true murderer and if he is charged then so be it. At least his blood will not be on my hands. The beast who killed Gloria we may hate for ever, but he is her *son*. Her *only* child. And I do not want to be the one who sees him hanged like his father before him. He was everything Gloria had lived for, Edith. Her dream had been that her son would come to fetch her and take her to live with him away from London somewhere.'

'I understand all you're saying Aunt Nao, but he grew from being her adorable child to become the greedy monster he is. Cold and calculating.'

'I know. But we *must* abide by what I know she would have wished. That I, her only *real* friend, would not be the one to see him hanged. If fate brings it about that is something else.' Lifting her eyes, Naomi looked into Edie's face. 'We have to let some things go, my darling. Imagine if it had been you. Can you *honestly* tell me with your hand on your heart that you would want Maggie to be hanged for having taken your life?'

'Of course I wouldn't want that but she would never do such a thing.'

'And what of Peppito? If he were to see his father turn bad the way Gloria's son had done . . . and then go off the rails himself. Would you wish to see him meet the same fate as the man you want me to shop to the police?'

'Stop it, Nao. I don't want to hear another word of this rubbish. You can't compare us with that family. I can't believe you're saying all this. The man murdered his own mother. A woman whom he let live a lonely life with no thoughts of spending time with her. Why would you want to protect him? I think you've lost the plot.'

'We are all from the same mould, Edie. Human beings who are reliant on fate from the moment we take our first breath of air. Gloria's son will pay for what he has done for the rest of his life. Guilt is the worst burden of all.'

'No, he won't pay for the rest of his life! He won't care. He will put it all behind him. His type do that. Shift the guilt to somewhere else!'

'I don't agree. He might well be on a high now with his mind on the money and nothing else. But I very much doubt that he will sleep at night. If he is arrested and executed without my intervention then at least it will not be *me* who has sent him to the gallows. I will *not* intervene. I will *not* be the one who sends her beloved son to the hangman.' With that, Naomi cupped her face and murmured, 'Please don't shout at me again, Edie. Try to understand why I cannot betray what I know Gloria would have as her last wish. To leave her son alone.'

'All right,' said Edie, showing the flat of her hand. 'I'll go along with it for now, but if my Maggie's young husband is taken in for questioning over this – my loyalties will be with him. My son-in-law. My grandson's dad.'

'Of course, darling. Whatever you say,' murmured Naomi, her pale drawn face showing her age.

8

Back in his rented house in Jamaica Street on this lazy Saturday afternoon, James Drake watched as fluffy white clouds drifted slowly out of the way of the sun. In an old, worn and slightly torn brown leather armchair he sipped a glass of port as he planned his next move. Four days had passed since he had put his mother to rest and he felt better for it, with no sense of guilt or remorse. As far as he was concerned she would be more comfortable in the next world than existing in her miserable soulless flat, where she had spent days and nights alone in silence as if she were a hermit in a refuge, rather than a woman at home. He saw her as one of life's washouts – too stupid to enjoy what it had to offer. She had had a small fortune tucked away for years and yet had spread margarine on her sliced bread when she could have had butter and eaten fatty meat when she could have had lean. And, worse than that, she had always smelled the same – of Lifebuoy toilet soap or lavender.

Lifting his eyes from the floor to a small grimy side table he couldn't help smiling. He had counted the money and stacked it in neat piles. Four thousand, seven hundred and fifty pounds . . . and it was all his, to do with as he pleased. His mother had stood between him and this wonderful sense of release for years, and now, instead of feeling the slightest sense of guilt at her death he drank in the joy of new-found freedom. A burden had lifted from his shoulders. It had only taken a matter of seconds to carry out the act which he had been rehearsing inside his head since the day he had bullied her into telling him where his father's key to the safety deposit box was. The fruits of his labour had given him not only a small fortune but had freed him at last of his roots. Now he could be whatever he chose to be, his own person, without the shadow of an absurd brainless mother, for whom he had no feelings, hovering in the background of his mind and debasing his very existence. As a child he had had to listen to her constantly telling him how precious was life and how his father shouldn't have been taken from them to be hung like a chicken in a butcher's shop window. This she had said over and over once her husband had gone to the gallows some twenty-three years ago, when he himself was a child of no more than four or five years old. Even though he had left home once he had left school at the age of fifteen, his mother had continued to haunt him, no matter where he was lodging. Having started his career as a casual labourer Drake eventually became one of the finest bricklayers in the trade and there had been no shortage of work and this had not changed. But *he* had. On the day he reached his twenty-first birthday he had made a pledge that no matter how he was to make a living he would no longer toil and sweat like a pig. He was quite aware that he had come from middle-class stock and that his paternal grandfather had cut off this line of the family before his mother, Gloria, had even given birth to him.

The reasons had been clear-cut: his father, James Drake senior, had been a great burden to *his* parents and had brought shame on the family name with his heavy gambling, drinking and womanising. Now, more than ever, Gloria's son, who felt no remorse at having murdered her, wanted to use his inheritance, as he saw it, to create the right image before he turned up on the doorstep of his grandparents' grand house in Knightsbridge. With his good looks and stature he felt certain that once he was wearing a made-to-measure suit from Savile Row he would cut a dash. Having travelled and lived in different parts of Great Britain for the past seven years, he had learned how to listen and to alter his accent according to the company and his was not exactly broad cockney but neither was it the Queen's English. Some people had an ear for music; he had an ear for dialect and the rhythm of speech.

Pouring himself another glass of port, Drake congratulated himself on committing the perfect crime and without his mother suffering too much. To his mind he had saved Gloria the heartache she would have felt, had he taken her treasure away while she was still alive. He felt no remorse at the way he had bullied her to get the information he needed because as far as he was concerned, the money was rightfully his. The key which had finally surfaced had led him to a letter penned by his father explaining where he had stored his ill-gotten gains. In the old locked trunk. He raised his glass to the world and congratulated himself on his brilliant accomplishment. If anyone were to suggest to him that he was a psychopath he would laugh in their face. Only twice before had he killed and each time it had been something that he had not wanted to do but had done for the sake of self-preservation. He had had to protect himself once from a jealous husband and then from a prostitute in Glasgow who had threatened to have her pimp see to him if he did not pay for the extra services which he had requested. And each time, he had walked away from the scene leaving no sign of ever having been there. He had no regrets and continued to believe in his own philosophy: *We are each in charge of our own destiny.*

For almost two years now he had lived with thrift and frugality while he moved from one lodging room to another as he travelled around Great Britain from England to Scotland and then Ireland and eventually to Wales. In each place he stopped for at least six months to see if any of the places were somewhere he could hang his hat. This period of not working had not come from a sudden inspiration to travel but a plan which he had had for a long time. To see the lay of the land across Britain before he put down his roots and made a home away from the grime of London. But in the end he had come to the conclusion that the capital was the place for him after all and that soon he would be ready to ease his way into a world to which he should have been born and bred. Had it not been for his father's bad behaviour he would not be living amidst the common people who made him feel sick.

Glancing out of the window again he saw that the lad who had touched his car on his last sighting of him was with his black friend and standing too close to his Jaguar for his liking and he was annoyed by Malcolm who was laughing as he watched Billy using the window as a mirror while he combed his hair.

Drake knew they were baiting him and if he didn't have bigger fish to fry he would have gone outside and stood on his doorstep to stare them out until one of them made a move towards him. He would then use one head as a weapon to crack against the other. Content to sit back and watch them he lit a small cigar to go with his port but found that his temper was sparking a little as the West Indian first glanced at his window and then peered in. This being too much for him he stood up, placed his drink on a shelf and went to open the front door.

Blowing a perfect smoke ring he stared at Malcolm with an oily smile and then glared at Billy, saying, 'The car's not for sale. And even if it was – you wouldn't be able to afford it.'

'I wouldn't want it, mate,' said Billy, glad that the mystery man had come out at last. 'Too heavy on petrol.'

'Is that right?' he sniffed. 'Well, something seems to attract you to it.'

'Not a problem, is it?' said Billy.

'No. There are no rules on this street. Make of that what you will.' He looked from Billy to Malcolm. 'No rules whatsoever.' With that he shut the door in their faces and stood in the doorway of the front room so that he could see out but they could not see in. He felt a rush of adrenaline as the lads talked quietly to each other while looking at the window into which they could not see. Drake never kept a light on when the curtains were open because he liked to be anonymous – to see and yet not be seen. Speculation where his mother's death was concerned would abound in the local press and on the street and he was the only single living person who knew exactly what had happened.

He remembered reading in the *East London Advertiser* that there had been a house fire across the Whitechapel Road and that two old-timers had been rescued seconds before the house

collapsed. In the local pub which he sometimes used, the conversations had been varying as to why the pensioners had sat
inside and not wanted to leave. With notions and sentiments
flying, a few too opinionated for their own good had been
adamant that if the couple had wanted to go hand in hand to
their maker and had started the fire themselves, no-one had
the right to stop them and that the flash boy who had gone in
and dragged them out against their will had interfered with
what might have been the old people's hearts' desire . . . to go
to heaven together. Drake imagined similar scenes and conversation when the locals would be arguing the toss over *his* mother,
whether she had set fire to herself or had it truly been an accident. He could almost hear it now.

'Omniscience is power,' he whispered as he settled back in
his armchair. 'I am the only one who knows what happened
in that flat. The whore's mysterious death nor the jealous
Glaswegian's come anywhere close to this flawless crime.'
Then, to the sound of jeering he heard some lads in the street
yelling the word *Weirdo* outside his front door and as he stood
up and looked out of the window he saw one of them stick up
two fingers while the other showed a fist, and was immediately
thrown back into his past: the school playground, the bullies,
and their laughter when they used to circle him. Taking the
rise out of his short trousers that came down to his knees, his
sparkling white shirt, hand-knitted patterned sleeveless jumper
to match his knitted long grey socks, they could have no idea
the effect it would have on him later in life. 'Look at me now
though, eh?' he chuckled. 'Who's sorry *now*? Not me you ignorant little bastards. You taught me to be what I am.'

Remembering his tormentors he began to quietly laugh at
the thought of where they might be living and what kind of
jobs they were slaving away at now. In this easy mood he allowed
the worst of his childhood to drift back into his mind. He
recalled the time when a gang of boys had been chasing him
through the back streets of Shoreditch and how terrified he
had been. His heart started to softly pound as it all came

flooding back. He had pleaded with his aggressors, offered to pay tuppence a day if they left him alone but they had been like wild animals out for the kill. When he had confessed that he was asthmatic they were fired up by his weakness rather than sympathetic and while it turned out to be a mistake to have told them this, as far as he was concerned, it was something which had shaped his strength of character in the end.

Once the bullies had got him onto the ground one of them would grab his hair and pull so hard that the back of his head touched his spine leaving his Adam's apple vulnerable for what, in those early days of his life he had come to expect – a quick thump with the side of a hand in exactly the right place to cause excruciating pain and to make him retch. Then would come the blows from fists and feet as he lay curled into a ball on the ground trying to protect his face and his crotch. There had been nothing he could do other than to take all that came his way until either an adult came along and stopped it or if the blood they had drawn had flowed too much causing his attackers to panic and run for their lives. But until they had drawn blood they would not, could not, stop.

Drake as a boy had known why he had been a target. The story of his father having been hanged for shooting a policeman had grown out of all proportion where street gossip was concerned and instead of the coward that his father had been, his reputation had grown as one of the hardest men in the East End and any lad who could beat up the son of a notorious criminal gained credibility in the school playground and on the street.

At the age of eleven, when the war was in full swing, Drake and his mother, Gloria, had been evacuated to the countryside of Shropshire. They had both loved the rambling farm on which they stayed until 1945, when peacetime arrived, and he was thirteen years old. With just over a year to go before he could leave school the bullying in the school playground from his old enemies continued where it had left off until something inside his head finally snapped. Then, single-handed, he beat one of the biggest of them senseless and left him unconscious and half alive. The lad had been taken to hospital by ambulance and from that day onwards Drake was never approached by the bullies again but eyed with caution and kept at arm's length, a different stigma surrounding him. One of lunacy and one which had women leaning over the garden fence whispering, '*Like father like son,*' without having any idea just how close to the truth they were.

In 1950 a letter of conscription dropped onto the doormat of the two up two down terraced house where he and his mother Gloria now lived in the back streets of Aldgate. He had been called up for National Service but his medical at the Army Centre had showed that he was not clear of asthma and he had been relieved to discover that, because of this, he had failed his medical. By then he was no longer a hod-carrier on building sites but a fully accomplished bricklayer and laying bricks to perfection was not all that he had learned during those earlier teenage years. He had learned how to listen, how to keep his mouth shut and how to earn easy money from wealthy successful gamblers – the bookmakers – men who avoided paying tax and hid their money under floorboards and in the back of cupboards. Things couldn't have been better, especially since he also had the looks that women would die for. He seemed destined to follow in his father's footsteps by taking money from wealthy married women in return for passion.

His glass empty, Drake leaned his head back into the comfortable armchair, closed his eyes and let the sound of the boys playing football outside in Jamaica Street go above his head. Then, with no other thoughts in mind other than to move in wealthier circles again, perhaps once he had won his grandparents' affection, he drifted off into a light sleep to be woken an hour later by the excited yelling and shouts of the lads outside as they announced the arrival of the coppers.

Rubbing the sleep from his eyes Drake pulled himself up from the chair, crossed the room and went to open the street door to see what was going on. Surrounded by street kids was a police car which had pulled up outside the house where the flash black and white lads hung out. Out of curiosity and self preservation he went straight into his kitchen and filled a bucket of water and together with this, a sponge and chamois leather, went outside into the street. If this was a general house to house enquiry, which he didn't think it was, it would be short-sighted of him to look as if he were hiding away instead of innocently, if not mischievously, coming out to do what a normal man would do – clean his car. Keeping a furtive eye on the house, Drake was quietly amused to see both lads who had dared touch his car, Billy Smith and Malcolm Turner, being quietly escorted from the premises and into the back of the police car and going quietly. 'Lambs to the slaughter,' he murmured before quietly laughing. He had no idea why they were being arrested and didn't care but it did seem ironic. He had walked away from committing the worst imaginable crime and with his pockets lined, and the boys who had probably done no more than a bit of shop-lifting were now in the back of a police car on their way to the station to be grilled.

Back in his small neat kitchen cum scullery, Drake tipped the bucket of water down the butler sink and weighed up the benefits of moving on against the disadvantages. He guessed that the authorities would soon make an effort to find him since he was Gloria's next-of-kin, if only to inform him of her death. So if he were to suddenly move on, it might look a touch suspicious if he hadn't gone to see his mother before he left the area; especially since he was only ten minutes away by car. He opened a bottle of beer and went back to his armchair in the front room to reflect on all possibilities before he made a judgement. Seeing the police in uniform and so close by had had an effect on him and he had a feeling he wasn't going to be able to shake it off that easily. He didn't want them knocking on *his* door so wondered if he should go to them before they came to him.

Going over his movements from the moment he had parked his car under the arches close to where his mother lived up until later on when he arrived in Brushfield Street to have supper cum breakfast, apart from the girl on the stairs who behaved as if she was either sleepwalking or some kind of weirdo or blind, nobody had any idea that he had been into his mother's flat that night. He was confident that he hadn't left any clues to indicate that he'd been there. He had worn gloves and walked in and out again without staying a second longer than he had to. So why had there been a nagging worry in the pit of his gut which had not gone away? What tiny mistake could he have possibly made? His mother had been asleep in the dark when he went in and had made no sounds other than muffled cries which the neighbours either side could not possibly have heard. The heater next to her bed was foolproof and his mother's neighbour would testify that she had all but lost the plot. Why else would a woman in her late fifties sit stark naked in a kitchen sink by the window?

No matter how many times he went over things, still he felt uneasy and that something wasn't right. He felt as if he might have left something behind and yet there was nothing *to* have left. So what could it be, he wondered as he finished his beer and ran it all through his mind again and came up with no reason for him to worry, except for what his next move might be and whether he should waste any time sitting around. Then it clicked. This was a sunny Saturday afternoon, a time when a son might go to visit his mother for a cup of tea and a slice of cake. With adrenaline pumping he took the stairs two at a time and went into his bedroom and to the big old-fashioned walnut wardrobe.

His choice of clothes had to be right and nothing flashy. He pushed the wire coat hangers along until he came to a beige cardigan he had planned to throw away and a biscuit-coloured open-neck short-sleeve shirt. These garments, with his grey summer slacks, he thought should look boring and insignificant and more importantly, should the simple-minded girl who had been wandering around in the night see him she would probably not recognise him in his new guise. Once he had changed, he opened his jar of Brylcreem, rubbed a little into his hands which he then pushed through his hair before making a straight side parting and a middle-aged look. Checking himself in the mirror he was satisfied. Everything blended to create a boring quiet kind of a guy. Amused by his new appearance, he smiled and congratulated his reflection. He then pulled on a pair of horn-rimmed glasses which were some years old to complete the look. Now he was ready to go out and be the solitary son going to visit his widowed mother. He had no reason to fear the police because he had never been caught doing anything wrong in his entire life. Lessons learned from his father's carelessness. The fact that he had been to visit Gloria in the flat more often of late didn't worry him because he hadn't looked quite the way he did today. So, if anyone had given a description of a man seen coming and going he would not fit the bill.

Once out of his house he closed the door quietly behind him, ignored his beautiful car, and strolled along Jamaica Street as if he were run-of-the-mill and somebody's boring uncle. Making his way through the back turnings he passed all sorts of people out for a stroll and smiled benignly at those who smiled at him in that good old-fashioned East End way. When he arrived at Stepney Green Underground station he paused for a second, not sure whether to cut through to the back streets via Globe Road or walk along Mile End and turn at the department store, Wickhams, which would take him along Cleveland Way and past the house where a girl he had once courted lived, the lovely virgin Mary, sweet and innocent, who laughed when she was embarrassed and shed a tear when she was happy.

The vision of one of her older brothers coming to the door should he knock soon pushed away any notions of rekindling that innocent fleeting courtship from his mind. Five tall and brawny dockers who watched over their three younger sisters as if they were Madonnas were not men to mess with. Sighing at the thought of a life that could have been, he turned into Globe Road remembering how he used to fantasise about one day marrying someone so innocent and simple. Now in his late twenties he blamed life for cheating him of enjoying a settled marriage with children which might have been the case had his father not been hanged for murder when he should have been given a medal for having the guts to shoot an overly zealous copper. At least that's how he saw it.

Once he arrived at the Barcroft Estate he slowed his pace so that by the time he walked into the grounds of Scott House where his mother had lived he would be seen as someone with all the Sunday time in the world and with nothing playing on his mind. There were a few children playing hopscotch and a couple of women gossiping in the grounds but other than that there was no sign of panic or worry over a murder having been committed, which confirmed Drake's belief that he *had* performed the perfect crime. As he walked up the stairs, secretly bemused by this ridiculous visit to his mother who he knew was dead, he hardly noticed the girl of seventeen passing him on the stairs. It wasn't until he was on the next flight that he looked behind to see the back of her as she continued on her way in a world of her own that he realised who it was: the girl who had walked past him on the night he had smothered his mother's sleeping face with a pillow. In daytime the girl looked normal and this worried him, but more importantly she had not acknowledged him, so his phoney appearance had worked. Other than a polite nod and a queer smile she had behaved as if he were a stranger to this block of flats.

Satisfied with himself, Drake continued up the stairs confident that he had pulled off, without a hitch, something that he had been planning since he had at last found the key to his father's fortune beneath Gloria's bed. Once on the fourth floor a new thought crossed his mind. Why not apply for the rent book to his mother's flat to be changed into his name? He liked the idea of living on the uppermost balcony. It suited his penchant for having a fine view of the skyline and of the plebeians below and if he were to live here, he could look down on the common folk, other than those who lived on this floor, who he would treat in the same way as he handled the scum in Jamaica Street.

He rang his mother's doorbell with a sense of extreme gratification aroused by this new thought which in itself was a good thing. It would not do to look worried or concerned should a neighbour come out as he hoped. His plan was to have everyone believe that he knew nothing of the tragedy and like all his well-laid plans it seemed to be working. His mother's neighbour, who lived just two doors along, having heard someone arriving onto this floor was out like a shot and approaching him.

'If you're the insurance man you won't find anyone in there. Are you the insurance man?'

'No,' said Drake, his very best manner to the fore. 'As a matter of fact I'm simply paying my once a month visit.'

'Paying a visit? You'll be lucky. She's been gawn for five days now. Hasn't no-one told you?'

'Gone,' said Drake, smiling. 'Surely she hasn't at last taken my advice and booked a holiday at Butlins?'

'Don't you get the local paper? All right, there was only a few lines in this week's but they'll 'ave a full report next Friday, don't you worry.'

'A full report? I don't follow.'

'You will soon. And all dressed in black as you follow the coffin if you go in for that sort of thing. Burnt alive in 'er bed, she was. That poor woman. She was the only neighbour in this block that I talked to. The name's Sarah James and my 'usband works for the railway, in the offices. I thought the police would 'ave let you know she was gone, if you're a relative. Are you?'

'I'm Gloria's son actually . . . and I think you have made a ghastly embarrassing mistake.' Using his will-power not to crack even the slightest hint of a smile at this gossip, Drake sported a hostile expression. 'I think you must have the wrong person. I saw my mother just over a week ago and she was in very good health.'

'I'm not disputing that, am I? Who said anyfing about that? She might 'ave been in good 'ealth but she wasn't right in the 'ead. So . . . you're the son she always bragged about. First *I've* seen of yer. Some say she set fire to 'er own bed wiv a two-bar electric fire. I'm sorry it 'ad to be me that 'as 'ad to break the news like this. I'm not a well woman since this 'appened and now you're making me feel worse. Your mother thought the world of me. You'd best come in for a cup of tea and I'll tell you all about it. My place is not a palace but you won't find a speck of dirt.'

'My mother truly *has* passed away?' gasped Drake, clasping his forehead. 'You must be wrong. Tell me you're thinking of a different neighbour. I beg you.'

'Beg all you like but that won't bring 'er back. It happened and that's all there is to it. I've had to accept death four times during my lifetime of people who were close to me.

'The council cleaned up after the firemen 'ad been and the police. But I offered to go in and sort 'er stuff out and that. Get rid of clothes that was burnt or full of smoke – once the fingerprint people had been and gone.'

'Please . . . don't say any more.' Drake covered his face with both hands, saying, 'I don't suppose you would mind if I asked you for a glass of water would you? I feel quiet faint. I'm afraid this is all proving too much for me.'

'Well, what can you expect? But then men are weak when it comes to this sort of thing. My husband seems to think that anyone close to 'im will live for ever. I'll get the key and we can go in your late mother's flat.

'I washed up the cups and glasses out of the cupboard. They might 'ave looked clean but I'm a bit fussier than most. But that's no reflection on your mother. God rest 'er soul. She always said that I was the best friend she'd ever 'ad. She said I was kind and I could 'ave anyfing from that flat that I wanted. Well, as if I would accept anyfing from the poor cow. She never 'ad much as it was. Everyfing was old-fashioned and she would only drink tea out of a bone china cup. That's why I never asked 'er in. Mine are not bone china.'

'Mummy was rather particular, I know,' said Drake, gripping the edge of the balcony and weeping. 'If you could get the key . . .'

'Wait there,' said the gossip, 'I'll fetch it. But I warn yer . . . I might pass out if I come in there with yer. What with all the memories. Every time I step inside that passage I get a tight pain in the chest. I shall do my best not to today though, for your sake . . . broke my heart this 'as.'

'Thank you,' whispered Drake.

The woman let out a long and deep sigh. 'Trouble *always* troubles me. Singles me out it does. But there we are, I'm the salt of the earth and that's all there is to it.' She turned around and went back to her flat, slowly shaking her head.

Glancing over the balcony while he was waiting Drake realised just how clearly he could see now that he was wearing his glasses outside in the open air. Normally he only used them to drive his precious car. Trees which had been planted when this estate was first built had grown quite a bit and were in full leaf and he could see the leaves clearly whereas before now they had always been pleasant shades of misty green. The song of a blackbird suddenly rang through the air and he could see it perched proudly on the far end of the balcony. Yes, thought Blake, this would be a pleasant place to live, up in the sky, in the peace and quiet.

His sense of all things being well however was suddenly dashed, for walking arm in arm into the grounds was a young couple and although he hadn't seen the girl before he had certainly seen the young black man. Normally, without his glasses, he would never have recognised him and here he was with a lovely fair-haired girl on his arm. Asked if he were colour prejudiced Drake would be the first to stand and lie to put himself in a good light. He couldn't care less one way or the other about foreigners. But this was no ordinary foreigner. This was one who he had seen coming and going from the house along the road with the flash white boy who used the mirror of his car when combing his hair. He instinctively pulled back in case Errol should glance up and recognise him which was the last thing he wanted.

'I really should get another key cut,' said Sarah James as she approached him. 'If I should lose this one that flat'd soon be thick wiv dust and crawling alive.'

'I absolutely agree,' said Drake, preoccupied.

Turning the key in the lock the gossip pushed the door open and let out a groan. 'See? It smells already and I only give it a spring clean yesterday. But death's a funny thing. Hangs around for months, as does smoke.' She looked up at Gloria's son and couldn't quite make him out. She had expected a full burst of tears with him falling to his knees, heartbroken, but there was no sign of it now that the initial shedding of one or two tears was over. 'I can put the kettle on if you like. There's a half packet of tea in the cupboard. I never touched none of the groceries. I won't be accused of pilfering.'

'No, thank you,' murmured Drake. 'I couldn't swallow it. My poor mother . . .' he sighed as he sailed a hand through the air, forcing out a few more tears. 'She loved her little flat. She *was* happy here, wasn't she?'

'Who can tell?' said the woman, her arms folded. 'Who knows what really goes on inside someone's mind? She was very lonely and cold in the winter . . . and hungry too, I dare say. I like living in this block excepting for all the foreigners that are coming in. Irish, Scots, Polish . . .'

'Cold in the winter and hungry? Oh dear Lord . . . if only I was here when Mummy needed me. I hadn't realised. She put on such a brave face.'

'Yes,' said Sarah James, not in the least interested in his self-pity. 'Foreigners are everywhere you look. The Italian family 'ave gone mind you and good riddance. She always cooked with garlic that one. Stunk the balcony out for days on end. The German Jews are not too bad . . . they keep themselves to themselves. There are plenty of Jews everywhere, but that's nothing new. I've always said, we might just as well be in Israel, not that I'd want to be. They do say down at the laundry that it's not only the Pakistanis who don't use their left hand for eating, if you know what I mean.'

'I agree with *all* you say,' said Drake, slowly shaking his head, although, I must say, I just saw a young Jamaican coming into this block with a lovely white girl on his arm and it did make rather a charming picture.' He smiled gently at her as he wiped another lone tear from his face. 'Perhaps we're wrong, you and I? Who knows?'

'I don't think *so*. That'll be her pals downstairs; nothing shocks me now when it comes to that family, nothing. The woman gave 'er own baby away to 'er daughter to look after. Poor little orphan – he'll never know who his dad is because I bet the real mother doesn't know, and as for them blacks and Italians coming and going . . . they're in and out of that flat on the second floor like yo-yo's. The little boy's an 'alf-cast. She reckons it's not but you can't kid me. Black hair and brown eyes? I wasn't born yesterday. She put it about that the father was the man she was engaged to. Dennis someone or the other. If that's the case why'd he bugger off before the kid was born? That's what I'd like to know.'

'So the West Indian I just saw doesn't live in these flats?' said Blake probing as he dried his eyes with a new sparkling white handkerchief.

'Not *live* exactly, no, but it wouldn't surprise me if she's letting out a room on the quiet. What I can't make out is how that girl you saw hanging on his arm got to be employed at the public library. Living with a black man? Disgraceful. That wouldn't 'ave 'appened in my day.

'I blame her down on the second floor. Edie Birch and 'er daughter who mixed with Greeks, Cypriots, Maltese and the Turks before she married an Italian at sixteen. Couldn't wait to get between the sheets with 'em . . . like mother, like daughter.' She sniffed and then peered at Drake. 'Don't you wanna see your mother's bedroom? Where she was burned alive? I've done me best to make it look like a shrine. My great great grand-mother was a Catholic.'

'No. I'd rather not,' he said, feigning another spate of grief. 'But thank you for all the work you've done. It's very kind of you.'

'Someone 'as to do it. Most of the neighbours 'ave been in to pay their respects now. Those that are not made of stone that is. Some haven't bothered but they can answer to their maker when *they* kick the bucket. No respect for the dead, that's the trouble.'

'I don't understand. People come to pay their respects. Surely . . . she's not lying out *here*, in this flat . . . in the bedroom?'

'Of course she's not! She's in the morgue. All stitched up

by now, I expect. Now they've probed and taken bits they can use. No . . . people just like to come and say a prayer by her bedside that's all – and if you think it's morbid curiosity you're wrong – and the box wasn't meant for people to put money in for *me* neither. It's so we can buy 'er a decent wreath – from the neighbours. It mounts up all the time so I do take out a bit for cleaning materials and a bunch of flowers for the vase I put in her bedroom. I scrubbed the place from top to bottom once all the official people said I could. And I put the carpet sweeper over the place *every* day once we've closed. And rub a polish cloth over the furniture.'

'Once you've closed?' Drake was beginning to admire this woman.

'That's right. I've had to have opening and closing times or else it'd be a full-time job. I let people come in from ten in the morning 'til four in the afternoon. I never expect 'em to tip me but there you are, if they must they must. I'll buy a nice wreath from Columbia Road market out of the money. Can't get fresher than flowers from the market.'

'Well, I think you've been very kind and very neighbourly,' said Drake, smiling inwardly as he drew his wallet from his inside pocket. 'Not many people would do as you've done and I want you to know that I appreciate it.' He pulled a five-pound note out and looked compassionately into her face. 'Will you accept this as a gesture of goodwill and the only way I can think of to say thank you for being a good friend to my mother during *this* life and even now . . . now that she's passed into the *next*?'

'Well,' said the gossip quietly, her arms folded beneath her bosom, 'I wouldn't like people to fink I was doing it for money.'

'Of course you're not doing it for that. Goodness me . . . you could earn far more if you were employed in a care home, looking after the elderly, which I'm sure you must be cut out for. No. You mustn't ever let people think that. Let's keep this . . . and the box . . . between ourselves.'

'But they know about the box. I've not kept any secrets.'

'I'm sure no-one would ever think it . . . but there should

be quite a bit left over once you've paid for the wreath and so
on and I think *you* should have it.' He put up the flat of his
hand playing his part beautifully. 'I won't take no for an answer.
And as for my dear mother – she was never one for showy
weddings and funerals . . . and she always said to me . . . that
when her life here was at an end she would rather I didn't
attend the funeral. That it would break her heart to think of
me standing by her coffin.

'So . . . I shall abide by her wishes and remember her as she
was when I last saw her alive. We took tea on the back balcony
and talked about just everything. She was placed in a home as
a small child you know and doesn't have any family . . . other
than myself. This is why we were so close and why I shall, even
though it pains me to do so, abide by her wishes and go away.
Once I've been to the police station.'

'Police station!' Sarah James pulled back, her eyes wide and
frightened. 'I haven't done anyfing wrong! I've done all I can
to—'

'Of course you haven't done anything wrong . . . it's just that
I must present *myself* to them. No doubt there will be a tiny
bit in the corner of *The Times* telling me to contact a certain
solicitor. You know the kind of thing.' He didn't think that there
would be since he had led an elusive life moving from one
place to another and since he believed there would be no will
left by Gloria, a solicitor would have no need to search for
him. He wanted to go to the police simply to show the face of
a heartbroken son before he left town.

'Oh, I see what you mean,' said Sarah James, patting her
bosom. 'I see.'

'I don't think I shall come back to this flat any more so
please take anything you think you could use or would like. I
feel sure that my mother would want you to have it. I had
considered moving in myself at one point but I don't think I
could bear it.' In truth he couldn't face having this woman as
a neighbour. She knew too much about everyone's business.

'Well, if you think so . . . that would be very nice. There are some things that I might take.' She glanced furtively at Drake and then said, 'It's been a terrible shock for me, living so close by and what with this talk of it not being an accident . . .'

Drake narrowed his eyes as he looked into her face '*Not* an accident? Are you saying they think that *my* mother took her *own* life? Surely not?'

'Oh no . . . I'm not saying that. No. She wasn't the type. Not brave enough. No. Some say that it might 'ave been murder. Someone after 'er money. I don't take much notice of rumours. I've got no time for it and I've got enough on my plate than to stand around listening to idle gossip.'

'Murdered? For her money?' he said, slowly shaking his head and smiling. 'My mother was as poor as a church mouse. I topped up her widow's pension, naturally. But that didn't make her a wealthy woman.'

'Some say she had money under the bed.'

'Really? How strange people are. If only she had been wealthy. Well . . . as you infer, some people do have nothing better to do with their time than to try and turn something so tragic into something darker,' said Drake, hiding the worry now invading him.

'Oooh, I *know*. You don't 'ave to tell me. Idle hands breed idle minds. You could tell by the way she dressed that she 'ad to scrimp and scrape. I'm not one for keeping up with trends but she was very old-fashioned.'

'Yes, she was,' he said, wiping another crocodile tear from the corner of his eye. 'But tell me . . . what makes the rumour-mongers think she would have savings and hidden them? Unless of course she didn't like living here and was putting her pennies aside so that she could afford to move somewhere else?'

'Of course she wasn't gonna move. She *loved* her little flat. You don't wanna listen to gossip. Just because her pillow was on the chair? What does that prove? Nothing in my books.'

Drake felt as if lightning had struck through his very core. 'I don't understand. What on earth could a pillow have to do with the demise of my poor mother?'

'Well, far be it for me to speculate but by all accounts, according to the post-mortem and the postman, she never died of smoke getting in 'er lungs. Which is why I said in the first place that she was burnt to death. She was a bit on the slow side. Too slow to wake up to fire if you ask me.'

'And the pillow?'

'What about the pillow?'

'Exactly. *What* of it?'

'You mean you want me to spell it out?' Sarah James looked at the man as if he had sawdust for brains.

'Well yes, I'm afraid I do,' murmured Drake, gazing sadly at her. 'I'm in deep shock I suppose . . . so if I seem a little dull . . . please forgive me. To suddenly find that one is an orphan . . .'

'Well . . . if the pillow was on the chair and not under 'er head . . . then it might well 'ave been used to suffocate 'er. Before whoever it was that took the money from under the bed – and then put the electric fire right next to it. Touching the bed clothes is what I heard.'

'Oh my God . . . that would be cold-blooded cruel murder. Is this what people are saying about my mother?'

'Well, why else wasn't the pillow underneath 'er head?'

'Mrs James . . . if my memory serves me right . . . my mother didn't use a pillow. She always said it gave her neck ache when she woke in the mornings. She stopped using a pillow a very long time ago.'

'I'm only repeating what I've heard – and you did ask.'

Drake feigned a look of respect of her wisdom. 'And this is what *you* think happened?'

'Course not. Bloody daft idea. Your mother never knew what she was doing 'alf the time. She should 'ave bin in a home for the simple minded really. No. It was 'er own fault I'm sorry to say. She just 'ad the fire too close to 'er bed and fell asleep. The smoke must 'ave made 'er unconscious. Nice way to go if your time's up.'

'Well, that is a comforting way of putting it. Thank you so much. I appreciate your tact.' He placed a hand on his forehead and closed his eyes. 'This is all a bit too much to take in.'

'I offered you a cup of tea; I can't do fairer than that.'

'Oh, please . . . don't be offended. Look . . . I think it best if I just go for a long walk to try and take all of this in.' He placed a hand on her arm and gently squeezed it. 'I agree with all you've said but tell me . . . the Jamaican . . . does he often come to these flats?'

'Course he does. Trying to worm 'is way in. He went into your mother's flat once. They were all in there. Why do you ask that?'

'Into my mother's flat?' said Drake, seeing a chance of sowing a seed. 'I know I shouldn't think such things but—'

'In fact . . . I heard that they've been in and out more than once. But I wouldn't put my own hand on the Bible with something that's only hearsay. No. I'm not one for gossips.'

'Of course you aren't.'

'It's them little black children I feel sorry for. Ten in a bed? Dreadful.'

'Indeed. If *only* their children were allowed to play in the grounds with our white children, where they could be watched over. I have heard that back in their own country as soon as a baby can walk he is left to play in the jungle and swing as free as you like from tree to tree.'

'I didn't know that but it doesn't surprise me. They're not the same as us.'

'No, indeed. They have rituals instead of church services . . . sacrificial offerings of animals . . . and, of course . . . old people.'

'I never knew that either but I can see what you're getting at. Edie Birch seems to like 'em. The Italians and the Jamaican, that's why that little boy's an 'alf cast. Your mother gave the child a five-pound note you know and his mother told him to come up here and give it back. I thought that was very hurtful. I nearly wept when I heard about that. I mean, a pound note is very generous.'

'A one-pound note? I thought you said—'

'Oh, I don't know, five or one what difference do it make!'

'None. None at all. The gesture was the same.'

'Then the Jamaican and the Italian arrived apparently. I'm sorry I was at the bag wash now. I could 'ave kept an eye on them. Call me what you want but I wish none of the foreigners 'ad ever been allowed in. They're ruining this country.'

'I couldn't agree more,' said Drake, his mind working over-time. 'Do you think they might have thought that my poor mother had money to give away? Because she had been charitable?'

'They knew she wasn't right in the head, that much I can say. Too simple for her own good. They soon figured that out I expect.'

'Mrs James . . . have you spoken with the police over this yet? Have they asked you any questions?'

'Not as many as they should have done. And all I can say is that it's their loss. Let them ignore me at their peril.'

'Well, all I can say is that I would be so very grateful if you were to tell them about the Jamaican's coming to my mother's flat. It might throw a little light on things if anything untoward had gone on.'

'Trouble is, it then might be me who sees them behind bars . . .' Black magic was on her mind.

'And you'd rather not be a hero. I perfectly understand. But I would be obliged if you were to mention this to the police. If you could explain how they came up here and so on – to harass my mother. One or two of them behind bars wouldn't solve the immigration problem but it would help. If my mother's death wasn't an accident the police *must* be told who came and went . . . and if she had secret savings under the bed I would lay my best hand that it will now be in the coffers of . . . well . . . I think you know what I'm saying.'

'I never said it wasn't an accident! I don't want no asper-sions cast at me. My husband works for the railway in their offices. I have to protect his reputation.'

'Of course you have, but . . . I am beginning to wonder if anything untoward did happen in this flat. I hope I'm wrong, of course I do . . . but if anything else should turn up to show that all is not what it seems – I think you should say something to the police – to help them in their inquiry and to protect your good name. Withholding evidence is taken seriously. And beside which, you never know who might be next.'

'Next?' The woman pulled back and placed a hand protectively against her throat.

'I don't want to alarm you . . . please don't think that but . . . you and your husband are obviously a class above the other people who live in this block – with him being a professional gentleman I would hate to hear later on of you having also been burned in *your* bed because whoever did this to my mother may think that you have savings hidden away too. On the other hand, if your other neighbours are right and my mother was not murdered for the financial gain we must consider the alternative . . . a ritual. A sacrifice to the black gods perhaps?'

'There's only one God and he's white,' said the gossip, the fear now showing in her eyes.

'I wish I could believe that,' said Drake. 'I wish I could believe it.' He then squeezed the woman's arm, wished her well and left the flat, satisfied that he had laid enough seeds for this tattler to spread. His next step was to go to the police and put on his best performance of a grieving son, who had only just learned of the cruel blow that fate had dealt him. But first and foremost he had to get out of this building without coming face to face with the West Indian whom he had seen more than once in Jamaica Street and who would possibly recognise him as the man with the Jag who was today in the guise of a staid young man.

Rita and Errol, out for an early Saturday evening stroll and on their way to visit Maggie and Tony on the Ocean Estate, were calling on Jessie and Tom first. They had been told by Errol's uncle Joe to find out if there might be another cottage in need of renovation, up for sale in the Norfolk village, similar to the one Billy had described to them. Unlike Jessie and Tom's son, who had shown no interest whatsoever, Errol's uncle had been fired up when they had told him in passing about how cheap property in East Anglia was. They arrived onto the second floor and Rita felt that they should at least pop in to say hello to Edie even if they didn't stop for a cup of coffee. Of course Edie was pleased to see them, even though she had been enjoying a quiet time in front of the television.

Now, in her kitchen as she waited for the kettle she listened to the young couple's hopes, plans and dreams. Even though she felt that they were reaching for the sky, she didn't want to dampen their bubbly spirit as they chatted happily to her. This lovely mood in Edie's kitchen was about to be disrupted. Jessie was on her way down and the echoing sound of stiletto heels on the stone staircase could be heard. In a somewhat anxious state she rapped on the kitchen window as she passed and Edie went to let her in, wondering what could have happened. It was totally out of character for Jessie to knock on her window pane. When she opened the door she knew straight away that something was wrong. Jessie's dark blue eyes were bright and angry, her face flushed.

'You're not gonna believe this, Edie!' she said as she stormed into the flat heading for the kitchen where she stood with her hands on her hips looking at Rita and Errol, stony faced. 'I thought it was your voices I heard in here. This is a bit of luck!'

'You all right, Jessie?' said Rita as she came into the room.

'No, I'm not, as a matter of fact!' She folded her arms defiantly and looked at Errol with an expression to kill. 'I take it you don't know that my son and *your* cousin have been arrested?'

'You're joking,' said Rita.

'My cousin has been arrested?' Errol could hardly believe it. 'Why?'

Jessie shot him a look to kill. 'You tell me!'

'What happened, Jess?' was all that Edie could think of to say but she received an order rather than an answer.

'Sit down, Edie and I'll tell you,' said Jessie, her face even more flushed now. 'My son has been arrested! With Malcolm!' She turned and looked into Errol's worried face. 'What do you know about this?'

'Why don't *you* sit down, Jessie and tell us *all* about it,' said

Errol, completely in control of his anger. He didn't like to be treated as if he was guilty of something and he didn't like the way Jessie had broken bad news about his cousin. Or that she was laying the blame for whatever he and Billy had done on his shoulders. 'You are talking about my cousin Malcolm you know . . . as well as your son.'

'Errol's right, Jess,' said Edie as she turned around to smile at her friend. 'I'll make you a nice cup of tea, shall I?'

'I don't want one, thanks.'

'What about you, Errol?'

'No, I quite all right thank you, Edie.'

'I will though, please, Edie. In a cocoa mug and not a little cup.'

Edie almost melted as she looked into Rita's face. She looked so worried, so young and so vulnerable. 'And a couple of chocolate biscuits?' she said before smiling and giving her a wink.

'Please,' said Rita.

'So Jess . . . why have Billy and Malcolm been arrested? And what have me, Maggie or Tony got to do with it?'

'Who said they did have, Edie? I never said that!'

'No, but you've stormed in here like a bull in a china shop so I presume that you think that in some way it's our fault that Billy's been arrested. No?'

'I don't know, Edie, do I? All I do know is that they were both taken from Jamaica Street and they're being held at Arbour Square. I wish to God I'd never heard of the bloody street. It's because of Errol going on about it that Billy went there in the first place and now he's there most of the time!'

'And why do you think that the boys have been arrested, Jess? And how did you find out? Through the grapevine . . . which isn't always that reliable?'

'No. From Arbour Square. I got a phone call. I was allowed to talk to my son, for a minute, lucky old me!'

'And?'

'They're both in for questioning because they went into Gloria's flat—'

'Malcolm never went in there,' said Errol. 'I went up to the woman wit' Tony. And I know that Billy was not around at the time. She invite us in when in truth we didn't want to go.'

'Never mind that now,' said Rita. 'Why would they arrest them just for going into her flat? I don't understand.'

'That's all he could tell me so I'm in the dark. They've taken them in for questioning, that much I do know. Because of all the rumours, possibly. Gossip about money beneath Gloria's bed!'

'But it can't be that. Malcolm never went into her flat.'

'All right! So maybe they got that bit wrong. But the gist of it is . . . that they want to question both Malcolm and Billy!'

'Jess, calm down,' said Edie. 'Try to think clearly. What did Billy say exactly?'

'He said that the police believe that Gloria had that money hidden away under 'er bed. They've been questioned about it and now they're being held. Tom will hit the roof over this!'

'Christ almighty . . .' murmured Rita. 'I wish I'd never got up this morning. So does this mean that they really do think that someone set light to the flat on purpose?'

'It's been *rumoured*, Rita. I've not taken any notice of it and neither should you. It's nonsense. We've *all* been questioned,' said Edie.

'But *not* arrested, Edie. You wouldn't be this casual about it if it was your Maggie they pulled in. That's my son in that station. And in a cell soon, no doubt. Once they've finished bullying 'im!' She turned to Rita, 'It's all your fault! Fetching all of your friends round!'

'Do you mean her *black* friends, Jessie?' said Errol, showing that he was disappointed with this scenario.

'No, I don't and don't you start with all that prejudice crap, Errol! My Billy is in *prison*!'

'No, he's not, Jessie! They've taken him in for questioning, that's all. If they think there was foul play up there in Gloria's flat, we'll all be asked in to answer questions. There's a murder inquiry going on let's not forget.'

The room fell silent as each of them looked at Edie. It was Rita who broke the silence. 'You said murder, Edie.'

'Well, that's what it looks like to the police.'

'But how did they know about the treasure chest beneath the bed?' said Jessie. 'It was only us few that she told it to when we were all in here that afternoon for tea. None of us believed the silly woman . . . may she rest in peace.'

'I mentioned it to the police when they came here. I said that she'd said it that one time – and only that one time . . . I told them she was a bit on the daft side and I told them what she said about her husband having been hanged for murder. They knew about that in any case.'

'So it *was* true?'

'Yes Jessie, it was. So if that was true it's very likely that the money in the trunk was real as well.' Edie looked from one to the other. 'You must have all known about the rumours flying . . . Sarah James 'as bin having a field day up there. Charging people to look at the death bed and throwing in her penny-worth of rubbish about it not being an accident as well, no doubt. Don't tell me you haven't heard that, Jessie? The woman lives on your landing, for God's sake.'

'I don't entertain her, Edie. I won't smile at her or nod. I ignore her and she snubs me and that's the way I like it. But . . . if she has pointed the finger at my Billy because of it, so help me, I will kill that woman.'

'She won't have done. She's a harmful gossip. And besides . . . the police wouldn't take too much notice of someone like her. They know as much about all of us as they need to.'

'Meaning?' said Jessie.

'Just that and no more.'

'That won't do, Edie. You're holding something back.'

'I'm *not*. But if you want to know what I really think I'll tell you.'

'Go on then.'

'I think that someone did kill poor old Gloria for her money that she never wanted anyway. And yes, I do believe that the pillow they found on the chair is proof. That was the one mistake that the heartless bastard made. Not that that's the be all and end all. The forensic report showed that she died before the fire started. Something to do with no smoke in the lungs . . . I don't know.'

'This is all news to me,' murmured Rita, now as white as a sheet. 'Does Maggie know they think it was murder?'

'Probably not, Reet. It only happened days ago and I've not seen Mags or Tony this week. They're decorating the living room between them. Tony's wallpapering and she's painting the woodwork.'

Rita turned to look into Errol's face and knew that he was thinking what she was thinking. 'It was you they meant to take in for questioning, not Malcolm. You went up there with Tony and went in the flat. They'll want to question you.'

'It does look that way. But I can't see why they have to take Billy in. What he done?'

'Well,' said Edie, 'when the police were here, his name came up but then all the names came up. I told you – they seem to know about everyone in the East End. Well, in our circle anyway.'

'Well, what did they say about him, Edie?'

'I don't know, Jess. I can't remember.'

'Well, *try!*'

'It was something to do with Nao . . . that was it. The fire. The fire in Cotton Street. They knew that Billy was the one who got Ben and Nao to come out.' Edie leaned back in her chair, pleased that she had remembered.

'And?' said Jessie. 'What did that have to do with this?'

Edie looked down at the floor and shrugged. 'They made a joke of it. Kind of. Said that fires seem to happen around Billy. That kind of a thing.'

'Suggesting that he lights them?'

'Joking over it, Jess . . . that's all.'

'That's all. They accuse my son of being a bloody head case and you never told me.'

'No. It was a passing comment. They know Tom so mentioned his son. I told you – they know everything about all of us.'

'And your husband? Do they know all about him as well? Harry?'

'Only what I told them. That he was missing presumed dead during the war.' Edie avoided her friend's accusing eyes. 'I was hardly gonna go all through that in detail, was I? What they don't know they can't punish me for.'

Rita flopped down onto the other kitchen chair, drained by all she was hearing. 'I can't believe this is happening. I thought the three of you: Laura, Jessie and Edie were the three best friends of all time.'

'We are!' snapped Jessie. 'If we wasn't we wouldn't be able to be honest with each other!'

'All right! Don't bite my head off.'

'I'm sorry Rita, I didn't mean to. It's having an impact on all of us.'

'Never mind,' said Errol. 'My cousin's in prison and my uncle Joe should know about it. And I the one they want not my cousin. I'm going back home to Hackney, Rita. You want to come with me?'

'No, sweetheart. You go and tell Uncle Joe what's happened and I'll wait in my flat. You'll come and tell me what's happening to Malcolm, though, eh?'

The sudden rapping on the window and Maggie's high-pitched voice made all them jump. 'Mum, open the door! Quick!'

'Oh my God . . . what's happened now,' said Edie, rushing from the room.

Rita pinched her lips together and took hold of Errol's hand. 'What's happening to all of us, Errol? What's going on?' He was too mystified to answer her. His cousin was on his mind. His cousin – a black man in a white man's police station – being questioned about a murder. He put his arm around Rita and squeezed her tenderly.

Edie came back into the kitchen, the strain showing on her face. 'She's throwing up into the lavatory pan. If she's pregnant again . . .'

'I'd best go,' said Jessie. She looked at her wrist watch. 'Tom should be in soon from snooker. He's gonna do his nut over this. Still, by the time we get to the police station I might 'ave managed to calm him down.'

'You'd best calm yourself down first, Jessie,' said Edie.

'I can't. I am so angry over this. How *dare* they do this? Billy's got nothing to do with any of it. He's never been in Gloria's flat.'

Maggie arrived in the kitchen, her face as white as a sheet. 'Sorry about that Mum, but I've had a bit of a shock.' She immediately burst into tears, saying, 'Tony's been arrested. A police car pulled up and took him away . . . and Peppie was there and everything!'

'Where's Peppie now?' snapped Edie.

'Why do they need to question Tony at the station about the accident . . . about Gloria and the fire?'

'Maggie – where is Peppie?'

'Gone in with a neighbour. His little friend's house. He's all right. He'll be fine with her.' She turned to Jessie. 'Is Tom in, Jess? I want him to come with me. He'll know what to do. What to say. We can get him out on bail, can't we? That's what people do, isn't it?'

'Slow down, Maggie love,' said Jessie. 'Me and Tom will be going in any case. They've taken Billy and Malcolm in as well.'

'*What?*'

'It's all right. None of them 'ave done anything so they'll all be in their own beds tonight. You can bet on it.'

'How can you be so calm, Jessie?'

'I wasn't . . . till you arrived with your news.' She smiled. 'Now I can see the ridiculous side of this. I'll see you all later.' With that Jessie left a lot calmer than when she had arrived. At least it wasn't only her son who was being interrogated by the police.

'I don't understand. The police are arresting our blokes. My husband, Jessie's son . . . and Errol's cousin. What's going on?' Maggie turned on Errol. 'What *have* they been up to!'

'Murder,' he said breaking into a lovely smile. 'It seem like they all plotted together and murdered an old woman for her money.' He could now see the farcical side of it. 'We can't turn our back on them for a minute. Eh eh. They *real* bad people.'

'Reet . . . tell him this isn't funny. Tony might be locked in a cell by now for all we know.'

'Oh, shut up,' said Rita softly. 'Where's your sense of humour gone? If this wasn't ludicrous it would be grave . . . but it is and so it's not. So stop acting like your aunt Nao. You never 'ave been and never will be a drama queen. I suppose you are carrying agen – that's why you're in this state.'

'No, I'm not! It was from shock that I chucked up. It happened on the way here as well if you must know. But don't worry about it. You're all right. Errol's right by your side, safe and sound.' Her face went pale again and with her hand pressed against her mouth she ran out of the room, retching.

'They say the sun gonna shine the whole day tomorrow,' said Errol, trying to lighten the atmosphere. 'Pity we all be locked up in a dark dungeon with only bread and water, eh?'

'Many a true word spoken in jest, Errol,' said Edie, 'many a true word.'

'Well,' said Rita, 'let's make hay while today's sun is shining. Come on, Errol. We've got your cousin to sort out. God knows what your uncle's gonna make of this.'

Going hand in hand down the stairs, the couple stood aside and smiled as they moved aside to give space to an old man who was passing, on his way down. He stopped for a breather and then said, 'Isn't it lovely,' his blue eyes twinkling. 'A lovely summer's day.'

'It certainly is,' said Rita, her heart going out to the familiar old-timer, Sid the singing tramp, who looked as if he had enough to complain about but never did. He continued going cautiously down the steps, holding onto the iron handrail, his accordion balanced in front and his knapsack on his back.

'Mind how you go,' said Rita.

'Oooh, I shall my dear girl, I shall. Never you mind.' He

then stopped, turned his head and looked up at them, saying, 'You know I swear I heard a cuckoo this morning first thing. Wouldn't that be something? If the cuckoo nested under the arches with the sparrows. It's possible,' he continued as he carried on his way. 'Anything is possible if you don't let things get you down. Always look on the bright side of life. It's not a bad world when you take everything into account.'

Smiling at Errol, Rita spoke in a quiet voice. 'We'll be like that one day.'

'I suppose so.' Errol brushed a kiss across her cheek. 'And I will still love my white girl as much as I do now.'

'And I'll still love my black boy.' Then suddenly stopping she narrowed her eyes and creased her brow, saying, 'I wonder what old Sid was doing here?'

'Who?' said Errol, puzzled by her concern.

'Never mind,' said Rita. 'It's just another place to sleep as far as he's concerned.'

Walking out into the grounds of Scott House with Errol holding her arm, all that Rita wanted now was to be back in her own flat, on her little settee having a cup of tea so that she and her sweetheart could quietly discuss what was the most sensible and best thing for them to do. She didn't want Errol to present himself at Arbour Square police station but the idea was pervading her thoughts and she knew it would be on his mind too. If he insisted on going she was going to have to try and talk him out of it. She couldn't see the point of him telling an officer that it had been himself who had gone into Gloria's flat with Tony and not his cousin Malcolm. One of Naomi's clichés was floating through her mind and right now she understood the meaning of it, whereas before she hadn't: *'Don't trouble trouble 'til trouble troubles you.'* It couldn't be more clear to her.

Convincing Errol to take this approach however, would not be easy as he had already made up his mind. As they strolled across the grounds discussing the pros and cons, she heard Jessie call her name from the balcony of the fourth floor. Craning her neck and shielding her eyes from the sun with a hand, Rita gave a wave and waited to hear what she had to say now.

'I've just had a phone call!' Jessie shouted. 'Billy's on his way home!'

'Good!' Rita shouted back. 'What about Malcolm?'

'Still in there! But I'm sure it won't be for much longer!'

'How do you know? Did Billy say?'

'No! But it can't be! Can it?'

Rita raised a hand to Jessie and then turned to Errol, hoping that this news might win him over. 'There we are then, honey bun – they're bound to let Malcolm go as well. So there's no need for you to poke your lovely nose in, is there – because I know that's playing on your mind.'

'You t'ink so?'

'Talk properly, Errol.' Rita snapped. 'This is no time to muck about.'

'I talk the way I feel like talking. And it don't sound like it *positive* at all. Not in my cousin's favour, anyhow. I don't like it, Rita. I don't like it one little bit. I think we should go to the station before we tell Uncle Joe that they take Malcolm in for questioning.'

'Why? You just said you wanted to tell your uncle before he hears it from someone else.'

'Well, I had a change of heart, girl.'

'And if they keep you in?'

'Why they want to do that, eh? They let Billy go. Stop worrying so much.'

'I'll come with you then.'

'No. It look better if I go alone. And that is my final word on it.' He smiled and winked at her as he placed an arm around her slim waist and continued en route to Rita's little flat. 'I can't sit back and do nothing, Rita,' he said. 'I can't do that.'

'But we won't be doing nothing if we sit down and talk it through. That's all I'm saying. Don't rush into anyfing. And as for Uncle Joe . . . you can tell 'im all about it once Malcolm's been released. Which will be today going by what

Jessie said. They never kept Billy in there for that long, did they?'

'Maybe you right but Uncle Joe would be very hurt if it go wrong and they keep him in. We talking about his only son, you know. He t'ink the world of that boy.'

'He's not a boy, Errol. He's a young man – and a year older than you are. You're the first person Malcolm's gonna want to see, I reckon. And he knows you're taking the afternoon off to be with me so he's bound to come to my place as soon as they release 'im.'

'You is right there, girl. That is something to consider. He could do that. We really close you know.' Errol sighed heavily and slowly shook his head. 'He more like a brother than a cousin.'

'All the more reason to be there for him when he comes. He'll be gutted to find me on my own in the flat. It's your shoulder he'll want to cry on, not mine.'

'True.' He glanced at her lovely face and smiled. 'I wonder you can be bothered wit' me at times. I seem to bring trouble one way or another to disrupt your life.'

'No, you don't. What're you talking about? Disrupt my life. What life did I 'ave before you came along? If anyfing it's got calmer – never mind that I love you and you love me.'

Errol kissed her lightly on the cheek, his entire body filled with love for his beautiful white girl with the blue eyes. 'Yeah. We have each other and that all important. I happy with that . . . except for little t'ing.'

'What's that?'

'When you gonna wash out that colour from your beautiful white hair?'

'I can't wash it out, you dope. It's permanent. But look . . .' She leaned forward and pointed to her hair parting. 'See . . . the blonde's growing through agen.'

'Good. So you won't ever colour it again, eh?'

'I might do. It's a bit boring having no colour in it at all. I just wanted to liven it up a bit. I can't climb mountains but I can dye my own hair and make a good job of it.'

'Sweetheart, I think you just could climb the biggest mountain in the world if you had the mind to, but I don't think you very good as a hairdresser.'

'We'll both climb a mountain, Errol. Together. Show the world that blacks and whites can love each other and be happy.'

'And one day when it all calm and we married – we have children to prove it.'

'Yeah . . . little milk-chocolate babies.'

His arm around her shoulders Errol squeezed his sweetheart and kissed her lightly on the cheek, his secret still intact. Inside his jacket pocket he had forty pounds which he had borrowed from his uncle Joe to buy Rita an engagement ring, which he would give to her on her next birthday in two weeks' time. As they turned into the street where she lived he was still looking into her face, but the look of love in his eyes was not returned. Rita's attention was elsewhere; a police car was parked outside the house in which she lived. Following her point of vision cautiously, having seen the startled expression on her face, Errol's heart sank. 'It look like we have visitors,' he murmured. 'They leave no stone unturned it seems.'

'This is ridiculous. I'm gonna give them a piece of my mind, Errol.'

'No, Rita. Stay quiet and calm and imagine that the officers are your relatives doing their job. It will help. Trust me.' He gripped her arm and encouraged her to slow her pace as they walked towards the police car.

'You reckon? We'll see. Look at the nosy bastards down the street. Trying to look as if they stand there chatting like that every day.'

'Pretend that they do . . . and act natural and try not to antagonise the police or it will make matters worse for me you know. You learn how to be subservient when a black man in a white country.'

'Don't say fings like that. This is hardly a white country and probably never was. A right mixed bunch we are.'

'True,' he said, sucking his teeth. 'Very true. Now smile, my sugar plum. Smile demurely.'

They arrived at Rita's front door and each of them looked into the window of the police car, a sedate expression on both faces. 'Not here to arrest me, I hope,' said Rita, offering a friendly smile.

Both officers got out of the vehicle and focused on Errol saying, 'Errol Turner by any chance?'

'That's me sir, yes.' He showed a concerned look. 'Not bad news I hope?'

'If we could go inside, sir,' said one of the policemen. Then glancing at Rita added, 'I understand that this is where you live.'

'That's right. It is. Why?'

'I think it might be better if we conducted our conversation in your flat.' He glanced sideways at the onlookers.

'Whatever,' said Rita, pushing the key into the lock. 'Good job I tidied up this morning. Me having guests from Her Majesty's services.' She caught a look to kill from Errol and then smiled at one of the officers. 'Don't mind me. I'm not used to policemen waiting for me to come home.'

The officers said nothing as they followed Rita up the flight of stairs and into her rented rooms with Errol trailing behind, concerned but not overly worried about this call. He had done nothing wrong so felt sure that they would not be here for long. Once inside her flat however, Rita was nervous. She wasn't quite sure how to behave so she asked if they would like a cup of tea and when they politely refused she sat down on the small settee and spoke light-heartedly, saying, 'Well, sit down then, you're making the place look untidy.'

'This isn't a social call miss and we're not actually here to see you,' said the elder of the two officers who looked from her to Errol. 'It's just a routine enquiry, sir. We'd like you to accompany us to the station.'

'To Arbour Square,' said Errol knowingly. 'Where my cousin is being questioned?'

'My, how word flies in these parts,' the second officer mused.

'We just made a social call on some friends in Scott House and learned that Malcolm is being held and questioned . . . along with his friend, Billy.'

'*His* friend, sir?'

'*Our* friend, officer,' said Rita, irritated by their manner. They were in her home after all and they had come uninvited. Still she held her temper. 'Billy Smith's mother was quite annoyed actually. We were calling on my best friend's mother, Edie Birch, and Jessie came down from her flat, fuming. It's to do with that woman isn't it? The one whose flat caught fire?'

The officer glanced at his wrist watch and then looked into Errol's face. 'It shouldn't take long sir. So, if you wouldn't mind—'

'What about me?' Rita blurted out. 'If you're taking my future husband then I should come, too. Unless this is a proper arrest. Is it?'

'We shan't be needing you for the moment, madam, if at all.'

'Well, why do you need Errol then? He's not done anyfing wrong. Why is he being singled out? Because just like his cousin, he's black?'

'Rita . . . don't start all of that . . .' said Errol.

Ignoring Rita, the man showed a stern face and then said, 'After you, sir.'

'No. This ain't right! We want a solicitor!' Rita stood up and placed her hands firmly on her hips. 'If you've not got a warrant you're not taking him!'

Errol quietly chuckled and looked from the officer to Rita. 'Come on, sweetheart. Don't make a song and dance about it. They want me to answer a few questions. It's not a problem. I went into your neighbour's flat with Billy and they a bit concerned that we might have had *ulterior* motive.' Errol looked from one officer to the other. 'I can't say that I know any more than my friend Billy or my cousin but if I can be of assistance . . . then let us go.'

'This is mad! All right, it's a shame that Gloria died like that but let's not forget that she was off 'er rocker! It's a wonder she ain't burned the entire block of flats down by now. I wouldn't trust someone like that with a box of matches in my home!'

Leaving Rita to fume, Errol went quietly with the officers and a touch bemused by this scenario. He knew he had done nothing wrong so had nothing to hide – and a ride through the East End in the back of a squad car held no shame for him. If anything he felt a bit like a film star playing out a role in a B movie. Had they put handcuffs on him however that would be a different thing entirely. Once he was comfortably in the back seat of the vehicle he smiled at the thought of Rita cursing and swearing to herself and probably throwing a few things about. Her fiery temper could erupt over nothing, and even though this arrest was more than enough reason to make her cross, it wasn't the right time nor the place for this girl of his dreams to show her *couldn't care less* attitude. Privately, Errol had been relieved that she was not going with him to the police station.

By the time the police car had arrived at Arbour Square, Tony was already on his way home, a planned strategy by the police to sweep one particular group of lads in on the same morning and to have Tony there prior to Errol. They had wanted *his* version of the visit to Gloria's flat before the lads had had time to sit down and hatch a correlating story. As far as the chief inspector on the case was concerned Tony Baroncini was innocent and from a family with a spotlessly clean record. Billy Smith on the other hand was the only son of a man, Tom Smith, who had served time in the army prison for deserting in the face of the enemy during the war, and then a few years later, a prison sentence for fraud and deception.

As for the family from Jamaica . . . even though they had a clean record and all three of the Turners were hard working, they would need a substantial sum of money to refurbish the properties in Jamaica Street. Having made their enquiries the police knew that Uncle Joe worked very long hours on his small square of pavement outside the old Cameo cinema where he pitched up at the crack of dawn as the Cherry Blossom shoeshine man. To them the shilling thrown into his box would hardly amount to much but they were wrong. He was a good shoe-polisher and had earned a reputation as the best in town so had a very long list of clients who were only too pleased to drop a half-crown into his box. At the end of a normal day Joe could be sure to take home at least fifty half-crowns in the winter which amounted to around six pounds a day. During the summer time and with the tourists thick in that area he could expect to double it.

The interview room in the police station was fairly small with just two chairs either side of a small wooden table. Once the officer had reported to his sergeant his grounds for bringing Errol in for questioning, another male officer was called to search him. He was then read his rights. They were not accusing him yet of having anything to do with the fire which resulted in the death of Gloria. Errol, however, was nervous and worried; he hadn't expected it to be like this.

'If you're co-operative,' said the detective inspector, 'this shouldn't take too long.' The serious tone of his voice sent an icy cold shiver down Errol's spine and he felt intimidated by the austere atmosphere.

'I don't wish to sound naive, sir,' said Errol, his throat by now quite dry. 'But I can't say I truly know why I have been brought here.' A deliberate silence was left to hang in the room as the inspector looked directly into his face.

'You've been brought in under suspicion of aiding and abet-ting a robbery which turned into a murder case. You knew from hearsay that the deceased woman kept a small fortune in a trunk beneath her bed. We gather that you weren't the only one who knew that but—'

'I didn't know that. I don't even know the woman.'

'But you went up to her flat to visit her. And when she invited you in, you accepted. Is this something you make a habit of? Visiting elderly widows?'

'No, sir.'

'So this was an exception?'

'Yes, sir. I went up to the woman's flat with my friend, Tony. His five-year-old son—'

'Had been given a pound note and he wanted to make sure that the lad gave it back. Even though he had been taken up there by his child minder who, by all accounts, is a very capable young lady.'

'Yes, sir. But the boy's father was disturbed and wanted to make it clear to the woman that it wasn't the right thing to do – and that she shouldn't encourage the child to take money from a stranger.'

'Very commendable I'm sure but you can see what it looks like.'

'No, sir, I can't say that I do.'

'The word intimidating comes to mind.'

'No, sir. Tony was never intimidating. The woman she make no fuss about it. I t'ink she was very happy to have a visitor or two. I t'ink she one very lonely woman,' he said, as beads of sweat broke out on his forehead.

The inspector leaned back in his chair and studied Errol's face. 'And that was the first and last time you went into her home?'

'Yes, sir.'

'And what about your friend, Tony Baroncini?'

'As far as I know he never went back up there. He had no cause. His little boy accepted that it was a very bad t'ing to take money from someone whether it a stranger or someone he know from the area. To make up for the disappointment, his father take him to the sweet shop and buy him some candy.'

'And you went with him?'

'I did, sir. For the same reason I had gone with him to the woman's flat. We friends and we sometimes go around in a pair. My girlfriend Rita and Tony's wife Maggie have been that close ever since they were chil'ren.'

'So I gather. And while you were in the flat the deceased never mentioned the money she had in that trunk?'

'No, sir. We only there for a few minutes . . . and even then out of good manners. I t'ink the woman would have been insulted had we remained on the doorstep. My own mother would have behaved in a very similar way.'

'Hospitality you mean?'

'Yes, sir.'

'Mmm. I understand that you and your cousin and uncle have suddenly become property magnates? Two houses and a shop . . . in Jamaica Street. Nothing wrong with that of course but those houses are in a bit of a state. I would have thought it would take quite a bit of revenue to fix them up.' Another silence fell between them. 'And money's not that easy to come by. Tailors working in the East End don't earn that much . . . nor do people working on the buses . . . or polishing shoes on a kerbside.'

'We work hard and long hours, sir. My uncle Joe save every penny he can.' Errol was beginning to get angry now. 'My cousin Malcolm do overtime and he work on a Sunday morning in the marketplace, helping out on a busy grocery pitch in Petticoat Lane. We work hard to survive but that no bad t'ing. Most people in Jamaica are used to hard work. And we can't expect to be given a council house or an apartment. We aware of the housing situation . . . so we save for a deposit and then secure a loan. A mortgage. In order to buy ourselves some-where decent to live. I can't see the wrong in it.'

'No, I'm sure you can't. You know what I think?' The detective inspector leaned across the table a little closer to Errol. 'I think you and your friend, Tony Baroncini, went up to that woman's flat with all the good intentions you describe. But then, this woman, who was a bit on the simple side from what I can make out . . . tried to impress you so you'd be her friends. I think she told you in the same way as she told Jessie Smith, Edie Birch . . . and Laura Jackson, during a coffee morning, that she had thousands of pounds. Buying friendship is what they call it. Desperate not to be lonely would be my interpretation.'

'The woman never mentioned anyt'ing about having money.

We invited into the flat and stay a couple of minutes while she fuss over the boy, and then we come out. I can't say what she might have told the women at the coffee morning. I have no problem with what women talk about when they getting together.'

Nodding slowly as if in deep thought the inspector finally said, 'You're not planning to move out of the area or go for a holiday to your homeland, are you?'

'No, sir.'

'Good. Because we may need you to help us in our enquiries again.' The formidable officer stood up and stared down at Errol. 'I should think twice about the people you mix with. I should think that most of the men in Scott House have seen the inside of a prison at one time or another.'

'I can't say I would know about that, sir,' said Errol as he stood up and offered his hand to receive only a cold hard stare. The officer was making it clear by the expression on his face and look in his eyes that formalities apart he had no intention of shaking the hand of a man under suspicion of murder. Black or white.

'Like I say . . . don't go jumping on a ship just yet, will you?' The inspector glanced at his assisting officer, saying, 'Show Mr Turner out would you, Sergeant.'

Errol's heart was telling him to say something but his head was telling him something else: don't ask questions, don't expect respect, just go quietly out of this place which is what he did and once outside he sucked in the fresh air and relaxed. Even though he understood that the treatment he had received was no different from any other person under suspicion of robbing an old lady still it rankled. For a moment in that room he had actually felt guilty for going into the woman's flat – even though it had been innocent and out of respect of her wish for some company.

With nothing much else on his mind, except Malcolm and how they might have treated him, he made his way to Jamaica Street since he was so close by, where he hoped to find his cousin so that they could laugh at the ridiculous drama. Rita would worry but she would have to wait. Stepping up his pace he wove in and out of people who were out for an afternoon stroll and as he did so his shoulder bumped against a gentleman who glanced at him and immediately turned his face away clearly wanting no apology. Respecting the man's rights, Errol shrugged and continued on his way, a little ahead of the gentleman who seemed as if he was hanging back now instead of walking at the pace he had been going. For some reason Errol felt as if the man's eyes were focused on him and he wanted to turn around but he had had enough for one day. He realised that his nerves were dishevelled and his imagination a touch vivid since the somewhat hostile interrogation by the police. Pushing his hands deep into his pockets, his shoulders hunched, he went on his way bringing to mind his gentle family and his lovely Rita to rid himself of the feeling inside of having been treated unjustly and with suspicion. He didn't want to go to sleep that night worrying about what might be going to happen to him the next day.

Drake, in contrast, was in a buoyant mood. He had spotted Errol going into one of the interviewing rooms at the station and guessed that the man who had just brushed past him, by his demeanour, had been under fierce interrogation, unlike himself. His voluntary visit to assist them in their enquiries into the death of his poor mother had turned out to be quite amicable with a handshake and commiseration at the end of it. Having a quick brain it hadn't taken him many seconds to realise the way the mind of the police officer was working. He had been asked if he was familiar with any West Indian families and whether he knew a young white man called Billy Smith who lived with his parents in Scott House. He guessed this had to be the flash boy who loafed around in Jamaica Street. To keep himself completely out of the picture that was gradually being painted at the station, he had slowly shaken his head, saying he had never heard the name before and then told the officer that he now wished that he had taken more interest in his late mother's neighbours and friends, squeezing a little more sympathy out of them.

Before they had had a chance to bring his late father into
the scenario he had volunteered it himself, casually dropping
in the information while shedding a tear for his dear departed
mother, saying that if only his wretched father had been a good
man to her and taken care of both of them as he should have,
he felt sure that his mother would still be alive today. By the
time he had left the building he had given an excellent performance of a son devastated by what had happened to his mother
in what he could only presume was a dreadful accident: a
tragedy. He also told the same tale to them as he had to Sarah
James the gossip, that it had always been his mother's wish that
he never went to her funeral and that he was to remember her
as she was when she was alive and full of fun.

He told the inspector in passing that he would make arrange-
ments for a quiet respectable burial with no fuss or frill but a
special wreath from himself of white roses, her favourite flowers.
To his mind his convincing performance deserved an Oscar
and all he had left to do was see a local undertaker and pay
for them to make the necessary preparations for a plain funeral
and to see it through for him. His only desire now was to get
away from this deprived area and begin a new life somewhere
else, preferably with his wealthy grandparents who hopefully
would welcome him into the fold. With all things looking good
he now realised that there was no longer a need to grab at the
chance of securing the council flat for himself; an idea which
he had gone hot and cold on more than once. He had the
money from the trunk which would see him comfortably through
quite a few years, until he had his feet on the plush carpet of
his father's rich family.

It hadn't taken long for the news of the arrests of the lads to
reach Naomi's ears and having summoned both Ben and Joey,
they had debated this, that and the other on the subject of who
might have murdered Gloria for her money – if murdered she
had been. Of course, Naomi knew more than she was letting
on, but now that they had pulled Tony and the nice West Indian

lad in as well as Jessie's son she felt that she was going to have to admit that she knew more and that she was going to tell the police about Gloria's son having found the key to the chest in the safety box at King's Cross station. She had so far not confessed the part that she had played in covering up vital evidence to anyone other than Edie. Her worry now was that it might be too late, because once at the station the police officers would very possibly laugh in her face or be extremely cross with her – and see her as an old woman there to protect her great-niece's husband and his friends by trumping up a story – a fantasy from an ageing thespian would cut no ice whether she had an old chum there or not.

Filing past Edie's window the troupe of friends all thought the flat was too quiet for a time like this when everything seemed to be happening at once. It was by now early evening. Naomi knocked on Edie's door even though she could see no lights on. It seemed wrong to let herself in with her spare key kept for emergencies. A shuffling in the passage however, brought a smile to the faces of all three of them, who were ready for a decent cup of tea. When Edie opened the door, yawning, Naomi saw how pale and tired she looked and drew her breath in sharply. 'Oh, my poor darling,' she murmured, 'you look awful.'

'Thanks.' Edie stood aside and waved them in. 'I dozed off in the armchair. I've not been sleeping all that well lately,' then added with a touch of sarcasm, 'I can't think why.'

'Well,' said Naomi as she led the boys into the front room, 'at least you are well enough to be facetious Edith and that's no bad thing.'

'Take no notice,' said Ben as he passed Edie, 'I don't. When she's like this and it's a peaceful summer afternoon I think of fishing rods, baskets, reels and waders.'

'You should be so lucky,' moaned Joey, following him through. 'For us poorer ones it was a bamboo rod and a line from the ironmonger for eightpence, a float, weight and hook and a length of gut from Woolworth's.'

'I suppose you all want a cup of tea?' said Edie, closing the
street door behind them.

'Yes, that would be lovely, Edie,' said Joey, 'but only if you
let me make it. Is it a deal?'

'It's a deal.' Edie yawned again and went back into her living
room and flopped down into the free armchair and peered at
Naomi through sleepy eyes. 'So . . . what's new?'

'Well, that rather depends on how much you know, Edie,'
said Naomi, her head tilted to one side as she considered her
niece's expression, wondering whether she was tired or deeply
worried.

'You know about the arrests?'

'We heard that practically all the lads have been questioned
but they weren't held for long. Correct?' asked Ben.

'Unless anything else has transpired while I've been asleep,
that's the nuts and bolts of it.'

'So they're clear of any suspicion?'

'It does look that way.'

Ben turned to Naomi and quietly chuckled. 'What did I tell
you? I told you there was nothing to worry over, you silly cow.'
He slowly shook his head and rolled his eyes. 'She's been on
edge ever since we heard.'

Edie glanced at Naomi and then focused on the outside
world through the open door of the veranda. 'I'm not surprised.
Have you told Ben, Nao? All that you told me? About Gloria's
son.'

'Told me what about Gloria's son?'

'Darling, I really don't think that Ben wants to hear all of
that nonsense.'

'Yes, I do. See what I mean? Give her an inch and she takes
a yard. Let her answer one question for you now and then and
you lose your right to speak up for yourself.'

Edie was not in the mood for her aunt's theatricals or her
ridiculous principles which weren't worth a pinch of salt when
the serious side of life slaps you in the face and leaves you
waiting for the next blow. 'Gloria's son probably set fire to his

mother's bed,' she said coolly. He had bullied his mother on previous visits until one way or another he managed to get her to remember where she had hidden, for security reasons, a missing key to a safety box at King's Cross. And in that safety box was a letter penned by her husband together with another key to the trunk under her bed, where his money had been stored.

'It's fairly obvious that Gloria's son must have crept into her flat in the dead of night soon afterwards and suffocated his mother with her own pillow before taking gold sovereigns and a few thousand pounds from the trunk, and that he then placed an electric fire close enough to be almost touching her silky bedspread and walked calmly away laughing – leaving a trail of trouble behind for us lot. I think that just about sums it up, Nao, don't you?' Silence filled the room as Ben looked from Edie to Naomi. They could hear Joey rattling about in the kitchen and singing 'I Believe'. Clearly he was pleased to be in the kitchen out of it.

'Oh, dear,' whispered Naomi, her eyes fixed on the floor. 'I was wrong and you were right. You must do whatever you think best . . . if any of those young men are called in a second time it would be a disgrace.'

'No. *You* are going to do what's best, Aunt Nao. I'll come with you to the station and you can make a clean breast of it.' Rubbing her tired face with both hands, Edie continued. 'We all love my aunt, Ben, but we can't all go along with her senti-ments. It's mad to protect the feelings of the dead. It has to be.'

'Far be it for me to ask, but what are you talking about, Edie?'

'Aunt Nao couldn't bear the thought of Gloria's son being hanged, because Gloria might not rest in peace over it and that she would not complain, *if* she could speak to us from the other world, about having her life which was just beginning to blossom, cut short by her beloved son. Well, bollocks to that is all I can say.'

'That's one way of putting it,' said Ben.

'So you want us both to go to Arbour Square, Edith . . . is this what you're saying?'

'Naomi . . . could I have made it any plainer? This *is* what we are going to do.'

'Goodness, you are in spirit, my darling. What is it? What's happened now?'

'You *know* what's happened! My son-in-law's name has been tarnished! Never mind poor Errol and Malcolm . . . not to mention Jessie's son, Billy. It's a mess!'

'Yes . . . I see what you are saying, my darling. It has all got rather out of hand.'

'Oh, at last,' sighed Edie. 'We'll go after a cup of tea.'

'It takes a bit longer for the penny to drop where Nao's concerned but my mind's racing,' said Ben. He turned to face Naomi and shifted in his seat as he rubbed his chin thought-fully. 'We're gonna have to mull this over carefully.'

'What do you think I've been doing, Ben?' said Edie. 'In the end my brain hurt and I couldn't keep my eyes open any more. Fortunately Nao's old enough to get away with being muddled . . . or at least act that way.'

'Tell me something I don't know. It's good you've had a doze Edie and are alert enough to have us see clearly. We'll work something out, don't you worry.' At that point Joey arrived carrying a tray with everything on it that they needed, while singing . . . *'I believe for every drop of rain that falls . . . a flower grows . . .'*

'I shouldn't worry too much over it, my darling . . . because at the end of the day . . . it was not I or any of us here who are guilty of murder – if murder it be. Right will always out in the end. On this you may trust me.'

The room fell silent again as each of them gazed at the love-able woman who had always depended on her ability to get through any tight corners by using her theatrical charm which, together with her sensuality had, for most times, worked. But Naomi's charm would melt no ice outside her realm, if the police decided she was withholding important information to do with murder.

Having packed his clothes into a suitcase, apart from a clean shirt and underwear for the next day, James Drake was enjoying a glass of port and a small cigar in the front room of the house in Jamaica Street. Now that the world was his oyster he couldn't quite make up his mind where to hang his hat next. He had toyed with the idea of going to Ireland and then Wales and he was now wondering if he should leave Britain altogether. He intended to get out of Stepney the very next day and stay inside this house until he was ready to get into his car and not look back. Now that his mother was dead he felt as if a burden had finally been lifted from his shoulders and the only thing that concerned him now was the flash white boy who mixed with the self-assured Jamaicans, living just a few doors away, who were too close for comfort. If one of them had seen him in Scott House at any time and it dawned on them as to who was the son of Gloria – they might just start to blab and make things a little tricky for him.

To be on the safe side, he had told the police officer at Arbour Square, when paying his courtesy visit, that he was living temporarily in a small family-run boarding house in Essex and that he was soon to be moving up north, to a place where he had secured a contract for overseeing a new factory which was going to be built. Since the officer at the station had had no reason to question his movements he had wished him well and given his condolences over the death of his poor mother. So, all in all, Drake was quite pleased with himself and his perform-ance at the station. He wondered what his father would have made of it all. He imagined him floating through the air with like-minded ghosts who had also been given the death sentence. Then, looking around himself Drake made a snap decision for no particular reason to leave this house and to leave it now.

Fifteen minutes later he was driving towards the Blackwall Tunnel with no plan in mind other than to be miles away from the dirt and deprivation and the common working class. Coming out of the dark tunnel and cruising into the early evening sun he sucked in warm air. '*At last,*' he told himself, '*at long long last. I shall be of the class which I should have had bestowed upon me at birth.*'

Had Drake kept to his original plan however, of leaving the next day, he would have been feeling even more smug and confident. A police car had pulled up outside Errol's house in Jamaica Street in search of Errol, to re-arrest him on suspicion of murder. Soon after he had left the police station earlier that day new evidence had surfaced. His fingerprints taken on his first arrest matched those found on the handle of the bedroom in Gloria's flat. On the day that he had dropped in with Tony he had asked permission to use the bathroom, which had been granted, but he had opened the wrong door at first. The door to her bedroom.

This time Errol would not be released but detained in a cell in the station and grilled heavily in an attempt to break him and get a confession which the detective inspector felt certain was there to be extracted. Evidence that to his mind meant a strong finger of suspicion pointed at the young Jamaican murdering an old woman for her money.

In her rented rooms, Rita, having smoked more cigarettes than was good for her, paced the floor waiting for Errol to come back. She could not rid herself of a sense of gloom and was anxious, to say the least. Over and over she had been telling herself that she should have gone with him or at least followed in a taxi. When the sound of her doorbell rang through the flat she let out a cry of relief. Believing that this was Errol she ran down the stairs and opened the door with a lovely welcoming smile on her face. It was not her sweetheart however but Uncle Joe standing on the step. From his expression she knew that her worrying had not been for nothing and feared that the worst had happened. That Errol had been detained.

'Joe . . . please, please don't tell me they've locked him up.'

'Rita . . . I can't stand here on the doorstep another second more. Let me come in, eh?'

'Of course. I'm sorry. Come on up.' She was rushing her words even though she could see that Errol's uncle was still in a state of shock, his healthy glow now jaded.

'I tell you girl . . . this break my heart and that the truth.' He used the handrail to all but pull himself up the flight of stairs and Rita could see that his hands were trembling.

'It'll be all right, Joe,' she said, following him up the stairs. 'Errol's not done anyfing wrong let's not forget. So he'll be okay. They'll let him come home.'

'Whatever you say, darlin'.' Joe stepped into the small living room and pulled his handkerchief from his pocket and wiped the tears from his eyes. 'I hope to God you right, Rita, but it look real bad, you know. Real serious.'

Once she had settled him on the settee and given him a glass of water she pulled up a chair directly opposite and sat down with their knees close to touching. 'Now just tell me, nice and easy, what's happened now?'

'You mean you can't guess?' The grief-stricken gentleman gazed into her lovely innocent blue eyes. 'They arrest my nephew again and take him to the station . . . and they not about to let him go free. You see what I'm saying?'

'What do you mean, again? They took him from here but that was the *first* and only time.'

'It was. But once he come out of the police station he took himself to Jamaica Street and don't ask me why because I have no idea. But it make no difference. They come to my house in any case and I tell them he not home and that he was most probably here, wit' you. Then they ask about Jamaica Street and all of that and I wasn't expecting it. And then they start on my shoeshine patch and how I could make a lot of money from polishing boots. They make me feel like I done something really bad. Like I was guilty of something, too.'

Rita took Joe's trembling hands in hers and squeezed them. 'But sweetheart . . . how do you *know* that Errol's been arrested for a second time?.'

'They allow him to make one phone call and he call me.

They keeping him in a cell and they accuse him of murdering that woman.'

'But that's stupid! You must have got it wrong, Joe.'

'Nevertheless they keeping him locked up, Rita.'

'What proof or right have they got to hold 'im?' Rita stood up and paced the floor, wringing her hands. 'Well, if this is the case and they think they're gonna walk all over 'im, they're mistaken. I'm going to the station and if you feel like it you can come with me to get him out of there. They're taking downright liberties and I'm not standing for it.'

'Girl . . .' said Joe, slowly shaking his head and all but choking on his words. 'Rita . . . he not coming home. He asked me to come and let you know what was going on. He tell me that they found that fingerprints on the door handle of the woman's bedroom match the ones they took from him earlier today. You see what I'm saying?'

'They're lying,' said Rita, the wind suddenly gone from her sails. 'They're lying, Joe. They must be.'

'No, Rita. Errol he tell to me on the phone not to let that temper of yours get all of us into trouble. He say to tell you to stay calm and cool and to come back home wit' me . . . or go to your friend's home – to Maggie's house. He don't want you here by yourself wit' all this grief and sadness and worry.'

'Okay . . .' said Rita, 'fair enough. I'll keep my cool. But I won't come with you Joe, thanks all the same for the offer. I'll go to see Edie. Maggie's mother. I think that'll be best. Because Errol never said anything about Tony being arrested as well, did he?'

'No, I can't say that he did, child. He the only one they lock up in a cell.' Again he fought to keep his emotions in check for the sake of Rita.

'Right . . . so it's not a good idea for me to go to Tony and Maggie's. Because it wouldn't surprise me if this house isn't being watched. If I go there it might look suspicious. As if we're trying to collaborate on a story or something.'

'Because Tony also went to the woman house who dead?'

'Exactly. They went up there together once. I reckon they would expect me to go round Tony's . . . if Errol is guilty. Tony and Maggie are my mates, so of course I would go to them for help in trying to concoct an alibi for that time when the boys went up there. And that's where I would 'ave gone if Errol never came home and you hadn't come round, Joe.'

'I can't say I follow, Rita. What you trying to say, girl?'

'That I'm going to stick with my gut feeling and not go to see Tony over this. Edie Birch 'as been like a second mother to me since I was small and especially once my mum emigrated. So it would look perfectly natural for me to run to her now that you've called to tell me what's happened.'

'Whatever you think, Rita. I be at home if you want to call me on the telephone.'

'But will you be all right going back to Hackney by yourself? You are shaken up, Joe. You could stop here and have a nap if you wanted.'

'Eh eh. I can't do that. Malcolm out you see, so he can't know what happened. In any case I catch a bus from the Cambridgeheath Road and that only a few minute walk away.' He pulled himself up onto his feet and offered a weak smile. 'You know somet'ing? I do feel better now I here wit' you. Errol know what is good for me. Getting me to come and let you know.'

Hugging him, Rita told him not to worry and that right will out in the end and that Errol was innocent and law-abiding and would soon be free. He smiled softly at her but she could tell his heart was heavy. She walked him to the street door and waved goodbye and then went back upstairs and into the privacy of her home to let out her true feelings as the pent-up tears flowed. It wasn't a question of her sweetheart not being released soon, she felt sure he would be, but the thought of what he would be going through in that cell was breaking her heart . . . and what he had had to suffer while they had been grilling him. Errol was not a tough street guy and probably too tender-hearted for his own good. The thought of police officers being horrible to him made her want to punch her fist through the wall.

Walking at a slow pace to Edie's she arrived under the arches and her blood ran cold again. There had always been a cell-like feeling in this dark dank arched place under the railway bridge and now with the sun going behind a cloud and Errol locked away she felt scared of it for the first time in her life. She stepped up her pace and continued on her way, still asking herself how Errol's fingerprints would have been on the handle into Gloria's bedroom – if it was true and the police weren't framing him. Her thoughts flying from one thing to another she rushed up the stairs to the second floor, passing Sid the Singing Tramp, who on seeing her distraught and tear-stained face began to sing the words to the song, 'Smile'.

His beautiful voice echoing through the stone stairwell stopped her in her tracks. She turned back to look at him as he continued on his way up the next flight, singing, until he arrived at his new-found sleeping spot. On the second floor ready to go into Edie's, Rita was uplifted when she saw Jessie with her lovely daughter, Emma. 'Oh, Jess . . .' she said, her face creased as she held back her tears. 'They've re-arrested Errol and he's bin locked up in a cell.'

'That don't surprise me, Reet,' Jessie smiled. 'They have to have a scapegoat. Come on. Into Edie's. I've got something to tell both of you. Well . . . Emma has, not me.'

'I don't understand,' said Rita, puzzled and hurt that Jessie could look so relaxed and happy. 'Didn't you hear what I just said?'

'It's all right, Reet. Don't you worry,' said Emma, placing an arm around her friend.

'Not now, Emma!' said Rita. 'There's a time and place for everything and this is neither.'

But Emma was upset for Rita and couldn't stop herself from whispering, 'It is all right, Reet. I promise. I saw a man coming down the stairs on the night Gloria died and I've seen him again, since. Mum thinks he might have had something to do with the fire. It was Gloria's son. After her money.'

Rita stared at her, saying, 'But how could you have seen him? It must 'ave been well past midnight.'

'It was. I was sleepwalking. I never remembered much about it at first, I never do, but then when I saw the man again – when I was sitting on the wall down there and he was walking out of the grounds – I woke up properly. I didn't say anything before because Mum's been going on about me seeing a psychiatrist over it and I didn't want to.'

'So why now?'

'Because of our Billy being taken in for questioning. And now your Errol. I'll tell the police about seeing that man coming down from our floor on the night Gloria died. That should help Errol, shouldn't it? I only just heard that he's been arrested again. Dad said he'd drive me and Mum to Arbour Square and stay with me while I make a statement. Then we can fetch Errol home with us.'

'Oh, Emma . . . I don't fink so. I don't wanna put you down but you were sleepwalking. The police won't buy it. And you'd be laughed out of court if you even made it that far.'

'It's worth a try, surely?'

'I doubt it. But let's go into Edie's and see what she makes of it.'

As predicted, Edie saw this in the same light as Rita and after going over it more than once in the kitchen, her mood had sunk back to where it had been before she had been confronted by Emma and Jessie. The fact that they now had Emma's and Naomi's side of the story to tell meant something to them but deep down they knew that it would sound as if they had suddenly concocted both stories simply to get Errol off the hook. Unfortunately, Emma's dad Tom was known to the local police as a Jack the Lad and by storming into Arbour Square station they might actually do more damage than good. They were going to have to sit it out and wait to see what transpired over the next few days. If the police let Errol go because they hadn't evidence against him then it might be better to let sleeping dogs lie. On the other hand, if he was detained with no bail offered then they could fight with every pound they had to get the best solicitor they could find. Even Tom had to agree once it had been put to him that this was going to have to be a waiting game with no surety that Emma could be used as a witness.

Coming down from his flat on the fourth floor, Tom's mind was racing as to what was for the best. His girl was involved now whether he liked it or not. She was a prime witness and even though he hated the thought of her having to admit publicly that which she would prefer to keep in the dark, it was going to have to be done. After all, sleepwalking was a complaint and not a crime. Arriving at the second floor, his mind clouded with worry, he came face to face with the gentleman who was known locally as Sid the Singing Tramp who stood in front of him, a broad and devilish smile on his face.

'I don't suppose you've seen my brother, have you?' he said.

'Fuck me,' was Tom's bewildered response. 'What are you doin' here?'

'I could ask you the same question,' said the man, smiling gently. 'Why here, when you could have stayed on at High House with me?

'I came to London while you were serving a sentence for taking my brother's identity and spending my funds and living in my house. You did me a big favour you know. I wouldn't believe he had thrown himself off of a train. But you came into my life and changed all of that. You living at High House as if you were him. It's why I visited you in prison. To make certain that my brother had really gone. He was all I had, once mother died. We were very close.'

'So what the hell are you doing in the East End? A dump like this compared to where you could be living like a king?'

'At High House? No. Too lonely. It's still there you know – with your name on it. Once I'm dead and buried it's yours . . . perhaps. I'm not sure if you would be better off there than here.'

Quietly laughing and not taking this in, Tom was pleased to

see the old boy, the brother of the man who had jumped in front of a train at King's Cross just after the war was over. 'Have you still got that convertible Triumph Roadster garaged at High House? I loved that, you know. That long cream bonnet with two large chrome head lamps. I was a king for a while . . . driving around in that as if I owned it.'

'You still can if you like. It's there where you left it – in the garage.'

'No, thanks, mate. Come on. You look as if you've fallen on hard times. Come and have a cup of tea in Edie's.'

'No,' said the old boy, showing the flat of his hand. 'And I've not fallen on hard times. I've chosen to be a free man. Money can be like chains you know. Tie you up in knots if you let it. I never married so don't have a wife and a family. I never had that but you have. I moved out of that bloody damn great house in Suffolk and came here to the East End once you told me where you lived, when I came to visit you in prison. I couldn't have done a better thing. I'm free to roam and sing and do as I bloody well please. Thanks to you.'

Gutted by the genuine sincere look on the old boy's face, Tom could think of nothing to say. Even though he was dressed in the guise of a tramp and looked natural and happy playing the part, here was a gentleman of means who had lived in grand houses, Archibald John Thomas's brother, a recluse, who had always kept himself to himself. 'I loved living in that little mansion of yours,' Tom chuckled. 'In fact it spoilt me for the country. I'm soon to move up to a little village in Norfolk. That's what living like a lord for a while at High House did for me.'

'And this is what it did for me,' said Sid, the name he went by now. 'You brought energy into my life. I didn't want to live like a lord for goodness' sake. It was stifling. I'm a free man and I love it. Everyone knows me, you know. And they trust me with their children who always like to jig to my old accordion in the Bethnal Green gardens.'

'Who's living in the house now?' said Tom, his curiosity

piqued even though he felt as if he had suddenly been blasted back into a bit of his past he wanted to forget.

'The Salvation Army use it for their headquarters and I charge two pounds a week so that it isn't seen as charity.'

'You'd get a lot more than that on the private market, you know,' said Tom, grinning.

'And what would I do with the money? I can't give it away – people would start to look at me differently. No . . .' he said, thoughtfully. 'I feel the same about the house in Grafton Way, too. I let the charity organisation use that. Number thirty-seven, wasn't it?'

'I can't remember,' said Tom, looking at this tramp as if he were a saint. He was the owner of two magnificent houses, one in London and one in the country. The Tudor house being the one he stayed in for a while, where from every window he had a view of the beautiful gardens. Inside the grand house were heavy oak beams, pammet tiles, leaded light windows and two huge inglenook fireplaces, with nearly all of the furniture being antique and mostly carved, black oak, against the grey/blue walls with deep red and gold curtains.

This is where Tom had lived like a prince and spent this man's money as if there had been no tomorrow. And here he was, smiling at him, and dressed in shabby clothes. But happy. 'You're a lovely man as well as a lucky one,' said Tom. 'You deserve your new-found freedom to come and go as you please with the option to live like a king if you want.'

'Oh, I don't think I would ever return to my old way of life. Goodness me, no. They say I'm an eccentric and that suits me fine. You know I was of a mind to will High House to you.'

'I remember you telling me. When they let me out of prison. I stayed with you for a while, if you remember?'

'Of course I remember. Happy days,' he said, chuckling. 'I'm not sure now what I shall do. We'll just have to wait and see.'

'Never mind all that. Will you come and share a pot of tea with me?'

'No. Oh dear, no. Mustn't do that. It's one step back to the world I've escaped from. Total freedom with no commitments whatsoever. You can't do these things by half, you know. It's all or nothing.'

'I'm sure it is.' Tom was still having to pinch himself. This was like some weird kind of a dream. 'So you're Sid the Singing Tramp? Well, well, well. You have shocked me.'

'Good. I keep my ear to the ground, you know. And I see what I see. Right now I'm on my way to Bethnal Green police station. Why walk all the way to Arbour Square when I can go just round the corner?'

'Why's that?' said Tom. 'Why are you going to the station?'

'To tell them that I saw the man who started the fire. He drives a blue Jaguar and in my pocket is the registration number. The coloured lad will be home soon. Tell them all to stop tearing their heart and hair out. I saw and heard it all.'

'And you think the police will take you seriously?'

'Of course they will. Blue blood, dear friend, blue blood.'

'You're a tramp for Christ's sake,' said Tom, laughing.

'Indeed . . . but a wealthy tramp with property. Don't forget the hotel where I lived for a few years. I owned that, too. I shouldn't tell your family too much about me. About all you will inherit one day if I think it's right for you to. My brother would not have given you free rein to his hold-all on that train if you hadn't been kind to him. I like you, Tom Smith,' he said, showing his perfectly clean set of teeth as he smiled. 'I always did.'

With that, the old man turned away and walked down the stairs on his way to see that James Drake would receive all he deserved for murdering his own mother.

Going into Edie's flat Tom had to force himself not to laugh out loud. Still shaking his head in disbelief, he said, 'It's all right. You can all stop worrying. Errol will be back soon and Gloria's son will be under arrest. It was her own son who killed her, so I s'pose she must have had a small fortune tucked away. Time will tell,' he said, 'Only time will tell.'

Jessie narrowed her eyes and stared at him, puzzled. 'You're being serious.'

'I am, Jess. But don't ask me how I know or who I've just been talking to because you won't believe it.' He looked from her to Edie. 'I'm going up to our flat now but you can take it as read that you won't hear anything else about Gloria and the fire. Not from the police, anyway. You'll be reading it in the paper soon though, no doubt.'

Leaving them to stare after him Tom walked from the kitchen into the passage, feeling good inside. Warm. An old tramp had just spoken to him and he felt as if he had just been touched by a god. Never mind that all the time when he had heard people refer to him as Sid the Singing Tramp it had been his one-time benefactor they were talking about. Tom was now reminded of the Mile End Gate; a period in his life he had always wanted to forget, when he had been so jealous of Max and walked out on Jessie and his children over it.

'Jesus Christ,' he murmured and then smiled broadly as he pulled Edie's street door shut behind him. 'He's like someone straight out of the Bible. Living the way others preach but don't practise.' There was no doubt in his mind that the old man would see Errol walk free. 'Archibald John Thomas's brother . . . is now Sid the Singing Tramp,' said Tom, before laughing out loud, his emotions getting the better of him. 'So all's well that ends well, Tom. All's well that ends well.'

Epilogue

Edie, taken by complete surprise when her husband, Harry, turns up out of the blue to explain why he had gone off the rails, listens passively to him in her sitting room on a Sunday afternoon. She eventually agrees to take him back after he has apologised profusely and insisted that he had never stopped loving her and had not been able to get her out of his mind. She moves into the house in Holborn that he is renting with an option to purchase. Harry's small business of importing goods from the Canary Islands continues to grow and looks to be successful. The couple who were so devoted to each other before the second world war ripped them apart are in love again.

Jessie and Tom move home, taking Emma with them to Elmshill, where she will train at a local village school and also study in Norwich to become a school teacher. Billy, having none of it, stays with the lads in Stepney but finds the lure of the Norfolk countryside drawing him there every other weekend. Dolly, Jessie's sister, settles down very quickly to writing the series she hopes to see on the television one day. East Enders in Kent: *The Hop Pickers*.

Laura goes to the hop fields in Kent to discover that it will be the last time. Picking machines are to take over from people. Her love affair with Richard Wright ends and Jack's girlfriend Patsy goes back home to Leicester to have his baby, a boy called Jac.

Naomi and her troupe of friends do put on a show at Christmas and Larry sells the Grand Star knowing it will be turned into a bingo hall. With a little of the proceeds he does take the old die-hards to Butlins for a wonderful week's holiday. On Barcoft Estate, families come and go, but Laura and Jack with their daughter Kay continue to live there. Sarah James, the gossip, keeps an eye on everyone and Naomi, Harriet, Ben, Joey, Larry, Becky and Nathan continue to run the tea dances and visit each other as a group weekly, to play cards in each other's homes . . . taking it in turn to make sandwiches and a hot drink with something on the side. Harriet's diary has been passed to Dolly for her to write a book about the midwife and how Harriet's sister-in-law, Whitechapel Mary, had come close to being a victim of 'Jack the Ripper'.

Errol buys Rita a lovely engagement ring, a small diamond solitaire. Uncle Joe, Malcolm and Errol find that living in Jamaica Street is good and enjoy their little back yards where jasmine grows wild. Eventually racial intimidation calms down again with the arrival of the swinging sixties and those who continue to wave the red white and blue flag for the wrong reasons are a small minority.